By JACKSON CORDD

NOVELS
Cleats in Clay
Shamrock Green

NOVELLAS
Duanta Beads
Lavender Skies

Published by DREAMSPINNER PRESS
http://www.dreamspinnerpress.com

Shamrock GREEN

Jackson Cordd

Dreamspinner Press

Published by
Dreamspinner Press
5032 Capital Circle SW
Suite 2, PMB# 279
Tallahassee, FL 32305-7886
USA
http://www.dreamspinnerpress.com/

Shamrock Green
© 2014 Jackson Cordd.

Cover Art
© 2014 Paul Richmond.
http://www.paulrichmondstudio.com
Cover content is for illustrative purposes only and any person depicted on the cover is a model.

ISBN: 978-1-62798-637-3
Digital ISBN: 978-1-62798-638-0

Printed in the United States of America
First Edition
April 2014

I dedicate this work to my Irish ancestors, hearty and stubborn souls who have managed over the centuries to create a beautiful oasis on top of a small hunk of granite rising out of the ocean. I like to think that they had some help from the Fae....

Chapter 1

HANK WANDERED deeper into the National Museum of Ireland, freezing in his tracks when he saw the metal feline on display. A skilled artist had crafted the beautiful piece from circular bands of brass and bronze. He slowly stepped closer to the case for a better view. The pattern of the yellow-orange metal designs made the figure look remarkably like a life-sized marmalade tabby cat sitting on his haunches on top of a wooden shoe box. The cat's head angled to one side, as though he were preparing to lick his shoulder. The figurine's eyes, cut from some kind of green gemstone, glowed with fiery life in the up-lit case.

As he neared the display, Hank glanced at the placard which indicated this was a clockwork piece entitled *Dancing Phouka* by Cona Philmo. Recognizing that name from working in his parent's antique business, Hank knew of the renowned watchmaker of the 1920s era, but he'd never known the Portuguese artist had also made clockwork pieces.

What a strange thing to find in a Dublin museum, Hank thought as he examined the cat through the glass. Well, it didn't look *exactly* like a cat. Proportionally, his tail seemed a little too short and his shoulders seemed a bit too broad for a typical feline. Maybe those were just structural concessions the designer had made to accommodate the moving metal gears and bits inside.

Hank noticed a small button installed next to the sign. As he reached out his hand to it, a movement from the edge of the room snagged Hank's attention. Ignoring the sudden chill he felt, Hank glanced at the corner, but saw only dark shadows. He peered around the rest of the small alcove and saw he was alone.

Hank pushed the button.

A movie of the clockwork in action appeared on a screen along the back wall of the display case. The metallic sounds of a music-box rendition of the song "Greensleeves" tinkled out as Hank watched in awe. The metal phouka first stretched out a paw, then tiny metal claws extended from its paw-pads before the clockwork cat stood up. With an hypnotically smooth movement, the phouka figurine then lifted to stand on his back legs. While the tune still played, the clockwork cat rotated his hips and lifted his front paws, like a slow-moving belly dancer. Hank watched in fascination.

As the song came to an end, the clockwork figure dropped back to all four paws before returning to the sitting position. After a slight flick of its tail, the music ended.

Hank stood in stunned silence. *Granny would have loved this.* Even though his eyes welled up at the thought, he smiled. It had always been his Granny's dream to visit the homeland of their ancestors, but circumstances had never allowed for it before she passed on. Hank had scheduled this trip partly as a memorial in her honor.

Blinking heavily, he turned and read the descriptive placard.

> *Reported to have been the first work ever created by Cona Philmo, this clockwork music box is a shining example of early twentieth Century craftsmanship.*
>
> *The Phouka, thought to be the mythical cousins of Leprechauns, are often said to hide amongst humans in various disguises. Folklore speaks fondly of phouka, who were believed to be playfully benign, and sometimes even beneficial to humans. Cona could often be heard bragging that a live model posed for this unusual work.*
>
> *(1969) Due to the delicate nature of the metalwork, the museum no longer runs the music box. Instead, please enjoy the movie of the clockwork in action.*

Glancing at his watch, Hank saw that he still had about twenty minutes before it was time to meet the rest of the tour group in the museum's front lobby. He scrunched his tired toes inside his sneakers as he looked at the small bench by the wall. He walked over and sat down to rest his feet before heading back through the maze to the front doors.

He stretched out his legs and flexed his ankles with a soft groan. Then, he lifted his feet and scrunched his toes again, working the tired muscles of his calves. Not that Hank hadn't enjoyed every minute of his tour through Ireland, but he decided that next time he traveled, he would rethink the whole "tour bus" idea. He reached down and put his finger under the laces of his right sneaker and pulled up on the knot to try and loosen the shoe's grip a little. The problem with the bus was how the group scurried so quickly from one town to the next, leaving Hank feeling as though he never had time to catch his breath in any one place. Or rest his feet. Maybe he was getting too old for a week's worth of walking around.

He pulled at the knot of his other shoe before glancing up again at the glowing green eyes of the bronze and brass figurine. From this angle, the phouka's eyes seemed to be gazing back at him.

Fighting the strange feeling that someone was watching him, Hank peered around the empty room again. His gaze snagged briefly on the shadows in the dark corner, but he failed to see anything. *Quit being goosey,* he scolded himself. *I'm just tired,* he thought reassuringly.

He stood and took one last admiring glance at the Cona clockwork before walking out of the room.

HANK FOUND most of the tour group already milling about when he made it to the lobby. He smiled as he approached the Fergusons, the friendly older couple here from Boston. On the first night at dinner, Hank had learned from Florence Ferguson that the couple was visiting Ireland on their thirty-fifth wedding anniversary.

Florence smiled warmly back. "I think we're ready to go home now," she said to Hank in a whisper, her clipped New England accent making the words sound conspiratorial. "Eight days is a long time away from home when you're all old and creaky."

Hank flashed her a crooked grin. "Ya don't look much older than I am," he complimented in his Texas drawl.

As Paul, the tour guide, stepped to the front of the group and began his head count, Florence whispered back, "You're a sweet liar, and I doubt you're even thirty. Trust me, after fifty, everything starts sliding downhill."

Paul leaned on his fancy-looking cane as he glanced at his wristwatch. "Missing two," he announced as he scrutinized the group.

A loud feminine chuckle from the left drew everyone's attention to the restroom alcove, where "the sisters" hurried up to join the group. After watching them for a week, Hank still wasn't sure what to make of them. He'd guess the pair of women from Portland to be in their late forties, and their frequent disappearances to local bathrooms made Hank suspect they might be partaking of a bit of drugs. Cocaine probably.

"Did you see those dresses?" the blonder sister asked as she ran up next to Hank. Was it Bea, or Clara? Hank never had gotten their names straight.

"No, I didn't make it to that part," Hank replied as Paul resumed a new head count.

"So much fabric," the other sister threw in. "How could women wear so much? It makes my skin itch just to think about it."

He nodded as he suppressed a chuckle. It was more likely something else that made Clara's, or was it Bea's, skin itch.

Hank withheld any judgment. In typical Texan form, he left them to their own business. After all, the ladies were on vacation, and their extra recreational activities hadn't caused any problems on the tour. Lord knows, Hank wasn't one who could start throwing stones about alternative lifestyles.

With a new head count of twelve, Paul nodded his approval before sweeping his arm toward the front door and the tour van that waited outside.

Being one of the youngest in the tour group, Hank stood still like a gentleman and let the others pass through the door first.

All in all, it isn't a bad group of people to spend time with, Hank thought, though he did feel a little left out sometimes. He was the only single traveler on the tour. Except for one young family with their eight-year-old daughter, the rest of the group was made up of pairs.

One of the more boisterous members of the tour group, Crissy spoke with a loud Australian accent as she approached the museum doors. "I hope we get some *real* food tonight. That stew we had for dinner last night didn't fill me up *a'tall*."

"The schedule said it's dinner *and* a show," Florence replied warmly as she held the door open for Crissy. "I bet they'll have wine too," she added with a wink. It seemed Hank wasn't the only one who noticed Crissy enjoyed her alcohol.

Crissy nodded approvingly as she stepped outside.

As Hank brought up the rear, a hand on his shoulder nearly made him jump.

He turned to see Paul smile at him as he gave his shoulder another pat before resting his hand there in a fatherly gesture. "Just one last night," Paul said in his formal-sounding Irish accent. "Not much time left to enjoy the island. We're rolling out at six tomorrow morning."

"Ugh," Hank groaned. "*Another* early morning."

"You can sleep when you get home," Paul said warmly as he steered Hank to the museum exit.

"Vacations are supposed to be relaxing," Hank replied as Paul held the door open for him. "I feel like I need another vacation just to recover from this one."

Paul chuckled. "Can't say we haven't kept you busy." He followed Hank to the tour van.

HOURS LATER, Hank trotted down the sidewalk and around the corner as the tour van pulled away from the restaurant. Paul had been none too happy with him when Hank left on foot instead of piling into the van for the return trip to the hotel, but he had no plans to spend his last night in Ireland sleeping away in a hotel room. He had carefully studied the maps before dinner to find his later destination. The loud nightlife of Dublin awaited, just a few blocks away in the Temple Bar district.

Slowing his pace a little as he rounded another corner, Hank took one last drag of his cigarette before tossing the smoldering butt into the grated street gutter as he stepped past.

Walking faster in the damp chill of late evening as he headed down Dame Street, Hank stuffed his hands into the pockets of the rugby hoodie he'd gotten days before at one of the tourist shops.

He kept a brisk pace as he moved toward the bustling corner ahead. Growing up in a small town, he never did like being out on city streets at night. The unfamiliar urban terrain left him feeling exposed and vulnerable.

That sensation of being watched continued to follow him. A quick glance back showed nothing but a faint, gloomy fog hanging in the night. The gray mist seemed to grow thicker as he got closer to the river.

As he started to cross the street, Hank noticed a tall thug strolling on the opposite sidewalk. A look of danger radiated off the guy as he strutted quickly down the walk in tight acid-washed jeans and a dark leather jacket. The tribal piercings on his scruffy face stood out bone-white in the gloomy dark.

Hank walked a little slower and stuck to his own sidewalk in order to give the thug a wide berth. No sense in asking for trouble while walking the streets of a foreign city at night. Hank breathed a little easier when the intimidating guy turned at the corner.

It didn't take much longer for Hank to find his way to the safety of a flashing pink neon sign over the rainbow painted door of a corner pub. If the pink neon and pride rainbow weren't enough of a hint, the loud thumping of the incessant diva-dance music escaping from inside would have clued Hank in to the fact that he had finally found his people.

He took a deep, relaxing breath at the sight. Hank fingered the new Claddagh ring he wore on his right hand with its heart facing outward, to signify he was single and available. With a grin, he entered the gay pub.

Inside a small entry hall, the counter was manned by a handsome, burly bouncer. Hank smiled and flashed the ring at him. "How much?" he asked when he noticed the cash register.

The bouncer showed no interest in his ring. "Won't charge a cover now," he replied in a brogue. "But you'z better make it quick. Pub closes in ten minutes."

"Ten minutes?" Hank balked as he looked at the door. "But, it's not even midnight yet."

"Aye. The pub closes at midnight," the bouncer repeated drearily.

"Well, fuckin' A," Hank drawled. "What am I supposed to do now?"

"Could always try the Boilerhouse," the bouncer offered with a shrug. "Blue door down at the end of the west street. Open twenty-four hours."

Hank paused in the entryway. The Boilerhouse was another name his research of gay venues had turned up, but he'd quickly dismissed the idea of visiting a bathhouse. Something about those places had always felt a little sleazy to Hank. "Do any of the other pubs stay open later?"

The bouncer shook his head. "No. The other late one also shuts at midnight."

Fuckin' A, Hank thought again as he left the pub. Stepping onto the street and turning to the west, he studied the entrance to the street the bouncer had mentioned. The narrow opening between the buildings was shrouded by a foggy gloom this late at night, which would normally feel spooky and intimidating to Hank, but something about the way the pink neon's glow reflected in the fog made it feel warm.

Turning around, he glanced back the way he had come, but he could hardly see more than a few feet past the pub as the heavy, night fog continued to roll off the nearby river, secluding the street in a thickening barrier.

Hank looked back to the side street. The flashing pink mist thinned in the middle, showing an ocean-colored door near the end of the short walk. The pink fog seemed to welcome Hank.

What the hell, Hank decided as he walked down the street and turned into the alley. *Let's try a bathhouse.*

Chapter 2

WRAPPING THE towel tighter around his waist, Hank entered the steam room on the second floor. Heavy vapors swirled in the dimly lit space, making it nearly impossible for him to see. The room's only source of light seemed to be the frosted glass door that had closed behind him. He took two steps into the clouded dusk and stood unobtrusively near the wall.

When his eyes adjusted to the foggy dim, Hank could see two figures sitting on a bench that flanked the opposite wall, but he couldn't make out any details. One vague figure was a thin guy leaning forward with his elbows resting on his knees in a closed posture. The other shape was much bulkier, more of a bear. He leaned back and spread open the gap in the towel wrapped around his waist, fondling himself. As the bear stroked his hand under the towel, he spread his legs wider apart to signal an invitation.

Hank didn't find either figure very appealing, but at least the room was warm. His entire week in Ireland had been marred with clouds and a spitting drizzle that rarely found enough gumption to turn into real rain. The afternoons barely made it to seventy degrees, or twenty-one degrees Celsius as advertised by the little clock display of the tour van, quite a far cry from the ninety-eight-degree heat of June Hank had left behind in Texas.

The warm steam brought blessed relief after the eight nights of damp chill that seemed to settle into his joints and stiffen his journey-weary muscles. Leaning back into the wall, Hank let out a grateful sigh as he relaxed against the tiles. He could feel the first signs of a glistening sweat as the heat enveloping him warmed his skin and penetrated deeper into his tissues. He shifted his weight from one foot to the other. His arches were still tired after the brisk walk through the Temple Bar district. More aggravation on top of eight previous days of much walking and hiking around the sights and towns where his tour bus stopped.

The room's illumination suddenly increased when someone pulled open the door and stepped inside. Hank scanned the faces of the guys on the bench in front of him. The thin guy was definitely a twink, barely twenty-one, and the bear was probably pushing sixty. He felt no desire whatsoever for either man.

Before the door closed, he turned to glance at the new occupant. This nicely shaped silhouette was in his midthirties and not too tall, maybe five-ten—someone much more within Hank's range of appeal. Hank flashed him a smile as the door slipped closed and the dusky dark returned.

Thirtyish guy took a tentative step forward as his eyes acclimated. He took another step forward as Hank shifted his weight to the other foot. Hank looked up at the man's face, but the thick mist obscured any details. While taking another step closer, the guy reached out his hand and lightly touched Hank's left shoulder.

Hank leaned toward the hand in silent supplication. The man's fingers lightly stroked the top of his shoulder and up the side of Hank's neck. An involuntary sigh escaped from Hank as the gentle touching aroused him. The thin towel wrapped kilt-like around Hank's waist offered no resistance to his swelling erection.

Stepping around, the guy stood facing Hank and put his other hand on Hank's right shoulder. With both hands, he lightly kneaded at the bulge of knotted muscles on the sides of Hank's neck resulting from the long week of carrying a heavy duffel bag.

Hank pushed himself from the wall to stand at his full height, short though he was, and reached his hand up to gently grasp and squeeze the shapely bicep of the man's right arm. As Hank reached for the man's clavicle with his other hand, thirtyish guy removed his hands and pulled back, moving along the wall toward the room's corner. He hesitated a brief moment at the back wall, then disappeared.

Hank walked to the corner and soon realized the wall he had been leaning against was merely a divider and at the corner, a gap opened into another room behind him. Trying to move nonchalantly, he followed the guy through the opening. He paused just inside the doorway. This room captured even less light, making it nearly pitch-black. After a moment of visual acclimation, Hank could barely see the vaguest of shapes in front of him.

He walked to a bench discernable in the darkness. As he moved, a hand brushed against his butt while something else, maybe a hip, grazed his lower arm. When he neared the bench, a hand gently closed around his wrist and pulled him forward. Hank sat on the edge of the bench next to the shadowy figure turned sideways and reclining in the corner.

Another hand reached out and joined the hand around his wrist, slowly gliding and squeezing as it measured upward along Hank's arm until it reached his armpit. A deep, masculine voice whispered, "Tá tú mionfhear."

"Uh, 'scuse me?" Hank replied.

The hand stroking his arm paused. With a strong Irish accent, the voice asked, "No Gaelic?"

"No," Hank drawled in his Texas tongue. "I don't know any Gaelic. What did ya say?"

The man released his grip on Hank's arm and slid his fingers along the shoulder to Hank's neck. Hank felt hardened calluses on the thumb and fingers of the stranger's hand, and he quickly realized this wasn't the smooth hand of thirtyish guy.

Gently cupping Hank's head, the hand pulled Hank forward. Hank turned sideways on the bench to face the mysterious man in the corner, then scooted closer, until his hip rested against the shadowy figure's hip.

Near Hank's ear, the Irish voice whispered, "I said, you are such a tiny man."

The lyrical sounds of the Irish voice whispering so near sent a slight shiver of pleasure through Hank. "Not tiny, I'm five foot four. Don't ask me how many centimeters, coz I shur don't know that."

Hank felt the bursts of breath near his ear as the man quietly chuckled. "We usually measure height in meters," the voice whispered back. "I would guess one-point-six, or 160 centimeters, if a bigger number makes you feel better." The hand slid from Hank's neck and around to the front, slowly sliding down to Hank's chest. "Where are you from?"

The combination of the man's touch and exotic accent sent a stronger shiver through Hank. "The US," Hank drawled in a shaky voice. "Texas, out in the boonies."

The hand on his chest paused. "Are you afraid, Tex?" the strong Irish voice whispered in question.

As the lyrical words sent another shiver through Hank, he realized the contradiction hidden in the voice. It seemed so deep and strong, like it was used to bellowing with the calls of an army drill sergeant, but the lowered whisper tempered it with a softer gentleness. Hank reached into the darkness and found a stubbly chin. "No," he replied firmly, as he stroked the firm prickly jaw with his fingers.

"Then, why does your voice tremble?"

Hank shrugged, but of course his new friend wouldn't be able to see it in the misty dark. "Excitement. Anticipation, I guess."

"Enough excitement to tremble?" the Irish voice asked. "How old are you, Tex?"

From the open side of the room, Hank felt another hand reach out from the dark and touch his knee. Then that hand wrapped around and squeezed at his calf almost hard enough to hurt. Hank reached down and slapped at the hand, pushing it away. The hand returned again, this time on his thigh, but it gently sat without the squeeze. Hank turned back to the corner and answered, "I'm forty-one."

The hand on his thigh quickly disappeared. The stranger's hand on his chest didn't hesitate; it continued exploring the tuft of hair over his sternum and moved toward one of Hank's nipples.

"I see," the strong voice replied, sounding almost amused. "And does Tex have a wife waiting for him in the States?"

"No, I'm queer as a three-dollar bill. Why would you think that?"

The shadowy figure chuckled and shifted before lips brushed against his ear. The intimate touch caused a quiver all over Hank's spine.

In a very gentle whisper, the Irish voice replied, "I'm still a bit puzzled. A man over forty shouldn't find sex quite so exciting anymore." The hand moved from his chest up to the back of Hank's head and followed his skull up to the top, feeling Hank's short hair that curled slightly in the high humidity. "Is your boyfriend here? Or husband maybe?"

"Don't have one."

"But you seem so attractive. You're not throwing blarney at me, I hope."

"No," Hank argued. "I did kiss the Blarney Stone yesterday, but it's the truth." He moved his hand across his new friend's ear and around to the back of his neck, feeling the same short stubble he had felt on the jaw. He brought his hand up and over, finding the same buzzed stubble all over the stranger's head.

"You were in Cork yesterday?" the Irish man asked from the darkness.

"Yes," Hank answered as the shadowy figure shifted again. The lips gently brushed against his ear, then kissed it lightly before a warm, moist tongue lightly explored the ridges and valleys of cartilage. "Oh," Hank said with a sighing tone as a jolting quiver raced down his spine and swelled his cock almost instantly.

Hank pulled his brain back into gear as the mouth explored his earlobe, then suckled lightly at his jaw. What was it about this man? He'd never in his life felt anything like this. With just a few whispered words or a gentle touch, this shadowy figure had the power to reduce him to quivering gelatin.

"Why?" the man asked in his ear.

"Why what?"

"How come you are still single?" the whispery voice inquired.

"I just am."

"Aye jeust ahm," the man replied with a teasing tone, trying to match Hank's Texas drawl.

"Hush," Hank scolded, reaching out and swatting the shadowy figure somewhere on the upper arm. "Yer not bein' nice."

The man chuckled warmly. "You are *so* bloody cute." He reached up and stroked at Hank's cheek. "I think you're blushing, aren't you."

"Hush," Hank hissed as his cheeks warmed and tightened with what he knew was indeed a blush.

He chuckled again. "You didn't really answer my question, love."

"Just too selective, I guess," Hank said as he reached out and found the man's hand in the darkness. "I live in a smaller town, not much to pick from there."

"Certainly there are other gay men in Texas, other places to find them," the Irish man pointed out from the dark.

"Oh sure, I could drive to Dallas or Austin, or even Houston, if I just wanted to get off, but what's the point? All that expense and road time just for a few seconds of pleasure?" Hank moved his grasp to the tips of the man's fingers, feeling the hardened calluses that marred each finger.

"I see." The hand on Hank's cheek slid down and cradled his jaw. "Yet, here you are, Tex, in a bathhouse. Why?"

"It's not such a big deal, dude," Hank replied in a tone bordering on defensive.

"Dude," the man repeated with another amused chuckle. "Maybe not, or maybe it is. It's quite a puzzle, don't you think?"

"Call it an act of desperation, then. The dinner show ran long tonight, and by the time I made it out to the bars, they were closing. Who ever heard of shutting down a bar at midnight? On a Saturday night even?"

"What time do the bars close in Texas?" the Irish man asked as the hand gently stroked Hank's smooth jaw, moving forward to his chin.

"Close at 2:00 a.m., and that's prob'ly only because they're required to by law. They'd prob'ly stay open all night if they could."

A thumb stretched up and stroked at Hank's lip as the Irish man gently asked, "Why desperation?"

Someone groped at his foot in the dark. Hank pulled up his knees and scooted his back against the wall. "I wasn't about to leave Ireland without touching at least one Irish pecker."

The man chuckled as the shadowy figure adjusted position. "I see. And how many peckers have you touched tonight?"

"None, yet," Hank admitted.

"Don't try to blarney me. Even Texas guys don't go to a bathhouse just to look," the man said, sounding a little miffed.

"It's the truth," Hank reassured. "This is the closest I've gotten so far tonight."

"And why?" the man asked in a whisper.

"I'm not exactly a gay dreamboat. I don't fit the tall-dark-handsome or the hairy-bear molds, so I don't generate much interest."

"I see," he replied.

Hank reached up and took the man's other hand away from his jaw, examining the fingers and finding calluses on this hand as well. "What kinda work do you do?"

"Boring work," the man dismissed flatly as the figure leaned farther forward. Hank soon felt a warm breath on his ear, followed quickly by the exploring tongue. He sighed as he collapsed against the wall, feeling jolts with every flick and caress of the soft tongue as it moved over his ear ridges. Hank stroked the man's buzzed head, rubbing the stubbly hairs and trying not to moan too loudly.

A quiet fizzing noise started, signaling another round of steam. The room started feeling much warmer as the humidity increased.

The tongue and lips pulled back. "And what brings you to Ireland?" the man asked as the hand drifted farther down Hank's torso toward his navel.

"Vacation. Kinda checking on family roots," Hank explained as he moved his hand along the side of shadowy figure's head and down to his shoulder, where he found very strong and firm muscles on a frame that felt somewhere between thin and average.

"I see," the man cooed as his hand stroked across Hank's ticklish and twitching stomach. "You have Irish family?"

"Immigrants on both Mom's and Dad's sides. My last name is Lear, which was changed by my great-plus-grandfather on arrival, from O'Leary."

"And your first name is?"

"Hank. It's a nickname for Harrison." Hank moved his hand around the ball of the shoulder and down to a firm bicep. "And what's yours?"

"Pah—" the voice said before hesitating. "Darren."

Darren reached down with both hands and cradled his torso just above the hips, gently gripping and sliding up to his armpits. The steam room was getting so hot, Hank was starting to feel light-headed. He cleared his throat and asked, "What *were* you going to say your name was?"

"You noticed that, huh?" Darren said with a chuckle. "I was going to say Paddy."

"Ah. I gather that's the Irish version of John Doe." Hank reached out both hands and framed the sides of Darren's chest, placing a thumb on each nipple and gently rubbing them. His cock twitched from the joyous moan Darren uttered. Hank leaned toward the shadowy figure's head and whispered, "But you decided not to lie."

"I know," Darren whispered back with his Irish accent. "For some reason, I felt the need to be honest."

Lips brushed against his nose, and Hank smelled the distinctive aroma of Guinness ale before the lips found his. Moving his hand behind Darren's head, Hank pulled him into a strong kiss, opening his mouth and welcoming the flavor of Darren's breath and tongue spiced with the heady Irish ale. Darren moved his hands to Hank's shoulder blades, pulling him closer with a gentle strength as their tongues playfully explored. The heat of the room continued to increase.

Darren broke the kiss and moved his mouth to Hank's ear. "Tahg— Come home with me?" he whispered in a hesitant tone.

The increasing heat of the steam room was pushing Hank past light-headed into woozy. He would have to leave and cool off for a few minutes before he passed out. "I can't. I have to catch a plane later today."

"When?"

"Have to be back at the hotel by 5:00 a.m. to finish packing and grab the bus to the airport."

Darren pulled back his arm. Hank could see the tiny luminous glow from the hands and digits on his wristwatch. It seemed unusual Darren didn't have a digital watch, like most people Hank knew.

With a tone of disappointment, Darren told him, "That's only a few hours from now."

Hank started to answer, but the woozy state was quickly leading to nausea. He *had* to leave. Now. "Sorry, I'm getting too hot, I have to get out of here," he blurted as he crawled to the edge of the bench.

"Come home with me," Darren asked again as he reached out and patted Hank's hand.

"Can't," Hank said as he struggled to his feet and felt his way along the wall to the gap. He rounded the corner and made it to the door, blinking as he burst out into the light that seemed so bright.

AS THE tiny man scurried away, Darren pushed against the wall and stood up, peeking over the divider wall in time to see Tex exit the steam room. Darren felt a pang of loss when he saw how adorably handsome the little blond guy was. He stared at the exit as the door closed again. He wanted so much to chase after that man, but knew it was eminently safer, here in the dark. Too many consequences were likely if Darren showed his face in the light.

Besides, the man is leaving the country soon, he reminded himself, trying to feel convinced of his decision as he sat back on the bench. The steam roiled around him in agitation as it hissed out of the wall.

HANK SQUINTED in the bright fluorescent lights as he moved across the room past the gurgling hot tub and leaned against the wall near the showers. He took deep breaths of the cooler air to try and settle his stomach, all the while keeping his eyes on the steam room door.

Even if he'd had all the time in the world, Hank wasn't about to agree to go home with someone sight unseen, so to speak. Groping in the dark could only go so far in learning about a person, and he had no idea how old Darren was and only the vaguest notion of what he looked like. Hank watched the door, but no one else exited. Hank shifted his weight to the other tired foot. He had expected Darren would follow right behind him and felt disappointed that he hadn't.

After another minute, the steam room door swung open, but it was thirtyish guy exiting. Although he was kind of hunky with his ear-length black hair and bright-blue eyes framed by a clean shaven face, Hank knew it wasn't Darren.

Thirtyish guy glanced his way briefly. Then he averted his gaze and lifted his nose in a show of noninterest, before he walked down the hall to the toilets.

Hank felt like that was the story of his love life. Guys might be interested in the gloomy dark, but upon seeing how short, and more recently old, he was in full illumination, those same guys quickly lost interest. Not that Hank thought of his forty-one years as old, but much of the gay community tended to be shallow and regarded thirty-five as pushing the age barrier.

Two more guys emerged over the next five minutes, but none had the buzzed head and beard of Darren. Obviously, he hadn't been *truly* interested in Hank, and had quickly found another guy to share his affections.

Chiding himself for feeling let down, Hank pushed off the wall and wandered to the stairs. Darren seemed too young for him, anyway. He might as well venture up and see what could be found on the higher levels of the Dublin bathhouse.

THE TOP of the landing led to a dark-blue-painted hall. After a few twisty corners, the hall opened into a TV room with the sights and sounds of a pornographic movie pouring into the theater-like space. Hank stopped and leaned over the back of the bleacher-style box of enclosed seating platforms to watch the show. The video playing was the typical pair of twenty-five-ish guys with perfect bodies going down on each other.

Hank glanced at the older guy reclining on the top bench. He looked to be in his late forties and balding on top, but he had deep-green eyes and a nice body that he clearly kept in shape. Hank watched him masturbate his uncut cock, feeling a bit of interest in the older guy, until the guy reached over and roughly grabbed Hank's hand, trying to forcefully pull it down to his crotch. Hank quickly yanked his arm back with a scowl and continued down the hall around the next bend. Any signs of pain or use of aggression were instant turnoffs for Hank.

As he stumbled around the dark corner, Hank found himself in nearly pitch-black darkness again. He took tiny steps as he groped forward, hoping the lecherous guy wasn't following him. He felt terrycloth and a leg leaned into his touch. Hank moved his hand farther to the right and finally found the smooth wall. He followed it forward a few more steps, stopped moving, and looked back. He didn't see any silhouette behind him, so hopefully the aggressive guy had stayed in the TV room.

Hank stood still and listened. The sounds of slurping and sliding accompanied grunts and groans from farther in the room. From the number of sounds, the dark room seemed to be a bustling hive of activity. It was Saturday night, after all. Hank felt a sudden chill of being observed.

To his left, an irritated Irish accent called out, "Ouch. Watch it, you clumsy fecker."

From somewhere in the dark, Hank thought he felt something squishy and cold crawling by his foot, then he felt something like stiff bristles. He quickly yanked his foot up.

Not wanting to contemplate what was on the floor, he quickly turned to leave the way he had come in, but a silhouette appearing at the end of the hall made him freeze. He thought the lecher might have decided to follow him after all, but then he noticed how tall the approaching figure was. He didn't recall the older man being more than, maybe, five foot eight. This shadowy figure had to be at least six foot tall.

With the slight backlighting, Hank could see the figure extend an arm and grope for the wall. The figure found it and began moving forward, bumping right into Hank. As the figure's other hand reached out and touched his shoulder, Hank noticed the luminescent glow of the analog watch. The other hand slid down the wall until it touched the top of Hank's head. The fingers rubbed lightly through his hair.

"Tex?" the voice of Darren whispered nearby.

Feeling both thrilled and irritated, Hank replied in a sharp sarcastic tone, "Ya forgot my name already?"

"That was unkind," Darren replied in a slightly hurt tone. "Harrison Texas Hank Tex Lear O'Leary. How could I forget such a name?"

Hank couldn't help but chuckle at the long string of names. "Well, you seemed to forget me quick enough once I left the steam room. I waited for you to follow me, Darren, but you didn't." Hank reached up and clasped the hand that rested on his shoulder. "Why is it we keep meeting in the dark?"

"You picked this place," Darren said as he moved his hand from Hank's head down to his ear. "I simply followed when I saw you come in."

"So, you saw me? How'd you know it was me?"

"You are the only tiny man I've seen here."

Hank rolled his eyes, even though Darren couldn't see it in the darkened conditions. "Don't call me tiny, it feels a bit insulting."

Darren leaned down and put his mouth next to Hank's ear before whispering, "Apologies. I don't mean it as an insult."

"I know you don't, but still…." Hank let the statement trail off as Darren's tongue explored the crevices of his ear again.

Darren slid his hand down Hank's side to the towel, groping gently until he found Hank's solid erection poking out of the gap of the terrycloth.

Hank reached forward, gleefully surprised by the firm warm stomach his fingers encountered. He stroked his hands farther down as Darren widened his stance and separated his legs. Hank reached inside the gap of the towel and found an uncircumcised penis standing firm and waiting for his hand. The dick seemed to swell in his grasp.

Darren examined Hank's cock first with one hand, then used both hands to explore along the head. With calloused fingers, he touched and rubbed. "I certainly won't call you tiny anymore. Are you Jewish?"

"No," Hank answered as he examined Darren's foreskin with his fingers. "Just an American thing. For a while doctors thought it was a matter of public cleanliness and safety to circumcise all baby boys. And they often did it without even asking the parent's permission."

"I see," Darren said with a disheartened tone. "How unpleasant."

"It's not like I remember it, or anything. I guess that's one advantage to being a baby." Hank squeezed at the solid hooded cock in his hands. He loved the way it bent gracefully upward, like it was seeking Darren's navel. With that kind of a curve, it would probably hit right on his prostate button if Darren penetrated him in a facing position.

Stop it. Don't think about it, Hank scolded himself.

As if reading his mind, Darren slid his hand with a slow glide under the towel around Hank's thigh and to his butt. He rubbed and lightly clenched at the firm cheek under his hand. "Is this okay?"

"Ah, yeah," Hank choked out in a shaky voice as Darren leaned down and suckled on the side of his neck.

Darren groped farther around to the cleavage of Hank's ass, gently stroking at the crevice with his fingers as he pushed his hard cock against Hank's hip. "Certain about that?" he asked with a hint of concern as he pulled his mouth away.

Hank bent forward and widened his legs, opening himself further to Darren's hand. "Very," he said as he leaned up and kissed Darren's mouth. This man tasted so damn good. The fingers lightly teasing his anus felt oh-so great. Hank's engine was cranking up in ways it hadn't in many years.

Darren removed his hand, then broke the kiss long enough to moisten one of his fingers with his mouth. He returned the hand to Hank's ass as he kissed him again. Ever so carefully, he worked his slickened finger inside of Hank, until Hank broke the kiss with a groan.

Darren backed the finger out a bit. "You're so bloody tight. Am I too fast?"

Hank pushed back against the finger. "Hell no. I just forgot what it feels like. It's been about fifteen years since I've had anybody inside me."

Wiggling the finger in deeper, Darren asked next to his ear, "You're mostly a top?"

"Mostly celibate," Hank replied before another surge of pleasure made him moan.

"Are you a damn priest?"

"No. The celibacy was involuntary, I can assure you." Hank tried to relax and open himself to further probing as he reached forward and grasped Darren's ready and able cock. "Are you mostly a top?"

"Versatile," Darren replied as he withdrew his finger.

Hank sighed with frustration. *Don't even think about letting this man screw me. I don't even know what he looks like yet. And* definitely *not in the middle of a bathhouse.* Hank pulled back and released Darren's cock. "I want to see you."

"Come home with me, then," Darren offered again with a husky whisper. "We can see and explore every millimeter of each other that way. You deserve so much more than a quick-off in the dark."

Hank took a firm hold of Darren's hand and tried to lead him back to the lighted hallway, but Darren resisted. "Why don't you want me to see you? Is it the height difference? Coz I already noticed that. And it doesn't bother me at all."

"I didn't imagine it would," Darren replied as he held his ground without elaborating.

Hank tugged at his hand. "Then, let me see you."

"Is it that important?" Darren asked with a tone that sounded almost wounded.

"The more you resist," Hank drawled as he pulled at Darren. "The more it makes me think yer tryin' to hide some terrible disfigurement, or something."

"Trust me, I'm not," Darren said quickly, his accent sounding thicker. "You sound so bloody hot when you get all riled up, like one of those Ewings from that oil telly show."

"Ya haven't seen me riled, yet," Hank warned as he tugged again.

Darren pulled on his arm and drew him close. "Bump your flight. Stay another night."

"*Bump my flight?*" Hank asked in disbelief. "My ticket's already paid for. With a travel agency. I don't think I can do that without losing a lot of money."

Darren pulled him into a firm but gentle hug and kissed his forehead. "You are so *bloody* cute." He kissed Hank's forehead again. "And yes, you can. Airlines do it all the time." Bending and kneeling slightly until his mouth was right next to Hank's ear, he whispered in a husky Irish voice, "Teigh liom abhaile? Come home with me. Please?"

The firm embrace and lyrical Gaelic words sent a surge coursing through Hank's body. He leaned against Darren to keep from collapsing. "Jeezus. What are ya doin' to me?" Hank uttered in a quiet hiss.

"Something nice, I hope," Darren whispered back. "Please? I promise you won't regret it."

"No," Hank said strongly as he pulled himself away. "I can't do that. I won't make that kind of a promise until I at least see the goods first."

Darren stood. "If we must, then let it be," he conceded with a tone of resignation.

Hank took his hand and walked along the wall, keeping his eyes on Darren as they approached the lighted hall.

As more light fell on Darren in a slow reveal, Hank first noticed the darker blotches that covered his arms and chest, like maybe discolored burn scars? But Hank hadn't felt any scars when he had rubbed Darren's upper body.

More light revealed Darren had a rounded face with only the slightest traces of thirtiness. He was blessed with a smaller rounded nose, almost boyish in appearance. Then, with another step back, more light showed the ginger-brown color of the stubble covering his head and jaw. Hank also saw a thin bone stuck in an eyebrow piercing over Darren's left eye and one of those large, tribal, bone earrings stabbed through his right earlobe. *How could I have missed that?* Hank wondered, before he realized Darren had always kept his left side facing him.

Once fully in the lit corner, Hank could see that Darren's upper-body blotches were actually a huge tableau of colorful tattoo panels separated by intricate ropes of Celtic-knot borders covering his upper arms, chest and back.

This wasn't at all what Hank expected. The overall sight was so thuggishly gangster, completely at drastic odds with the gentle nature of the man Hank had grown so fond of in the dark. Then, with a sudden realization, Hank recognized Darren as the leather-jacket-wearing thug he had seen on the opposite sidewalk of Dame Street just a few hours before.

Hank tried to hold a poker face as he looked over Darren, but some disdain must have leaked through.

With a frown, Darren pulled his hand out of Hank's grasp. "Go ahead. You can run now."

"I'm not running," Hank replied as he studied Darren's face more closely. A nagging thought kept itching in his mind. Underneath all the thuggy accoutrements, he thought he recognized something else familiar about Darren. Yet, he couldn't quite place it.

"You look very shocked."

"Well, it's surely not what I expected, and it *is* a bit of a surprise, but that doesn't mean it scares me."

Darren offered a weak smile, showing only the slightest glimmer of hope. "I really don't scare you?"

"No," Hank said with a firm headshake. "Now, if I hadn't talked to you first, and you just approached me out of nowhere, it would be a different story," Hank replied, wondering if he should mention that he *had* avoided Darren on the street earlier in the evening.

Darren smiled with more confidence.

Hank reached up to the tattooed chest, tracing his finger along the tight and twisted lines of a Celtic knot inked into Darren's skin. "How long did it take to get all this work done?"

"Years," Darren answered without elaborating.

"How much did all this cost?"

"A guil—friend of the family is a tattoo artist, and I let him practice on me when he was first learning the trade. He still likes to use me as a guinea pig, trying out new techniques and such. So it was cost-free."

Hank admired the exquisite details. "It doesn't *look* like he needs to practice. This is fantastic work."

Darren grinned as he gazed down at Hank with bright, rich green eyes. "I'll tell him you said so." After a brief hesitation, Darren quickly asked, "Bump your flight?"

With a tight smile, Hank replied, "After seeing in the light just how short and old I am, I'm surprised yer still asking."

"Why? Any man who wouldn't want to take your cuteness home must be insane."

Hank smirked. "Well then, there's *lots and lots* of insane men in the world." Hank looked up the hallway when he saw movement from the corner of his eye. A thin twinkie started down the hall, but upon seeing Darren glare at him, he suddenly decided he needed to go the other way. The abrupt about-face nearly made Hank chuckle.

"Bump your flight?" Darren asked again as he glanced down at his watch.

Hank also looked at the watch. Almost immediately, now that he could see it in full light, he realized it was a frigging Cona. A platinum Cona, emblazoned with a world map and depicting all twenty-four time zones. One of the most expensive watches ever made. He shot his eyes back at Darren with shock that melded into a growing suspicion. How did this thug manage to get a Cona Philmo platinum watch?

"What?" Darren asked with a confused and worried tone when he saw the smolder in Hank's eyes.

"Really?" Hank grabbed Darren's hand and raised it to display the watch. "A Cona?" Hank tossed his hand away as he took a step back. "What kind of shit did you pull to get your hands on one?"

Darren's face collapsed into a pained expression. "Quieter. Please?" he implored in a nearly begging tone. "You recognize it? How?"

"Ya think coz I'm from Texas that makes me some clueless bumpkin?" Hank accused in a harsh whisper.

"No," Darren quietly said as he shook his head and leaned down closer. "Most people don't recognize it for what it is."

"Well, I ain't like most people, if ya haven't noticed."

"Oh yes," Darren replied with a wry smile. Darren glanced back at the hallway with a vulnerable gaze. "There's a dance bar downstairs, in the basement. More private. Let's go for a sit?"

"I'm not goin' anywhere 'til you cough up some answers," Hank drawled a little louder.

"Please? Downstairs?" Darren begged again in a hushed whisper as he stroked his fingers along Hank's arm.

"Fine, whatever," Hank agreed reluctantly as Darren's fingers gently rubbed his forearm, but he still smoldered with a trace of suspicion.

Chapter 3

HANK FOLLOWED as Darren led them down three flights of stairs to the main floor. Loud dance music greeted them as they descended a spiral staircase to a tiny room with a small bar flanked by four barstools. The space was empty, not counting the fiery-haired DJ who stood before a mixing board in the corner. Darren motioned for Hank to sit next to him as he lowered himself to a stool.

The DJ abandoned the music equipment in the corner and stepped behind the bar. "What's your poison?" he asked in an almost generic accent, bearing only the slightest touches of Irish inflection.

"Guinness?" Darren asked, looking over at Hank.

"Sure, whatever," Hank flatly replied.

The DJ/barkeep grabbed two pint glasses and filled each from the tap until the frothy heads reached the top. Then he set the glasses down for the required rest time.

Darren turned to Hank. "I have *certainly* noticed you aren't like most people," he said, resuming their previous conversation. "Why do you think I asked you home?"

Hank shrugged. "I didn't think twice about it. I figured it was just part of yer MO."

"Emmoh?"

"Modus operandi, yer typical way of doin' things."

Darren burst into a round of chuckles. "Bloody hell, love. If you knew me better, you'd know that was the farthest thing from the truth."

"But, I *don't* know you," Hank replied in a tired tone as he glanced at the watch on Darren's wrist. "Not that you've even bothered to answer my question."

Darren looked at the barkeep, watching as he picked up the first glass to finish topping off the Guinness. He turned to Hank, but before he could speak, a thumping ruckus drew their attention to the staircase. They turned and watched as a very inebriated guy stomped and stumbled his way down the last few spiral steps.

The drunk paused at the bottom, then peered around the basement bar. His gaze froze when his eyes landed on Darren. He suddenly straightened and covered his mouth as he squealed like a twelve-year-old girl. "Darr?" he yelled out in half question, half accusation as he rushed toward the bar.

Glaring coldly, Darren rotated on the barstool until the huge bone ear piercing was prominently displayed, then barked out, "What the fuck did you call me?"

The drunk screeched to a halt and turned ghostly pale as fear crawled over his features. "Uh," he stammered as he backed away. "Sorry, thought you'z somebody else." He turned and quickly crawled his way back up the spiral steps.

The barkeep eyed them closely as he set down the full glasses on the bar. Hank turned and stared at Darren. That voice, the drill-sergeant bark Darren had just used was no surprise. Hank had already sensed that power, but the display of rough thug he'd just witnessed *did* surprise him. Had he just seen a glimpse of the *real* Darren?

Darren reached out for the glass, but the barkeep glared at him. "That's eight euro, lad."

"Oh, right," Darren said as he reached down instinctively to his butt and found nothing but terrycloth. "Shite," he replied as he stood. "I'll be right back." While Darren unclasped the little wrist strap that held his locker key, Hank noticed the locker number "234" imprinted on the band. Darren stood and quickly ascended the stairs for the lockers.

Hank looked over at the barkeep when he sensed the man staring at him. "What?" he asked defensively.

The man tightened his lips into a tiny smile. "Nothing," he said generically.

Hank's thoughts wandered back to Darren. Was the gentle voice in the dark just a façade? A carefully crafted lure? Or was the gruff display he'd just witnessed the real façade? Hank shook his head. The details about this guy just weren't adding up. He gazed up at the clock and saw 3:04 a.m. Only two hours left to get laid, then get back to the hotel. An hour and a half, more realistically, since he'd have to factor in walking time.

Glancing back at the stairs, Hank contemplated leaving. He still had time to head back upstairs and find some action. Yet, he turned his gaze back to the pints on the bar. *I'll drink the man's beer, then get back to it. I'm too tired and too short of time to deal with all this confusing bullshit*, Hank decided as he heard the rapid thumping of steps on the staircase.

Darren rushed back to his seat and handed the barkeep a twenty-euro bill. He picked up his glass and turned to Hank. "Drink," he urged.

Hank picked up his glass and blew at the foamy head before taking a sip of the dark brew. "Ya know, this shit's actually pretty damn good."

The barkeep set down the change. As Darren pushed two euro coins back to the barkeep, he replied, "Tex, don't tell me this is your first Guinness?"

"Nah, been drinkin' 'em all week. I hope I'll be able to find it back home," he replied as his gaze wandered back to the offensive watch.

Darren followed Hank's gaze, then watched the barkeep return to the music equipment in the corner. He looked at Hank with a tight smile, saying, "I can't tell you here. Bump your flight and come home with me, and I promise I'll explain everything."

Hank turned to him with a weary stare. "What's this obsession with you draggin' me home? Do you wanna fuck me that badly?"

Darren's face scrunched into a pout. "Bloody hell! If all I wanted was a fuck, I'd have maneuvered you into one of the upstairs cubicle-rooms an hour ago."

"Really? Then yer a psycho serial killer and I'm the next pigeon on the menu?"

Sucking in a breath, Darren look scalded. "*What*? How could you *think* such a thing?"

"What am I supposed to think?" Hank asked with a weary shrug. "You won't tell me a goddamned thing, other than, 'Come home with me and all the secrets of the universe will be revealed.' *Really*?"

An expression of utter defeat slumped over Darren's face. He took two huge gulps of his pint, then set the remainder on the bar. "Obviously, this situation is fucked beyond salvage." He stood and spoke crisply. "Enjoy your pint, Harrison, and I hope you remember Eire fondly," he said as warmly as he could before walking briskly to the staircase and ascending rapidly.

Hank turned on his stool and watched the shapely thighs, then calves of Darren climb up until he vanished from sight. A part of him, actually a damn-big part, screamed that it was a huge mistake to let this man walk away. Yet, the rest of him was too tired and confused to care.

He gazed up at the clock on the wall, watching the digital colon between the hour and minute blink with each new second, counting away the few remaining hours of his time in Ireland.

Hank took a gulp of his ale.

When he arrived in Ireland, he'd thought of this trip as being his own sort of "eat-pray-love" adventure. The eating and praying parts of the equation had turned out surprisingly remarkable. Hank cracked a smile as he recalled the dinners and music, the busy streets, quiet museums, and ancient ruins that had fed his palate and soul.

Unfortunately, it was the "love" part that proved elusive. *Of course, that shouldn't be any big surprise,* Hank realized with a scowl. Throughout his life, love had always been a reclusive bitch. It always felt like Cupid had lost the name of "Harrison Shay Lear" somewhere in the paperwork on his desk, and after all these years, he still hadn't found it.

Turning back to his beer, he took two slow sips, then set the pint glass down on the bar with a clink. He didn't want any more. As he stood to leave, Hank's gaze fell on the ten-euro bill still sitting on the bar. Darren had left his change behind. Was it meant as a tip, or had

Darren forgotten the money? He paused, staring at the bill and debating whether or not to pick it up. With a sigh, Hank finally decided it wasn't his problem, and left the bill behind as he walked to the stairs.

He glanced back at the clock, reading 3:16 a.m. He unclasped the band holding his locker key around his wrist as he climbed the first step. Enough time to grab a smoke and a quickie before he had to leave. If he couldn't find love, at least he could go enjoy himself.

When he put his foot on the second step, the volume of the dance music suddenly dropped. He turned to look at the DJ/barkeep.

"You going after him?" the man behind the music machine asked.

"No," Hank replied as he stared at the nosey guy. "What's it to you?"

The man simply looked at him with that tight-lipped smile.

"Does that mean you think I should?"

The man held the same smile as something smoldered in his eyes.

"*Don't* answer me then, I didn't ask ya anyway," Hank yelled as he climbed up the rest of the steps. The loud music returned.

"Jeezus," Hank muttered as he walked across the lobby to the locker room. "The nerve of some people." He found his locker and opened it long enough to retrieve one cigarette from the pack and grab the book of matches he'd picked up in the pub at lunch. No sense in risking losing a lighter. He closed the locker door with a clang.

ONCE ON the second floor, Hank went to the balcony exit to the designated smoking area. He stepped outside. Putting the cigarette into his mouth, he bent down to open the matches and a sudden flame in his face startled him. After jumping back, he lit his cigarette from the fancy-looking silver lighter. Maybe his luck was turning and this kind stranger would be worth pursuing. Hank drawled out, "Thank you," as he looked up to the face of his benefactor. Darren smiled sheepishly back at him.

Part of Hank felt ecstatic over finding him once more, but he also felt irritated over having to deal with this thug again. He stared at Darren as he took a heavy drag from his cigarette.

Darren held up the short stub of his own burning smoke. "I'm almost done, then I'll leave you be."

Hank glanced around at the empty benches of the balcony. "No, you won't." He pointed to the corner. "Sit yer ass down and talk to me."

Darren walked over to the corner and sat down by one of the outdoor ashtrays.

"We're alone here," Hank said as he walked up and stood before him. "You can answer some questions." He smelled an aroma, something spicy that made him think of food, as he stared at Darren.

Darren took a quick drag of his smoke. "What questions?" he asked, holding up his palms in surrender.

"I still want to know about that damn watch," Hank said firmly. "How did ya get hold of it?"

"Before I answer that," Darren countered in his smooth Irish accent as he crossed his legs. "I'd like to hear how you recognize it."

Hank tapped his foot in aggravation. Leave it to this asshole to set up a stalemate. "Fine, I'll tell ya, then ya better answer me."

Darren held up his palms. "Promise."

"My parents run an antique store," Hank said as he paced in front of Darren. "I help them sometimes with research, and I happened to see that watch, or one like it anyway, in one of the auction bulletins." Hank stopped in front of him. "That Cona watch was one of only seven ever made, and sold for over a million dollars." He gave a hard stare at Darren. "Your turn."

Darren sucked the last drag from his cigarette, stamped out the butt in the ashtray, then fidgeted with his towel before finally looking up at Hank. "How about you tell me where you think I got it?"

Hank scowled at him. "*More* games? Screw you," Hank barked out as he threw the book of matches at Darren, hitting him in the chest. "Yer either an expertly talented thief, or high up in the mafia. Or something equally as shady." Hank took another huge drag of his smoke. "In any case," he said as he stamped out the half-used cigarette in the ashtray. "Since yer not gonna be honest with me, I'm done with you," he announced as he turned to leave.

"Please?" Darren implored quietly. "None of that is true."

Hank stopped, then turned around. "Okay then, what *is* the truth?"

Darren hesitated. "I bought it."

"You *bought* it?" Hank wobbled his head in complete disbelief.

"Yes," Darren repeated quietly. "What was the name of the buyer at that auction?"

Hank pursed his lips at Darren. "Good try. They don't post the names of buyers, only the sellers. If you knew anything about how auctions work, you'd already know that."

"Then, what can I say to put you at ease?" Darren asked with a quiet shrug.

Hank let out a sigh. "I don't think there *is* anything you can say."

Darren stood. "Which makes this a rather pointless conversation," he said with a tone of failure as he walked past Hank and stepped back into the building.

Hank stomped his bare foot and growled aloud in frustration. *Who the hell does this guy think he is? And why the hell do I even care?* he wondered as he growled up at the darkened skylight.

A cold draft from between the slats reminded Hank that he was standing essentially outdoors, nearly naked. He gruffed out loud as he went back inside. He glanced around the hallway for a clock. Not seeing one, he remembered noticing a clock near the steam room.

Ignoring the parade of nearly naked male flesh surrounding him as he went up another level, Hank made his way to the main room. As he walked down the hall, he heard a quiet wolf whistle. It couldn't be meant for him—he was much too short and old for that kind of attention—so he ignored it and kept walking.

Once in the main room, he stopped and looked up at the clock, reading 3:42 a.m. He still had nearly an hour before he had to leave, but the thought of cruising had lost its appeal. That asshole Darren had him so twisted up, he couldn't even enjoy himself anymore. "Fuckin' A," he muttered quietly. Sighing, Hank decided he might as well just call it a night.

Hank turned and went into the shower alcove, removing his towel and placing it on the wall hook before stepping up to one of the shower heads in the wall. He had to examine it a moment before finding the push button to turn on the water. A warm stream shot down on him for sixty seconds before the water flow stopped. Growling in frustration, he punched the button again and tried to get himself actually wet.

After two more punches, he squirted some of the soap from the dispenser onto his hand and lathered up his body. He turned as he scrubbed at himself and happened to notice the drunk from earlier, despite still wearing his towel, leaning against the tiled wall under one of the other shower heads.

Typically reserved, Hank normally wouldn't socially approach a stranger while soapy and naked, but without even considering the move, Hank marched over to the drunk. "Hey dude," he said loudly.

The drunk turned his head and blinked at him. "Go away, you noisy feck," he said as he punched the shower button again.

Ignoring the order, Hank took a step closer. "When ya saw that guy downstairs, who did ya think it was?"

"Who?" the drunk asked as he blinked in confusion.

"Down in the club, that guy you called 'Darr.' Who did you think it was?"

"Oh," the drunk said as his eyes showed a little life. "Him. I thought he looked like Darr O'Connell."

That name didn't ring any bells with Hank. "And who's that?" he asked as he reached out and punched the button for the drunk.

"Who?"

"Darr O'Connell," Hank said louder. "Who is he?"

The drunk looked at Hank like he was a stupid child. "Lead singer of Celtic Cantrips. Now go away, you make too much noise."

Hank walked slowly back to the shower station he had used earlier. "Celtic Cantrips" was a name he *did* know. Not only had he heard of the group, he even owned one of their CDs and a whole slew of their mp3 songs on his laptop. He often found himself listening to their captivating and haunting music.

He punched the button to rinse off, feeling like a complete idiot. Hank should have realized those calluses on Darren's fingers were guitar-playing artifacts; Hank's uncle had similar marks. That strong voice came not from barking orders, but from being a professional singer. Darren's dodginess and that desire for darkness and privacy was his way of trying to enjoy himself without being recognized in a public setting.

Hank punched the button again and continued to rinse. *I treated him like complete shit, accusing him of being a thief in the mafia.* Hank groaned aloud at the thought. *Could I have been any more of a snippy bitch?*

He reviewed the evening in his mind as he punched the button one last time to rinse the last traces of soap from his feet. A few of the details Hank still found confusing. *Why the obsessive desire to drag me home? Was his music career the "everything" Darren had promised to explain?* That just didn't seem to fit. Darren could have mentioned his career earlier; he could even have been vague and merely said he was a singer in a band. Hank would have been satisfied with that answer. The high level of deception just didn't seem to jibe with the simple facts. There must be more to this situation.

Hank retrieved the towel from the hook and dried himself. *There doesn't necessarily have to be more*, he realized. *The isolation of being famous can easily leave people feeling out of touch and paranoid. Darren could just be overprotective of himself and his group.*

Wrapping the moist towel around himself, Hank headed to the locker room. With a sudden thought of maybe finding him again, he scanned the numbers until he found 234. The locker door stood open and vacant. Darren had already left.

Hank let out a weary sigh. *Not that it matters now,* he thought as he headed to the other end of the locker room and his clothes. *In just a few hours, I'll be on a plane, zooming home and leaving Ireland far behind me.*

Chapter 4

STANDING IN line at the exit, Darren unclasped, then yanked the horrible Cona watch off his arm and stuffed it into his jeans pocket. The next time he saw Brigand, he would throw the offensive thing in his face. *Imbued with magic my arse,* he thought as he turned in his towel and locker key. *All the bloody watch did was bollocks-up my night.*

Darren remembered to check his phone as he left the bathhouse. He fished it from his jacket pocket and turned it on as he started walking north, toward the canal. The busy intersection there had a cabstand, which often held a waiting taxi.

While he walked, Darren glanced at his phone and saw the notice of nine missed calls. He scrolled through the list, seeing nearly all of them were from his sister. *Bloody hell, not another crisis weekend.* He started to dial her number, but the phone vibrated in his hand with another incoming call from her. "What?" he answered gruffly.

"I was calling to ask *you* what. Your stone is pinging like crazy. What the hell's going on with you?" Anne asked with an edge of excitement to her voice.

"Other than a shitty evening? Not much."

"Darr," his sister said anxiously. "Something's going on. What do you mean by shitty?"

"Just… shitty, is all. I met a fantastically great bloke, but it didn't work out."

"You *met* someone?" Anne asked with that excited edge again. "What's he like?"

"It doesn't matter," Darren said in a wounded tone. "He's going home, back to the States, in about two hours."

"States?" Anne echoed in his ear. He could hear her fumbling around with things; then she screamed in his ear, "No fucking way. You *can't* let him leave."

"Why not? It's his choice," Darren said. "I can't *make* him like me."

"*Stop him!*" Anne screamed at him before disconnecting.

Darren looked up from his phone. He had made it to the street corner cabstand, but unfortunately, no cabs were in sight.

His sister could be quirky, sometimes even flaky, but he'd never before heard her sound so fanatical about something. He turned around and walked back to the bathhouse. He could at least catch Tex on his way out, then maybe talk to him again.

AS HE turned in his towel and key, Hank looked at the Claddagh ring he'd put back on his right ring finger. It seemed like such an impulsive purchase now, yet when Hank had seen the ring in the antique shop, the very distinctness of it had grabbed his attention. Most Claddagh rings were simple metal designs, but this one was fashioned from shiny silver and the two hands clasped a heart-shaped, green glass stone. Fifty euro might be a lot for such a simple ring, since it didn't even have a precious gem, but at the time, it didn't seem like enough as Hank eagerly handed over the cash and bought the ring. He was amazed to find the ring fit perfectly without any resizing. Hank had felt happy to find a meaningful piece of Ireland to bring home.

Moving forward in line, Hank rubbed at the ring with his shirttail, but still couldn't seem to remove that strange tarnish. Maybe the antique dealer had used some funky stuff to try and clean it previously, which left behind a mottled pinkish residue on the silver. When he got home, he'd have to ask his mom how to clean it properly. Hank tucked his shirttail back in as he stepped up to the window.

Checkout completed, Hank left the bathhouse and turned south for the long walk back to his hotel. The drizzle was spitting just enough to be miserable, and he still had plenty of time, so he pulled up his hood, then set a slower pace as he crossed Dame Street and turned east.

BACK AT the bathhouse, Darren paused outside the entrance. He should probably wait here, he decided. Leaning against the wall, he fished the pack of clove cigarettes from his jacket and sparked up. It wasn't that paying another twenty-euro admission was a great imposition, but if he went back into the maze of hallways and rooms, he would likely miss Hank altogether. Hank would be leaving soon for his hotel, and Darren could catch him on his way out.

Darren thought fondly about the little man as he took another drag and recalled their discussions in the steam room and later upstairs. At the time, he almost couldn't believe the answers from Hank. Not that Hank's situation was so incredible, but in a strange way, he was echoing the same answers Darren would have given to those questions. The underlying circumstances for Hank and him were completely different, but their situations resulted in the same sense of isolation and lack of love life. *Two peas in neighbor pods,* Darren mused, liking the poetry of the words. *That phrase might have potential to develop into a song.*

Taking another heavy drag, he let his mind drift back to those whispered moments in the dark with Hank. That hesitant frankness in the man's voice, Hank's vulnerable shivers when they had kissed— those things seemed to almost leave a branded mark on Darren's heart.

As Darren dropped the smoldering butt in the gutter, his phone rang again. "What?" he answered.

"Whatever you're doing," Anne's voice scolded him, "it's not working; things are cooling off."

"What do you mean?"

"I mean, it's like he's moving farther away. Did you not stop him?"

"I haven't found him yet," Darren said. "He must have slipped out and I missed him."

"Then, go find him. Where would he go?"

Looking up and down the street, Darren replied, "Back to his hotel most likely, but I don't know where that is."

"Shite, you've got to find him, Darr," Anne said.

"I just want to go home. Is this really that bloody important?"

"Yes!" Anne nearly screamed. "Hotels, hotels," she repeated to herself. "There's that cluster of hotels just south of St. Stephen's that are popular with tourists. Maybe there?"

Darren pushed off the wall and started walking south. "Cluster? How many makes a cluster?"

"Oh, five or six. With the connection you have, you should be able to pin him down."

"Connection?" Darren asked with a tone of doubt.

"Your stone wouldn't have reacted that way if you *didn't* build a connection, love."

After crossing Dame Street, Darren paused, then turned east. "I doubt that. We didn't really connect at all, didn't seem like."

"Quit arguing. Just open your instincts and find him," Anne commanded before breaking the call again.

"Bollocks," Darren cursed out as he put the phone back in his pocket. No matter how many times he scolded her for it, Anne couldn't seem to learn polite phone manners, like saying good-bye. He continued walking briskly toward the large park called St. Stephen's Green.

AFTER TURNING right at the next intersection, Hank continued southeast. His thoughts kept wandering back to Darren as his fingers absently caressed the ring. Part of him wanted very much to turn around and go find him. It wasn't just that Hank felt he owed Darren an apology; his craving seemed to go much deeper than that. *If I had more time, maybe,* he told himself. *Once I get home, maybe I can find an e-mail address or something, and I can get in touch with him that way.*

Hank barely glanced at the two men sitting on a stoop as he walked by. He didn't give them a thought, until one of the guys yelled out in an Irish accent, "Hey, look at the princess, afraid of getting his hair wet."

Normally, Hank would have done the safe thing and just kept walking, maybe a little faster. Yet, nothing seemed normal tonight as he found himself reaching up to yank the hood off and turn around. He took two steps forward to the stoop. "I don't give a shit about my hair gettin' wet," he spat out. "I'm tryin' not to catch cold on my long walk back to the hotel, in this miserable chill you Irish jokingly call a summer," he drawled out rather sharply.

With widened eyes, the boys crouched back onto the steps. Now that he had a closer look, Hank realized they *were* just boys, barely sixteen or so.

"Sorry," one of the boys squeaked out. "We were only messin'. No offense?"

Hank had no idea what the boy meant by "messin'," but he softened at the attempted apology. "Yeah, whatever," he said as he put the hood back on his head and turned to continue his walk.

"Hey mate," the other boy called from behind. "Think you could do us a favor?"

Hank turned around. "What do you mean?"

The boys stood. "There's an off-license—"

"A Spar," the first boy cut in.

"Just up the street. Think you could get us a liter?"

Studying them, Hank asked, "Of what?"

"Bushmills," the first boy said.

Hank shook his head. These Irish boys might have the potential for real trouble if they got tanked-up on whiskey. "How about," he offered as a compromise, "I get two bottles of Guinness."

"Okay," the boys happily agreed. One boy reached for his pocket.

With a dismissive wave, Hank said, "On me. I got some euros to unload before I leave, anyway." Hank started back up the street to the store.

"You're a real mate," one of the guys replied behind him.

Stepping into the small convenience store, Hank removed the hood as he moved to the refrigerated section and picked up two half-liter-sized bottles of the promised brew and carried them to the counter. The older, rotund lady peered at him as she rang up the beers. She cleared her throat. In an accent that sounded almost Swedish, she asked, "Those lads wouldn't happen to still be hanging around?"

Hank tried to smile innocently. "What lads?"

"Right," she replied with a tight smile. "Six euro twenty." After fishing in his wallet, Hank handed her a ten-euro bill. As she handed over the change, the clerk said, "You tell them to find a rubbish bin. If I find those empty bottles in the gutter later, I'll tan their hides."

"Sure," Hank replied as he picked up the bottles and carried them out.

He found the boys back on the stoop and handed each a bottle. "And ya better find a trash can when yer done. That clerk said she'd beat you if you leave the bottles layin' around."

The boys crouched back at the thought. "Okay, we will. Thanks, mate."

"Don't cause any trouble," Hank said as he pulled the hood back up and started his walk again. He continued to the next major street, then turned south, flanking the Green. He'd lost some time with his little side journey to buy the beer, so he picked up his pace as he absently fingered the Claddagh ring.

DARREN FOUND his steps quickening as he turned and followed the next street southeast. Up ahead, two boys sat on the steps of a row house. The boys quickly hid something between them as he approached. Darren stopped and asked, "You lads didn't happen to see a tiny man pass by here?"

"Tiny man?" one of the boys replied in a mocking tone.

"Naturally," the other boy said as he turned to his friend. "He'd be out looking for leprechauns, you see." Both boys burst into chuckles at the joke.

"Cut the shite," Darren growled as he stuffed his hands into his jeans pockets. "A short guy, probably walking fast?"

"And why would that be?" the second boy asked the first before turning to Darren. "Wouldn't be running from *you*, would he?"

"No," Darren said. "He's flying back to the States. I have to catch him first, before he leaves."

"Why?" the first boy asked.

Feeling the watch against his fingers, Darren had a sudden inspiration. He yanked the watch from his pocket and held it up for display. "He left his watch behind and I'm trying to return it."

"Looks expensive," the first boy said as he peered over. The boys shared questioning glances. Then the second said as he pointed toward the Green, "He went that way, then turned right."

"Thanks," Darren said as he put the watch back in his pocket and walked faster down the street.

At the end of the walk, he took the right turn and picked up his pace. He followed the street down about three blocks; then he suddenly stopped. He glanced around, noticing that across the road, a gate stood open, leading into St. Stephen's Green. Darren followed his instincts. He crossed the street, but stopped before he reached the gate. He looked to the south, and saw the tall building of the Hyatt Hotel just a few blocks farther along. Something inside Darren felt that was the right place, so he trotted the remaining distance to the hotel.

Parked on the side drive, a black tour van was being loaded with suitcases as Darren rushed to the front entrance and walked across the lobby to the counter.

"Good morning," a tired young girl said without enthusiasm. "How may I help?" A slight tightness hardened her features when she looked up at the intimidating bone jewelry adorning his face.

"I'm looking for a guest," Darren told her. "Last name Lear, first might be Hank or Harrison."

"Of course," the girl replied crisply as she turned to the computer and typed in the details. "We do have a Hank Lear, scheduled to check out this morning."

"That's him," Darren merrily said with a nod, proud of himself for finding him. "What's his room number?"

The girl scowled at him. "I can't divulge that information," she said flatly. She pointed to the colored phones in the corner. "I can ring him on the yellow courtesy phone."

"Of course," Darren said. "Thank you." He forced himself to walk instead of running to the phone and picked up the receiver. For some reason, the thought of speaking with Hank again had him feeling a bit giddy.

The phone buzzed in his ear, three, four times, and continued buzzing. *Shite,* Darren thought as he hung up the receiver. *I couldn't have missed him again? Maybe he's just in the bath? Or maybe he's eating a breakfast?*

Glancing around the lobby, he walked to the front and looked inside the little café. He saw only one patron inside, and it wasn't Hank.

Darren felt useless just standing around the lobby. When the girl behind the counter turned away, he darted inside the stairwell and raced upstairs. He paused at the landing of floor one, and opened himself up, looking for Hank's hotel room. His instincts told him *up.* He raced to the next landing, and listened. *Up.* At the next landing, his instincts said *forward and right.*

After stepping into the hallway, Darren moved slowly past the row of hotel doors. He stopped when he reached 307. Listening, he heard no sound, so he lightly rapped on the door. He heard no movements inside, and the door remained unopened.

"Imigh sa diabhal!" Darren muttered under his breath. He must be at the wrong room, for his instincts were now telling him *down.* He should have known better than to trust his sister's crazy advice. He turned in defeat and slowly dragged himself back to the stairway.

HANK STEPPED off the elevator, his wheeled suitcase making a whizzing clatter as he dragged it quickly through the tiled lobby. He could see through the windows that George the driver already had the van parked outside and was busy loading the bags for the trip to the airport. Hank stepped outside and rolled the bag down the steps with a bump, bump, bump, before hurrying to the van.

"Mr. Lear, right on time," George said with a cheery smile.

"Yeah," Hank mumbled tiredly as he handed off the suitcase. The van driver overflowed with mirth and obviously hadn't stayed up all night.

"Grab your seat, and we'll be heading to the airport shortly," George instructed.

Hank walked to the van door, patting his pockets to make sure he had his wallet and passport. He also felt the room key still in his back pocket. "Damn," he said, turning back to George. "I forgot to check out."

"Make it quick," George called as Hank ran back to the lobby.

At the lobby counter, he handed over the key. "Checking out of 307," he told the girl as she took the plastic card and swiped it in the reader.

The hostess smiled at him. "No extra charges, Mr. Lear. Hope you enjoyed your stay with us." She suddenly said, "Oh, there was a lad looking for you a few minutes ago. I think he went into the café."

"Okay, thanks," Hank replied as he headed to the café, puzzled over who might be looking for him. He stepped into the small restaurant and saw Paul, the tour guide, finishing off a cup of tea.

Paul waved when he looked up. "Hank. Nice to see you made it back. George is loading up now."

"Already gave him my bag," Hank said as he stepped up next to Paul.

"Good, all good, then." He flashed a warm smile at Hank as he leaned on his cane and stood from the counter. "I hope you've enjoyed your stay, and speak fondly of Ireland when you go home."

Hank nodded, remembering Darren had said nearly the same thing to him before leaving the dance bar, and wondered if it was some sort of standard good-bye.

"Well then," Paul said as he reached out in a fatherly way and patted Hank's shoulder. "Let's get you on that van." He gently cradled Hank's shoulder before he guided them out of the café and into the lobby.

DESPONDENT, DARREN walked slowly out of the stairwell and across the lobby. He was expecting his phone to ring any minute, with another admonishing call from his sister. That conversation wasn't one he looked forward to. Anne would fly off the rails when she learned of his failure.

He walked through the lobby, glancing up to see the tour van was still parked outside. Darren felt a sudden spark of hope. Maybe Tex hadn't left yet? He quickened his pace as he got to the exit doors. Stepping outside, he scanned the van's windows, looking at the seated passengers. Not spotting him, he looked at the group clustered around the van's baggage door and saw him chatting with two other guys. "Tex!" he yelled out warmly as he ran down the steps.

With absolute surprise in his eyes, Hank looked up at Darren as he ran toward him. "Darren?"

"Bless the stars, I found you," Darren said as he leaned forward as if to hug Hank, but he pulled himself back before embracing.

"What are you doing here?" Hank asked as the hand tightened on his shoulder. He'd completely forgotten Paul's hand rested there.

"Time to go," Paul said. He glared at Darren and continued to pull Hank toward the van door. "Say your good-byes, we have a schedule to keep."

Darren stared back at Paul briefly before turning his attention back to Hank. "Please?"

Hank tried to pull away from the fingers that dug into his shoulder like a vulture's talon. "I owe ya an apology," Hank said to Darren.

In a cool tone, Paul said, "Get in the van, Hank. We must leave now."

Darren glared at Paul. "Just two fucking minutes," he barked. "If you don't mind?" he added with a polite smile.

Hank tried to pull away again, but he couldn't shake Paul's tightening grip from his shoulder. He reached out his right hand to Darren, grabbing at his wrist. The Claddagh ring on Hank's finger felt nicely warm when it touched Darren's skin. Paul abruptly pulled away, releasing his grip on Hank's shoulder.

George nearly whined, "We must go-oh."

Paul reached out to Hank again as Darren and Hank gazed silently at each other, but pulled back without touching him. "Mr. Lear, get in the van," he ordered again.

Hank took a step forward without breaking Darren's gaze, moving farther from Paul. "No. Fetch my bag back."

George hopped from one foot to the other. "It's already loaded. All the bags are loaded, can't be unloaded," he repeated in a strange sing-song kind of voice.

Darren broke the gaze and stared at Paul. "His bag," he said firmly.

Paul's features hardened to steel. "The bag, George."

George continued hopping. "But, it's loaded, he's almost home."

"Get the man's bag," Paul said with a glare at George.

Scurrying to the baggage compartment, George continued muttering, "All the bags are loaded, isn't time to unload." He found Hank's suitcase and pulled it out, dropping it on the sidewalk with a careless thump.

Hank walked over and popped up the long handle, then wheeled the bag away from the van. He glanced at George, who looked like a terribly unhappy puppy.

Paul looked down at Hank, trying to smile warmly. "This is quite unorthodox, and most assuredly a mistake. You shouldn't miss your flight."

"I can find another plane," Hank said without taking his eyes from Darren. The Claddagh ring around his finger felt warmly comforting.

Darren glanced back at the hotel. "The café?" he asked Hank.

Hank nodded and the pair started up the steps. George whined something behind them.

PAUL GLARED at George. "Calm yourself."

George stopped hopping. "But, he's almost home. Almost gone. He's *not* leaving now."

Paul gave him another hard glare. "This can still be dealt with. Just calm yourself."

Walking quickly, Paul entered the lobby right behind Hank and Darren. He fished in his pocket and pulled out a very fancy-looking business card. "I still advise against this, Mr. Lear. But if you find yourself in need of anything, transportation home, lodging, please call me. I have connections and can get things done."

Hank took the card. "Okay, I'll remember that."

Paul hovered a brief moment before turning and walking out of the hotel.

Approaching the van, Paul glared at the agitated George and yanked out his cell phone. *Useless sycophant,* he thought as he shook his head at the bouncing man. He punched one of the speed-dial buttons and held the phone to his ear.

"Plan A failed," he said curtly.

Paul listened, then nodded. "He's being shielded by some scummer currently. Will make a move at the first opportunity."

After hanging up the phone, he glared at George again. "To the van. Let's get the rest of these people home."

George scurried over and closed the baggage compartment door, then rushed into the van and started it. Paul stepped in behind him, staring back at the café windows as the van pulled away from the hotel.

Chαpτer 5

AS HANK absently slipped Paul's business card into his back jeans pocket, Darren led them into the café and motioned to one of the booths. Hank parked his suitcase at the end of the seat and pushed down the retractable handle to get it out of the way.

With a tired sigh as he sat, Darren smiled. "I'm *so* glad I found you. I was beginning to think I wouldn't. Now, what was that about an apology?"

Hank fished around in his duffel bag, retrieving his plane tickets. "Sorry, I should take care of this first," he said with a weak smile. "You sure about this 'bumping' thing?"

Darren nodded. "Let me," he said, reaching out and taking the tickets. He read over the information. "Aer Lingus?" he asked with a wide grin. "This will be easy, then." Darren fished out his phone and dialed the toll-free number printed on the bottom. After many strings of Gaelic syllables, each one sending a strange jolt through Hank, Darren hung up and smiled. "Bumped it to Tuesday. Same flight and times."

"And how much is that gonna cost me?" Hank wondered aloud.

"I got some sympathy. Only the twenty-euro rescheduling fee," Darren said as he set his phone on the table. He still expected a call from his sister at any moment.

"Thank you," Hank said as he took the tickets and put them into the side pocket of his duffel. He zipped up the bag and dropped his hands to his lap.

A waitress wearing some strange, green, costumey frock stepped up to the table. "Top o' the morning,'" she said with a cheery smile.

"Deirfiúr," Darren replied in Gaelic with a disapproving look. "None of the tourist shite for us."

The waitress smiled back with an expression that looked more genuine. "The Full Irish?" she asked.

Hank shook his head. "Just some black coffee for me." He looked over at Darren.

"Coffee," Darren agreed with a nod. "And what kind of pie do you have at hand?"

"Strawberry, I think," the waitress said.

"And a bit of pie, with two forks," Darren asked with a smile.

The waitress left. Darren looked at Hank, who gazed back at him. "Now, that apology?"

"I'm sorry. I realized I'd acted like a complete asshole, but you'd already left when I tried to find you again."

Darren nodded. "And how did you come about this realization?"

"I talked to one of the guys and found out who you were."

Darren's expression collapsed. "I see," he replied quietly, pulling his arms in and crossing them in front of his chest. "So. Now I'm just a celebrity."

"No." Hank shook his head violently. "It's not like *that* at all. I just knew then that you *would* have been able to afford the watch, so you weren't lying to me." He absently twirled the Claddagh ring on his finger. "I don't care about that." He smiled sheepishly. "I mean, other than I think it's cool. I *love* Celtic Cantrips."

Darren held his face flat. "You've heard of us, out in Texas?"

"Yes, at least, *I* have. That song of yours, 'Bluestone in the Water' has got to be one of my all-time favorite songs."

With a curt nod, Darren lowered his arms to the table and asked, "What other songs?"

Hank smiled. "Well, 'Faery Fungus Jig,' 'Hawthorne Tears,' 'Pyre at Sunrise.'" He shrugged. "Can't think of any others, off the top of my head."

DARREN SMILED. It seemed odd that Hank would pick the tunes from his group's repertoire that were based on Celtic and Wiccan ceremonial songs.

The waitress returned with a tray and set down their mugs of coffee. "We're out of the strawberry," she apologized. "Did bring an apple, if that's okay?"

Darren looked at Hank, who nodded. "Yes, apple will be nice."

She set down the slice of apple pie, two forks, and a bowl of whipped cream. "Anything else?" Both men shook their heads, so she left them to their food.

Darren picked up one of the forks, pulled off the corner of the pie, and ate it. "Any other songs?"

Hank hesitated, then grabbed the other fork. "Oh, 'Meadow Moonglow,'" he announced as he cut off his own piece of pie and ate it. "How could I forget that one?"

Darren nodded, noticing the silver glint of a ring on Hank's right hand. The title he'd mentioned was another ceremonial song. The group had one more, a much more obscure title that never made it on any popular tunes lists, and now he was curious to see if Hank would name it as well. He took another bite of pie.

Hank picked up his mug to take a sip of coffee, but put it back down quickly. It was still much too hot to drink. Instead, he took another bite of the apple pie. "And 'Bog's Bridge' is strangely haunting, but, it's kinda depressing, too."

Darren nodded with a wider smile, not quite sure what it meant that Hank had nailed them all. It would probably be the sort of thing his sister would get all goo-goo over, cooking up another of her bizarre theories. He glanced at his phone, surprised Anne had yet to call again.

Setting down his fork, Hank looked at Darren. "Have you given up on the idea of dragging me home? Ya haven't mentioned it in about ten minutes now…." He let his comment dangle.

Darren chuckled as he took another bit of the apple pie, then shrugged as he chewed. "Since you're staying longer, I'm sure we'll eventually get there. And besides, it's a bit moot now."

"Moot?" Hank looked at him as he fiddled with his ring. "What do ya mean?"

"My reason for being so insistent. I wanted you to agree to go home with me, before seeing me or knowing who I was, so I could be sure it was Darren you were interested in, and not 'Darr the Celebrity.'"

Hank nodded. "Yeah, I can understand that. And you don't think I am? Interested in 'Darr,' I mean?"

Darren nodded as he took a sip from his mug. "You don't seem all starry-eyed. Why is that?"

"Well, I guess being around the auction world has kind of jaded me. Not that I met many celebrities, but I did meet lots of guys with more money than sense, and the attitude to go with it. Made me realize that despite their money or fame, they were petty humans, just like the rest of us."

Quietly, Darren nodded along in agreement.

Hank took another bit of pie, dipping it liberally in the whipped cream this time before eating it. "So, I'm guessing you date a lot."

As he took another bit of pie, Darren frowned. "Not really. Not hardly at all, actually. There are a few gay pubs that have darker areas, and I've tried meeting guys there. Inevitably though, at some point, the whole 'Oh my stars, you're Darr' moment happens. Kills the mood for me, after that."

"Oh? You don't like the groupies?"

"Would you?" Darren asked, turning the question around on Hank.

"I guess, maybe not."

"Oh, the attention is very fun and flattering, for about five minutes. But then, you know they are just pining after some idealized version of who they *think* you should be, and don't give a thatch for who you *really* are."

Hank sat his fork down and looked right at Darren. "Okay, Mr. Mild-Mannered-Citizen Darren. I have another question about that watch."

"Sprite's spit," Darren cursed as he rolled his eyes. "Not the bloody *watch* again." He looked back at Hank. "Fine then, ask your question."

"Celtic Cantrips has a bit of a reputation for being all conservationist and green conscious. Unless that's all just a bunch of marketing bullshit, which might explain why you spent such an extravagant amount of money on a stupid watch. Those two pictures just don't seem to jibe."

Darren nodded. "I agree, it *is* an obscene sum to spend on a timepiece. But, in a way, it actually is a bit of conservation." After fishing the watch from his pocket, Darren held it over the table for Hank to see. "These are *very* custom watches. Notice the day/night indicator window with that wheel in it? The daytime side of the wheel is fashioned from a piece of Irish Bluestone. The nighttime side is made from Kilkenny black marble. And the band of rose color around the time zones, that's a bit of the rare Cork red marble."

Hank nodded. "That seems like quite a bit of Ireland. Unusual to have all those stone bits in a watch," he mused.

"Rumor is, the bluestone bit is a piece taken from the Blarney Stone, but who can say?" Darren set the watch on the table and looked at Hank. "How much do you know about Cona Philmo?"

"Not much," Hank admitted with a shrug. "I know he's considered a genius watchmaker. Got very reclusive and eccentric as he got older. And he was Portuguese, or had something to do with Portugal."

"There is *much* more to the story," Darren said as he picked up the watch and put it back in his jeans pocket. "But this isn't the place to tell it. Come—"

"Home with me and all the secrets of the universe will be revealed," Hank cut in with a wry grin. "Yeah, I heard that line earlier today. Or yesterday, or whatever." He grabbed his mug and took several sips of coffee. "But okay. Lead the way."

"No rush," Darren told him, taking the second-to-last bite of pie. "We can finish our coffee first. And I can at least tell the first part of the story."

"I'm all ears," Hank said as he took the remaining bit of pie.

"He was actually born Conrad Philmore, but when he wanted to build an artistic name for himself in clockworks, I guess that name seemed too ordinarily Irish, so he changed it to Cona Philmo. Many of his earlier clockworks strongly showed his Irish heritage, such as the *Dancing Phouka*."

"Right," Hank agreed with a nod. "I saw that clockwork piece at the museum by Trinity College. But the museum didn't mention he was Irish. Kinda makes more sense why they'd have some of his pieces, though."

"Well," Darren started as he picked up his mug. "As you may recall, if you've heard any history while here, there was a bit of a dustup between the Irish and the British Crown right after World War I. During all that turmoil, Cona feared persecution as an Irish nationalist, and that's when he fled to Portugal. It was there that Cona changed his focus and began working solely on wristwatches. So, when a new Portugal watchmaker bursts onto the scene in the 1920s, with the last name Philmo, most people assumed he was Portuguese."

"Like I did," Hank said.

"Easy mistake," Darren agreed with a nod as he sipped at his mug. "And Cona wasn't known to go out of his way to correct people, either."

The waitress appeared with a glass carafe of steaming coffee and filled up their mugs. "Would you like another slice of pie? Anything else?" she asked warmly as she picked up the empty plate.

The steam seemed to dance and roll merrily out of the carafe as she leaned forward.

"No thanks," Darren said with a smile. "We'll just have a spot more coffee and chat a bit, if that's okay?"

The waitress glanced around the empty cafe. "No hurry, lads," she answered with a smile before heading back to the kitchen.

Darren glanced down at his phone, then up at Hank. "Could you excuse me for just a moment? I've been expecting a ring from my sister...."

"Oh, go ahead," Hank said. "An American wouldn't even bother to ask."

"Truly?" Darren picked up the phone before sliding out of the booth. "That seems a bit rude."

Hank chuckled. "I thought we had a reputation for bein' rude."

"I'll be right back," Darren promised as he stepped toward the lobby.

TURNING IN the booth, Hank watched him—watched Darren's fine ass rippling under his jeans as he stepped through the doors. That rough-and-tumble look of Darren's clothing and face jewelry still struck him as odd. It didn't at all seem to fit the man Hank was coming to know and trust. And... like. Hank couldn't bring himself to admit to more than that. Not after only knowing the guy two or three hours.

Hank turned back in his seat and looked out the café windows at the sights of Dublin as it awakened from its slumber. More people and vehicles scurried around on the streets as the dawn grew brighter. Maybe it was four hours now?

As he scanned the manicured greenery surrounding the hotel, his gaze landed on a tall clump of clovers in one of the flower boxes. The shamrock looked so wild and out of place in the tailored surroundings. He watched a swirling mist that hovered over the clover as the sun warmed the dew on the triform green leaves.

ONCE IN the lobby, Darren punched the speed dial for Anne. She answered on the first ring. "You found him," she said merrily.

"Yes, we're having coffee. I got him to stay until Tuesday."

Anne tsked in his ear. "At least it's a start. Why are you calling?"

"I expected you'd call any minute, so I wanted to get it out of the way."

"No need. From the way your stone is humming now, I knew all was good."

"Now," Darren said as he sat in one of the lounge chairs. "Are you going to tell me why he's so bloody important?"

"I'm still working on that, and I'm not ready to discuss it. Don't tell me you're not happy he's staying."

Darren wobbled his head. "In a way, I am."

"But...," Anne prompted.

"But, I don't know what to do with him now."

"Surely you're messin' with me. I thought you had that mature, adult stuff well practiced."

"What do you mean?" Darren asked.

"Do I have to be crude?" Anne asked in his ear. "Take him home for a shag, then keep an eye on him."

"But I don't want to do that if he's just going to leave. You don't know what kind of position that will put me in."

"Don't be concerned about that. Show him a good time. Keep him occupied until Brigand gets here, at least," Anne told him as he heard the background noises of cards being shuffled around.

"Easy for you to say, you're not the one at risk."

After a pause, she replied in a musing tone. "I see." Anne paused briefly again. "That's true. I'm not the one with my heart on the line. But look at it this way, Darr—you can't hope to win if you don't roll the dice."

Darren sat up sharply. "This isn't some bloody game."

"Maybe not, or maybe it is."

"Fine," Darren conceded with a sigh. "Hank is so full of questions, though. What should I tell him?"

"I don't see any reason not to tell him everything, but that's up to you. Follow your instincts."

Darren scowled. "Quit saying that. My instincts aren't worth much."

"Darr," she said softly. "You've always been so much stronger than you've ever wanted to believe. I've never understood why you doubt yourself so."

"I've never had the gifts, not like the rest of you," Darren admitted.

"True, you're not all flashy and dramatic. That doesn't mean you have less, just different," Anne told him.

"Whatever," he said quietly, wanting to end the topic that made him feel self-conscious.

"All right, then. Take the lad home."

"Hank," Darren told her.

"What?" his sister asked in his ear.

"His name is Hank," Darren repeated. "The way you called him 'lad' makes him sound like some one-off I snatched up."

"Take *Hank* home, then. And enjoy yourself."

Before Darren could reply, the phone clicked in his ear as his sister hung up.

He scowled at the phone as he stood. He slipped it into his jacket pocket as he crossed the lobby back to the cafe.

FROM HER camouflage of misty clover leaves, the tiny green pixie watched through the windows as the tall one returned to the table. She would normally never venture this far out from St. Stephen's Green, but the strong scent of magic had enticed her, drawing her to the hotel. She saw the short one smile as the tall one sat down, and a fresh scent of magic emanated forth.

HANK SMILED as Darren sat down in the booth across from him. "Everything okay?"

"Oh, quite," Darren replied with his own smile. "I didn't mean to be gone for so long."

"No problem, I know how family is," Hank reassured.

"Where were we?"

"You'd just told me how Cona Philmo became a famous Portuguese watchmaker," Hank explained. "But, now I'm curious about your phone call. That wouldn't happen to be the same sister that plays keyboards in your group, would it?"

"Anne," Darren replied with a nod. "Yes, she's my only sibling."

Hank fidgeted a moment before briefly glancing at Darren, then turned his eyes away. "Would it be rude if I asked...?"

"About the wheelchair?"

Hank nodded quickly.

"She was born with spina bifida myelomeningocele. It's where the spinal cord isn't totally sealed inside the vertebrae and left exposed.

After many surgeries to repair her back, she does have reduced sensation and motor control from about midthigh down. So, technically, she isn't a paraplegic, but she's been in the chair her whole life."

"I'm sorry," Hank said quietly, offering his right hand across the table.

Without looking down, Darren reached out and took his hand. "It's just one of those things," he explained as he glanced down at the Claddagh ring.

The waitress suddenly appeared with her steaming carafe. She looked at their clasped hands on the table. "Refills?" she asked with a crooked smile.

As Hank self-consciously pulled his hand away, he thought he saw sudden movement out of the corner of his eye. He looked up at the cloud of steam wafting from the open top of the carafe, but saw only the rolling-hot mist. "Yes please," he told the waitress.

The waitress filled Hank's mug, then moved the carafe to Darren's mug. "Don't mind me," she said as she poured. "My cousin's gay, so I've heard all about these things."

"Thanks," Darren said.

With a smile and a nod, she headed back to the counter.

Darren gazed at Hank. "Can I see the ring?" he asked.

"Sure," Hank replied as he lifted his hands from his lap and set his right hand on the table.

DARREN REACHED out his finger and lightly touched the green, heart-shaped stone as he studied the intricate details of the extraordinary ring. The crown at the top of the heart wasn't the typical royal crown; this one was more like the old-fashioned torque of Celtic renown. "Where did you get this?" he asked in amazement.

"Just a trinket I found in an antique store, in Galway," Hank replied dismissively. "Prob'ly paid *way* too much for it."

"I thought you knew about antiques?" Darren asked as he pushed at the stone, marveling over the pink sparkling iridescence of the silver spangold metal.

"Mom is the jewelry expert. I usually deal with furniture, American manufacture, mostly."

"I daresay, your mom is going to swoon when she sees this." Darren looked up into Hank's eyes. "You really have no idea?"

Hank shrugged. "I only hope it's worth at least the fifty euro I plunked down for it."

Darren looked down at the ring. "You're truly serious. You certain the clerk didn't misread the tag?"

"It didn't have a tag, and I'm pretty sure it was the shop owner that quoted the price and rang it up." Hank looked down and studied the ring more closely. "What's so special about it?"

"You never heard of spangold? It was discovered when early jewelers experimented with alloys of gold, silver, and copper. That's how you get what's often called rose gold, like what was popular in Russia for a time."

Hank looked down at the metal of the ring. "But, that's not what this is."

"No," Darren agreed. "This type of spangold was created with a special and difficult finishing process. The Celtic smiths claimed that millennia ago, the leprechauns taught them a secret method, which has not been successfully replicated in many generations. They believed the special pink iridescence showed the blessing of the sprites."

"Sprites?"

"They're like water faeries," Darren explained. "The few jewelry pieces successfully created were highly revered among the Celts."

He glanced up when he heard the door open, and a large group of groggy-looking tourists filed into the café. The waitress quickly appeared and ushered them to tables as they yawned and begged for coffee.

He glanced back to Hank. "I think it's time to go, find someplace more private."

HANK LOOKED at the tourist group, who seemed to grow noisier as they awakened further. He finished off his mug. "Of course. Lead the way." He scooted out of the booth and popped up the handle of his suitcase, then watched as Darren discreetly concealed two fifty-euro bills under his coffee mug, leaving only the generic corners sticking out.

Darren motioned to the door and quietly said, "She deserves it, and I doubt those blokes will leave a damn thing behind."

"I agree," Hank said with a warm smile as he followed Darren through the lobby and outside to the curb.

With a wave of his hand, Darren soon flagged down a taxi. They crawled into the vehicle as the cabby threw Hank's suitcase into the trunk.

STILL CONCEALED in the clover, the pixie watched as the taxicab drove off. She knew it wouldn't be safe to try and follow; she already risked too much being so near the dangerous concentrations of iron. She frowned up at the sprite who hid in the misty cloud draping the clover, sharing an unspoken thought. Best to return across the street to the safety of St. Stephen's Green.

Chapter 6

DARREN TOLD the driver, "Uiscí Mianra Estates, off Merrion Square South."

The driver raised an eyebrow at the swanky address in the oldest part of town as he pulled away from the curb and pushed his way into the traffic lane.

"What's that mean?" Hank asked.

"It's Gaelic for 'mineral waters.' The family estate is named after the nearby hot springs."

"Cool." Hank settled closer to Darren.

Darren smiled sheepishly at Hank. "Assuming you want to go home with me now? Or should I tell him someplace else?"

"Your place is fine," Hank said. "I was kinda expecting it, at this point."

Frowning slightly, Darren turned his attention out the cab window.

"What?" Hank asked. "You seem, disappointed, or something."

"You don't sound like you're looking forward to it."

"I'm tired," Hank said with a shrug. "Sorry if I'm not all bouncing with enthusiasm. But, I *am* looking forward to it."

Darren tentatively ventured his hand over to surround Hank's. "I'm a bit tired as well. Not used to staying up quite this late."

"Oh? I thought all rock stars partied 'til dawn," Hank teased.

With a scowl, Darren gently squeezed Hank's hand. "I'm not a rock star. I'm a folk singer. Not quite the same thing."

Hank chuckled. "An internationally known folk singer, with extravagant, and no doubt expensive, videos all over the Internet, huge world tours, gaggles of groupies, and probably even a stalker or two. Nothing rock star about that. Not at all."

Darren sighed. "I try not to think about all that shite and just be a singer."

The cab lurched to the left as the driver cursed out something and merged into another roundabout. Hank glanced out the window at the thickening traffic. The streets of Dublin seemed worse than London, as though the city layout had been designed long before the invention of the compass or ruler.

When he'd first seen a map, Hank frowned at the way the short stretches of road banged into each other at peculiar angles, then veered off in some other obtuse direction. And of course, it seemed the streets changed names at each intersection. *Walking* through town was enough of a confusing experience. Hank was certainly glad he wasn't trying to *drive* through it, especially since all that spaghetti-like mess was topped by the fact that they drove on the wrong side of the road.

Smiling at Darren, Hank asked, "When's your next gig?"

"We always take time during the Sol—Midsummer. We won't start up again until July."

Hank gave Darren's hand a squeeze and used his thumb to caress the calluses on the tips of Darren's fingers. "You do more than sing. You also play some guitar," he commented.

"Hopefully, I do more than just play some."

"Oh, you definitely do. That guitar solo of yours in 'Bog's Bridge' nearly brings me to tears every time I hear it. Each note just seems to drip with sorrow."

Darren nodded. "That's actually taken from the very old Celtic song 'Siog Tórramh', which translates as: 'Faeries' Funeral.'"

"Oh, that must be why it's so sad. I didn't know faeries could die."

"Yes, they can," Darren said with a nod. "And it's usually because of something man does. That Celtic song is the story of a stubborn farmer that chops down the faery tree taking up space in his field, and the green faery who dies when she tries to stop him. He hits her with his iron axe and it kills her. The farmer then grows a great bounty in his field, but the townsfolk shun him, and it all rots without him earning a cent from it. In the end, he plants a new hawthorn tree in his field, hoping to appease the Fae. The faeries appear that night and host a wake for the green faery around the sapling."

"Wow," Hank said with wonder. "That's quite a story. Why did you change the lyrics? It sounds like that would be such a powerful song," he asked as he gazed up at Darren.

Darren paused, not sure how to frame the answer for that question. It wasn't that he feared being truthful with Hank, but he felt that it would involve a lengthy explanation in order for Hank to truly understand the reasons, and he didn't feel this was the proper place for such a long discussion. He took a deep breath and shrugged. "The short answer is, out of respect. If you can wait, I'll give you the longer answer later."

"I can wait," Hank replied with a nod. "I can understand respect."

The cab screeched to a halt. Hank looked out the window as the driver barked out something. Darren dug his wallet out of his jacket pocket and handed the driver a hundred-euro bill. "Keep it," he told the cabbie.

"Thanks, mate," the cabbie replied in a vaguely Australian accent before he darted out, ran to the rear trunk, then retrieved Hank's suitcase as the men crawled out of the taxi.

Hank wasn't sure what he'd expected to see, but this looked like just another row of dingy old brownstones crammed into a city street. For some reason, he was thinking of something a little more upscale. He soon scolded himself for responding like one of those groupies, expecting Darren to be something other than himself. The down-to-earth nature of the man Hank was learning about would definitely be at home in a simple brownstone apartment.

"This way." Darren motioned down the sidewalk as he picked up Hank's bag.

"You don't have to carry my bag," Hank said as he followed.

"You're my guest," Darren said, intoning that was more than enough explanation.

"It has wheels," Hank pointed out.

"Lahzy Americans," Darren teased with a heavy Irish accent as he smirked. "You'd put wheels on'ta yer own feet, if they'd 'a stick."

"Whatever, dude," Hank replied with his own smirk. "We call them rollerblades."

Darren carried the suitcase past a stoop and entered a wooden gate set at street level, then led Hank through a short passage that opened into a courtyard.

The burgeoning greenery in the space nearly made Hank gasp. Everywhere he looked, potted plants, small trees, and huge tangles of vines crawling the walls competed for their place in the sun. A large, ornate fountain of handcrafted terracotta dominated the central space. It spurted and gurgled jets of water as the frozen poses of terracotta faeries of various species appeared to dance and leap around the bowls. He paused as the sight nearly stole his breath.

Darren looked back and saw the grin on Hank's face. "I'm guessing you like it."

"Oh, for sure," Hank replied when he found his voice. "It's, like, an unexpected surprise."

"Aren't surprises typically unexpected?" Darren teased.

Hank playfully scowled. "Hush up, yer bein' mean again."

With a grin, Darren led them around the fountain, to a lime-green door in the wall at the other side. He set down the suitcase to free his hand, then fished the keys from his jeans pocket and unlocked the door. He took hold of the doorknob and turned it, but found himself pausing to look back at Hank. This suddenly felt to Darren like a very pregnant moment, as if it were the precipice of some point of no return.

Hank sensed the moment as well and met Darren's serious gaze. He took a deep breath, then said simply, "I'm ready."

With a nod, Darren pushed open the door, took Hank's suitcase, then carried it into the entry. Hank stepped in behind him.

THE LITTLE brownie shivered from the chill of freezing in place so close to the water spray. He crawled off the lip of the fountain bowl and dropped to the ground, before darting faster than the human eye could follow across the paving bricks and up to the door. He zipped back and forth near the doorway, drenching himself in those traces of ancient magic that still lingered in the air. At a faint sound from inside, the brownie reflexively zoomed to the wall and leaped into the ivy, scrambling nearly halfway up before realizing it was a false alarm. Since he was already so close, he skirted along another branch and hung at the edge of the wooden window frame, peeking in at the two men and trying to catch another whiff of that tantalizing magic.

THE HUMANS might not have seen the brownie, but the catlike phouka, who lounged curled around a clay pot in the corner, noticed the brownie.

Brownies taste better than mice, the phouka recalled as he watched the wriggling ivy leaves. *But the little buggers are sooo much trouble to catch,* he also recalled as he lazily stretched out his paw. *Not worth the trouble, really*, the phouka decided as he curled back against the warm pot with a yawn. Unusual for a phouka, his marmalade fur shined in the warm sun as he returned to dozing.

HANK FOLLOWED Darren down a tunnel-like entry hall into a huge room that seemed to suffer an identity crisis. Long shelves stuffed with books lined the walls like a library, yet one corner held a pair of fancy-looking settees with matching side tables and lamps more fitting within a formal parlor. On the opposite side, a broad dining table flanked a long wall covered with ornate wallpaper. The center of the room stood vacantly open like a ballroom, except for the large expanse of an intricately detailed rug covering the wooden floorboards. Hank glanced around the various zones, not sure what to think.

"I know," Darren apologized as he set the suitcase down by the settee. "It's a mess."

"Not really," Hank said as he wandered over to the shelves. "It looks well organized."

"But, needs a good dusting," Darren admitted as he ran his finger along one of the bookshelves, leaving a visible trail. "I tend to neglect it." Darren motioned to the settee as he pulled off his leather jacket and left it on the back of one of the dining chairs. "Please, have a seat and let me excuse myself for the bath a few minutes."

"Sure," Hank said as he smiled. "Go take care of your business."

"I'll be back soon," he promised as he left through the doorway by the dining table.

Hank considered sitting, but thought better of it. As tired as he was, he feared falling asleep, so walking seemed like a safer option. He approached the bookshelves and glanced over the titles. The first section looked to be all history books, most of them so old they had real leather covers. The titles seemed to focus heavily on Irish and Celtic history, and Hank wondered if Darren had actually read all of these books. He guessed he probably had when he recalled how knowledgeable Darren had seemed on the many different subjects they had discussed in the cafe.

Stepping to the next shelf, Hank saw this section centered on music. Different volumes on music theory, sheet music, printed scores, and rhyming books populated the area.

The next shelf was devoted to mythology. He found many books on Celtic and Irish myths, along with some British and even a few Nordic volumes. From the amount of wear on the spines and lack of dust, Hank guessed these books were also well read by Darren.

"Feel free to read anything you want," Darren said from behind him.

Hank turned and stopped when he looked up at Darren. With the bone jewelry gone and his cheeks and jaw freshly shaven, Hank now saw the emerald-eyed, cherubic face of Darr O'Connell that he recognized from the Celtic Cantrip CD covers. Hank studied his right ear, surprised not to see a large hole where the fat bone had stabbed through just moments ago.

Pointing at Darren's ear, Hank asked, "That bone thing doesn't leave a mark?"

Darren looked momentarily puzzled, then said "Oh, *that*," as he fished the bone earring out of his pocket and handed it to Hank. "It's merely an illusion. The two regular post pieces meet together to look like one giant bone."

"Ah, I get it. So it's like a disguise. What about the eyebrow one?"

"Oh, that's actually pierced. I just normally wear a very small ring in it," Darren explained as he leaned down for Hank to get a better look.

Hank looked at the eyebrow and its thin golden hoop; then his gaze drifted to Darren's eyes. He took a step closer. "And now, that you've finally lured me into your lair...."

"You want your answers," Darren finished the sentence as he pulled back and stood up. "Where do I start?"

Hank had really wanted a kiss, but he put aside his disappointment as he twirled his Claddagh ring. "At the beginning is usually the best place to start."

Darren frowned at that thought. "But that will make for a *very* long story." Darren dropped onto one of the settees and motioned for Hank to sit in the other one. "If you'll indulge me, let me start with a few of my own questions, and just play it by ear from there?"

"Sure," Hank agreed as he stepped to the other settee, but he changed his mind and sat himself down right next to Darren.

"How much do you know about Celtic mythology?"

"Hardly any, I'd guess," Hank said. "Only heard some brief mentions of leprechauns and faeries from Granny when I was growing up."

"And did she also mention the ceremonies?"

"No, nothing like that. Many of the family, including my parents, were strict Methodists, so if she believed in that kind of thing, she never told me about it."

"Yet, you seem to have an affinity for their music," Darren mused aloud.

"What do you mean?"

"I just thought it odd, that the CC songs you named as being favorites, are all based upon, or downright stolen from, ceremonial songs."

Hank shrugged. "It's prob'ly just coincidence, that I happen to like those certain songs."

"I see," Darren said. "And, how often do you experience that kind of coincidence in your life?"

"Really dude, I think yer tryin' to read more into it than there is."

Darren raised his pierced brow at Hank. "Well then, *dude*," Darren said sarcastically as he stood and went to a small cabinet by the dining table. He dug around inside and retrieved some small object. "Do you mind if I take a closer look at that ring of yours?"

"Of course not," Hank said as he slipped the Claddagh ring from his finger.

Darren took the ring, then centered an old-fashioned jeweler's loupe against his eye as he stepped to the brighter lamp. He studied the ring, noticing, as he'd expected, the tiny, angular, swirled defects in the green stone set into the spangold band. This stone was no simple piece of glass or common quartz. He also saw, from the magnified view, the torque crowning the heart bore the shaped insignia of the Shay family. He casually turned the ring over to the back side, not really expecting anything, but gasped in amazement when he saw the secret Celtic mark of the green faery etched on the heart's back side.

"What?" Hank asked curiously. "You found somethin' interesting?"

Darren opened his eye and let the jeweler's loupe drop to his waiting palm. He threw a firm look at Hank. "I don't think I should tell you," he said as he returned the ring.

"Why not?" Hank asked sharply as he absently slipped the ring back onto his finger. "It's *my* ring."

Darren paced back to the cabinet to put away the loupe. "That's true. But you didn't have a very receptive attitude a few moments ago."

"I'm receptive," Hank defended. "I'm just not gonna fall for some load of bullshit."

Darren stood in front of him and raised his pierced brow again. "That's precisely the attitude I meant."

"Okay, then." Hank softened. "I'll try to keep an open mind."

"You will have to do more than just *try*," Darren said before he sighed.

"Okay," Hank said with a deep breath. "Open mind. I promise."

Darren looked at him skeptically as he tried to determine how best to explain it. "I guess I should start by filling in a few details. The first being that Philmore—Cona Philmo was my grandfather."

"Oh. So that's how you know so much about him."

"Yes, and the jewelry skills have continued in the family lineage. So, I do know a bit about Irish and Celtic jewelry." Darren paused for a deep breath, then changed direction. "That little dustup I mentioned, right after World War I—there's a bit more to the story than most people know," he explained. He gazed at Hank's eyes, trying to gauge his reaction as he continued. "You see, for centuries—"

The keyboard solo of the CC song "Meadow Moonglow" twinkling from Darren's phone rudely interrupted. "Bloody shite," Darren cursed as he got up to find his jacket. "That's Anne," he told Hank as he retrieved the phone from his pocket. "Please excuse me."

"Sure," Hank said as Darren disappeared into the hall by the dining table.

DARREN PACED all the way to the end of the hall near the bath before answering the phone. "What?" he asked harshly.

"Really Darr, you can be so rude," his sister scolded. "Where are you?"

"At home, with Hank. I was just starting to explain some things when you interrupted."

"Oh, sorry about that," Anne replied sincerely. "Just wanted to let you know Brigand is here, and we want to meet Hank."

"I can talk to him and bring him by tomorrow," Darren offered.

"No, as in *now*," she said.

Darren shook his head. "That's a lousy idea. I think I need to prep him a bit first, before he starts meeting anybody."

"But, Brigand is being insistent."

"I don't care if Brigand thinks the moon is crashing down," he said harshly. Then his tone softened. "Trust me, Anne. He's an American, who was raised outside the belief. He'll just balk and clam up if we start throwing everything at him. He's barely receptive as it is."

Anne paused. "Your attitude seems a bit stronger. Have you learned something from him?"

"Not directly. Earlier this week, he found a spangold ring in a Galway antique store. The owner sold it to him for fifty euro."

Anne gasped in his ear. "My stars! How incredible," she muttered as Darren heard the shuffling of cards. "Any antique dealer would know how *rare* those are. Why sell it for so cheap, to a *foreigner*, no less?"

"That's not even the half of it," Darren said into the phone before pausing. "It has an Eirestone in it."

"Well shite!" she cursed. "Did Hank say this dealer was both blind and stupid?"

"No, Hank seemed to think he was very kind and competent."

"*Kind* isn't the word for it," Anne replied. "He must be quite thrilled with that."

"Not really," Darren said with a headshake. "Hank has no idea what he bought."

"Truly? Then you should tell him."

"I was starting to, before somebody called me," Darren said. "So, what's the latest verdict?"

"Have your talk, then bring him by for lunch. I can sell Brigand on that delay, most likely," his sister said calmly.

"How about dinner?" Darren counteroffered. "I still haven't had any sleep yet, and I can get Hank at least somewhat up to speed before then."

"Hmm," Anne said with a pause. "Brigand will have words about that, but that seems reasonable."

"You can handle Brigand," Darren assured. "Now, let me get back to Hank."

"Yes," she replied absently. "You deal with your man, and I'll handle mine. Oh, and don't shag him yet," Anne added.

"Why not?" Darren asked as he wearily leaned against the wall. "Just hours ago, you said I should. Now you're being a flake."

"Cards change," she replied. "See you at dinner," Anne said before hanging up.

Darren returned to the great room as he stuffed his phone into his jeans pocket. He was thinking through what would be most important for Hank to know when he stepped through the doorway. Hank was slumped into the corner of the settee, his steady breathing making soft snores. *Bollocks*, Darren cursed to himself. He'd spent so long on the phone, the exhausted man had fallen asleep on him.

Darren briefly considered waking him, before he decided that a little sleep might actually be a good idea. He lightly stroked his finger along Hank's forehead. "Just sleep away," he sang softly as he leaned down and picked up the little man. Hank stirred slightly as Darren cradled him in his arms and carried him into the hall and the first bedroom, but Darren's soothing coos of "Just sleep away" calmed him.

Darren laid him on the bed, then crawled up next to him.

Hank scooted closer and cuddled tightly against him. Darren ignored their growing erections and closed his eyes as he hugged Hank, letting the slow rhythm of Hank's breathing lull him into his own slumber.

ON HER thin, spiderlike legs, Skeena raised up from her hiding place in the ceiling corner of the spare bedroom where the two men slept. One of a rare and reclusive species that no human had ever documented, she had lived unseen for many years inside this house, feeding off the quiet, faint traces of energy that still bled from the walls. But this new vibration seemed so loud. She scurried across the crown molding to the doorway. Much too loud for her delicate senses. With quick movements, she scrambled across the doorframe and down the hallway ceiling, seeking a refuge far away from this new pulsing energy.

Skeena had no understanding of the failed experiment conducted by Cona which had yanked her from her home; such details would be far beyond her capacity to comprehend. But since her unexpected arrival in this dangerous, alien world, she had managed to survive, and her instincts drove her to continue surviving.

Chapter 7

SOME TIME later, Darren bolted awake. He paused, listening for the phone or door buzzer, or whatever had woken him, when another loud snore drew his attention to Hank. At some point in his sleep, Hank had rolled onto his back, and now made the most horrendous sounds with his breathing.

Darren glanced around before recalling that he didn't have a clock in this spare bedroom. He fished his phone from his pocket, then hit the button to awaken the screen and reveal the time; 1:07 p.m. appeared in the corner of his phone.

As Hank made the noise of sawing another log, Darren guessed that four hours was probably not enough sleep for him, so he nudged Hank to roll him to his side.

Darren reclined back beside Hank but found himself wide awake, so he gingerly crawled from the bed and stretched.

He glanced at Hank curled on the mattress. *The man might appreciate having his bags handy when he wakes,* Darren thought as he went to the great room and retrieved the suitcase and duffel bag. He left them next to the bed, then went to the bath and relieved himself.

TWITCHING HIS ears, the phouka cursed the growing level of sound. He opened his eyes to see a small gathering of faeries fluttering about near the ivy at the window. *Bloody noisy insects,* he thought as he stretched out. *What could be so bloody interesting to draw them out in droves like this?* Sitting up, the phouka sniffed the air with his catlike nose. That remnant of ancient magic still lingered faintly in the courtyard. *Interesting.* The phouka stood and strolled closer to the doorway, still sniffing. *Very interesting.* The source of the magic seemed to be inside the house.

He glared up at the buzzing throng of faeries. They weren't much more than bugs being drawn to a bright light, in his opinion. *This magic could be much more useful to someone else,* the phouka thought as he turned and walked to the gate. *Maybe even a good bargaining chip. Someone might trade for such valuable information.*

The phouka shimmied his broad shoulders under the wooden gate. He flicked his short tail and paused on the sidewalk, sniffing the air. With a determined scamper, he turned and ran in the direction of St. Stephen's Green.

DARREN RETURNED to the spare bedroom, stopping in the doorway and looking over Hank as he slept. He grinned at the way Hank's bed hair pushed up on one side, making him look so adorably cute.

He chuckled softly when he remembered that strange American phrase, "queer as a three-dollar bill," Hank had used to describe himself. Even though that description was applicable for Darren as well, he had encountered very few men in his life that he felt would be worth pursuing. Yet, none of those previous suitors came close to meeting the level of desire he felt for this slumbering American.

He found himself puzzling over the bigger situation. He *knew* Anne wasn't telling him everything. Of course, she rarely did. His sister treated the information gleaned from her readings as dispensable on a "need-to-know" basis. But, whatever she saw regarding Hank, it must be big news, if she felt the need to drag Brigand into it. Which left Darren feeling a bit slighted, because his own sister didn't trust him enough to share the details with him.

His mind pondered the upcoming dinner, trying to determine what details might be best to mention to Hank before he encountered Brigand and Anne. He should probably begin with explaining the ring, since the two dinner hosts would, no doubt, want to examine it and question Hank about it.

The ring might actually be a nice segue, Darren thought. He stepped away from the doorframe and down the hall to his own bedroom. After opening his antique dresser, then working the hidden latch inside, he retrieved the square clamshell-style jewelry box from the secret compartment. He'd always felt the bold style of the stained glass box was a bit loud, but his great-grandmother had cherished her 1905 birthday gift from Louis Tiffany.

He carefully carried the pendant box into the great room, then set it on the dining table. Not able to resist, he popped open the lid for a peek inside at the necklace. The gnarled branches of the spangold faery tree glistened with rosy-gold opalescence against the bed of black velvet underneath.

Darren reached down and touched the heart-shaped bluestone set within the trunk of the tree. *How many coincidences will it take for a man like Hank to start believing?* he wondered as he closed the lid of the pendant box. Leaving the box on the table, he went back to the spare bedroom.

BREATHING HEAVILY, the phouka soon found who he searched for. "How's it cuttin' this day?" he asked the dullahan as he approached. He felt relieved to see the elder fae in a human guise, the normal form of the dullahan was quite… disconcerting. Talking to a decapitated head always felt a bit queer.

The dullahan snarled down at him. "Go away, cat."

"Awh, now that's no way to treat a friend," the phouka purred.

"I've never been friends with you, or any phouka," he said coldly.

"Obviously, after what happened—" The phouka cut himself off with a shake of his head. "Water under the bridge. I'm not here to discuss that. I have some valuable information," the cat teased as he leaned down to groom his shoulder.

The dullahan paused. "And, what value do you place on this tidbit of yours?"

"Just that you use your sword, for a mere moment, to pierce the veil wide enough for me to feed. I'm tired of this cursed form, but the veil is too thick now to draw enough magic to change."

"Really?" The dullahan laughed. "You think that's a simple, little thing? Piercing the veil?"

"I never said it was simple, I just know that you are capable," the phouka said as he sat back on his haunches.

"Tell me your little bit of gossip," the dullahan replied with a wicked smile, "and I'll decide if it's worth that much."

"Let me feed, and then I will tell you."

The dullahan laughed with horrible cackles, sounding a bit like the crushing of bones under horse's hooves. He glared down at the phouka. "I think not. Go away, silly cat." When he sat on the sidewalk without moving, the dullahan kicked out his foot and nearly hit the phouka, who was only saved by his catlike reflexes.

"Fine then," the phouka spat out. "Your loss."

"Make your leave," the dullahan yelled. "And don't ever again presume to show your face in my presence."

Not wanting to look defeated, the phouka slowly sauntered away as he flicked his short tail in the air behind him.

AS DARREN approached the spare bedroom door, he saw Hank sitting up in the bed, rubbing his eyes and yawning. "Sorry. How long did I sleep?"

"A bit over four hours," Darren told him as he stepped into the room. "I brought in your bags," he said as he pointed to the side of the bed. "In case you want to spruce up," he added with an amused smile.

"Maybe later." Hank dropped back onto the bed. "I didn't mean to pass out on you."

"Not a problem," Darren reassured as he sat on the edge of the mattress. "I also grabbed a nap after I brought you in here."

Hank stretched out his arms as another yawn escaped. "This bed is big enough for two…," Hank said with a flirty grin. "Lay back down here, and we can… nap some more."

"I'm afraid we shall have to stall anything until later. You may recall that phone call from Anne? We've been invited to dinner."

"*We?*" Hank drawled as he sat up. "You mean, you've already told her about me?"

"Yes, when I was trying to find you this morning."

Hank looked at him with an incredulous expression. "Is there someplace I can grab a smoke?" Hank asked as he crawled to the edge of the bed.

"Oh, of course. We can go to the kitchen," Darren said as he led the way down the hall.

He pointed to a glass ashtray on a tiny café table as he stepped across the efficiency-sized cooking area and turned on the exhaust fan. Hank took a seat after lighting up a cigarette.

Darren took a pack of the clove cigarettes from one of the kitchen drawers and lit up his own before joining Hank at the table.

"So," Hank said after taking a drag. "Your sister. She approved of ya stalking me?"

"Actually, she suggested it, telling me not to let you get away."

Hank just shook his head.

"You act as though you don't believe me."

"Well, ya must be pretty damn close to your sister, then. I'm trying to picture that conversation. 'Hey Sis. I met a dude in a gay bathhouse, who gave me shit about my watch before disappearing. What should I do?'" Hank took another drag. "I can't imagine saying anything like that to any of *my* family."

"Actually, Tex," Darren said as he exhaled, filling the air with the spicy smell of burning cloves. "*She* called *me* as I walked out the door, wanting to know what was going on," he explained as he studied Hank for his reaction.

Hank looked back at him. "From the way you say it so casually, I'm guessing that sort of thing happens a lot. Are you two twins?"

"No, I'm two years older. Why ask that?" Darren replied, his Irish accent making the words sound somehow formal.

"Oh," Hank said, reacting to the answer. "I've heard stories about how twins can have a weird telepathy thing—just wondering if that's what it was."

Darren stubbed out his cigarette and took a deep breath. "It isn't exactly like that. Anne tends to be that way with everybody." He hesitated, not sure what else to say.

"Oh?" Hank asked with a tone of simple curiosity.

"You see, she has a bit of a gift, especially with the tarot. Have you heard of that?"

Hank tried not to look insulted. "Yes, even us bumpkin Americans have heard of tarot cards and fortune-tellers."

Darren felt the warm metal of the ring in his palm. He glanced down with a bit of surprise to find his hand grasping Hank's. He'd never even had the thought to take his hand, but here they were, holding hands. "She's not a fortune-teller, not like the tinkers."

"Tinkers?" Hank asked as he appeared to puzzle over the word.

"Travelers? Gypsies?" Darren offered, before Hank nodded. "Anne doesn't really see the future very well, per se. It's more like she sees the seams of how the present fits together and can lead to possible futures."

"You're saying, she's some kind of psychic," Hank said flatly as he smashed the remains of his cigarette.

"Something like that," Darren said with a warm smile. "You don't seem too happy with that answer."

"Well, just tryin' to wrap my head around it. Tryin' to be open-minded."

Darren paused a moment to give Hank time to process. He soon cleared his throat and said, "She's not the only one in the family with gifts."

"Let me guess," Hank said sarcastically. "You can levitate and shoot fireworks out of your butt?"

"No," Darren replied as he frowned. "I wasn't talking about me. I don't really have one. Our mother did. She had a strong affinity with animals. It was said that her touch could soothe and tame any kind of beast."

"Doesn't sound very practical, unless she worked for the circus."

Darren scowled at Hank's flippant tone. "You're not being very receptive," he said firmly.

"Maybe not," Hank replied before letting out a sigh. "I have the feeling you're leading up to some big-assed revelation. Just tell me whatever the hell it is."

Darren flinched back. "In order for you to comprehend it, I need to fill in some details first."

"*Comprehend?*" Hank asked in a hurt tone. "I'm not some freakin' four-year-old. And I'm getting tired of these games."

"Games? I'm just trying to—"

"Just spit it out already," Hank said firmly.

"Fine," Darren said as he leaned back. "I haven't confirmed it for certain, but I believe that Claddagh ring you found is part of a wedding set created in 1234 ACE, that went missing during the Tempest."

Hank's brow crinkled in confusion.

"See," Darren told him. "You can't understand that without the background details to explain it."

"Well, by all means," Hank said in a sarcastic reply. "Fill me in."

"You don't sound very open-minded."

"Really? And what *should* I sound like?" Hank asked as he pulled his hand away from Darren's grasp. "I'm trying to keep from choking on the stench of bullshit from all this."

"Bullshit?" Darren's jaw worked as he tried to come up with a retort. "*Why* would you think it's bullshit? What would I possibly have to gain from a blarney story?"

"People gain pleasure from all kinds of twisted things," Hank replied firmly.

Darren tried to keep the hurt from showing on his face. Without a word, he stood and walked to the stove, reached up, and turned off the exhaust fan, then walked out of the kitchen.

HANK GLANCED around the tiny cooking space as he waited for Darren to return. *Maybe I am being a bit harsh,* he realized as he sat there. He'd reacted without thinking, the words from Hank's mouth sounding so much like something his dad would say. In his weariness, he had spoken like his uptight, closed-minded father out of some kind of instinct.

After stewing a few minutes, he felt the need for the restroom. Hank left the kitchen and went into the hallway. He peeked into the great room but didn't see Darren there, so he headed farther down the hall. Through the doorway at the end, he could see the porcelain edge and claw foot of a bathtub, so he walked to that room.

As he passed another bedroom, he looked in and saw Darren, clenching his fists as he paced near the bed. Hank continued to the bathroom.

He quickly relieved himself, then stopped at the mirror. After passing out, his hair was all scrunched and pushed up on one side like some kind of strange pompadour. No wonder Darren had suggested a sprucing up. Feeling a touch of embarrassment, Hank tried to wet down the unruly hairstyle and finger-comb it to something more acceptable.

SOMEWHERE ELSE in Dublin, in the empty tour van parked at the side of the road, Paul handed one of his business cards to George. "Mr. Lear has one just like this. Do your thing and find him."

"Find him," George repeated as he took the card. He took a deep breath as he closed his eyes and clutched the card to his chest. His face smoothed to a blank expression.

"You remember Hank," Paul guided. "Find Hank."

"Find him, find him," George muttered a moment before his brow began crinkling into a frown. "He's… not."

"Hank Lear, find him," Paul urged again.

"Find…. He's…. Find…. Not…. He's not," George muttered as his face scrunched up into a confused frown.

"He's not in Ireland anymore?" Paul asked, trying to understand George's mutterings.

"Yes…? But not," George declared as he opened his eyes.

Paul scowled at him. "Yes or no? Either he left the island, or he didn't. It can't be both." Paul sighed as he looked at the silent George. "Which is it?"

"Neither?" George replied in a questioning tone.

"*Neither?*" Paul yelled out like a groan. "He can't be neither!"

George sank back into the chair, looking terribly wounded. "He's… not," the man muttered again.

Paul softened when he saw the stress on George's face. "It's okay, George. We'll figure this out."

"Okay."

"It doesn't feel like he left Ireland?"

George shook his head.

"Has he left Dublin?"

After a brief hesitation, George shook his head again.

"Bulging bollocks," Paul cursed. "Is he cloaked? Is that why you can't pin him down?"

George paused, then nodded hesitantly. "Hiding. He's hiding good."

"Well then," Paul replied with a wicked grin. "Let's not look for Hank at all. Let's look for the magic."

"Okay," George agreed.

"So, close your eyes and do your thing. Find the *magic* hiding Hank."

"Find the magic, the magic, find…," George muttered. "Over east, over south, over water, old town." George blinked and sat up.

Paul grinned. "Very good, George," he praised with a pat on the shoulder. "Drive us to old town."

With a happy smile, George started the "Coiste Suaimhneach Tours" van, then carefully pulled into traffic.

Tapping his cane rhythmically on the floor of the van, Paul continued thinking aloud. "Maybe we could plant a bit of doubt and keep him from getting too chummy with those O'Connell—"

"Seeds of doubt," George said as he drove. "Seeds of doubt—"

FEELING A bit more composed, Hank left the bathroom, then went to the bedroom where he'd seen Darren pacing. From all the music paraphernalia inside, he guessed it to be Darren's bedroom.

Darren stopped in his tracks and looked at him without saying anything.

"Okay," Hank said, smiling slightly with a weak apology. "I'm trying to stay open-minded. Tell me about this wedding back in 1234."

After appraising him a moment, Darren motioned to the bed. Hank stepped in and sat on the edge of the mattress as he fought back a yawn.

Darren looked down at him. "It was a very important wedding among private circles. At that time, Ireland had been spiritually divided roughly between east and west, each half controlled by a strong family. The marriage would join these two families, uniting Ireland in spirit."

"And what happened? You mentioned something about a tempest."

"Oh, that's not until a century later."

Hank smiled tightly at the long stretch of time, but he had promised to be open-minded, so he let Darren proceed without interruption. Unfortunately, a seed of doubt found fertile ground in Hank's mind.

"The wedding," Darren continued, "and the union, went off without a hitch. The families of the Connell and the Shay formed a powerful alliance that—"

At the mention of his middle name, that seed of doubt sprouted into something larger. Hank leapt to his feet. "What the *hell* dude? Did you snoop in my wallet while I slept?" he accused pointedly.

"No," Darren replied in confusion. "Why would I *do* that?"

Hank stormed to the doorway as those doubts continued to grow and blossom. The rational part of him that felt he was overreacting got a brief foothold. He forced himself to stop and turn around. "How the hell else would you find out what my middle name was? Then, to try and use it against me." At the voicing of his concerns, the doubt grew again, overwhelming his rational side. "Screw you," Hank spat out before stomping down the hallway.

"*What?*" Darren asked as Hank stormed off. "Wait! What are you talking about?" Darren asked as he chased after Hank.

Spurred on by more growing doubt, Hank ignored his questions as he charged down the hall then turned the corner into the great room. The stained glass box on the dining table seemed to jump into his gaze, but he ignored that too and continued his charge to the front door.

DARREN MADE it to the great room in time to see the front door slam shut. "Bloody diabhal," he spat out, cursing the devil in Gaelic.

Stopping, he leaned against the dining table. *Was Hank trying to say he was a Connell? Is that his middle name? Are we distant cousins?* Darren let out a groan of frustration. *How much more bollocksed could this situation get?* He dug his cell phone from his pocket, expecting a ring from Anne at any moment.

HANK STOMPED through the courtyard and out the gate almost to the street before he stopped. He really had no idea what he was doing. His flight from the house had been pure reactionary adrenaline. He stood on the sidewalk and calmed himself. As the planted doubts faded, he was left feeling more ashamed and a bit stupid at the way he had reacted.

Another one of Dad's signature moves, you idiot, Hank scolded himself as he turned.

A loud honk drew his attention back to the street. He saw the familiar satiny-black van, emblazoned with "Coiste Suaimhneach Tours" along its side. The van pulled to a stop at the curb, and the door opened. From inside the stair-stepped doorway, Paul motioned for Hank to come forward.

What the hell? Hank thought as he took a step closer to the van. *What is Paul doing here?* he wondered as he took another step forward.

"Mr. Lear," Paul yelled warmly from inside the van. "I was so *concerned* to learn you hadn't booked again in the hotel. Why don't you come back and we'll get you checked in for another night?" he asked as he motioned Hank forward again.

Hank took another step. "How did you find me?" he wondered aloud as he looked at Paul and lifted his foot for another step.

Paul just smiled and waved him forward.

A tiny alarm bell quietly pinged somewhere in Hank's mind. *Why isn't Paul stepping off the bus?* he suddenly wondered. *And how the hell* did *they find me?* he asked himself as that alarm bell grew a little louder. Hank planted his foot and stopped walking. "My suitcase is still inside. Why don't you come help me with it?" he asked.

Paul shook his head, remaining on the van step. "Come on aboard, and we can send someone to collect your bag later."

As the Claddagh ring on his finger grew warmer, the hairs on the back of his neck stood up. "No thanks," Hank said. "I already have a place for the night."

Paul looked up and glanced past Hank. Hank turned to see Darren standing in the courtyard with the gate open.

Darren glanced between Hank and Paul, his face full of confused curiosity.

"Come back to the hotel, Mr. Lear," Paul insisted. "You will be much safer there."

Hank took a step back. "No. Like I said, I've already made arrangements."

Paul's face scrunched into a scowl. "You are being quite contrary, young man. Get inside this van."

Pushing the wooden gate further open, Darren glared at Paul. "Hank said no," he yelled toward the van. "It's time for you to leave. Pull away from my curb before I call the Gardai," he threatened, holding up his cell phone.

Paul turned and barked something to George, who closed the door and pulled the van into the street, slowly driving away.

Hank felt a strange sense of relief as the van turned the corner. He turned around and returned to the courtyard.

Darren looked at him in puzzlement as he approached. "Did you call him?"

"No," Hank said. "He just showed up right after I got to the sidewalk."

"Huh," Darren said. "If you don't mind my saying so, that guy gives me the creeps."

"I'm starting to agree with you," Hank replied as he followed Darren back to the house.

AFTER THE lime-green door of Darren's flat closed, the phouka jumped down from his perch on the wall. *My, my, my...*, he purred to himself as he sauntered to the fountain for a drink. All that running around earlier in the day had left him thirsty. While he lapped with his tongue, he looked at the door. *This day is proving even more interesting,* he mused, before finding a warm place to curl up. *I think I should keep an eye on things here for a while.*

Chapter 8

HANK FOLLOWED Darren back into the great room.

Darren took a seat on the little settee. "Now then," he asked with a firm face. "Care to explain what prompted that little outburst?"

Hank stiffened where he stood. "You never answered *my* question. Fair's fair."

"But I *did*. I told you I did not snoop into your wallet, as you accused."

"Then how did you find out my middle name?"

"I did not, and I still *do not* know your middle name," Darren replied, his Irish accent making the words seem somehow like a formal declaration. "What is it?"

Hank paced across the floor before he decided to answer. "It's Shay."

Darren sat slack-jawed at the revelation, before he burst into laughter. "And the tale grows more twisted," he said.

Hank stepped up to him. "What do you mean?"

"On that little ring of yours, the torque that crowns the heart has a folded-down corner on its central peak. Otherwise known as the insignia of the Shay family."

Hank stood frozen as he processed the new facts. "Then," he said as he sank down onto the other settee. "You're saying... that this ring…." He held up his hand and studied the Claddagh closely. "It once belonged to one of my ancestors? Here in Ireland? In 1234?"

Darren nodded. "Assuming your family continued the tradition of using maternal maiden names as a middle name, that's *precisely* what I'm saying."

Hank sat and studied the ring in silence.

"Did your family continue the tradition?"

"I guess so," Hank finally said. "Granny's maiden name was Shay."

Darren chuckled. "The same Granny who told you of faeries and leprechauns?"

Hank nodded.

"Ah. Yet I suppose, these are nothing but a few more coincidences," Darren replied with a crooked smile. "Simple, meaningless facts."

Hank quietly studied the ring a moment more. "Okay," he said, then took a deep breath. "Tell me more about this ring."

"It was commissioned by the Connell groom as a gift to his Shay bride."

"Connell?" Hank asked as he looked over at Darren. "As in, O'Connell?"

Darren nodded. "They were my ancestors. Not quick to jump onto a new trend, the O' prefix didn't really get started with my family until later."

Hank clenched his jaw. "What else?"

"We've already discussed the spangold and its significance. Another unique feature is the setting, which is an Eirestone."

"Eirestone?"

"Not surprised you haven't heard of it. They are unique. Well then," Darren said as he took a breath. "Do you want the long version, or the short one?"

Hank shrugged as he chuckled. "What the hell, hit me with the long one."

DARREN TRIED not to smile at the little hints that Hank was growing more receptive. "The old story goes, that back in the mid-800s, my ancestor, Dorian Neil, returned home after a journey. He was approaching his house right about sunset, when a terrible wail screamed on the wind. Thinking it was the howl of a banshee, he hurried to the house, fearing someone's pending death. As he drew near, he saw the banshee hovering in the garden. She didn't vanish or flee as they typically do. Instead, she pointed down to the ground with a long bony finger and let out another wail." Darren paused. "No snide comments yet?"

Hank smiled tightly. "Open-minded, like I promised."

"Well, then." Darren smiled and continued. "As he ran up to the garden gate, the banshee faded away. He ran to the spot where she pointed, and found a peculiar round rock. It seemed to be granite, but felt much too light to be of solid rock—"

"A geode," Hank said.

Darren grinned. "No cheating now…. Guessing the rock was hollow, he had to try three hammers, each successively larger and heavier than the last, before the rock finally burst open. Inside, the sparkling green crystals looked like nothing he had ever seen before."

"Like I said," Hank replied.

Darren smirked at him. "Not one to pass up a lucrative opportunity, Dorian tried using the green crystals in his fledgling jewelry business. He had to search high and low to find tools strong enough to work them into stones, but he finally did, and made a bit of money with what he dubbed his Eirestone trinkets. As his supply dwindled, he scoured the surrounding countryside, looking for more of the geodes, but none were ever found. Only a tiny piece of that geode is left."

"So, it's a special green quartz?"

"No," Darren said as he shook his head. "Recent tests of the geode show it to be green diamond. One of the rarest kinds."

"Green *diamond*? In a geode? That's too incredible to believe," Hank said as he scrunched his brow.

Darren chuckled. "I thought you'd argue about the banshee, instead you focus on the geode."

"Obviously, the banshee is pure fiction, but a geode is real."

Darren raised his pierced eyebrow. "What happened to open-minded?"

"Whatever," Hank said as he looked at the green gem in the Claddagh ring. "So, this is a green diamond?"

"Yes. Over the years, many had suspected the Eirestone was diamond, and modern tests finally proved it."

"Okay. Is that all of the story?"

"About the geode? Yes," Darren said.

"No, I mean, about that wedding and all. This ring."

Darren paused. Hank may be growing a little more receptive, but he didn't want to risk pushing him too far. "A few more details, but I expect those can wait."

"Okay," Hank agreed.

Darren stood. "I think it's time for a kitchen break," he announced.

"Good idea." Hank stood and followed him.

Darren retrieved two bottles of sparkling water from the small refrigerator and set them on the kitchen table before lighting another clove cigarette. Hank lit up his own, then grabbed one of the water bottles and opened it for a sip. He tried not to scowl. "I don't know if I'll ever get used to this," he said as he set down the bottle. "At home, that bubbly water is usually a mixer."

"I could add something more, if you wish," Darren offered with a shrug.

Hank shook his head as he took another drag of his cigarette. "Don't wanna be all drunk when I meet your sister."

"Probably not wise," Darren agreed with a chuckle. "But, I suspect, you're cute when you're drunk."

"Hush up there," Hank replied in a southern-belle falsetto as he batted his eyelashes. "Such a devilish thing for a man to say."

"I can assure you," Darren replied in his deep baritone. "I have only the best intentions at heart."

Hank dropped back to his normal voice. "Who said I was thinking about your heart?" he teased.

"Now, now. No time for that. Anne will probably ring at any moment, expecting us over."

"So you keep saying," Hank replied. "Maybe we should just head over now and get it over with. Or, did you have some other revelations to hit me with first?"

Darren paused as he thought about the pendant. *Should I show that to Hank now? Or wait until we return?*

"Go ahead," Hank prompted. "Might as well lay it all out now."

"Might as well." Darren decided aloud as he stood and left the room. He returned with the stained glass box and set it on the table in front of Hank. He placed his hand on top of the lid when Hank reached forward to open it. "I'm almost afraid to let you see this," he admitted. "I worry about your reaction."

"What is it?" Hank asked as he gazed up into Darren's eyes. "Why would you be worried?"

"Well, as you Texans would say, this is one big-assed clusterfuck of a coincidence."

Hank chuckled. "Maybe a Texas marine would say that. I can't imagine my mother ever saying such a thing. What movie did that line come from?"

"Some sci-fi show, with aliens in it," Darren replied quietly as he kept his hand firmly on the lid.

"What is it?" Hank asked again in a softer tone.

After the briefest pause, Darren lifted the lid to reveal the pendant inside. Hank gasped aloud when he saw it. Darren quickly closed the lid when the keyboard music of "Meadow Moonglow" echoed from the living room. "Time for dinner," he announced as he picked up the box and carried it with him to answer the phone.

HANK DOWNED the rest of the water before following Darren. He'd had only the briefest glimpse of the sparkly tree, but thought it was one of the most hauntingly beautiful things he had ever seen.

"On our way," Darren said into the phone before ending the call.

"Should I grab a jacket?" Hank asked as he stepped toward the front door.

"If you wish, but I don't think you'll need it," Darren replied as he gently took Hank's arm and steered him to the other side of the living room. He opened a door in the opposite wall that led outside into another courtyard, only this space didn't have a large fountain in the middle. Instead, one of the Tuscany-style wall fountains gurgled near another wooden gate. Darren stepped across the way to a bright-yellow door and knocked once before opening it.

Hank followed him through the doorway.

ONCE INSIDE the new apartment, Hank nearly ran into a tall, thin giant of a man.

"Brigand," Darren introduced. "This is Hank."

"Pleasure," Brigand greeted with a deep bass voice as he closed the door behind them. He ushered them farther into the parlor, where Anne waited.

She nodded as the group stepped into the Victorian-styled room. Even though she was only two years Darren's junior, she looked much younger and quite frail sitting in the old-fashioned medical chair.

Hank tried not to stare too much, but he couldn't keep his eyes off the ornate, antique wheelchair Anne sat in. The carved wooden chair was much narrower than more modern styles, and looked like a fancy dining chair that had a metal wheel stuck on each side. In the antique world, this style was often referred to as a "house" chair. She probably needed a chair with a smaller footprint, to fit the narrower halls and doorways of this older building.

Hank diverted his eyes to the rest of the room as Anne wheeled forward.

"Welcome, Hank, I'm Anne," she greeted as she pulled up to what looked like a coffee table with leg extensions to raise it higher. "Ham, or turkey?"

"'Scuse me?" Hank asked, thrown by the strange question.

"We're ordering deli," Brigand added as he smiled at Hank. "What kind of sandwich would you like?"

"Either one would be fine," Hank answered as he looked over the room. The decor seemed so old-fashioned, and the deep reds, maroons, and somber yellows in Victorian patterns made Hank think of old ghost-story movies, full of gypsy fortune-tellers and séances. Knowing what he did about her, Hank wondered if Anne styled the room to intentionally create that effect.

Darren motioned for Hank to sit on the sofa. "Ham and swiss with mayonnaise and lettuce, for me."

Hank stepped up to the sofa and patted the seat with his hand. It looked so old and worn, he expected to see a plume of dust rise up from the cushion, but none appeared from the clean fabric. He sat down gingerly on the edge of the sofa.

While Brigand dialed his cell phone and placed the food order, Darren sat down next to Hank, close enough for their legs to touch.

Fearing such closeness might be inappropriate in front of Darren's sister, Hank glanced at Anne. She didn't seem to notice. Instead, all of her attention was focused on what looked like a handful of gravel scattered on the table in front of her.

Darren reached down and lightly patted Hank's leg. "Relax," he whispered softly. "Everything is fine. You look like you're ready to bolt."

Hank shrugged and glanced at Brigand. He looked much older than what Hank had thought Anne's boyfriend would be. His raven-dark hair showed visible gray in the temples, contradicting the vigor of youth which sparkled in his bright blue eyes.

"What year did it change?" Anne asked loudly at Hank.

"'Scuse me?"

Darren scowled. "Anne, please. He's a guest. Hank's probably accustomed to civilized folk who speak in complete, coherent sentences."

Anne smiled impatiently and looked at Hank. "Do you know what year your last name changed from O'Leary to Lear?"

"Not really sure," Hank answered as he shook his head. "Maybe, four generations ago? When they lived in New York."

Anne glanced back down at the rocks on the table. "Would that be 1849? Or, does that date have some other significance?"

Hank shrugged in reply. The way Anne continued scrutinizing him, he really wanted a cigarette right about now. He glanced around the room for an ashtray. On a round table nestled in the corner, he saw a large bowl full of sand. On second glance, the tall, thin stones sticking up from the sand in a circular pattern reminded Hank of Stonehenge. *Probably* not *an ashtray*, he decided. *I should step back out to the courtyard.*

"Well?" Anne asked loudly as she continued peering at Hank.

"Anne." Darren cut in as he threw a glare in her direction. "You're being quite rude now." He looked imploringly over to Brigand, then leaned closer to Hank. "Just relax," he whispered in a singing tone as he rubbed Hank's thigh. "Relax."

As Hank felt Darren massage his leg, the gentle touch and soft voice seemed to draw the tension from his shoulders and spine.

Brigand stepped forward. "I think you may be getting sidetracked, Anne. Put away the stones."

With a pout, Anne wheeled herself back from the table, then zoomed to the sofa, nearly running over Hank's foot. She screeched to a stop and thrust her hands out expectantly to Hank. "Let's see that ring of yours."

After one quick pat on Hank's leg, Darren said quietly, "Excuse us a moment, please." He stood and grabbed the handle on the back of Anne's chair. "A word," he said firmly to his sister as he wheeled her from the room, disappearing down the hallway amidst her protests.

Brigand gave a warm smile to Hank as he sat on the nearby settee. "Apologies. She's actually a normal person, she just gets quite excited and caught up in strange details, sometimes."

Hank merely shrugged in reply. He'd believe her normalcy when he actually saw it.

With full Irish civility, Brigand smiled at Hank. "May I inquire about the ring?"

"Sure, I guess," Hank said as he offered his hand to Brigand for a better look.

Brigand studied the spangold band on Hank's finger for a moment. "Do you recall the name of the merchant from whom you purchased this?"

Hank shook his head. "I don't think he told me his name. I just remember it was a small shop off the main strip, in sort of an alley."

"Perhaps, you recall the name of the shop?" Brigand asked hopefully.

"No, I sure don't," Hank replied. When he saw Brigand's disappointment, he added, "I just remember it had a funky-looking 'F' on the hanging sign outside."

"I see."

Brigand sat quietly a moment, staring off as if in deep thought.

"So," Hank asked, trying to think of conversation. "How long have you and Anne been together?"

"Together?" Brigand asked in surprise. "Oh, dear Lord no. Anne and I aren't a couple. I'm the—an old friend of the family, I guess you'd say."

"How old?" Hank found himself asking as he, once again, noticed the gray hair.

Brigand peered back with a tight smile. "Younger than I *should* be."

Hank shook his head at the strange reply as he looked closer at Brigand. "Things like that answer just lead me to think there's a whole *bunch* of shit you guys aren't telling me. What, exactly, the fuck is going on?"

Recoiling a little, Brigand dropped his gaze to the floor. "I don't know what you mean."

"Bullshit," Hank said firmly. "You know quite well what I mean. Tell me."

"But, Darr said—," Brigand let slip before he clamped his mouth closed.

"Darren said *what*?"

Frowning, Brigand quickly stood and left the room through a doorway that showed a peek of a kitchen beyond before the door closed.

Hank threw his arms in the air. "Is this some kind of asylum? I'm surrounded by crazy people," he complained to the empty room.

SKEENA PULLED in her spiderlike body and cowered in the secluded corner of the bookcase where she had taken refuge. She didn't have enough consciousness to understand Hank's words, but if she had, she would have agreed wholeheartedly with the sentiment. Things had suddenly grown much too loud and crazy for her delicate senses.

Yet, right now would not be a safe time to move. She pulled her legs in tighter to wait it out.

IN THE library, Darren continued confronting Anne. "I warned you before, Hank is barely following along. Your little display of tizzy rudeness didn't help any." He kneeled in front of her chair and softened his face as he asked again. "So, *tell* me. What did you see in that very first reading this morning that drove you so bonkers?"

Anne crinkled her brow. "I don't really know for certain. That's why I'm asking questions, trying to suss it out."

Darren patted her arm soothingly. "The questions aren't the problem, Anne. You need to get a grip and be more civil."

"I know. But, with the Solstice coming, this just seems so monumentally important."

"What do you mean?" Darren asked as he sank down to sit on the floor. "What does Hank have to do with the Solstice?"

Anne tightened her face. "That's what I'm *trying* to figure out," she nearly yelled as she wrung her hands in her lap.

"Okay," Darren said quietly as he rubbed across Anne's arm. "It's okay. Just take a breath, and we'll discuss this."

"Okay," Anne agreed, sounding more calm.

Darren soothingly patted her arm. "Now, start by telling me about the Solstice."

Anne frowned. "I think… no, I *feel* it's make-or-break this time. We face a very real chance of the portal completely closing this year. Sealed for good."

"And?" Darren asked with a look of serious concern. "You got that from your reading this morning?"

"Partly. I've been seeing it for weeks, though."

"*Weeks?*" Darren hissed as he stood up. "And you didn't mention this sooner?"

"I'm only seeing it as a possibility, and I keep seeing there's an out. I was trying to understand more before I said anything," Anne defended.

Darren paced to the bar. He stopped himself before he actually grabbed the whisky bottle. "This 'out,'" he wondered aloud as he turned to face Anne. "You think Hank is involved?"

"I don't know. All I can say is things changed so drastically after you met him. It would only seem logical he's in the middle of it, somehow."

"Changed?" Darren asked as he stepped back to her. "How?"

"Hard to describe. It's like the sudden change of being in the cinema watching *Casablanca*, then you go to the toilets and return to find *Star Wars* on the screen instead."

Darren knelt beside her again and rubbed her arm. "Okay, Anne. Very slowly, tell me exactly what you saw this morning."

Anne sighed in frustration. "It wasn't that kind of reading. It was more… vague impressions. Sensations." She shook her head. "I don't think I can really explain it."

HANK LOOKED to the hallway, then at the closed kitchen door. It seemed no one was returning soon, so he stood and made his way to the courtyard door. He could at least grab a smoke while he was waiting for somebody to show up.

He stepped out to Anne's smaller courtyard, then lit up a cigarette, trying to ignore the strong feeling that he was being manipulated by these people somehow.

Inexplicable touches of doubt still lingered. Darren had turned out to be nothing but a confusing contradiction since the moment they'd met. *Even being captivatingly attractive, is Darren worth the price of all this aggravation?* Despite the fact that Darren seemed to be sitting on a whole trunk full of secrets, Hank also couldn't ignore the way the man made him feel.

Near the gurgling fountain, he noticed the orange tabby cat reclining on the ground, sunning in a ray of afternoon light.

Afternoon? Hank thought. *I know it's much later than that.* Then he remembered the latitude shift. In Ireland, he was so much closer to the North Pole than in Texas, and this near to Midsummer, the days lasted much longer than they did at home. Six in the evening still felt like afternoon to Hank's internal sundial. *Winters must be a bitch. The days must shorten to practically nothing.*

Hank had that strange feeling of being watched again. He took another drag from his cigarette and shivered as he tried to ignore it. Yet, something caught the corner of Hank's eye. He yanked his gaze to the shadowy corner on the opposite side of the courtyard, but didn't see anything. He glanced back to the cat, who had perked awake and now stared intently into the shadows. *Maybe there* is *something there.*

The cat lazily stretched out and reclined on the paving stones. He turned his head to glance at Hank with vivid green eyes, before he settled back into a nap. Hank would swear the cat had smiled at him.

Chapter 9

DARREN WHEELED Anne back to the parlor to find Brigand sitting alone on one of the settees. "Where's Hank?"

Brigand sat up straighter. "I thought he went to the library, looking for you two." He jumped to his feet. "Where would he have gone?"

Darren looked at the courtyard door as the buzzer squealed from the front door. "He might have gone back to my flat. Take care of the food, and I'll go check," he said as he walked to the courtyard exit.

Stepping outside, he saw Hank finishing a cigarette. Before Darren could speak, he felt a chill and instinctively looked to the dark corner of the courtyard. He caught only the briefest glimpse of rustling movement before it disappeared, but he feared he had seen the shadowy shape of a reaver, the English nickname his family used for the réamhfhíoraigh. Named for their foreshadowing habit of appearing in locations preceding a major disaster, the spiny sea slug-like creatures were known to be dangerous harbingers of doom and dark forces. Glancing nervously at Anne's door, Darren hoped he was mistaken.

He turned to Hank. "Dinner has arrived. Let's go back in."

Hank threw a hard look his direction. "What if I changed my mind?"

"About eating?" Darren asked, confused by the statement.

"No, about this whole goddamn mess. Maybe I should just go back to the hotel and grab a plane tomorrow."

"Please." Darren's expression fell sorrowfully as he stepped closer to Hank. "Don't do that. I don't want you to leave."

"*You*, or your sister?" Hank asked pointedly.

Darren reached down and stroked his hand softly across the top of the shorter man's head. "*I* don't want you to leave."

"Why not? Why should I stay?"

Darren paused, trying to push aside all thoughts of the surrounding circumstances and focus only on what he felt. "Because, all other shite aside, I don't want...," he said hesitantly as he sorted through it all. "There might be something special here, and I think we deserve the chance to find out."

Hank nodded slowly as he met Darren's gaze. Then, he glanced at the yellow door as he took a step closer to Darren. "I don't want to go back in there."

Darren reached out and wrapped his arms protectively around Hank's shoulders. "Then we won't," he said firmly as he guided Hank back to his flat. "This is just between us."

"Okay. Won't that piss them off though? If we don't come back?"

"I doubt it," Darren replied to the strange phrase. "I can't see as it will drive them to drink."

"What?" Hank drawled in confusion.

"They won't get drunk, or pissed as you said," Darren explained as he opened the door to his flat.

"No," Hank said with a chuckle as he followed inside. "Pissed *off*. As in angry."

"Oh," Darren replied as he closed the door. "Anger *will* probably result. But, I don't give a shite right now." Darren reached forward and pulled Hank into a tight hug. "I'm more concerned with you."

Hank wrapped his arms around Darren's back and nestled his head against Darren's chest, quietly enjoying the feel of strong arms around him as he inhaled his scent. "This is good," he said as he lifted his jaw and gazed at Darren.

Darren kissed his forehead, then angled down to his lips. Hank used his fingers to trace along the outline of Darren's shoulder blades as the two men lightly rubbed their noses and lips together.

Darren dropped his hands down to lightly massage Hank's back. "I agree. This is good." After a squeeze, he loosened his grip and leaned back to gaze at Hank. "I say, for the rest of the night, let's put everything else aside and just be two guys, enjoying each other's company."

Playfully, Hank stood on his toes and bit at Darren's nose. "Okay. Just two guys." He planted a soft kiss on Darren's lips. "Just between us."

Darren met his lips again briefly for another soft kiss. Then, he lifted Hank off his feet and danced them around to the front of the settee, where they both sat.

Hank brought his hand up and rubbed it across the short hairs on top of Darren's head. "I love feeling your buzzed hair," he said as he gazed at Darren.

In reply, Darren leaned forward and kissed Hank, putting more heat and passion into their embrace. Hank closed his eyes, opening himself up to feel the pleasure of the moment, but he soon found himself pulling back. Like a parched ground that had suffered drought for too many years, he felt flooded by too much sudden emotion, unable to absorb it all. Hank opened his eyes and looked at Darren. Before he could speak, a soft rapping at the courtyard door echoed into the great room.

"Pardon me," Darren said as he stood and crossed to the door. He opened the door just wide enough to stick his head out and found Anne sitting on the other side with a paper bag in her lap. "Yes?"

"I promise," she said quietly as she held up her hands in surrender. "No crazy. Give Hank my apologies."

"He's right here," Darren said as he pushed the door open wider, showing Hank sitting on the settee.

Leaning forward, Anne spoke in a louder voice, "I apologize for the outburst earlier. It's nice to meet you, Hank." She reached down to her lap and handed the bag to Darren. "Why don't we all get a good night sleep, and you come by tomorrow?"

"Sure," Hank replied. "We can do that."

Darren took the paper bag of deli food. "I'll call you first."

"Sounds fine," Anne agreed. "Have a good night." She waved before turning herself around and wheeling across the courtyard to her yellow door.

Darren closed the door behind her. "Are you hungry?"

"Now that you mention it," Hank replied as he stood. "Maybe a bit. I haven't eaten since the pie at the cafe." He followed Darren into the kitchen and sat at the table while Darren retrieved two beers before joining him.

From the bag, Darren handed Hank one of the sandwiches and a pack of chips, taking the remainder for himself.

"Not Guinness?" Hank asked as he picked up the green beer bottle.

"No, it's Harp, the other Irish beer. It's a very pale ale, almost like lager."

Hank took a sip and smiled approvingly before unwrapping his sandwich. "So," he said as he opened his bag of potato chips. "That tree necklace. Is that also part of the wedding set?"

Darren frowned as he chewed his first bite. "I thought we weren't going to discuss any of that tonight?"

"Well, we hafta talk about *some*thing."

"Yes," Darren answered. "The faery tree was the bride's gift to the groom. It's been handed down in our family ever since then."

"Hmm," Hank replied as he chewed. "That seems kinda weird, that *you'd* have it. I thought jewelry usually passed down to daughters."

"I guess it was always considered a more masculine trinket. It was passed down to me from my father."

"Oh, so your parents aren't still around?" Hank asked after he took a sip of the beer.

"No, Ma died shortly after giving birth to Anne, from complications. Da...." He paused as he looked at Hank. "How much of Ireland's recent history do you know?"

"Some, I guess," Hank said before taking another bite of his sandwich.

"Ever heard of 'The Troubles,' or 'Bloody Friday,' or 'The Dublin-Monaghan Bombs'?"

Hank took another sip of beer. "Wasn't 'The Troubles' mostly in the 1960s and '70s, with all that Catholic-versus-Protestant violence?"

Darren frowned as he chewed on a potato chip. "Well, not precisely. The argument was very complicated, and did spill over into religious conflicts when the churches for each side sort of fanned the flames a bit and the situation turned quite emotional. But the main political conflict had to do with merging Northern Ireland into the rest of the Irish Republic. Some in the North were quite happy with the semiautonomous State, and feared losing their self-control, while others yearned for one nation."

"Oh, I guess that makes more sense than it just being a religious war. Maybe they talked about that in the news, but I was too young to really follow it."

"Or, maybe not," Darren said as he took a sip of beer. "American television news has been known to be a bit... myopic when it comes to world events."

"Maybe so," Hank agreed as he took another bite. "But, what does that have to do with your father?"

"Da worked as a guard in the North Road station. He was there when the Monaghan car bomb went off just yards away. He was one of the casualties."

"Oh jeez," Hank said with a frown. "When was that?"

"May 17, 1974, otherwise known as 'Bloody Friday.'"

Hank paused and looked closer at Darren. "*Seventy*-four? How old are you?"

Darren smiled slightly. "How old do you think I am?"

"I had figured, maybe early thirties, at most," Hank replied with a shrug.

"Oh," Darren chuckled. "I suppose I should consider that a compliment. I just turned forty last week."

"*Forty?*" Hank smirked. "No way, dude."

"I'm surprised you're reacting that way. How many people peg you as being forty-one?"

Hank smiled tightly. "Oh." He took another sip of beer. "I suppose you're right." Noticing the color of his ring's Eirestone was the same as the green of the beer bottle, Hank set down the beer and looked closer at the ring. "So," he asked as he flashed the ring at Darren. "Does this mean that we're cousins?"

"Probably no more so than any two Irishman would be," Darren replied. "Many generations have ensued since the twelve hundreds. To continue carrying the Shay name, you would have to be the descendant of one of the bride's three brothers."

"Oh, right," Hank said as he ate his last chip. "Might be interesting to find out."

"Yes, that would be interesting," Darren said as he gathered up the empty wrappers and put them in the paper bag. "We could try to trace your genealogy, but depending on *when* your branch of the Shay left Ireland, some of the records are rather spotty."

"Spotty?"

"For instance," Darren explained as he threw the paper bag into the bin under the sink. "If they left during the Hunger, the records of that period weren't well documented."

"The Hunger," Hank replied with a crooked smile. "You Irish have such a polite way of understating things."

"And, what do you Americans call it?"

"'The Great Potato Famine' is what I remember it being called."

"Oh." Darren turned on the exhaust fan and got his pack of cloves from the kitchen drawer. "I can't see that there was anything *great* about the situation."

Hank fished out his own cigarettes and lit up. He looked at Darren. "I'm kinda surprised, with ya bein' a singer," he drawled out as he exhaled. "That you'd smoke."

"The cloves help my throat," Darren said as he returned to the table. "I know," he added with a frown. "That's just an excuse. I got into a rough crowd when I was younger, and just can't break the habit."

"A rough crowd? *You*?" Hank asked incredulously.

"After Da died, we moved around a bit from home to home," Darren explained.

"Some kind of foster care?"

"No, it was family, or friends of family, who would take us in for a time. Until we settled here with our Aunt Oli during secondary."

"Oh, that sucks," Hank said as he took Darren's hand. "What's secondary?"

"Later school age before university. I think you Americans would call it 'high school.'"

"High school sucks for everybody."

Darren nodded. "And," Darren said as he gazed down at his beer bottle, "I hate to admit it now, but I felt a bit left out, with Anne."

"How do you mean?"

"With her... issues, she garnered most of the attention. So, growing up, I got a bit rebellious and spent time in the alleys. I didn't find music until later."

"Alleys?" Hank asked. "What did you do there?"

Darren frowned. "You'd likely call them 'gangs,' but that denotes a little too much cohesion, I think. The alleys are where the rougher blokes congregate, surviving mostly by peddling drugs and petty thefts."

"Ah," Hank said with a tight smile. "So, that's how you pull off that rough look so well." He looked into Darren's eyes. "I didn't tell you before, but I saw you on Dame Street when I was heading to the pub last night. I was quite convinced you were a thug looking for trouble."

Darren chuckled as he smashed down the rest of his cigarette. "It's easy to be a scummer. Just scowl and growl frequently," he said as he scowled fiercely in demonstration.

Hank scrunched up his own face, trying to make a similar scowl. "Arrg," he groaned out, before chuckling. "Makes me feel like a movie pirate." Hank snuffed out his cigarette. "I know I must sound stupid, but, what's a scummer?"

"Not a stupid question at all," Darren replied. "'Scummer' is a common name for the street urchins."

Hank squeezed Darren's hand in his grasp. "That sounds like kind of an... intense childhood. Were you *out* back then?"

Darren dropped his gaze to their clasped hands. "Define 'out.'"

"I mean, knew you were gay and pursued guys?"

Clearing his throat, Darren kept his eyes on the table. "Well, if you didn't want to ply the trade of drugs or thievery, there's another way in the alleys to earn coin…."

"Oh," Hank replied quietly.

"So, using your definition, I was 'out,' but I kept my trysts under the guise of earning money. As you can imagine, the scummers aren't too fond of poofs." After a brief pause, Darren looked at Hank. "How did we veer off into such a dreary subject?"

Hank shrugged. "Just talking about the past, I guess."

"Well then," Darren said with a grin as he lightly squeezed Hank's hand. "Tell me about yours. What was it like, growing up in wild Texas?"

"*Wild*? I think you've been watchin' too many westerns. Texas is as modern as the rest of the world."

"Dagnabit," Darren teased in a drawl. "I was hopin' for some ropin' and Indian-raid stories."

Hank threw him a hard look.

"Sorry, couldn't resist," Darren apologized. "Tell me about your family."

"Fairly typical, for a small town. Oh, speaking of, do you have a phone I could use? I need to call Mom and let her know I'm not flying back yet. That plane should be landing in Dallas soon."

"Certainly," Darren said as he fished his phone from his pocket and held it out for Hank.

"You sure you want me to use your cell? It'll be international."

"Don't have a phone here in the flat. I don't mind," Darren said as he offered the cell phone again. "I have a good plan for that, because of touring so much."

"Thanks," Hank replied as he took Darren's phone. "How do I dial the US?"

"Zero, zero, one, then area code, then number," he explained as Hank punched out the numbers.

After two rings, Hank heard his mom's voice. "Hello?"

"Hey Mom, it's me."

"Hank? Where are ya callin' from? The caller ID just says a bunch of zeros. You aren't wastin' money callin' from the plane, are ya?"

"No Mom, I'm still in Ireland. I bumped my return flight 'til later in the week."

Hank heard his mom sigh. "Harrison? Why in tarnation would ya do a thing like that?"

"Well, I kinda met somebody, and I wanna hang around a few more days," Hank said hesitantly. When his mom didn't answer right away, Hank rushed on. "You know that music group Celtic Cantrips? I kinda met the lead singer, Darren."

"Oh," his mother replied firmly. "A singer."

"Don't be like that, he's a great guy, Mom."

"I see. And when are ya coming home?"

"Not until late Tuesday," Hank replied. "Don't worry, everything's great here."

"One of my sons calls me from a foreign country with no way home, and ya expect me not to worry?"

"Really Ma, you can be so melodramatic. I'm not stuck here, or anything. I have a ticket home. I'm just waiting a few extra days to use it."

"And you're sure about this singer? That type is known for all kinds of... mischief," his mom asked pointedly.

"Mom," Hank argued. "I didn't just fall off the turnip truck yesterday. He's not a player."

"You sure?"

"I'm sure. And I'm calling international on his cell phone, so we should keep it short."

"Well, I'll still worry. You be careful. Let me know when you get that flight home."

"I will. Say howdy to everybody for me," Hank said, as he thought he heard the clicking of computer keys from over the phone.

"Before ya hang up," his mom barked, "give me that phone number and the address where yer at."

Hank made a scribbling motion in the air. "Okay, give me a sec to find out."

Darren went to one of the drawers and returned with a small pad of paper and a pencil. Hank wrote "phone and address" across the top of the page, then handed the pencil to Darren.

"How'd you meet this singer, anyway?" his mom asked in his ear as Darren filled out the information on the pad.

"We met at a gym," Hank replied, fudging the answer a bit. "He thought I was cute and bought me a beer." He heard more clicking sounds.

"Darr O'Connell?" his mom asked.

"That's him."

"You sure he's not too young for you?"

"He's forty, Mom. Not too young. Did ya get on the Internet and google him?"

"Of course I did. How else am I gonna see his picture?"

Hank shook his head as he slid the pad over to read it. "You ready for the info?"

"Shoot," his mom replied.

Hank read the phone number and address, then had his mother repeat it back to him.

"I'm still not too sure about this," his mother admitted. "But, at least ya snagged a looker. Maybe you can drag him back home with ya."

"Who knows?" Hank replied with a shrug. "Gotta go."

"You be careful. Bye, Hank."

"Bye, Mom," Hank replied before he ended the call. He handed the phone back to Darren. "I'm surprised that went so well."

"Went *well*?" Darren asked in confusion. "Sounded like you were defending yourself a great deal."

"Oh, I figured she'd throw a right fit over me staying. But, she was more worried about me hanging out with a rock star, I think."

"I'm not a rock star," Darren repeated with a tired tone.

Hank smiled wryly back at him. "If ya say so."

Darren stood, then reached across the table for Hank's hand. "Let's go to the great room. These café chairs hurt my butt after a bit."

"Okee," Hank replied as he let Darren pull him to his feet.

BRIGAND FOUND Anne reading one of the dusty tomes in the library. "I'm on my way out," he told her from the doorway. "No luck on finding that antiquer in Galway, but still have some calls out."

"Oh?" Anne said with a surprised expression as she looked up from her book. "What time is it?"

"About 8:00 p.m." Brigand hesitated before asking, "Did you tell Darr about our research?"

"Not yet," Anne said with a shake of her head. "Darr needs to be solid, right now. Can't let him be having doubts, or it's all likely to fall apart."

"But, he should know—they should both know what's at stake here."

"And leave Darr staring over his shoulder for the bogeyman? He needs to keep focused on Hank for the time being. Or it will all be for naught." Anne rolled to the table and placed a bookmark on the page she was reading before closing the book and leaving it behind. She wheeled around to face Brigand. "I'll show you out."

Brigand stepped back and let her roll through the doorway before following. "I hope you're right."

Chapter 10

As Darren led him through the hall to the great room, Hank reached out and rubbed his hand across Darren's butt. Darren looked over with a crooked grin.

"Massaging helps with tired butts," Hank said in a flirty tone. "Don't want your tushy all sore from the café chair."

Darren led them to the shelves near the settees and lit a candle. "How about some music? What would you like?"

"Let me hear what *you* like. What would ya play if you were home alone?"

Darren fiddled with the music player, pulled up a list, then selected the "Fav40" option. He set the player to random shuffle and hit the enter key.

Hank looked surprised at hearing the swinging sounds of violins playing behind a peppy clarinet. He glanced at the music player and saw Artie Shaw's "Frenesi" on the display screen. "Big-band forties?"

"Yes, one of my favorite periods in American music, when ragtime and blues merged with orchestra and waltz to create a brand new sound." Darren stepped forward and held out his hand. "Care to dance?"

"I don't really know how, to this," Hank admitted.

Darren pulled Hank to his feet, then took Hank's right hand in his left, and placed his right hand on Hank's hip. "Just think of it like a waltz. The three-four time is the same."

"And what if I can't waltz?"

Darren tapped his hand on Hank's hip in rhythm to the music. Pat-pat-pat. "Let's start by swaying with each beat." Pat-pat-pat, he tapped out as he swayed Hank from the left to the right.

After a few bars, Hank seemed to catch the rhythm. With more guided instruction, Darren had Hank dancing a shaky box step before the song ended.

Hank smiled up. "This is kinda fun," he said cheerfully.

"That's why people do it," Darren teased.

The song ended, and the next began with a more somber clarinet playing a haunting melody. Hank looked at the player and saw "Nature Boy" before Darren smiled and pulled him in close for a slow dance. The song seemed vaguely familiar to Hank, but he couldn't place where he'd heard the sorrowful tune.

As they swayed to the slower beat of the throaty clarinet, Darren sang along with Nat in a harmonizing baritone. "There was a boy, a very strange enchanted boy…."

Hank noticed the growing smell of the spicy summer scent of sage from the candle as they continued to slow dance. He put the side of his face against Darren's chest, feeling and hearing the deep, comforting rumbles vibrating through Darren's body as he sang each note.

"… and then one day, a magic day he passed my way…."

Hank smirked at the lyrics as the song continued. It seemed that Darren was trying to seduce him.

"… is just to love, and be loved, in return."

When the song ended, the tinkling sounds of a slow ragtime piano started. Hank looked over to see Glenn Miller's "Moonlight Cocktail" on the player's display.

Darren pulled back and started another slow box step as some brassy trumpets joined the piano. Hank followed along with surer steps.

As the song progressed, Darren added in a few fancier dips and sways to their movements, smiling when Hank followed along easily. Darren winked. "I thought you said you couldn't dance."

"I haven't danced like this," Hank said as the song ended.

Darren grinned as the birdlike flute of "Bali Ha'i" twittering through the room. He pulled Hank close again. As he held him, Darren sang along to part of the lyrics with Perry Como. "... in your heart, you'll hear it call you, come away, come away...."

Hank closed his eyes as they moved slowly in a circle. He had to admit, it felt really nice to be so warmly serenaded by Darren.

"... here am I, your special island, come to me, come to me...."

Smirking again, Hank started to wonder about these song choices. There seemed to be an underlying theme to the melodies Darren had picked.

When the song ended, Hank looked up and started to say something, but the bagpipe-like sounds of a covered clarinet made him pause. This song had such an Irish feel to it. *Did Darren slip up on picking American 40s songs?* On the player's screen he saw Bing Crosby "Galway Bay." *Guess not,* Hank thought.

Darren glanced quizzically at the player. "Well, I'll be. I don't think I've ever heard this song before."

Hank chuckled. "How many songs do you have on there?"

"The player is one of the special ones, with extended memory, so who knows how many selections are on it." He shrugged at Hank as they danced. "Anne's constantly adding to it. She likes surprising me."

They swayed closer in a slower rhythm as Bing sang about the glories of western Ireland.

When Bing's song ended, a gravelly recording of a bluesy piano and guitar accompanied an African American female voice singing about a man. Hank glanced over to see Lil Green's "Romance in the Dark."

Darren pulled Hank closer and sang along. "... in the dark, I get such a thrill, when he presses fingertips upon my lips, and he begs me...."

"So," Hank asked. "Is there some subliminal message to these songs you picked?"

"I didn't pick them," Darren explained. "The player's on random shuffle."

"Really?"

"Go look, if you don't believe me," Darren said with a slightly wounded tone. "And, what about these tunes makes you ask that?"

"All the songs are about islands, dancing, and moonlight?"

Lil's song finished, and a plucked cello set a slow fox-trot beat for Peggy Lee's "I Don't Know Enough About You."

"This one's not," Darren argued.

Hank sang some of the lyrics along with Miss Lee. "... you've get me in a spin, oh what a stew I'm in...." Hank stopped singing and frowned. "Well, maybe not this one."

The next selection started and Bing Crosby sang "Moonlight Becomes You."

Darren chuckled. "Or, maybe you *do* have a point," he replied as he led them into another box-step waltz.

RUDELY AWAKENED again, the phouka opened his eyes. *What the bloody shite is going* on *in that house?* the phouka thought as he sat on his haunches and watched the activity around the courtyard.

It looked like dozens of new pixie arrivals were excitedly buzzing and whispering as they hovered near the house windows in the setting sun's gloom. He listened and heard them repeating the same two syllables as they fluttered about. "Prod Gal."

Prod Gal? The phouka puzzled over the strange words. It wasn't a phrase recognizable from any language he was familiar with, certainly not of Fae origin. Was it some strange English expression about poking a woman? He shook his head at how ridiculous that sounded—Ridiculous, even by silly human standards.

He stood up as the buzzing faeries continued their strange mantra. With all this commotion, he would need to find another place to sleep.

His tummy rumbled as he let out a yawn. *Maybe, grab some dinner first,* the phouka thought as he went to the wooden gate and shimmied through the gap and into the darkening street. *That little chapel by the Shamrock Green is usually quiet and good for hunting,* he decided as he turned and scampered down the walk.

WITH A pained groan, Anne managed to stand on her weak legs and maneuver from her house chair to the bed. She'd been lucky all these years to manage caring for herself without assistance, but as she got older, she feared her run of luck was reaching its end. Now, even the simplest things, like slipping out of her sweatpants and preparing for bed, had grown into lengthy and painful chores.

Anne knew her brother would be here in two shakes of a lamb's tail if she rang him, but she worried Darr already spent entirely too much of his time caring for her. She didn't want to grow to be even more of a burden, especially now that Darr had a chance of getting.... *Maybe it's time to hire a nurse.*

She tried not to groan again as she dropped her day clothes to the floor, then slipped on the oversized nightshirt. *Just part-time, of course.* She hadn't reached the point of being an invalid, but a little help with bedtime and mornings would be nice.

Finally changed for the night, Anne wriggled her way under the bedsheets and settled against the headboard. Careful not to twist her back, she retrieved her current fiction book from the nightstand for a bit of reading before going to sleep.

IN THE silent darkness of Anne's flat, Skeena finally relaxed as she stretched her legs. It might be best to seek another location. Yet, she sensed it would be difficult to hunt down another shelter with the kind of energy she needed to survive. Except for the occasional loud outbursts, this flat wasn't a *bad* place. She cautiously crawled from the interior of the bookcase to the wall, then quickly up to the ceiling. *Just find a quieter room,* her instincts urged as she scurried across the parlor ceiling to the hallway that led to the bedrooms.

DARREN CONTINUED singing along with Bing as they danced a slower waltz, "… You're all dressed up to go dreaming… and what a night to go dreaming, mind if I tag along…?"

Hank fought to hold back a yawn as they danced slower. The next song came up with a slow trumpet. Harry James's "I Had the Craziest Dream" showed on the player. Hank snickered. "Now, we're into dreams," he said quietly.

"It would seem so," Darren agreed as he pulled Hank closer and swayed against him. "… I found your lips close to mine, so I kissed you, and you didn't mind it at—"

Taking it as an invitation, Hank stood up on his tiptoes and planted his lips gently onto Darren's mouth, cutting off his words. Darren slid his hand around to Hank's back and returned the kiss as they continued a slow dance until the song ended.

The tinkling sounds of a xylophone played a gentle lullaby tune as The Pied Pipers's "Dream" echoed softly into the room.

Hank fought back another yawn as his dancing paused. "This song's putting me to sleep."

"It *has* been a long day," Darren agreed. "Maybe we should retire?"

"Oh, now yer tryin' to drag me to your bed?" Hank drawled with a tired grin.

"Only if you want," Darren said with a shrug. "Or, you could take the guest room."

"Would you prefer that?" Hank asked as he pushed up against Darren and felt his erection.

Darren pulled away and walked over to the mp3 player before turning it off. "I fear sleep will get the best of me soon, so it probably doesn't matter, either way."

Hank reached out and took Darren's hand. "Then, to *your* room," he said with a flirty smile as he tugged him toward the hallway. "Let's find out just how tired you are."

AFTER DIRECTING George to park a block farther away from the chapel, Paul frowned when he saw James, still dressed in his clergy attire, approaching the tour van. *Diabhe, could the man be any more conspicuous?*

Paul rushed forward and nearly pulled James inside the shelter of the van when he reached the door. "Imigh sa diabhal, can you not at least change your clothing?"

James scowled back as he sank down to a first-row seat on the coach. "Don't curse at me, and you know I hate the Gaelic. *You've* created such a mess of this, I don't think appearance matters now."

"*I've* made a mess? What happened last night? You said you could handle the observation, and look where we are now."

"It was rather foggy last night, my man reported," James offered as an explanation. "Mr. Lear slipped away. These things happen."

"Dia—" Paul cut off another curse. "I don't recall any fog in Temple Bar. I think your man may be incompetent. And now, Lear's somehow found an O'Connell. Whose mistake is that?"

"My dear Paul," James said in a soothing tone as he reached out and patted his arm. "Now is *not* the time to focus on blame."

Paul had to fight not to yank away from James's clammy hand. "Of course you'd say that," Paul spit back. "From the moment I saw that little American at the airport, I knew he was trouble, as I warned you, repeatedly. I've spent the last week tracking his every move, and *your* bloke goes and blows the game on the last whistle."

James stared back. "Even if this so-called legend of yours is true, how much can a clueless foreigner accomplish?" He pulled away his hand and leaned against the padded van seat. "I went out to the stone ring yesterday," he explained dismissively. "The portal is waning so close to death, all *we* have to do is interrupt their little Solstice Soirée, and the thing will close for good. End of story. I don't think it warrants so much concern."

"*My* legend? It was *your* devoted Katherine who turned up the initial research," Paul spit back as he fought to keep from screaming at the priest. "If even only a tiny portion of the tale is true, we should be *very* concerned. This may require more drastic action."

"Drastic?" James blanched at the word. "What are you suggesting?"

Paul smiled tightly. "Since you can't be bothered to muster any concern, maybe you should just go back to your little church and do whatever it is you do there." Paul stood and motioned to the door. "We wouldn't want to risk staining your collar."

James jumped to his feet with an intimidating glare. "Don't try going over my head with this. Just observe, for now. Taking such action could only worsen the circumstances." James walked down the steps and paused at the door. "A little patience is in order."

"Patience?" Paul echoed with a scowl. "The time for patience may be at an end."

"Just observe," James directed with a cold glare before stepping to the street.

Paul scowled at the stupid priest's back as he made his way down the walk. "And, what do you think?" he asked as he turned to George, who sat silently in the driver's seat.

"We need to watch Hank," the driver replied.

"Indeed, we do," Paul agreed. "Get us back to O'Connell's," he told George before he sat in the tour-guide seat on the front row.

FROM HIS shelter of the bushes, the phouka watched the little exchange on the tour bus. *Ah, dissention in the ranks,* he purred as the priest scurried angrily down the walk and the van drove away. *Could the dullahan be losing control?* With a smile, the phouka thought, *What a pity that would be.*

He reached up with his paw and cleaned away the feather tufts that remained from his dinner. *Maybe I should head back to that courtyard.* This all promised to be leading up to an interesting show.

AN HOUR later, Hank tossed awake in the bed again, rolling over to his stomach and scooting a bit farther from Darren. He was having trouble getting comfortable enough to sleep well.

Hank lay listening to Darren's steady breathing. The Irishman didn't seem to have any trouble passing out after their pleasant mutual activities.

Maybe, Hank thought, *it's just that I'm not used to having someone sleep next to me.* Darren's body heat seemed to radiate from him like a fireplace.

Then again, maybe it was the mattress, which was so much softer than Hank was used to. So soft that it made a peculiar hammock-like dip around Darren's body, leaving the rest of the bed sloping up to the edge. *It's like sleeping on a hillside.* Hank groaned as he repositioned his legs.

Or, maybe it's that faint whispering noise that's keeping me awake, he decided. It was such a strange, rhythmic sound, like a staccato triple beat that seemed to grow louder when he closed his eyes and drifted nearer to sleep.

He closed his eyes and tried to tune it in better. The syncopated murmur was so faint, it was hard to tell if it was coming from outside or somewhere else in the house. Hank repositioned his arm and the angle of his neck against the over-soft pillow. He ignored the sound as best he could until exhaustion eventually pulled him into slumber.

ANNE STARTLED awake from her dream. She lay still, almost paralyzed, puzzling over the sensation of being watched. The feeling soon passed, and she breathed easier.

That was peculiar, Anne thought as she carefully shifted her position in the bed. *And after such a strange dream, too.* She struggled to remember the details, but like her readings of late, the dream was composed of only random images and perceptions. The one persistent sensation, which gave her shivers to recall, was the feeling of being locked in a box. *An unpleasant sensation, to say the least,* she thought with a sigh as she closed her eyes again.

WHEN THE woman's breathing finally evened out with sleep, Skeena lifted herself from the screw on the light fixture she had clung to when the woman below had startled awake. She quickly made her way across the remainder of the ceiling and down the wall into the space behind the armoire. Once near the floor, she curled up her legs and settled into a resting pose near the faint energies emanating from below.

Not since shortly after her sudden arrival in the house had Skeena felt this close to the special energy. She reveled in its warmth.

Chapter 11

JAMES ROSE early the next morning. In typical fashion, he dropped to his knees at the side of the bed to recite his early prayers.

Business out of the way, he stood and passed through the silent rectory hallway to the water closet. He tried not to frown as his mind turned to Paul. *That man is such a shark,* he thought as he relieved himself. *But, daresay, a useful shark.*

That point, none could argue. When Katherine had turned up that nasty legend—James refused to call it a *prophecy,* as so many of the others liked to throw about—it was Paul who had come up with the idea of planting informants in all the tour groups. *A brilliant idea,* James admitted as he made his way to the tiny kitchen, *which has borne fruit. Now, we just have to keep it from ripening.*

Of course, James couldn't condone whatever "drastic" action Paul may have in mind. *But, if the man acts on his own... no use in crying over spilled milk, as they say.*

HANK AWOKE again to that strange whispering sound. He lay still a moment in the faint dawn light, tuning out the noise of Darren breathing beside him on the bed as he listened intently.

The whisper had such a strong rhythm, almost a two-syllable beat to it, but the syncopation seemed slower than it had been earlier. *Like a heartbeat,* Hank suddenly realized.

Swish-swish.

His ears fully perked, he crawled from the bed and stepped into the hallway before the next beat.

Swish. Swish.

Listening, he followed the sound as he walked through the hall, but the whispering seemed to die off when he stepped into the great room.

Frustrated, Hank stepped to the rug, but couldn't hear the sound anymore.

Deciding it was time for a smoke, he went back to Darren's room. While the Irishman continued to sleep, Hank retrieved his discarded clothes from the floor. He slipped on his jeans, shoes, and rugby hoodie, then ventured out the green door to the larger courtyard.

As he stepped outside, a sudden flurry of movement near the ivy drew his eye. Hank turned, but didn't see anything other than the green leaves in the early morning light. He fished his cigarette pack from his pocket and lit up. He turned and looked toward the center and nearly dropped the lighter from surprise.

Like some strange aura, a shimmery vapor surrounded the entire large fountain of terracotta bowls. *Guess I'm not in Texas anymore,* Hank thought as he marveled over the beautiful phenomena.

He couldn't take his eyes from the glistening fog that hovered in place over the fountain while he smoked. He studied it more closely, noticing little movements, like air currents stirring in the misty interior. The vapor writhed inside, as though it were a living thing.

Hank finished his cigarette, dropped it to the bricks, then stamped it out with his foot. He reached down, picked up the butt, and put it in his pocket for later disposal. He hated to be a litterbug. Quietly, he went back into Darren's house.

AFTER ANNE finished her long struggle to rise and dress herself, she rolled down the hall to the kitchen to start her pot of morning tea. While the water heated on the stove, she tried to shield her receptors from the confusing mess in the ether. She'd never before experienced this kind of problem with her gift.

Since Sunday morning, when Hank had entered Darr's life, the future appeared to be in some strange, unwritten flux. The details and possibilities changed so quickly from one moment to the next that it made her readings nearly impossible. She would just have to try and ignore the noise until things settled back into some kind of reasonable pattern.

Once the kettle whistled, Anne prepared her tea, rolled her chair to the table, and sipped gratefully at the hot liquid. *Maybe,* she thought as she sat. *Instead of the future, I should try and focus on the past. That may turn up some valuable clues,* she realized.

Also, a little psychometry might be useful, she thought with another sip. But, Anne wasn't nearly as good with the gift of reading objects as their Aunt had been. *Wouldn't hurt to try, though.* On that thought, she carefully placed her mug between her thighs and rolled down the hall to the library in search of her history books.

WITH A satisfying stretch, Darren got out of the bed and donned his linen lounging trousers and a plain T-shirt before making his way to the kitchen.

Hank smiled at him from where he sat at the table. "Good morning, sleepyhead."

"Morning," Darren replied as he found his pack of cloves and retrieved one. "Sleep well?"

"Not really. Noises kept waking me up."

"Sorry," Darren said sincerely as he sat in the other chair. "Do I snore?"

"No," Hank answered. "It wasn't *you* I was hearing. Just other strange noises from this old building that I'm not used to."

"Oh? What noises?"

"Some weird, whispery kind of sound. Kept hearing it all night long. I tried to track it down this morning, but never did."

"Really?" Darren asked. "I don't recall ever hearing such a noise. It could be the pump for the fountain, or some such."

"Maybe," Hank agreed. "It could be a pump that sounds like that."

"After living here this long, I must be so accustomed to the sound that I don't even hear it."

"How long have ya lived here?"

"About—" Darren paused as he thought. "—twenty-seven years? I think."

"Wow. Ya must have good rent control, then."

"Rent? Heavens no. Anne and I own the estate; our Uncle Kelley left it to us when he passed. This used to be Kelley's flat," Darren explained as he stubbed out his smoke.

"You own the whole building?" Hank asked as he glanced around.

"Yes, the O'Connell estate has been here in this block, in one form or another, nearly six hundred years."

"Jeez, how many apartments are there?"

"Oh, about half the building is actually the main house, where Anne lives now. Besides this flat and the one Brigand lives in, we have two other boarders," Darren said as he stood from the table. "Would you like some tea? Or coffee? I'm afraid I don't have much in the way of food to offer for breakfast. I can run out for something in a bit."

"Coffee's fine. I didn't realize the O'Connells were a wealthy family."

Darren frowned as he poured the water for the coffeemaker. "It may look good on paper, but most of the family fortune has been lost to one cause or another. With all the taxes and maintenance for this old structure, we barely break even with the two rentals." He turned back to Hank. "Milk, or sugar?"

Hank shook his head. "Just black." He waited until Darren finished setting up the coffeemaker before he cleared his throat. "So, who *is* this Brigand guy?"

Darren returned to the table, then hesitantly looked at Hank. "Anne and I are involved with a group that's working toward Irish prosperity. Brigand is the leader of our group."

Hank frowned. "Another vague answer. Why can't you just tell me?"

"Please?" Darren implored. "Let's avoid another repeat of yesterday. Can you trust me to explain things at a logical pace?"

"Then, please explain it. Why are you so hesitant? What are you afraid to tell me?"

Darren shook his head. "I'm not *afraid* to tell you anything."

"Well then," Hank asked pointedly. "What's the problem?"

"The issue is—" Darren paused to take a deep breath. "—I can explain until I'm blue in the face, but it won't matter until you're ready to believe."

Hank sighed heavily. "Believe *what?*"

The coffeemaker beeped to signal it was finished brewing. "One moment," Darren said as he stood and went to pour their coffees. "Let's move this someplace more comfortable," he said as he carried their mugs into the great room.

Hank followed him across the large space to the settees and sat down on one.

Darren handed him a mug and sat down next to him. "Why don't we take this from another angle," he suggested. "How up-to-date are you with the recent work in physics?"

"I like reading current science. So, I guess, a bit."

"Well, then you should be aware of the recent postulations by quantum mechanics and string theory, although that school seems to be losing a bit of its original luster. Both areas strongly indicate the certainty of multiple dimensions existing within the universe."

Hank nodded. "Right, I have heard things along those lines. But, what does that have to do with Irish history?"

Darren smiled. "It has *everything* to do with Irish history."

"How?" Hank asked as he scrunched his brow. "What do you mean by that?"

"Just for the sake of conversation, let's assume physicists are, indeed, correct with their postulations. It would be likely that some of these dimensions would be very near to our own 'space' so to speak." Darren studied Hank as he continued. "So near in fact, that there might be 'soft spots' where the two dimensions may interact."

"Okay." Hank nodded. "That seems possible. But you still haven't answered my question."

"Think a moment," he asked Hank as he pointed to the bookshelves of Irish history and mythology. "What is unique about Irish and Nordic mythology?"

Hank glanced over at the shelves. "I don't know."

"If you look at the past myths of other cultures, few of them claim to have actually met their gods. You don't see many stories of a mere mortal shaking hands with Hercules, or sharing a drink with Bacchus. Yet, Irish tales are littered with such accounts of the Fae interacting with common humans." Darren took a sip from his mug. "Even until quite recently."

Hank shook his head. "I'm not following."

"What if, due to some trick of geography, or heaven knows what, Ireland, Greenland, and Iceland all contain some of these 'soft spots' into another dimension?"

Hank paused a moment as he took a sip of his cooling coffee. "Okay, so you're saying that, these Fae are, like, real? Creatures from another dimension?"

Darren nodded.

Hank sipped his coffee, then frowned. "I'm sorry, dude, that's just a bit too much to swallow."

Darren's face fell in disappointment as he tried not to be upset with Hank's dismissal. He shouldn't have tried to push the American so fast, but Hank couldn't be patient enough to come around to things at a slower pace. At least Hank hadn't reacted by bolting, as he did before. Maybe that was a sign of progress.

Darren hoped he hadn't completely wrecked the situation. When his phone twinkled out the first bars of "Meadow Moonglow," it seemed likely that he had. He threw a stage smile at Hank as he answered his phone. "Aye?"

"Are you up and decent?" Anne's voice asked in his ear.

"Mostly," Darren teased.

"Then I'll be over in a moment. I need to borrow your bookshelves," Anne said before hanging up.

Darren stood. "Anne's coming over. Can you let her in while I pull on some more appropriate clothes?" he asked as he headed to his bedroom.

HANK DOWNED the rest of his coffee before going to the back door. A light rapping ensued before he could reach for the deadbolt knob. He opened the door and stood aside so Anne could roll her wheelchair into the room.

"Have you not slept?" Anne asked as she quickly looked over Hank before zipping around the settees and up to the bookshelves.

"Yes," Hank replied. "Of course I did."

"Then, why are you still wearing the same clothing?"

Hank flustered visibly. "Darren was still asleep when I got up, and I didn't want to rummage around in the suitcase, so I just pulled these back on," he defended.

"Anne," Darren said strongly as he returned and saw Hank still standing at the door. "Are you teasing our guest?"

She broke into a huge grin as she perused the titles on the bookshelf. "Sorry. He's too easy to tease," Anne said warmly as she rolled to the next shelf. "I thought you had a copy of *Neil's Chronicle*?"

"I do, but I lent that to Kathy some months back," Darren said as he smiled at Hank and motioned for him to sit again.

"Bloody hell, I was hoping to check something."

"Is it important?" Darren asked as he sat next to Hank. "It was over a year ago that she borrowed it, now that I think about it. She should be done with it."

"Yes," Anne said as she rolled around to face the men. "I would be ever so grateful if you could retrieve it."

"Then, I shall."

Hank shook his head. "You guys don't have to be so damn formal just 'cause I'm here."

"Fine by me," Anne said with a grin as she wheeled closer and studied them. "You two haven't shagged yet? I thought you would have, last night."

As Hank blushed, Darren frowned at his sister. "Anne, no need to be so personal."

"Whatever," she replied with a smile at Hank's red face. "Since the future is such a mess right now, I did have another thought...." She looked at Darren.

"Which is?"

She turned to Hank. "I'm not as good as Oli, but would you be opposed to a little psychometry?"

"Prob'ly," Hank replied as he pulled back reflexively. "How much does it hurt?"

Anne and Darren both chuckled. Darren took Hank's hand as he explained. "Psychometry is doing readings from the vibrations of objects. There's no pain involved."

"Oh," Hank replied. "I guess it's okay, then."

Anne smiled. "I would like to try your ring, if you don't mind. But before that, maybe something more personal. Like a necklace, or something you've worn often, and for a while."

"Sorry, this ring is the only jewelry I've worn in ages."

Anne frowned.

Hank reached down and patted his pockets. "How about this?" he asked as he reached in and removed his keychain. "I've had these keys forever."

Anne smiled as she took the chain with the battered Ford logo charm. "This will be perfect." She sat back in her chair and cradled the keychain in both hands.

"What do I need to do?" Hank asked.

"Shh," Darren said quietly as he squeezed gently at Hank's hand. "Just let her concentrate."

Her face slackened and she hummed softly.

CLOSING HER eyes, Anne pushed out the rest of the world and opened herself to the objects in her hands. Just as Aunt Oli had instructed, she let the vibration of the keys guide her mind to seeing and hearing their world.

In her mind's eye, she soon saw an image of a heavy gray fog. She relaxed and pushed deeper, trying to move past the obscuring haze. The fog shifted, then turned a pinkish color as it pulsed strangely.

Trying not to react with frustration, Anne opened wider. The foggy image shifted in color from pulsing pink, then briefly to a deep blue, then changed to a terracotta hue before she heard a buzzing noise. No other images emerged beyond the thick mist.

Thinking the reading was a failure, Anne soon sighed and opened her eyes. Darren asked, "Well?"

"No luck, too foggy," she said as she handed the keys back to Hank. "Maybe I can get more from the ring…."

Hank took the keys and slipped the Claddagh ring from his finger and handed it over. Anne studied the design a moment, noting the torque crown, before she clasped it in her hand and relaxed again.

As she opened up, the sensation of deep loneliness engulfed her as a flood of images bombarded her mind's eye, flashing rapidly like pages of a book fanning past much too quickly. She took a deep breath and willed the images to slow.

Several more images flashed by too briefly to comprehend; then it slowed to an image, like a video recording, of a hairy hand reaching out and taking the ring. At the same time, she felt a frigid gust of wind. Another rapid series of images followed. She willed the information to slow. A heavy gray fog appeared—the same image she had seen with Hank's keys.

More, she asked, hoping to see past what she thought was obscurity. The fog shimmered and briefly turned into a pulsing neon-pink cloud before shifting to an earthy terracotta, just as before. As the clay-colored fog swirled and danced, she heard a female voice singing to the tune of "Greensleeves," but the words were all wrong. "Go back, go back," the lyrics echoed.

Go back where? Anne wondered.

Her conscious thought broke the trance and everything fell away.

"Bloody hell." She cursed her perceived failure. She looked at Darren before handing the ring back to Hank. "I did get a bit more, but nothing that really made sense. Someone with more skill might have better luck."

"It was worth a try," Darren said. "What did you see?"

"Hard to say," Anne replied. "The ring has *such* a long history. I don't even know what might be relevant, so it makes it hard to focus."

HANK TOOK the ring and slipped it back onto his finger, thinking it was peculiar how cool the metal now felt after being in Anne's palm. He looked up to Anne. "What's it like?"

"Pardon?" Anne asked.

"Doing the readings. What's it like? What do you usually see?"

"Usually, it's very disorienting, like tuning into the middle of a telly program where you're trying to piece together what's happened in the story so far. At least, that's the way it feels for me."

"But, do you actually *see* things?"

Anne nodded. "Quite often there are visual images, and auditory ones, as well as sensations and emotions that come through. The emotions are usually the strongest part."

"You're saying my ring has emotions?"

Anne chuckled. "No, silly. But the wearer, or the environment it was in would have vibrating emotions the ring could pick up and carry."

"Like," Darren added, "how a guitar string continues to vibrate long after it's been plucked."

Anne shook out her hands violently and took in a deep breath. "Well then," she said as she turned to Hank. "Have you made your arrangements to stay until Sol—"

"No." Darren jumped in and cut her off. "I haven't broached *that* topic yet, Anne." He frowned at her. "Thank you very much for bringing it up," he added sarcastically.

"Sorry." She turned to Hank again. "It wouldn't be a problem for you to stay… until Sunday, I hope."

Hank thought on it a moment. He didn't have any pressing matters back home in Texas to attend to, but would he be comfortable staying in Dublin nearly another week? "Prob'ly not a problem," he told Anne. "Unless Darren gets tired of me hanging out around here."

Anne smiled wickedly. "*That's* not an issue, is it dear Darr?"

Darren threw her an exasperated look.

"What airline are you traveling with?"

"Aer Lingus," Hank replied.

"Well then," Anne chimed warmly as she patted Hank's knee. "Get me your ticket information and I'll get the arrangements made. They still owe me a favor, after that fiasco with my chair when we had our gig in Naples."

Hank glanced at Darren, who smiled warmly and nodded. Hank got up and went through the hall to the spare bedroom. Still fearing the possibility of wearing out his welcome in Darren's apartment, he dug around in his duffel bag and retrieved the airline tickets.

As he turned to leave, he remembered Anne's teasing remark about his clothes, so he dragged his suitcase onto the bed to tidy himself up a bit.

Feeling more presentable after refreshing his deodorant and changing into a clean shirt, Hank went back into the hallway, but slowed when he heard the intense whispering coming from the great room. No doubt the siblings were arguing about him. He hung back a moment and wondered if he should interrupt them. Maybe his staying longer was a bad idea if it would lead to so much friction.

The whispering stopped, so Hank stepped into the great room.

Anne smiled up at him as she wheeled to the end of the settees. "Let me take those, and I'll head over to my place and have this taken care of."

Reluctantly, Hank handed her the tickets. He looked at Darren. "You sure my staying won't be a problem?"

Darren smiled at him warmly. "Of course not. I'm grateful, actually. I had been planning to ask myself, but Anne can be as impatient as you, at times."

"I'm off for now," Anne called from the door as she pulled it open. "And don't forget that book! *Neil's Chronicle*," she yelled at Darren before closing the door behind herself.

Hank frowned. "Who says I'm impatient?"

Darren laughed. "I'm certainly not the first person that's ever pointed that out to you."

"Whatever," Hank replied as he stifled a yawn.

"Why don't you go for a lie down," Darren suggested as he stood. "Maybe sleep a bit more. I'll go to Kathy's and collect that book, before Anne has another tizzy."

"Yeah, I guess I could do that," Hank agreed. "My body clock is still all screwed up."

Darren slipped his arm around Hank's shoulder in a cradling hug as he walked them to the hallway. "Just sleep. Kathy can be quite chatty during our visits, so I'm likely to be gone a while." He leaned down and kissed Hank on the forehead. "Go sleep."

"Sure." Hank pulled Darren into a tight hug, then went down the hall to the guest room and crawled onto the bed. He didn't think he was tired enough to actually sleep, but his snores reverberated through the house soon after Darren left.

FROM HIS vantage point in the van, Paul watched as Darren left the house and walked to the corner. He turned to George. "And where do you suppose he's off to?"

George merely shrugged in reply.

"Maybe we should follow and find out."

"Not Hank? Isn't he alone now?" George asked with a frown.

"Won't matter, he's still under the protection of that house. We may have to come up with some way to lure him out. In the meantime, we should find out where that O'Connell lad is going."

George started the van and maneuvered onto the street as Darren crawled into a cab.

Chapter 12

ANNE MADE it to the door before a third knock. "What has you so excited?" she asked Brigand as she pulled the front door open and rolled back to let him enter.

"News on Hank's ring. He mentioned something about the shop's sign that proved to be a lead," Brigand explained as he followed Anne into the parlor. "Hank bought it from the Faerie's Goblet, the shop run by Chauncey O'Dowd. I'm waiting for him to ring back."

"That name sounds familiar, but he isn't one of the Antiquer's Guild?"

"No. He's worked with the Galway group in the past, but has never been a member, as far as I know."

"Oh," Anne replied with surprise. "Well then, I guess we'll have to wait for that ring-back and find out the man's story."

Brigand paused. "Forgive my ignorance, but I'm confused as to why it's so relevant."

"*Something*, obviously, happened in that shop for this O'Dowd man to sell the artifact to Hank. I'm curious what he knows."

"Still not picking up anything solid?"

"No." Anne shook her head. "And it's beginning to get rather irritating. I feel like I'm out of the loop."

"Let me know if there's any way I can help."

"Have you mentioned anything to the rest of the Guild yet?"

Brigand shook his head. "Unless you think there's something they should know right now, I'm holding off until we have more detail. I'm hoping we'll have something more solid to mention at the Guild meeting tonight."

"Sounds wisest," Anne agreed with a nod of her head. "I'm still working some sources. Darr's—"

The ringing of Brigand's cell phone interrupted their conversation. Brigand pulled the phone from his pocket and glanced at the display, then handed the phone to Anne. "It's O'Dowd. Maybe you should take it."

Anne took the phone. "Hello."

"G'day to you, this is Chauncey and I had a message to call this number. With whom am I speaking?"

"I'm Anne O'Connell."

"Well, blessed be, *the* Anne," the man replied with awe. "I've certainly heard your name among various circles. What can I do for you, Miss O'Connell?"

"I'm inquiring about a man that visited your shop sometime in the past week. You sold him a ring...," Anne dangled teasingly.

Chauncey chuckled in her ear. "Indeed, I did." He chuckled again. "And, I suppose you're curious as to *why* I would do such a thing?"

"Oh, that question has crossed my mind," Anne admitted.

"That particular ring has sat quietly in this shop for who knows how many decades, until that American walked through the door. As soon as he entered the shop, the ring started singing. And the young man zeroed right in on it, staring at that ring in the case."

"I see," Anne replied in a bemused tone.

"Naturally, it was obvious the two belonged to each other, so I quoted a reasonable price and sold him the ring."

"Naturally," Anne agreed. "And may I ask, Mr. O'Dowd, do you have a gift?"

Chauncey cleared his throat. "Some might say that. Nothing like yours, though." Hesitantly, he said, "I can do a bit of dousing, find lost things sometimes."

"That sounds like a very useful gift."

"Sometimes," he replied noncommittally.

"About this ring, you say it's been in your shop for decades?"

"It's been in the shop since I was a boy. I took over the business from my da, so the ring has been here at least fifty years."

"What else do you know about the ring?"

"Not much more. Da always thought it was merely a replica of the Shay bridal ring, and I did too, until it started singing. I was a bit surprised by that." Chauncey cleared his throat again. "May I ask, what prompted your call? I mean, did I do something ill-advised by giving up the ring?"

"Oh, heaven's no," Anne replied quickly. "I think, in the long run, it may be a very good thing. Actually, the man who bought the ring, Hank, ran into my brother yesterday, and we're just trying to sort all this out."

"Well then," he replied. "I'll leave you to it. I don't think I can offer any more, but do ring if any more questions come up."

"I will," Anne said sweetly. "And thank you so much for speaking with me, Mr. O'Dowd."

"My pleasure. Have a good day, Miss O'Connell."

"Good day," Anne said before hanging up and handing the phone back to Brigand.

"Anything helpful?"

"No," Anne replied before a sigh. "About what I expected. Chauncey said the ring sang to Hank, so he sold it to him. He didn't know any details about the ring, or Hank, other than that."

Brigand put the phone back in his pocket and stood up. "Anne, you still haven't explained how all this might fit together."

Anne smirked at him. "Believe me, if I had a clear idea, I'd certainly divulge it. But I don't. I'll have to keep digging."

"Right," Brigand replied. "I'll leave you be, then."

FOLLOWING DISCREETLY behind the cab until it arrived at the McPherson home, George pulled to a stop at the edge of the road and gripped the wheel. "Uh-oh," he muttered.

Paul patted his driver's shoulder. "Now, now. Nothing to fret over. I doubt Katherine is in any danger. This will most likely prove to be rather innocent, but, we'll stay a few moments, just in case."

DARREN CRAWLED from the cab after paying his fare. He followed the brick path to Kathy's stoop, then rang the buzzer.

The door soon opened. With a surprised expression on her wrinkled face, Kathy motioned Darren inside. "Mr. O'Connell. I hadn't been expecting anyone," she said as she tried to nonchalantly fluff up her gray hair as she led him into the sitting room. "Would you like tea? Or perhaps a soft drink?"

Darren shook his head. "No refreshments needed. And please, just call me Darr, like you used to," he replied as he took a seat on the large divan.

Kathy fluttered over him like a mother hen. "What brings you by?"

"I'm actually here about that book you borrowed."

"Oh?" Kathy dropped down to sit on the divan. "And which book is that, deary?"

"*Neil's Chronicle*. I lent it to you some time ago."

"A chronicle? Are you quite sure about that?" she asked with doubt in her voice. "That's not the sort of book I normally read."

"Do you not recall last May? You came by my flat after one of the Guild meetings and asked to check my shelves."

"Oh. Was that May of *last* year?" Kathy asked as she fluffed her hair again. "I do seem to remember something about that. But, didn't I return that book shortly after?"

Darren tried not to sigh in frustration. "Yes, you *did* return the fiction book you also borrowed that day, but you didn't return the chronicle."

"Well, good heavens," she exclaimed as she rose to her feet. "If you're sure that I have it, let me go check," she said as she wandered slowly to the bookcase by the window. She poked and fingered the spines of the books as she slowly peered over the titles. "Ah, here," she said in a cheery voice as she yanked the book off the shelf and brought it back to Darren. "And I apologize for my absentmindedness."

Darren took the book, then shook his head when he glanced at the title and saw *The Chronicles of Narnia.* He stood. "Unfortunately, Mrs. McPherson, this isn't the right book."

"That's not a chronicle?" she asked pointedly.

"Well, yes," Darren replied as he fidgeted on his feet. "But this isn't *Neil's Chronicle,* the book you borrowed. Do you mind if I take a peek at your shelves? Maybe it's hidden somewhere."

"Oh, deary," she replied with a tired tone. "Please do. I've had *quite* a trouble with things hiding from me lately."

Darren smiled and tried not to show any other expression as he passed the old woman on his way to the shelves. It was sad to see the years catch up to her like this. He could still remember what a vibrant woman she had been when he was a child.

At the bookcase, he quickly scanned the series of titles from one shelf to the next, but never found the book. He turned back to her with a stage smile. "Is there, perhaps, another bookcase in the home where it might turn up?"

"Where *what* might turn up?" she asked innocently.

"The book we're looking for, *Neil's Chronicle,*" Darren replied smoothly, trying to keep any frustration out of his voice.

"Oh. The only other place I keep books is on my nightstand by the bed. Should we check there?"

"That sounds like a fine idea," Darren said as he followed her up the narrow stairs to the second floor.

She led him down the hall to the facilities and motioned him in. "And remember young man, jiggle the handle after you flush, or it won't stop running."

With the brightest stage smile he could muster, Darren turned to Kathy. "Can we check your nightstand first, to see if that book is there?"

Mrs. McPherson looked up at him with a scolding expression. "Darr, you're much too young to be reading *my* bedtime books. You can read one from the case downstairs where I keep the children's things."

"Yes ma'am," Darren said reflexively while still holding his smile, even though her mental slips were nearly breaking his heart. He decided to buy some time to secretly browse on his own for where the book may have ended up. "I think I would like some tea, if you still have any of that ginger spice I remember."

Kathy beamed a smile. "Of course I still have that, you rascal. Follow me to the kitchen and we'll get the kettle on."

Darren stepped into the bathroom. "I'll be right behind you," he said before closing the door. He relieved himself, which went quickly since he didn't really *need* to go. After flushing, he played the trick with the handle before stepping into the empty hall.

He scurried to the opposite end and peeked inside Kathy's bedroom. He could see a stack of books on the nightstand, but they were all modern paperbacks, not like the leather-bound history book he sought. He glanced around the room without spotting any others.

On his way back to the stairs, he peeked into the spare rooms, just to make sure, but saw no other books. After descending, he found Kathy in the kitchen, setting out a plate of shortbread bars.

"The pot should be hot shortly," she explained as Darren took a seat at the linoleum-covered table.

Darren grabbed one of the bars, recalling, as he bit into it, that he hadn't eaten anything yet. And neither had Hank, he also realized. He suddenly felt like a terrible host. Guilt stole his appetite, so he started to put the bitten treat back on the plate.

A scolding glare from Kathy made him freeze. He put the remainder of the bar in his mouth and chewed, but the shortbread was like flavorless, dry sand in his mouth.

The kettle whistled, and Kathy soon brought over steaming mugs of the ginger tea. She sat down cheerfully. "It's been ages since you've stopped in, Darr. What brings you by?"

"Just collecting that book you borrowed, *Neil's Chronicle*. Do you know where it is?"

"A chronicle?" Kathy frowned. "I do hope that wasn't one of the books I loaned out. You know Emmy, that sweet lady down the street. She likes borrowing my books and drops by from time to time."

"I see," Darren replied, hoping none of his frustration showed through. "And, how often does she drop by?"

Kathy's face went lax as she stared over at the kettle by the sink. "Who dropped by, deary?" she asked with an innocent smile as she turned back to Darren.

HANK STARTLED awake.

He blinked as he stared at the space over the side of the bed. At about the height of a man's head, a small ball-shaped cloud of mist hovered.

He blinked again.

The strange, tiny cloud swirled. As he stared at it, the mist faded away.

Hank rose, still blinking. *I must still be dreaming,* he thought, but he was not reassured.

Hank settled back on the bed and closed his eyes. A grumbling from his stomach reminded him that they'd never had the breakfast Darren had mentioned. He rolled over, but hunger kept him awake. Maybe he should go rustle up some food.

Hank soon gave up on a nap and made his way to the kitchen.

FROM THEIR new, more secluded vantage point, Paul slapped George on the shoulder as they watched the O'Connell lad emerge empty-handed from Katherine's house. Darren rushed to the curb and the waiting cab. "See," Paul said with a grin. "Nothing to worry about."

"Should we follow?" the driver asked.

"Hm." Paul paused and thought for a moment. "No. Chances are that he's just heading back to his flat. I'll have a quick word with Katherine once he's around the corner."

The cab drove away. Once it was safely out of sight, Paul opened the van's door and, using his cane, teetered down the walk to her porch. He had to wait several minutes after pushing the buzzer before the door opened.

"Mr. Malloy," Kathy said in surprise. "You shouldn't be here," she said as she held the door partially closed without offering an invitation inside.

"Just wanted to check in. What did the O'Connell want?" Paul asked as he pushed his way past Katherine into the foyer.

"Looking for the chronicle," Kathy replied stiffly as she eased the front door nearly closed behind Paul but kept her hand on the knob. "I guess they finally realized it might be important."

"You didn't return it?"

"Of course not."

"And didn't that make him suspicious?" Paul asked pointedly.

"No, I dealt with it rather craftily." Kathy pulled open the door. "If there isn't anything else, I was on my way to the bath."

Paul put his hand on the door and pushed it closed until the bolt clicked. "*How* did you deal with it?"

"By going senile," she whined with a slight fear in her voice as Paul towered over her and pushed closer. She released the door knob and backed into the corner. "Honestly, he doesn't suspect a thing."

AFTER TURNING on the kitchenette exhaust fan and lighting up a cigarette, Hank poked around in search of food. He first checked the refrigerator, but besides the case of sparkling water, he found only a small bottle of milk, part of a six-pack of beer, and a squeeze container of some kind of nut butter.

Hank went to the cabinets. He found part of a loaf of bread on the mostly bare shelves. He glanced around the tiny counter space without finding a toaster.

In another cabinet, he found a metal box with some kind of soup crackers inside. He pulled out one of the round wafers and ate it. Although a little dry, he decided the crackers would be his best choice, so he took the metal box to the table.

He went back and checked the coffee pot. The sludgy brew had been sitting on the warmer all morning, but Hank didn't care. He looked in the cabinets again, but failed to find another mug.

The mugs they had used earlier in the morning must still be in the living room, so Hank went into the great room and picked them up from the coffee table. As he carried them back to the kitchen, he saw the stained glass jewelry box still sitting on the dining room table.

Hank stopped to stare at it. Now that Darren's hand wasn't covering the top, he could see the stained glass details on the lid. Fashioned from glittering blue glass in the center of the art-deco design, he saw another one of those funky F-shaped characters. Only, he realized, this one was backward, a mirror image of the strange "F" he had seen on the shop's sign in Galway. *And somewhere else?*

Hank struggled to recall where else he had seen that glyph, but his memory failed to conjure any further details. Yet, he *knew* he'd seen that shape somewhere before. Hank shook his head and returned to the kitchen. *I must have just seen it online somewhere when browsing the Internet, or something.*

He picked up the carafe and gave the blackened coffee a swirl before filling his mug. He was just sitting down to the tiny table for his improvised brunch when he heard a noise near the front door.

Hank stood, but Darren, carrying several brown paper bags, bustled into the kitchen before he could move from the table.

Darren deposited the paper bags onto the tabletop, frowning when he saw the tin of soup biscuits. "I hope that wasn't your lunch. I've brought real food. Well, pub food, anyway."

The aroma of fried potatoes and meat sent Hank's guts into a tumbling rumble. "Smells like food to me," he replied with a smile as Darren sat at the table and nudged one of the paper bags in his direction.

"The pub has roast beef on the board on Mondays. I hope that is acceptable," Darren explained as they dug into the bags of chips and sandwiches. "I realized while at Kathy's that we never had that breakfast."

"It's great." Hank bit into the sliced roast beef sandwich on some kind of whole-grain bread. He was so hungry, he hardly noticed the taste as he chewed ravenously. As he ate, he glanced around the table but didn't see anything other than the food bags. "Where's the book? Did you leave it in the living room?"

"Didn't get it," Darren said as he got up, went to the refrigerator, and grabbed two bottles of water. "We couldn't find the chronicle. Don't know if it's tucked away somewhere, or if she might have inadvertently loaned it out."

"Oh," Hank said as he chewed. After swallowing the bite, he ignored the water bottle, choosing to drink some of the old coffee instead. "Did ya at least have a nice visit?"

"Not really," Darren answered with a frown. "A bit sad, actually. The poor dear seems to be fading with age."

"Fading?" Hank asked after another bite.

"Starting to have trouble with memory as her age catches up. At one point, she thought it was the 1980s, and I was a young boy again." Darren ate his last chip, but left more than half the sandwich untouched as he sipped at his water bottle.

"Alzheimer's?"

"Maybe. Don't know. It *could* just be old age. Kathy must be in her late eighties, if not past ninety, at this point."

"I'm sorry," Hank said before he grabbed a few of his fries. "That sucks."

Darren shrugged vaguely. "It is the way of things." He watched as Hank devoured the last of his sandwich. "You must be hungry."

"Yeah," Hank replied with a smile when he realized all the food was gone. "I've just had a huge appetite since getting to Ireland. Must be all the running around we were doing."

Darren smiled back. "Did you get some sleep while I was gone?"

"A bit," Hank answered as he guzzled down the remaining coffee in the mug. He hesitated briefly before he finally said, "But, I did wake up rather suddenly."

"That noise again?"

"No." Hank hesitated again. "There was a cloud in the bedroom."

"A *what*?" Darren asked with a quietly serious tone as he leaned forward.

"Some kind of bluish cloud, or mist, about the size of a grapefruit. It kinda hovered in the air by the bed. Then it disappeared."

Darren's face got very serious. "It just hovered?"

"Yeah, the strangest thing."

"That *is* a bit unusual. If it was what I *think* it was. I can't recall anyone ever mentioning they saw a sprite in the house before."

"Sprite? One of those water faeries?"

Darren nodded. "There's been the occasional sighting of what we call green faeries, but no mention of sprites."

Hank took the other sparkling water bottle and opened it. He took a sip. "Have *you* seen one? One of the green faeries?"

Darren nodded in reply.

"What do they look like?"

"A bit like green butterflies. At least, that's how they looked to me. I haven't seen any *in* the house, just occasionally in the courtyard."

Hank glanced back with a crooked grin. "And, how do you know it *wasn't* just butterflies that ya saw?"

"Several differences. The wing shape wasn't quite right, for one. And instead of a solid color, their wings were quite a bit more translucent. Also, their bodies were larger, with some feminine curvature to the shape."

Hank took a sip of water as he pondered Darren's description. "When ya said 'How they looked to me,' what did ya mean? Other people see different things?"

"Yes," Darren said with a nod. "It seems that when describing the Fae, everyone sees something a little bit different. One theory I heard that sounds reasonable postulates that the Fae are actually some kind of nebulous energy, and what us *humans* see is just a projection—our minds trying to make sense of what we're looking at." Darren looked over at the empty coffee mug in front of Hank. "I can make a fresh pot, if you'd like."

Hank nodded. "That would be great."

Darren gathered up the papers and bags from their meal and took them to the waste bin as Hank fished out his pack of cigarettes.

Chapter 13

Once a new pot of coffee was set to brewing, Darren returned to the table and smiled at Hank. "Not that I'm wanting to put a jinx on it, but you seem to be much more agreeable this afternoon. Why is that?"

Hank gave a shrug as he tamped out his cigarette butt. "I've been thinking a lot about the last few days, and all these coincidences that just keep piling up into a big mountain. I'd be a fool to try and ignore all this stuff." He smiled at Darren. "And, you seem so confident in all this; your explanations have made a lot of sense."

"I see," Darren replied. "That wasn't the answer I expected to hear."

"Really? What did ya think I was gonna say?"

"That seeing the sprite made you rethink everything."

The coffee pot beeped. Darren picked up Hank's mug and took it to the counter for a refill.

"Well, that too," Hank admitted. "I guess we could call it the cherry on top. I think, maybe, that wasn't the first time I've seen one of those sprites."

"Oh?" Darren asked as he brought the mug back to Hank and set it in front of him. "When was this?"

"This morning, most recently. When that noise woke me up again about sunrise, I went out to the courtyard for a smoke. That fancy fountain of yours was surrounded by a strange cloud. I tried to convince myself it was just some weird, early morning weather thing. But now I'm thinking it was a sprite."

"The *whole* fountain?" Darren asked after he pulled his jaw closed. "That sounds like more than just *one* sprite." He pondered a moment, then gave a warm smile to Hank. "I suppose I shouldn't be surprised about it."

Hank set down the mug of hot coffee and reached across the table. "Why's that?"

Darren took Hank's hands, feeling their warmth as he clasped them softly. "If you recall, I did say there were a few more details about the wedding we could discuss later." Darren paused briefly as he organized his thoughts. "This isn't common knowledge, but my family has classified the Fae into two major groups: the green and the blue. Going all the way back to the first Neils, our family has been—how would you say—aligned? Well, cooperative anyway, with the Green Fae, what you would typically think of as faeries and pixies."

"Okay," Hank said. "What does that have to do with the wedding?"

"I mentioned that the marriage brought about the union of Eire in spirit. The Shay, they were aligned with the Blue Fae, the sprites and nymphs."

"And, since I'm a Shay," Hank thought aloud, "I have a thing with the sprites?"

"It would seem so."

Hank pondered that a moment. "What about all the other things? Like leprechauns, or phoukas, or others? Is there more besides the green and blue?"

"No, they tend to fall one way or the other. For instance, the leprechauns and brownies are also green, and the phouka are blue. I can only think of one type of Fae that are considered different—the dullahan. They've been referred to as red, or redcaps."

"Dullahan? I've never even heard of those."

Darren smiled as he warmly squeezed Hank's hands. "Of course you have. It was an American writer that made them famous, with his Sleepy Hollow story. Dullahan are headless horsemen—harbingers of justice. Washington Irving took quite a bit of license when he wrote the tale, turning the horseman into a vengeful spirit. A real dullahan would never target an innocent, like poor Ichabod."

"Yer pullin' my leg now," Hank drawled. "Those dullahan things *can't* be real."

"Why not?" Darren asked with a frown. "Why accept one thing, like the sprites, but not another?"

"Well, I've seen a sprite, for one thing. It's just easier to accept something simple, like a cloud or a butterfly, than some kind of headless monster. I mean, how would the damn thing even talk? If there's no air moving over the vocal cords—"

"Remember what I said about projections?" Darren cut in. "You're trying to interpret things too literally. They are *all* just nebulous energy, and many are known to be able to change their appearance. Likely, by a simple trick of changing the projection we see." Darren paused a moment to give his statement time to sink in before he continued. "I'm thinking, that cloud form of the sprites is probably the closest to what these creatures actually look like."

Hank sat quietly but nodded slightly as he pondered Darren's explanation. "Okay," Hank said as nodded again. "Then, why bother with all the projections? And why do they have such different forms?"

"Why do some women wear makeup and others not? It may be simply a matter of personal taste for them. I don't think that's the kind of question we could get an answer to. Or, at least, one that might make sense to us."

WHILE NOSING around the dumpster on the south side of the estate, the phouka froze when he sensed a presence approach. He glanced up to see the dullahan strolling his way.

"My friend," the dullahan said in greeting.

The phouka scowled. "Oh. *Now* I'm your friend?" He leaped onto the wooden railing and poised on the beam, scrutinizing him warily. "What is it that you want?"

"Just a minor favor." He smiled, showing white razor-like teeth. "And in exchange, I'll help you with your cursed form. I should be able to remove it."

"Really now?" the cat replied in a sarcastic tone. "Seeing as how you applied this cursed form in the first place, I would hope you could remove it."

"Yes." The dullahan tried to smile kindly, but he still looked treacherous. "Help with a small matter, and I'll remove it."

The phouka rose to his haunches and fluffed out his coat, distrust showing in every stiff hair of his marmalade fur as he considered the proposal. "And replace it with what?" The cat tensed and didn't give the dullahan time to reply. "I will certainly want to see the fine print first."

"But—" The dullahan tried to look sympathetic, without quite pulling it off. "Is this feline form not pleasing to the human eye?"

"You know bloody well this was not my desire. I wanted a pleasing *human* form, male preferably."

"Not *my* fault, if you weren't specific enough when we made our deal," he replied with a shrug. "Yet, such a wish can still be arranged...," the dullahan teased. "Just lure that American away from the estate, and I shall grant your desire."

"To what end?" the phouka asked suspiciously. "That last little favor I did for you turned out rather badly for many." The phouka shivered when he remembered the repercussions of the Tempest.

"No harm will befall the lad. He need simply be... detained for a time."

The phouka weighed the aspects of the proposal in his mind. "Detained?" he asked as he considered the task. "As in, kidnapped and held hostage?"

"I would not use those words."

The phouka gave a wry smile. "Of course not, but those are the words that *need* to be used, are they not?"

"If you want to get into technical details, they might apply," the dullahan said casually.

"Aye," the phouka replied. He pondered only briefly before his lips widened into a knowing grin—at least, as much of a grin as he could match with a cat's face. "A dodgy bastard, as always." He stood and strolled along the beam to get closer to the dullahan and stare him in the eye. "I was a fool to trust you once, so I won't be involved in your shenanigans a second time. Find some other errand boy," he replied dismissively, then jumped from the fence and scurried behind the dumpster.

"Think wisely on your choice," the dullahan called with only a trace of frustration in his voice. "I won't repeat this offer."

The phouka waited, hiding behind the steel dumpster until he sensed the dullahan depart. The dumpster probably didn't offer much protection, though. Like himself, the horseman would undoubtedly have built up a certain amount of immunity to iron after living in this world for so many centuries.

As he waited, he tried not to think about their previous bargain. "Guilt" would be too human a word to use, but the phouka did feel a certain amount of responsibility for his part in what led to the Tempest. Had he foreseen the consequences, he would not have agreed to help the dullahan on that occasion. Which left him wondering, *What is the dullahan out to accomplish now?*

Just as before, it seemed like a simple little request. But the phouka knew from the past that every action led to reactions and created repercussions which could soon snowball into major ramifications. And of course, there was no way to know if the dullahan was being completely honest when he promised no harm to the American.

Carefully, the phouka crawled from behind the dumpster and scurried to the walk. He quickly made his way to the terracotta courtyard. *How, exactly, does a dullahan define "harm?"* he wondered.

He felt concern as he shimmied under the wooden gate to the courtyard. The word "harm" seemed to leave much leeway for someone like the dullahan, who played fast and loose with definitions.

Picking a spot by the sun-warmed planter pots, he sat facing the flat's door. The few times he had seen the American, he'd seemed like a solid lad, not someone deserving of a dullahan's attention.

The phouka curled up with a sigh. There might not be anything the phouka could accomplish, if, or when, the horseman decided to act, but he could at least keep a watch on the situation.

AFTER DARREN left for his sister's, Hank sat alone in the living room. Or, he tried to sit, anyway.

Feeling restless, he stood up and paced to the bookshelves. He did see a few interesting titles when he scanned the huge selection of books, but the thought of sitting still and reading didn't feel appealing. *Maybe some music?*

Hank paced to the music player. After looking over the unfamiliar device, he thought it best not to mess with it. With a shrug, he walked back to the settee. He sat down again, but couldn't seem to sit still. His foot kept twitching, bouncing his knee up and down.

He glanced at the back door. Darren had been gone only a few minutes, but the time seemed to be stretching out, making the moments feel like long hours. Hank got up and paced to the kitchen.

GEORGE FROWNED as he sat in the van, clutching the business card to his chest. "It's not working."

Paul gave George a reassuring pat on the shoulder. "Keep at it. It takes time—like boiling a kettle. At first, nothing seems to be happening, until the pot suddenly hisses and whistles. Just think about how heavy and oppressive those walls are. The walls are closing in."

"Closing in...," George echoed as he closed his eyes. "Walls closing in...."

"Need to leave. Get outside," Paul continued guiding.

HANK PACED around the kitchen, noticing just how tiny this room was—and hot. He peeked in the refrigerator—empty. The room was starting to feel suffocating. He slammed the fridge door and trotted back to the living room.

A restlessness stirred in every muscle of his body. A terrible need to go somewhere, to do something, chewed at him. *But go where? Do what?*

As Hank paced across the rug in the great room, a sudden inspiration struck him. *I can fix the empty fridge,* he realized. He yanked his wallet out of his jeans pocket and looked inside. A quick glance showed at least thirty euros tucked away. *Darren had mentioned there was a market nearby... thirty should be enough to buy a few groceries... at least some eggs and cheese for omelets, or something.*

Happy to have a goal and a reason to leave the suddenly claustrophobic house, Hank grabbed his kelly-green hoodie and nearly ran out the front door as he pulled on the jacket.

Rushing around the terracotta fountain, he kept all of his attention focused on the front gate and nearly stepped on the cat's tail without even seeing it.

The cat lurched to his feet and pulled in his tail, giving Hank a glare.

"Sorry," Hank replied as he hurried to the gate, opened it, then stepped out to the street. Finally, he had made it outside.

Remembering that the cab had passed the market on the way to Darren's, Hank turned to the right, set a brisk pace to the corner, and soon found the market. With a happy smile, he pushed open the door and stepped inside.

Hank glanced around the interior of the shop. This place was a bit bigger than a convenience store, but still not nearly the size of a real American grocery store. Spotting the wall sign that said "Dairy," he walked in that direction to the outer wall.

Once he found the eggs, Hank puzzled over the container as he checked the price. Instead of the dozen eggs he was used to seeing, this case—in fact, *all* the egg cases—only held ten. *Must be some kind of metric convention,* he decided as he checked inside the carton for any broken ones.

Moving farther down the wall, he found the cheese and was once again surprised. In the American grocery stores, the upper wall would be filled with plastic hanging bags of shredded and sliced cheeses. But, in this Irish store, little wire shelves covered the wall with small blocks and tiny wheels of a mind-boggling assortment of cheeses. The lower refrigerator compartment held much larger wheels, most of which must have weighed over ten pounds. *Guess I'll have to grate my own,* Hank though as he selected one of the two-kilo blocks of British cheddar and checked the price.

With still more money to burn, Hank stepped farther down the wall to the meat section. After finding some sliced ham, he turned to the rest of the store.

After mostly marveling and occasionally feeling disgusted at some of the things he found in the butcher's section, Hank wandered through the market and selected a few more items, until he neared his thirty-euro mark.

AFTER A fast and friendly checkout, Hank carried the paper bag by its little jute handles back to the street. Turning left, he froze when he saw the front edge of a satiny-black van, visible around the corner of the dog-leg turn that led back to Darren's. A little alarm bell went off in his head.

"Run," said a voice from somewhere near his feet. He glanced down at the orange tabby cat looking up at him. *No way. That cat did not just talk.*

Hank picked up his foot and took a step to the left, but a plume of vapor shot up from the manhole cover in front of him, obscuring his view and making him pause again.

"The *other* way, you silly man," the voice from the street said.

Hank turned around and took a few steps down the sidewalk, moving farther away from Darren's house as he stared at the cat.

"Run!" the cat yelled at him.

Pulling the bag close, Hank took off in a quick jog down the walk. He felt the tiny hairs on the back of his neck bristle as he jogged to the next intersection, which veered off at a strange thirty-seven-degree angle. The light was red for crossing, so Hank turned to the right and continued along the same block at a slower pace. The Claddagh ring suddenly felt cold, and he had that peculiar feeling of being watched again.

Hank stepped up to a faster jog and was nearly at the next intersection when a blast of steam shot from one of the gutter pipes running down the brick wall in front of him. The vapor formed a sort of vague, triangular shape, pointing right. Hank turned and jogged into the alley, not slowing his pace until he reached the end.

The feeling of being watched returned, so he glanced around for some sign of refuge. Across the next street, he could see a walled-off park, with a gate standing open.

A loud blast of steam in the alley behind him drove him forward. He ran across the road and jogged to the gate. Slowing and panting heavily, he entered the large park.

The bristling hairs on the back of his neck warned him to keep moving.

Hank looked around for any spot to hide but didn't see any place secluded enough among the trees and grassy areas of the park. He looked to the left and saw two boys sitting on a little knoll near the bricked sidewalk. Hank smiled when recognition set in. He slipped his free arm out of the sleeve of his hoodie as he quickly jogged in their direction.

"Cover me," he told the stoop boys as he removed the hoodie and turned it inside out, so the white lining now showed on the outside. After pulling it back on, he grabbed a beer bottle from one of the boys and nestled in the grass behind them. He lay down on the ground, positioning the bag in front of his head, trying his best to look like a passed-out teenager. As he curled his head down and pulled the hood over his face, a spitting drizzle started, hovering over the park with a shadowy fog.

One of the boys started to say something, until a determined-looking Paul stormed through the gate. He slowed his steps as he entered the park. Then he leaned on his fancy cane, scrutinizing every nook and cranny of the gloomy trees as he slowly turned his head.

The blonder boy stood up, blocking Paul's view, and took a few swaying steps forward. "Hey mate," he slurred out loudly. "Think you'z can do us a solid?"

Paul glanced briefly in their direction, then crinkled his nose.

"Yeah, mate," the other boy threw in as he stood up. "Just a tiny little favor?" he whined as he stepped closer to Paul.

Crinkling his nose again, Paul brushed off his arms, as though he were covered with disgusting lint. "I don't have time for the likes of you," he spat as he quickly moved deeper into the park, disappearing around a copse of trees.

The boys sat down again, hiding Hank behind their bodies. They sat quietly until Hank felt the nape of his neck return to normal.

"Thanks," Hank said a moment later, when he tentatively sat up.

"No skin," the darker-haired boy replied dismissively. "We owe you'z one, any—"

The blonder boy cut in. "What's with getting chased by all the blokes? You'z running from the Gardai, or something?"

"No," Hank replied. "All what blokes?"

"First, there's the watch guy Saturday, then this one. And he sure looked like a Garda to me," the boy announced with an accusing stare.

"Oh, the watch guy musta been Darren, Darr O'Connell. He's cool." Hank angled his head toward the park gate. "*That* guy isn't a cop. He's actually my tour guide."

"Tour guide?" the darker-haired boy asked in disbelief. "You ditched your bus?"

"Something like that," Hank said with a tight smile. "I don't really know *what* his deal is."

The blonder boy looked over Hank. "You'z from the States?"

"Yeah, the great state of Texas. What gave me away?" he asked teasingly, with a heavier drawl.

The darker-haired boy laughed.

The blonder boy suddenly looked very serious. He leaned in a little closer. "Are you… are you the Prodigal?" he asked in nearly a whisper.

"The *what*?" Hank asked, thrown off by the unusual word. "My family's originally from Ireland," he mused aloud. "So, I guess you could say I'm a prodigal. Where in the world did that question come from?"

"You'z a foreigner, in cahoots with an O'Connell. Just had me wondering."

"About what?" Hank asked in all sincerity, hoping for a better explanation.

"I overheard my great-aunt on the phone, all excited about some Prodigal that's doing something big for the Solstice."

"Well, I don't know a thing about that," Hank spat out. That feeling of being manipulated crept over him again. All along, he'd felt that Darren and his sister had been pushing him toward something without bothering to give him any details. "When is this Solstice thing?"

"Tomorrow night," the blonder boy replied. "I'm Reg, and that's Colin," he introduced as he waved his hand at the darker-haired boy. "And you are…?"

Feeling overwhelmed with sudden suspicion, Hank tightened his smile. "Nobody important," he said flatly as he stood up and grabbed his paper bag. "Thanks for the cover."

Reg stood also. "Wait," he hissed as he glanced nervously around the park. "Where you heading?"

Hank paused. That was a good question. Despite the fact that they were being less than forthright, Darren's apartment still seemed like the safest place to go. And he should leave soon, before Paul decided to make another sweep of the park. "Back to the O'Connell house, I guess." He turned to the gate but stopped again. During his blind run down the streets and alleys, he'd lost his sense of direction and had no idea how to get back. He wasn't sure he'd be able to backtrack his steps and find the way. And Paul would doubtless also be retracing the route, right on his heels. He turned to Reg and looked him over. On second thought, he didn't see any reason not to trust these boys. "I'm Hank. You wouldn't happen to know where the O'Connell place is, would ya?"

"What's the name of the house?"

Hank thought aloud. "Husky Meenra," he said. Or something like that.

Colin spoke up when Reg shrugged. "You mean, Uiscí Mianra Estates? I know where that is. Not far."

Reg glanced around the park again. "Might be best if we walked you'z back."

"Sure, if ya want."

The boys gathered their things and headed to the gate. Reg quietly said, "Just follow along behind us. Stagger a little, and make lots of noise. People will steer clear if they think we're a bunch of drunk scallies."

"Gotcha," Hank replied as he stumbled forward like he'd missed his footing.

THE PHOUKA stuck to the shadowy space near the wall as he watched Hank and the boys leave. He'd found their conversation to be rather illuminating. For one thing, he now knew the word the pixies had been repeating in their buzzing chant must have been "Prodigal." *I wonder what else the little bugs might know?*

Keeping a wary eye out for Paul, he stretched his feline form, then sauntered from the border wall and headed to the hawthorn tree in another secluded corner. "Hello, pretty pixie," he called out with a purr as he rubbed against the trunk of the small tree.

"Hello, strange-body phouka," the yellow pixie replied as she left the branch and darted to him. "A phouka in strange body?" she repeated.

The cat shook his head. "Long story, maybe some other day. I hear talk of a prodigal...."

She buzzed and began bouncing in the air. "Prodigal, the Prodigal," she chimed out.

Several other pixies descended from the tree, also buzzing excitedly. All of them began speaking at once.

"... Prodigal...."

"... is here...."

"... returned...."

"... arrived...."

The phouka smiled up. "Why is this prodigal so important?"

"... here...."

"... come home...."

"... love...."

"... Prodigal...."

"... help...."

Even more pixies bounced down from the tree, joining the buzzing chorus. The phouka couldn't make out any more words. Their voices had become a continuous, droning buzz, like that of an excited hornet's nest.

He shook his head as their foray brought on a bloody headache. "Thanks," he offered, before turning back to the wall and following it to the green's exit.

Chapter 14

DARREN JUMPED up from the kitchen table when he heard the front door. He rushed and grabbed Hank as he stepped inside, eliciting a surprised squeal from the little man when he yanked him into a tight hug.

"Darren," Hank wheezed. "Can't breathe."

Darren loosened his grip and his expression fell from joy to concern as he glared down. "What the bloody devil? Why'd you run off?"

"I didn't," Hank replied while holding up the shopping bag. "Just ran to the market for some groceries," he said as he wriggled from Darren's arms and pushed past him toward the kitchen.

"The *market*?" Darren stomped behind him, now noticing all the visible seams from Hank's inside-out hoodie. "What happened? Anne and I both felt some negative force—"

Hank glared back as he removed the contents of the shopping bag. "I thought we were through with all these damn secrets.... Why don't *you* start my telling me about this Solstice thing."

"Solstice?"

"Yeah, *Solstice*," Hank spat out as he carefully inspected each egg in the carton before putting it in the refrigerator. "You guys seem to expect me to perform some big-assed horse-and-pony show there, without bothering to tell me about it."

"Tex.... Hank," Darren said quietly as he stepped up behind him. "I know Anne thought you should be at the Solstice, but I don't know any more than that. What's this horse-and-pony show you speak of?" He ran his finger along the exposed seam of the hoodie. "What happened at the market?"

Hank softened a little and leaned against the cabinet, but his face still showed anger. Darren opened his hand and caressed his palm gently along Hank's upper shoulder, waiting for him to calm. "Please, tell me?"

Hank turned around. "Well, it *is* a bit of a story," he said as he looked into Darren's eyes. "The kind of story Granny would have loved, with talking cats and steam that turned into arrows."

Darren sprouted a bemused smile as he massaged Hank's shoulder. "Talking cats?"

"Well, I think that orange tabby cat that's been hanging around outside might really be a phouka."

Darren nodded. "I think he was friends with Cona. But, go on. You were in the market...."

"It wasn't until I left the market. I stepped out, then I thought I saw Paul's tour van, and I suddenly got a real wiggy feeling. Then the cat, who I guess musta followed me there, told me to run. So I did. And I followed the blasts of steam that led me to a park by the hotel, where I ran into some boys I knew. They helped me hide when Paul showed up, then they helped me back to the house."

"I see," Darren replied with a warm smile. "At least you're safe now."

Hank smiled back, but then his lips tightened. "It was Reg, one of the boys, that asked if I was the Prodigal. And dammit all if ya didn't sidetrack me again. I'm supposed to be mad at ya."

"Asked if you were *what*?" Darren queried with concern.

"The Prodigal, whatever the hell that is," Hank replied as he slipped off the hoodie and reversed the sleeves to their proper place.

Darren hardened his expression as he leaned down and kissed Hank on the forehead. "Believe me, Hank, Anne has kept this from me. I would certainly have said something, had I known."

Hank gazed up. "Said *what*? You're scaring me now."

Darren wrapped his arm protectively around Hank and led him to the kitchen table. "*Now* I know why Anne wanted that chronicle," he muttered as he pulled out a chair for Hank to sit in.

While Hank put the hoodie on the back of the chair, Darren pulled out his cell phone, then hit the speed-dial button for Anne. "Get yourself over here now and start spilling," he said gruffly when she answered.

"Can't it wait?" Anne asked. "The Guild meeting starts in about forty-five minutes. People have already started arriving...."

"Fine," Darren replied as he looked at Hank. "But Hank's coming to the meeting, and you're putting it *all* on the table," he barked back before hanging up.

As Darren put his phone away and sat down, Hank stared at him, the anger returning to his gaze. "I'm tired of all this manipulative shit. Ya didn't even *ask* if I wanted to go to your stupid meeting."

"You're right. I'm sorry. But I thought you would want to hear the answers firsthand."

"What answers? Gawd, you people are driving me crazy."

Darren reached out and took Hank's hands. "I'll have to give a bit of history, so please let me finish, then I promise I'll answer any questions I can."

Hank nodded.

"I only remember once, reading about a legend regarding a Prodigal that would bring an end to the war. Those 'soft spots' I mentioned? There used to be more than a dozen portals, here in Ireland. But, sometime around 1000 ACE, a group calling themselves the 'True Swords' started speaking out about how unnatural the Fae were and began working to close the portals. Their first attempts were dramatically unsuccessful, but the True Swords soon realized the tight connection between the portals and the Irish belief in the Fae. You see, it's like a feedback loop. By weakening the belief in the Fae, the True Swords could weaken the portals themselves, and for the past century, that's been their ultimate goal."

Darren paused for a breath before continuing. "In that time, a core group of the families, most recently going by the name of 'Antiquer's Guild,' have been fighting against this destruction. But we've lost much ground in the last hundred years. Only one portal is left now, the one here in Dublin. Every year at the Solstice, we've been doing a ritual to help the portal stay open."

Darren sighed before he finished. "As to the legend, I know very little. I only saw a vague reference once to a Prodigal." With a frown, he added, "I'm guessing Anne knows much more than she's told either of us."

Hank thought over the story a moment. "So, is Paul one of these True Sword people?"

"About four-hundred years ago, they aligned with the church and now they use the name the 'True Cross,' but yes, I would suspect he is."

"Still doesn't really explain why he was chasing me, but okay." Hank paused a moment. "How's this Prodigal supposed to end the war? What are you guys expecting me to do?"

"I have no idea," Darren said with all sincerity. "Like I said, I never read the legend itself, only a reference to it."

Hank sat and shook his head. "Why does everybody else seem to know about this? Reg overheard his great-aunt talking about it. Is she in this 'Guild' of yours?"

"I have no idea who Reg, or his great-aunt, is."

"You met him." Hank looked up. "Oh. Maybe I forgot to mention it. Those boys I ran into at the park were the ones on the stoop when I was going back to the hotel. Named Reg and Colin."

Darren did remember the boys, but it was still rather dark when he had encountered them. "Is he Reg McPherson?"

Hank shrugged. "Never got his last name, come to think of it."

"Blond-haired, slightly husky kid?" Darren asked.

Hank nodded.

"Sounds like Reginald. About the right age. And you said his great-aunt was talking about the Prodigal?"

"That's what he said. He overheard her on the phone with somebody."

"I see," Darren replied, recalling that Kathy had said she'd never read *Neil's Chronicle*.

Hank intertwined his fingers with Darren's. "I don't like this...," he said under his breath. "I feel like I'm being pushed onto a stage, with a handful of scribbled notes; everyone is expecting a speech I haven't even rehearsed for."

Darren surrounded their twined hands with his right hand. "I promise. That won't happen. I won't let it."

"But, what am I supposed to do? I don't have a—whacha-call-it—a gift."

"I don't know," Darren replied with open sincerity.

"Well, what *is* this ritual thing you mentioned? What do you guys normally do? Am I supposed to help?"

"Possibly?" Darren responded with a hint of doubt as he scooted his chair closer to Hank. "When the portals started shrinking a few hundred years ago, they went into a sort of cyclic collapse centered around the Solstices. Over the course of a year, they open wider, then shrink, with the widest point taking place on Yule... winter," he added when Hank frowned, "and the narrowest point on Midsummer. Are you picturing that?"

"Yeah, I'm getting it. So, it gets a little bit smaller each year, and will eventually close altogether."

"Exactly. The Guild's early attempts to stop the collapse accomplished nothing, but Cona spent several years studying the phenomena, and said he came up with a solution. That was right before the True Cross took advantage of the post-World-War-I nationalist fervor and tried to have my grandfather arrested."

"The little 'dustup' you mentioned before."

"Right. And you know that Cona fled to Portugal. He steered clear of Irish politics for about a decade, then he sent a coded message to the Guild that his solution was almost complete. His message mentioned nine watches that, when used at the portals, would thin the veil again, reverse the collapse, and open the portals fully."

"So, you guys are using the watches, somehow."

"We're trying to," Darren said as he pulled his hands away from Hank's grasp. "About a month after the message, Cona returned to Ireland."

Darren fished in his pocket and pulled out the platinum watch. "Yet, before he could meet with the Guild, the house was broken into and he died from strange coma symptoms a few days later."

Hank looked at the table. "The *platinum* watches…," he cooed in a tone of growing understanding. "But, I thought Cona only made seven of them."

"Eight completed, actually. He died while working on the last one. He'd sent one ahead, along with that coded message to Brigand. Its existence was never made public."

"Brigand?" Hank asked. "The same—?"

The tinkling notes of "Meadow Moonglow" interrupted. Darren quickly answered the phone. "On the way," he said as he stood. Seeing the confused question on Hank's face, he replied, "I promise, we'll finish later."

He led Hank to the main house.

AS HANK followed Darren into Anne's parlor, he felt surprised. Unlike the huge crowd of people he'd been expecting, only a handful were gathered with Anne and Brigand.

Hank scanned the new faces, stopping when he recognized the barkeep/DJ guy from the bathhouse. For a more formal look, he had slicked back his hair with some kind of oil, making the red color darker, more like glowing embers. The guy stood and gave Hank a pleasant smile as he shook hands with Darren.

"Hank," Darren introduced. "This is Mike O'Reilly. I would assume you recognize him."

"Yeah, howdy," Hank replied as he shook Mike's hand.

"Glad it worked out," Mike said. "I wanted so badly to call you'z a stubborn arse, but I knew Darr was trying to be incognito, so I had to bite my tongue. Welcome to the Nine Families."

"Ten," Darren corrected as Anne rolled to her elevated coffee table.

Mike looked at Darren with a puzzled expression. "Ten?"

Before he could explain, Anne slapped her hand on the arm of her wheelchair and called the meeting to order. Darren took Hank's arm and pulled him to a seat on one of the divans.

Anne smiled at the small group. "Before we speak of the Solstice, I have a small bit I'd like to read first. It's translated from Middle Gaelic, so some of the rhyme is lost, but the meaning is intact." She picked up a sheet of paper from her lap. After clearing her throat, Anne read:

> *"With a song in his heart and old blood in his veins, the Prodigal will return to the shores.*
>
> *"Spangold as a shield, the mists he will wield, bringing the end of the long Sword's war.*
>
> *"But, none will rejoice, at the loss of the choice, and the moon will lose its shine.*
>
> *"Yet, noontime lament will leave them content, once the final deed is done."*

Anne set down the paper as she glanced at the crowd. "That was a quatrain from *Neil's Chronicle*." She looked at Hank and dramatically waved her hand at him. "That Prodigal, it would seem, is now among us."

Hank rolled his eyes as the others turned to gape at him. "Really, aren't ya stretching it a bit?" he asked as he looked at Anne. "What makes ya think this Prodigal is me?"

Anne smiled. "Aside from the fact that I saw it in my reading right after Darr met you, you're a returning Shay, who happened to stumble upon and acquire the lost Shay bridal ring. A *spangold* ring, I might add."

"A Shay?" Mike asked as he looked first at Hank, then at Darren. "Then, we really *are* ten families again."

One of the older ladies, with a hairdo that looked like a crooked beehive, leaned forward with a scrutinizing eye on Hank. "How, exactly, is he supposed to end this war? What's your gift, Shay lad?"

Hank shrugged and wilted back from the older lady's stare. "Don't have one."

The other lady sitting closest to him leaned to him, sniffing with her freckled nose. She sniffed again. "You certain about that? You have the aroma of *something* on you...."

Mike leaned forward. "Do you have a watch?"

Hank turned to Mike, knowing he meant one of Cona's platinum timepieces. "No, I don't have a watch." He looked over the rest of the group nervously. "And I don't have a gift, either."

Brigand stood and interjected himself. "Maybe," he said as he walked toward Anne and drew the group's attention, "we should focus a moment on the prophecy. It may hold some clues."

The old man in the corner sat up a little straighter and loudly said, "Don't know about that. Not only is the bloody thing vague, sounds to me like it's mostly bad news."

"Why say that?" the beehive lady questioned.

"With all that losing and lamenting, what else you'z gonna say?"

Mike cut in. "It's the Swords that will be lamenting."

"*None* will rejoice," the old man said with bared teeth as he sat forward. "Read it again, Anne."

Anne repeated the quatrain for the group.

Mike smiled. "If he's a Shay, then Hank should have an affinity with the blue. That must be the mist it's referring to; he can summon the sprites."

"Aye?" the old man barked. "And just what benefit will be accomplished by having a bunch of sprites flying about?"

The others sat in silence as Mike shrugged in reply.

The crooked-beehive lady looked at Anne. "What about that first line?" She turned to Hank. "That 'song in the heart' part. *Do* you have a song in your heart?"

Hank squirmed on the edge of the divan as he felt everyone's eyes fall on him. He shrugged and shrank in as everyone continued gazing at him. "I don't even know what that means."

Darren protectively rested his arm across Hank's shoulder. "I don't think it changes the game plan, ultimately." Darren squeezed Hank's shoulder affectionately before he rose to his feet and deflected attention from Hank. "We shall do as we've always done and use the watches. With my recent purchase, we'll have *eight* of them this year, which should make a significant difference in holding the portal open," he said with a hopeful smile.

"And," the old man countered as he also stood. "If it doesn't? What then?"

Brigand cut in. "I agree with Darr. With eight watches, we should at least be able to hold the portal open enough that it won't completely collapse. That will buy us until Yule to figure out Hank's possible role in this. The quatrain doesn't have any kind of time limits in it."

The ladies and Mike nodded in silent agreement.

Hank felt strangely queasy at the thought of staying in Ireland until Christmas. Which was what, he guessed, Brigand was implying with his suggestion. He glanced at Darren and hoped the slight grin he saw on his face came from the same thought.

Anne smiled at the group. "That seems most sensible, wouldn't you agree, Mr. O'Keefe?" she asked while looking right at the old man.

The old man softened a little under her gaze. "Of course. Can't see there's anything else *to* do...." He trailed off as he sat back down.

"Then, it's settled," Anne announced. "We shall meet in the green, say... 17:30 tomorrow?"

As the group nodded and many stood, Hank did the math in his head, realizing she meant 5:30 p.m.

Mike stepped over to Hank and looked down at his hand. "Can I see the ring?" he asked as he sat down.

"Sure." Hank held up his hand so Mike could get a better look.

"You weren't wearing this the other night; I would definitely have noticed."

"No, didn't want to risk any damage from hot tub or steam room chemicals," Hank replied as he looked at Darren.

Darren glanced around the group again, then stepped up to Brigand. "Kathy didn't make it? When I spoke to her earlier, she said she was coming."

Brigand shrugged. "I rang her a bit ago to see if she wanted a lift but didn't get an answer. I assumed she was on the way."

"Then, we should send someone to check on her. She was a bit out of sorts this afternoon."

Brigand nodded. "I'll ring her daughter-in-law and have her pop in. Excuse me," he said to the group as he dug his phone from his pocket and stepped into the kitchen.

Hank looked at Mike when he felt a stare.

Mike dropped his eyes quickly. "Sorry. I've just... I've never seen such blue eyes."

Feeling his cheeks warming, Hank shrugged off the compliment. "I thought most Irish had blue eyes."

"Yes," Mike agreed. "But not like yours. Yours are so deep, like the purest bay waters. Quite remarkable."

Darren stepped over and gave a wry smile as he lightly took Hank's arm and pulled him to his feet. "You must excuse us," he said to Mike. "It's time to make our leave."

"Oh certainly," Mike said as he jumped to his feet. "We should all get a good night's sleep. It was nice meeting you again, Hank Shay."

"It's Lear," Hank corrected. "Shay is my middle name."

As Darren and Hank moved toward the courtyard door, the older lady with the freckled nose intercepted them. She peered at the men, then sniffed at the air. "Don't know quite what, but I *do* smell some sensitivity in you."

"Uh, right," Hank said with a tight smile. He started to make a joke about his deodorant before Darren jumped in.

"Excuse us, Mrs. McCray," Darren replied politely. "We must be on our way."

"Good night, then," she said dismissively, but she didn't take her eyes off Hank as they went to the door and stepped outside.

ONCE BACK inside his flat, Darren breathed a sigh of relief as he closed the door behind them.

"Thanks for the rescue," Hank told him as he dropped onto the settee.

"I felt it was about to turn... intense." Darren smiled as he sat beside Hank. "Hopefully, that answered your questions."

"Sort of. I still don't know about this ritual ya guys do. Do you put on green robes and dance around a fire, or what?"

Darren smiled crookedly. "Nothing that elaborate, or quite so silly. We tune the watches to emit a specific tone, then chant and hum along with the sound. My supposition is, the watches are doing more than just making the noises, but that's all we are really aware of."

Hank nodded at the answer. "But I still don't know what in the hell y'all expect me to do. I don't think I'm that Prodigal guy yer looking for."

Darren grasped Hank's right hand. He could feel the warmth of the Claddagh ring's metal band against his palm. He caught Hank's gaze. "To be completely honest, I'm not as certain about this as Anne seems to be. Yet, my opinion may not be worth much. I haven't studied the ancient histories to quite the degree my sister has." Darren smiled warmly. "I *can* say, I don't expect anything from you, other than for you to be true to yourself."

"Well...." Hank sighed, sounding full of doubt. "I don't know if I should even tag along to this thing."

Darren wanted him to "tag along," if for no other reason than to provide moral support, but he didn't feel right trying to force Hank into accompanying them if he decided against it. He gave Hank's hand a gentle squeeze before he stood and pulled the other man to his feet. "Let me show you something," he explained as he led Hank across the great room. "Go get your jacket and I'll take you to the Shamrock Green."

"Where?" Hank asked as he went into the kitchen.

"It's the private green, like a garden, for the estate."

Chapter 15

HANK SLIPPED on his hoodie, then followed Darren as he led them outside to the terracotta courtyard. Even with the hazy drizzle of late evening, the sun's light seemed much brighter to Hank than it should have been for this time of night.

He glanced around but didn't see the tabby cat as Darren led him through the wooden gate. Darren turned left and set a brisk pace down the walk.

Hank trailed behind a few paces, admiring the scenery of Darren's backside. His shoulders looked strong and broad in that black leather jacket. And his butt—well. *It's a very nice butt,* Hank thought with a grin.

At the end of the walk, near some dumpsters, they crossed the street and approached another walled-off section. Noticing all the moss growth on the chunky-looking rocks that composed the enclosure, Hank guessed this wall was quite old. He followed Darren around the corner, and they soon reached another wooden gate.

After fishing in his pocket, Darren pulled out his key ring, then unlocked the new modern-styled bolted lock above the handle. He glanced furtively around the street as he took Hank's arm. He pushed open the gate, then quickly pushed Hank inside before closing it behind them.

Hank started to protest being manhandled, but the words caught in his throat as he gazed around the small hidden garden. Six huge hawthorn trees, much larger than any similar trees Hank had seen on the island, flanked the borders protectively. Their thin, gnarly branches, most bearing clumps of tiny white flowers, crossed each other, creating a solid upper canopy as they stretched to the sky.

Behind the trees and nearly obscuring the walls, massive growths of some kind of thick, thorny vines clung to the stone enclosure. Large pink flowers dotted the brambles everywhere. Hank thought the climbing greenery looked like raspberry vines on steroids.

Hank scanned the middle of the garden. Covering the ground like a thick shag carpet, a solid growth of shamrocks grew out from the center of a strange circle. Protruding up about three feet from the ground, ten thin-columned stones, reminiscent of Egyptian obelisks, framed a circle about eight feet in diameter. The ring of stones looked like a larger version of the "ashtray" in Anne's parlor.

He turned his gaze to the center of the stones, but his sight kept drifting off in other directions. No matter how hard he tried to focus inside the ring, his eyes refused to cooperate and kept sliding away in one direction or another. Darren chuckled as he continued his attempts.

"Don't try too hard, or you'll give yourself a headache." Darren took hold of his shoulders and rotated him to face the corner. "Just use your peripheral."

Hank turned his gaze to the wall and for a brief instant at the corner of his sight, saw a shimmering sort of silvery globe, about the size of a softball, hovering nearly two feet off the ground. Instinctively, he moved his eyes to try and look at it, and the image vanished.

He turned his gaze back to the wall and caught another glimpse of the portal. "It looks so small."

"Yes," Darren agreed. "And shrinking more as we speak. It won't reach its smallest point until tomorrow night."

Hank turned to look at Darren. "Why don't you guys do your thingy now, before it gets smaller?"

"I wish we could," Darren replied with a frown. "In the past, the Guild has tried the ritual at various times of the year, but there seems to be a brief window at the Solstices. That short moment, when the growth or shrink is reversing the cycle, is the only time our efforts have any effect."

"That sucks." Hank felt that was a lame thing to say, but he couldn't think of anything more eloquent. He noticed Darren peering at the vines.

Darren shrugged. "It seems they are shy tonight."

"Who?"

"The faeries. It's common to find several here in the garden."

"Oh. I prob'ly spooked them off."

"Doubtful," Darren said as he continued glancing around. "I gather this is a rather safe haven for them."

Hank smiled at Darren. The black leather jacket, in which he already looked so deliciously sexy, shimmered from the glistening silver light that mysteriously bathed the garden. He reached out to touch Darren's chest, but stopped his hand when he saw the Claddagh ring on his finger.

By the light of the portal, the Eirestone gleamed a vibrant green, and the pink opalescence of the spangold metal sparkled and danced with veiny lines. The colors pulsed and flowed across the metal in such a beautiful way, almost as if the ring were a living thing. The ring felt nicely warm on Hank's finger now.

"By the stars," Darren exclaimed. "Look at your ring."

"I am," Hank replied as he admired the flittering iridescence.

Hank looked up, then smiled at the expression of wonderment he saw on Darren's face. As he reached his right hand out and placed it around Darren's neck, he lifted up on his toes, then pulled him into a kiss. Darren surrounded him with his arms as their lips touched.

The heart-shaped Eirestone of the ring flashed with an emerald beam as they shared their kiss.

Hank reveled in the warmth as they deepened their embrace. Their tongues played together as Darren held him tighter, his strong arms cradling Hank close and caressing his back. As their kiss continued, a strong feeling of contentment flowed into Hank's heart. *Maybe Cupid has finally found me.*

As the wash of positive emotion flowed through, it overwhelmed the remaining seed of doubt in Hank, extinguishing it. Hank hugged Darren closer.

Flashing again, the Eirestone released a tiny gossamer string of emerald energy that drifted into the air. The winds carried the sparkling tendril into the greenery, where it collided with one of the white blossoms of the nearby hawthorn tree.

The bloom spasmed. Its long stamens curled inward as the energy penetrated the flower. Its petals darkened, charring as they shrank and withered from the surge.

Darren grinned as he pulled back. "Although I do enjoy it, I didn't bring you out here to snog. I thought you might want to see what we're trying to defend."

"It doesn't really seem like much," Hank replied as he tried in vain to look at the center of the stone ring directly. "Not even big enough to step through, or anything. Would it be such a big deal if it *did* close off?"

Frowning, Darren shook his head. "Not directly, I don't think. But, I'm always reminded of the Pandora's Box story. If the portal closes, it will also seal off all of the magical energy that leaks over into our world. Who's to say, if it's not that magic which fuels the occasional miracle and provides hope to humanity."

"Sounds a bit melodramatic." Hank shrugged. "I still don't know what I'm supposed to do about it."

"Don't concern yourself with doing anything. Just stand here with me—that's all I will ask."

As Hank nodded, he caught a whiff of a smoldering odor that made his nose wrinkle. He looked up, and Darren was also sniffing at the air. "Smells like something burning…."

They both turned their noses to the house. Darren stood on his toes and tried to look over the wall, before he rushed to the gate. Hank ran up behind. They both saw the flames as they stepped out of the garden. On the other side of the road, crackling tongues of fire stretched up from the dumpster, licking at the bricks and wooden window frames of the old brownstone.

"Bollocks!" Darren yelled out as they ran across the street. Without another word, they each grabbed one side of the dumpster and rolled it away from the house. They tried grabbing the lid that dangled on hinges along the back, but the temperature of the metal had already risen to a painful heat. Hank pulled the cuffs of his sleeves over his hands into makeshift gloves. Darren copied Hank's maneuver with his leather jacket; then a second attempt succeeded in getting the lid closed.

"Stay here," Darren yelled as he took off running back to his flat.

Hank stepped back from the dumpster, fearing some strange explosion would send sparks flying. He couldn't see any more flames; only a tiny bit of thick smoke oozed along the edge of the lid.

FARTHER DOWN the street, hidden by the darkened enclosure of another flat, the dullahan watched their valiant efforts with the dumpster. A wicked smile spread across his face. As he had hoped, the little distraction had lured them from the Shamrock Green in such a rush that the humans had forgotten to lock up.

Leaning onto his sword, he watched and waited for an opportunity.

A MOMENT later, Darren rushed down the walk, carrying a fire extinguisher. "Help with the lid."

With less effort this time, because the metal didn't seem quite as hot as it had before, they got the dumpster lid lifted open. Starved of oxygen, the vibrant flames were now gone, but Hank could still see a glowing smolder in the trash at the bottom.

Darren squirted a blast of chemicals at the burning embers. He stirred through the trash and used the extinguisher once more, just to make sure the fire was completely out.

"Careless scallies," Darren cursed under his breath. "We're lucky we noticed it so soon."

"Yeah," Hank agreed aloud, but he wasn't sure if luck had anything to do with it. The ring on his finger felt cold as he peered around, not seeing anyone on the nearby streets. He also hadn't noticed anyone when they'd passed through on their way to the garden earlier in the evening. *If the scallies were around, wouldn't we have seen them?*

Darren cradled the extinguisher in his arms and motioned with his head back toward the brownstone. "It should be safe. I imagine they've scattered kilometers away now."

"Sure," Hank replied as he glanced around again. Darren's idea of the scallies seemed like a nice explanation, but it felt wrong. The situation left nagging doubts in Hank.

"You don't agree?"

Before Hank could reply, he heard the haunting gong of a bell. It sounded with a deep reverberation, like one of those old-fashioned church bells. He saw Darren's expression scrunch up with worry.

"Imigh sa diabhal…." Darren muttered as he took Hank's arm and pulled him to the sidewalk, steering him toward the gate as the bell gonged again.

"Is that the fire alarm?" Hank wondered aloud.

"No, it's the tolling bell," Darren explained as they approached the terracotta courtyard. "It means one of the Guild has died."

As they hurried around the fountain, Darren fished out his cell phone and punched a speed dial number. His face scrunched again. "Katherine McPherson," he repeated to Hank as he hung up his phone.

Leaving the extinguisher in the living room as they passed through, Darren moved quickly across the room and out the side door to Anne's courtyard. After only a brief knock, he pushed the door open and they stepped inside.

Brigand rushed up to meet them. "Oh Darr, it is a terrible tragedy."

"What happened?"

"The daughter-in-law found her," Brigand explained. "The poor dear slipped when getting out of her bath, falling against the toilet and breaking her neck."

The ring on Hank's finger grew cold again as he listened to the account. He looked down to his hand and puzzled over the reaction as Darren and Brigand continued to talk. *That's twice now that the ring's—no, three times, that I've noticed,* Hank amended when he remembered his little post-shopping incident. The ring had also felt cold then, while he was being chased through the streets by Paul.

While Hank pondered the meaning of it, he realized there had been opposite instances when the metal band had felt soothingly warm to his skin—like in the garden. He couldn't recall any other specific moments with enough detail to see a pattern, but he doubted those temperature occurrences were random. Now that he realized these new properties of the Claddagh ring, he would have to pay more careful attention. Darren jostled his shoulder.

"I asked," Darren said. "Did you want to stay here, or head back to my flat? I may be here a bit, fussing over details."

"I'll just stay, if I won't be in the way."

"Take a look around," Darren said while motioning to the shelves of strange knickknacks. "You might find something interesting."

THE DULLAHAN let out a mighty sigh as he snuck into the green. The place looked just the same as it had on his last visit, thirty years ago, with its overgrown Irish rose vines and guardian hawthorn trees. It wasn't fair of them to keep this place under lock and key. Not that he would have any difficulty tearing their flimsy wall to bits if an urgent need truly arose; the humans couldn't keep him out *that* easily. His irritation stemmed from the fact that they were so arrogant to even try.

With a frown of puzzlement, the dullahan turned his attention to the stone ring. Unlike the mortals, he had no trouble seeing the silvery gateway. His senses were keenly aware of the power issuing from the hole in the veil between the dimensions. As he watched the pulsing globe, he felt himself in a bit of a quandary. He needed access to that energy to fully recharge, but since his goal was to close the portal, he didn't want to risk opening the gateway even more, as he likely would if he just stuck his sword directly into the portal.

When he looked at the ground, he smiled broadly. With his vision, he could see that the gossamer veil extended below the globe, all the way to the grassy earth. If he carefully cut at the bottom of the veil, such a rent would mend itself quickly without affecting the portal above it.

Kneeling into the blanket of clover, the dullahan laid his sword down flat upon the ground before he carefully slid it forward. With delicate maneuvering, he nudged the weapon and pierced an opening just large enough for the sword to enter. He gave a few more gentle pushes until he felt the energy flowing through the obsidian blade. He kept his hand on the hilt until the flow dissipated, charging himself for the Solstice. Since he could only guess at what opposition he might face, he would need all the power he could draw.

Once sated, he gingerly slid the sword backward, cautious not to widen the opening any further. With the blade removed, the tiny gap quickly sealed, healing itself before his eyes.

He looked at the small ball of energy hovering above the ground. This ugly thing did not belong here—all it did was encourage fraternization with the humans, something the dullahan found disgusting. Those petty creatures, with their unnatural use of metals, didn't deserve any of the Fae gifts his kind had bestowed over the centuries. Even if it took *another* century to accomplish, the dullahan would see to it that contact between these worlds ended.

When that deed is accomplished, the dullahan thought with a grin. *Then I'll be unfettered from pointless rules and can begin issuing some* real *justice on these worthless humans.*

As he stood, the dullahan brushed against the hanging hawthorn branches, sending a snowfall of white petals drifting to the ground. He scowled as he brushed a few clingy petals and the charred flower husk from his coat. As he turned, his feet absently crushed the flowers into the ground as he left the garden.

HANK SOON grew bored of looking over the array of new-age trinkets displayed on the shelves. Whatever it was Darren thought might catch his eye, he failed to find it.

Stifling a yawn, Hank wandered to the divans and sank down to one. He didn't want to intrude, yet he couldn't help but overhear snatches of the conversations as Anne and Brigand made their phone calls, notifying the others of the recent death in their group. Darren seemed to be playing secretary, reading between different notebooks for phone numbers and occasionally scratching down notes on a legal pad. Despite their busy chattering, a mournful gloom hovered over the room.

He reclined against the back of the divan and closed his eyes. Even with over a week of living in the Irish time zone, his body stubbornly refused to adjust. He took a few deeps breaths.

He opened his eyes when he heard Brigand's voice somewhere near.

"Hank," Brigand repeated. "I need to go feed my cat." He stepped closer to the divan. "Darr suggested we should speak. Why don't you accompany me? And we can discuss along the way."

"Oh, yeah," Hank replied blearily as he stood. "Sure. Lead the way." He followed Brigand through the house and out the front door.

Once outside, Brigand turned to the right and proceeded down the sidewalk to the next stoop. "I should start with an apology," he said as he unlocked his door.

"For what?"

"When you asked about my age, I was rather vague with my reply." Brigand ushered him inside.

Hank glanced around the dim space. The apartment felt as dark as a cave. He followed Brigand across a small living room and into a tiny kitchen. When they entered, a snow-white Persian cat appeared seemingly from nowhere and let out a yowl. Hank had to laugh at himself. For some reason, he'd expected a black cat.

"Yes, love. It's dinner time," Brigand cooed to his pet as he opened a cabinet and retrieved a can of cat food. He opened a drawer and fished out an opener. "To answer your question properly, I was born in 1892."

Hank started to object at such an outrageous number, but clamped his mouth closed before saying anything.

Brigand smiled as he emptied the food into the cat's bowl. The Persian whined impatiently at his feet. Brigand walked over and set the bowl down by the cat's water dish.

"So," Hank finally replied as the cat devoured its meal. "You actually knew Cona?"

Brigand let out a warm chuckle. "Oh yes, Conrad was born in 1891, also in County Cork."

"I thought he died in his late twenties, back in 1938."

"No, he was nearly fifty years old when he passed, but most thought he was much younger, because of our double blessing." Brigand motioned with his hand to the kitchen door. "Come sit a moment, and I'll explain."

Hank went into the small living room and sat in one of the wing-back chairs. He looked at Brigand as he sat nearby, and had trouble believing he was over a hundred years old. He looked to be, at most, nearing forty. "What do you mean by 'double blessing'?"

"I'm assuming Darr told you of the Shay-Connell wedding, so *that* blessing would be the first one."

Hank shook his head. "No, he never mentioned anything about a blessing."

"Well then, we should correct his oversight. The wedding celebration lasted nearly a week, and on the last night, the Fae presented the bride and groom, as well as all those in attendance, a special blessing. That event was the creation of what we now call 'The Ten Families.' But, the Fae would never divulge exactly *what* the blessing was.

"It took over a decade for the families to learn what the blessing entailed, not realizing the true nature of the gift until they failed to show any signs of aging."

"No signs of aging? Is that why we all look younger than our years?"

"Exactly. Although, we no longer possess the *full* blessing. You see, the wedding party would eventually come to understand that they had been gifted with immortality."

"Immortality? Darren certainly never mentioned that. Are they still around?" Hank asked, surprised at himself for even entertaining the notion.

Brigand frowned. "Didn't he, or Anne, ever tell you of the Tempest?"

"I've heard that name mentioned a few times, but never heard the story behind it."

"Ah," Brigand said before the Persian cat chose that moment to leap into his lap. He reclined into the chair and stroked the purring feline. "Then I should caution you, much of this story is based on speculation, since the Fae have been less than forthcoming about many details."

"Okay, I can hang with that," Hank replied.

"Not all of the Fae were happy about this blessing. It seems they have an unspoken agreement amongst themselves regarding their interactions with humans, a sort of noninterference policy. So, over the course of decades, tensions between different Fae factions grew. In 1313, when the bride was accused of infidelity after the Shay bridal ring disappeared, dissention among the families fueled the situation further and those heated escalations eventually led to a bit of a skirmish."

Hank grinned crookedly. "I'm guessing, with the Irish habit of understatement, that by skirmish, you *really* mean a war of some kind."

Brigand nodded. "It is the only time known to us that the Fae attacked each other. During all that ruckus, the family's blessing was revoked. Some believe the loss of the ring forfeited the gift, others think the responsible Fae voluntarily reversed the gift as a sort of cease-fire agreement. So, the families are no longer immortal, but we have been left with a touch of longevity."

Hank looked down at the spangold band on his finger. "So, this ring has been missing since 1313?"

"Yes," Brigand replied with a nod as he petted the cat in his lap. "Many believed it had been destroyed, so the ring's reappearance is a bit of a surprise."

Hank looked over at Brigand. "And, ya think it means something that I found it."

"Honestly, I can't say for certain. But I have difficulty believing it's merely a coincidence. I can't even speculate *what* it may mean, if it does have meaning."

"Oh," Hank replied quietly as he looked at the pearlescent ring again.

Brigand shooed the cat to the floor, then scooted to the edge of his seat. "We should probably return—"

"Wait," Hank interrupted. "You said something about having a *second* blessing, and you still haven't told me about Cona."

"Yes, of course," Brigand replied with a nod. "I had forgotten where the story was going." He reclined back into the chair. "Conrad and I were mates growing up, always goading each other into mischief. One afternoon, when I was fourteen, so he must have been fifteen at the time, we were goofing about at the portal ring. His family's home was near the circle in Mallow, and we played there often. This, of course, was before that portal closed."

Brigand suddenly paused and looked over. "Forgive my rudeness. This may take a bit of time to recite. Would you like a drink or some other refreshment?"

"No," Hank replied. "I'm fine." He leaned back and fought a yawn.

"Well then," Brigand said with a reminiscing smile. "I'll continue. We had been cautioned many times about the dangers of the portal, but being silly youngsters, he dared me to put my hand into it. After doing so, I returned the dare. Then he dared me to stick my head into the portal."

Hank sat up. "Did you?"

"Well, naturally. I couldn't let such a challenge slide. I put my head into it for a few seconds, which was long enough to learn how alien their dimension is."

"What was it like?"

"Difficult to explain. It felt thick and heavy, like being underwater. Sparkling globes and tendrils floated about, reminding me of jellyfish and seaweed, which enhanced the illusion of an undersea world. And I felt different *inside* my head too. That's the part that defies words."

The cat jumped into Brigand's lap again. "Then, I dared Conrad to do the same. Declaring that he could last longer than I did, he stuck his head into the portal. Which was a queer sight, how his head just disappeared from his body. I waited a minute, then two minutes, and grew concerned when he didn't withdraw, so I grabbed his shoulders and pulled him back."

Brigand stroked the white fur of the cat almost absently. "He stared at me with the most peculiar expression. So I said, 'Conrad, snap out of it.' Curling up his mouth, he replied, 'Cona is more representative of my essence,' before he turned and wandered toward the road, still seemingly in a daze."

"Was he alright?" Hank asked.

"Oh, he soon recovered, more or less. But the exposure to their world changed him somehow. Well, it changed both of us actually, but I wouldn't understand how I had been affected for a few years. Conrad though, he had always been clever with math and mechanics, but after the portal incident, he became compulsively obsessed with the subjects, spending many hours scribbling in his notebooks and tinkering with strange devices."

Hank sat back a moment. "And how were *you* affected?"

"Just physically, it would seem. I grew suspicious at eighteen, when I had yet to develop any facial hair. My family were known to be 'late bloomers,' so it wasn't until I reached twenty-one, still lacking any signs of a beard, and seeing that Conrad still looked less than eighteen, I realized that our aging clocks had been affected as well." Brigand sat up and shooed the cat from his lap a second time. "We really should return. We can discuss later, if you have any questions," he said as he stood and motioned to the front door.

Hank stood and followed him back to Anne's door.

Chapter 16

AFTER STIFLING another yawn, Hank said his good-nights to the group and returned to Darren's apartment. He went to the front bedroom and retrieved the bathroom kit from his suitcase, then took it down the hall. As he brushed his teeth, his thoughts wandered back to what Brigand had suggested earlier in the evening.

Well, Brigand hadn't outright *said* Hank should hang around in Ireland, but he had strongly implied Hank should stay until Christmas, with the hopes of figuring out a way to help at the next Solstice thing.

Can I do that? Should I do that? Hank asked himself while looking at his reflection as he scrubbed with the toothbrush. *What's the downside?*

After pondering a moment, he didn't really come up with one. He wasn't the kind of guy who was married to his work, and antique appraisal was the type of work he could do anywhere. Besides, with Darren's Guild connections in the antique business, it would probably be easy to get a local job. In fact, there may even be a need for an expert in American furniture here on this side of the ocean. He would probably have to apply for a green card, or whatever the Irish equivalent was, but since he did have a unique specialty, it would probably be easy to get one.

So, if work wouldn't be a problem, then the biggest complication would be trying to explain it all to his mother.

Hank frowned at himself in the mirror. *Really? I'm past forty and still worried about what Mother thinks?*

As he rinsed his toothbrush, he didn't have to consider the upside to staying. Spending more time with Darren would be rather… nice. *Although,* he realized, *that could easily turn into its own downside.* He was already quite infatuated with Darren, and staying around him longer would only… intensify the situation. Hank quickly shut down that train of thought. *If I stay, it will only be for the sake of this portal business.*

Once he'd swished his mouth clean with some water, Hank stared at his reflection. "Grow some balls already," he muttered to himself. *I'll never get* anything *in life if I don't take a chance on* something.

With everything in his kit packed away, Hank took it to Darren's bedroom and pulled off his clothes before crawling into bed. He stretched and closed his eyes, but his mind churned with possibilities as he yawned again.

ANNE HUNG up the phone and looked at Darren. "So, haven't you two shagged yet?"

"Anne," Darren exclaimed as he turned from Brigand to hide the blush on his cheeks. "Not appropriate…."

She smiled. "A simple 'no' would suffice. What are you waiting for?"

"I'm not *waiting* for anything. It just hasn't felt… right yet."

"Oh I see," Anne replied with a knowing smile.

"What do you mean by that?" Darren asked. "What is your sudden obsession with my sex life? If you've *seen* something, either tell me or be quiet about it."

"Who says that I *saw* anything?"

Darren threw an exasperated look at Brigand. "The way you keep prodding me makes me think you have. So spill, or shut up about it."

Anne pursed her lips as she dialed the next phone number. "Rude bastard…."

ONCE ALL the contacts had been called, Darren excused himself for the night, then quietly made his way into his bedroom. As he unbuttoned his shirt, he stood near the bed and looked at the reclined figure of Hank, barely visible in the gloom.

His mind wandered back to Anne's question. Darren wasn't going to admit it to his sister, but he did feel as though he were stalling, but not because he was waiting.

He was avoiding.

Or, trying to avoid, anyway. He felt it would be entirely too easy to fall in love with this man, which could only lead to painful consequences, since Hank would eventually leave. At some point in the future, the American would want to go home.

Darren slipped off his clothes and crawled as gently as possible into bed beside Hank.

As he lay on his side, facing away, Hank's breaths sounded like heavy sighs, so Darren suspected he was asleep. He softly scooted and spooned behind Hank's smaller body.

Hank eased back against him. "Everything all done?" he asked quietly.

"Yes," Darren said. "At least, as much as *can* be done tonight."

Hank nestled closer and clutched at Darren's draping arm. "I'm sorry. I bet the timing of this really sucks. I hope this doesn't screw up the… thingy later."

"Likely not, since she never had an active role in Solstice. Katherine wasn't from one of the families. She got involved through Michum, her husband, and stayed active in the Guild after his passing."

Hank wiggled his butt up against Darren's lap, feeling his solid presence, then chuckled. "You don't seem very tired."

"I am," Darren replied. "But, I also happen to be a male. Some things have a will of their own."

"That's true. Then I should let you go to sleep."

"I'm not as tired as I was yesterday…," Darren teased.

"Oh?" Hank rolled onto his back and reached his hand out to massage Darren's chest. In the dim moonlight that filled the room, the darker patches of tattoo ink that covered his upper body once again reminded Hank of burn scars.

"You have anything in mind?"

"Well, I still haven't tasted an Irishman," Hank replied as he rolled to face Darren.

"I see. I'd be willing to correct that oversight. Merely for the good of Irish-Texan relations, of course."

Hank leaned forward and kissed him, then lowered his mouth and lightly sucked on his chin. He continued farther down, licking and nibbling at Darren's inked skin as he scooted lower.

A BIT later, Hank struggled again with sleep. "Stupid-assed house," he grumbled as he rolled to his other side. He squeezed his eyes closed and pulled the pillow around his ears, trying to block out the sound, but that strange hum persisted. It seemed to echo all through the house like a vibration of some kind. As he listened, the tone of the sound seemed to lower slightly.

That's no frigging pump, Hank thought as he sat up. Looking at Darren, he saw the man continued sleeping, oblivious to the noise. *Maybe if I can figure out what the damn thing is, I can shut it off,* he decided before slipping out of bed and pulling on his jeans as the pitch dropped a tiny bit further.

Hank paused after stepping into the hall and turned his head from one side to the other in an attempt to isolate the humming's point of origin. He slowly moved down the hall toward the living room, listening intently. The pitch lowered more as he neared the end of the hallway.

Stepping into the living room, Hank looked up to see another one of the misty globes. *Or is it the same one?* he thought while he observed it hovering in the air.

As he watched the sprite, if that was indeed what he was looking at, the tone lowered again before the sound wavered and fell into the swoosh-swoosh pattern he had heard the night before. He stepped deeper into the room and approached the swirling cloud.

When he got within a yard of the sprite, it bobbed in the air, then slowly drifted across the room. Hank took slow steps and followed the misty cloud as it led him past the coffee tables and to the settees. It bobbed again. Then the sprite drifted to the bookshelf crammed with mythology books. That swishing sound seemed very close now. Hank followed and looked over the shelves for the source of the noise, but only saw cluttered volumes of leather-bound books. The sprite bobbed again before slowly drifting to the floor.

Hank dropped to his knees, peering intently over the lowest shelf, yet he only saw more books. "Where?" he asked aloud in frustration as he began pulling the books from the shelf and looking behind them.

The cloudy mist sort of shivered, then the vapors condensed into a tiny feminine-looking arm that protruded from the cloud. With its index finger, the hand pointed downward briefly before the mist evaporated away to nothing.

Hank looked at the rug and failed to see anything. He looked up and scanned the room as the swishing sound slowed and took on that heartbeat rhythm. No other misty clouds were visible. He looked at the rug again. The sprite was obviously trying to show him something, but he was at a loss as to what he was supposed to find. While scanning the dimly illuminated rug, Hank heard the swishing noise slow even further, then stop.

With a defeated sigh, he stood up and headed back to the bedroom. *At least the damn noise is gone. Maybe I can sleep now.*

ANNE WAS pulled awake by the strange vibration. She didn't hear any sounds, but she could feel pulsing tremors in the ether, as if some alien presence were intruding.

As she lay puzzling over the bizarre throbbing, she nearly laughed aloud when some dialog from the Star Wars movies entered her thoughts. She heard the elderly voice of Obi-Wan Kenobi recite in her mind, *"I sense a great disturbance in the force."*

Anne chuckled as she nodded. *Yes, I agree. A great disturbance indeed.*

Before she had time to consider the odd energy much further, the vibrations weakened, then faded out altogether, leaving her to puzzle over the brief intrusion as she drifted back to sleep.

LATER IN the morning, Hank woke to an intensely bright light.

He squinted as he rose. Looking at the windows, he noticed the thin beam of sunlight coming through the gap in the curtains, aimed right at his pillow. He let out a groan as he shifted closer to Darren and turned on his right side to avoid the sun. As he faced the slumbering man, Hank looked over the tableau of tattoos on his chest and admired the artwork for the first time in full daylight.

He zeroed in on the image of a faery above Darren's sternum. The line drawing of the stylized creature seemed almost hieroglyphic. Then, Hank suddenly noticed the image was actually created from those mysterious *F* characters. One mirror image *F* character of blue ink nestled next to an *F* character of green ink, and together the characters created the full figure.

So, that's *where I've seen it before,* Hank realized as he admired the work.

Darren let out a low snorting noise as he rolled over slightly. "Your staring makes it difficult to sleep," he huskily whispered out.

"Oh, sorry. I was just admiring your tattoos."

"Much to admire," Darren groggily replied. "Mike's done many over the years."

"As in, Mike O'Reilly?" Hank asked. "The guy from last night and the bathhouse?"

"Yes, one and the same."

Hank briefly studied one of the smaller panels showing a stylized drawing of what looked like a hexagon-shaped chalice. "What do these mean?"

"No meaning, as far as I know. Mike said that sometimes he sees the future when he draws, but who can say if that's true or not." Darren sat up and yawned. "I guess I'm through with sleep, since you continue to stare at me."

"Oh, sorry," Hank apologized. "But since you're awake now, I can tell you about last night."

"That noise again?"

"Yes, and another sprite."

"Oh? Do tell," Darren urged as he rubbed at his eye.

"It led me across the living room and over to your mythology bookshelf, then pointed at the ground."

Darren practically leaped from the bed and grabbed his lounging pants, pausing only long enough to pull them on before running into the hallway.

After quickly pulling on his own jeans, Hank followed Darren into the living room.

"HERE?" DARREN asked as he knelt down and peered at the lowest shelf of the bookcase. The front of the bookcase had a flat, covering panel stretching between the floor and the first shelf.

"Yeah, hovering a little toward the outer side."

Darren pulled out some of the books and set them on the floor, then used his thumb to thump along the sides and bottom of the cabinet. "Some of this older furniture has hidden compartments," he explained as he listened to the echoes while moving his hand and thumping along the corner seam. "Help with these," Darren said as he pulled more books off the shelf and handed them to Hank, who stacked them on the settee. Darren soon had the shelf completely uncovered.

Darren carefully explored the back seam, sounding with his thumb and poking with his fingers, but failed to find anything. He moved his attention to the front of the shelf and the panel, once again finding nothing unusual. He looked at the rug in front of the shelf. This section was rather plain and lacked any sort of design, so he quickly gave up on the notion of any secret messages hidden in the weave.

"Maybe something's *under* the bookcase?" Hank thought aloud when he saw Darren's frustration.

"Maybe," Darren agreed. He rose up on his knees and started pulling the books from the second shelf a few at a time and handing them to Hank. "We will have to empty the case first, before we try to move it."

After a few moments, they had the shelves emptied, then managed to pull and maneuver the heavy wooden case into the sitting room area. Glancing behind it, both men saw the slight circular dimple in the rug that had been concealed by the case.

"What's that?" Hank asked. "Something's under the rug?"

"Certainly appears that way." Darren motioned for Hank to help, and they carefully pulled the bookcase farther into the room to rest near the coffee table. "I never knew there was anything here," Darren said as he moved the side table away from the corner of the rug, then knelt down and lifted the fabric to peer underneath.

"Well, I'll be…," Darren muttered when he saw the round metal ring of a trap door. "I certainly never heard of a crawlspace in the flat."

"Looks like we'll have to move that second bookcase also," Hank said as he looked over Darren's shoulder and studied the outline of the door.

"And move the settee over a bit as well."

They spent the next thirty minutes moving more books and furniture, finally exposing enough of the rug to completely uncover the hidden door in the floor. Darren curled back the corner of the rug and stuck the edge under one of the settee's legs to hold it open. "I should grab a torch," he said as he darted to the hallway.

HANK FELT a touch disappointed when Darren returned with a big flashlight. He'd expected to see him carrying one of those action-movie torches, the kind with a burning rag on the end of a long stick.

Darren pulled the door open and revealed the dark opening to a root cellar. "You first?"

"You're the one with the light," Hank replied. "I'll follow you."

Grinning, Darren switched on the light and started down the stairs.

Hank trailed behind, surprised to find carefully laid stone steps leading into the cellar, and not rickety wooden stairs like he would expect to encounter in an American house.

As they descended, Darren reached out and pulled the dangling chain of one of those old-fashioned bare-bulb light fixtures mounted in the ceiling, but the long-dead lightbulb failed to spark to life. They had to rely on the beam of the flashlight as Darren moved it around, trying to reveal the interior.

When they reached the bottom of the steps, Hank noticed the buried room wasn't dank and cold, like he would expect from such a space. The temperature of the room was only slightly cooler than the living room above, and the air felt very dry—more like a dusty attic.

Slowly, Darren panned the shaft of light from right to left, illuminating the cabinets and shelves mounted along the walls of the cramped space. The thin coating of dust that covered the objects scattered along the shelves made it difficult to identify any of the items.

Darren stepped forward and carefully blew at the small obscured lumps spread across the cabinet. A plume of dust rose up to reveal tiny gears, cogs, and springs laid out along the surface. He took another deep breath and blew at the counter farther to the left, revealing an empty platinum watch housing. "My stars," Darren exclaimed as he stifled a sneeze. "The ninth watch. This must have been Cona's workspace." He blew at the shelf mounted above the cabinet, clearing the dust away to reveal a shiny, silvery figurine of a ballerina on top of a wooden box. "It was always assumed the watch was stolen by whomever had broken into the house."

Hank reached his hand out to the ballerina, but stopped before actually touching the delicate figurine. "Is this also platinum?"

"Don't think so," Darren replied before blowing on another section of the shelf. "That actually looks like ai-leeoo-min-eeum."

"Alien what?" Hank asked.

"Ai-leeoo-min-eeum, the metal of soft-drink cans."

"Oh, you mean *aluminum*," he replied, using the shorter, clipped vowels of the American pronunciation as he looked at the little bits and pieces of the watch. "Do you think you could fix it?"

"Possibly?" Darren answered with questioning doubt in his voice as he aimed the light at an array of partially assembled gears. "If it were merely a normal watch, I easily could, but certainly not before tonight. Just properly cleaning the pieces to prepare for assembly will take many hours. With the added complication of its *special* properties, I may never get it to function as intended."

"That sucks," Hank said as he reached out and took hold of the turning key at the base of the ballerina. He turned it a few clicks, and they watched as the ballerina kicked out one foot and twirled around in a slow circle before freezing in place again.

Darren panned the light around the shelves, pausing the beam briefly on another tall object. He illuminated the odd-looking device.

Hank noticed the strange configuration of circular pieces that, unlike everything else in this basement space, appeared free of dust. He stepped closer for a better look. The three circular bands that nestled inside each other at perpendicular angles weren't fashioned from metal; they looked more like some kind of ceramic material. He reached out and touched the base, which was a hexagonal-shaped column nearly a foot tall, on top of which the circular pieces rested. The strange thing reminded Hank a bit of the Emmy Awards statue. Peering closer at one face of the device revealed an engraving: another of those *F* characters.

"How peculiar," Darren said as he also touched the base. "Why would Cona build a gyroscope? And out of ivory?"

DURING THE brief moment when both men's hands were touching the base, the central ring of the gyroscope twitched slightly, but neither one noticed the tiny movements before Hank pulled back his hand.

"OH, IVORY," Hank said in realization as he looked closer at the circular bands. "It does look like those circles were carved from an elephant tusk."

Darren lifted the device off the table. It felt surprisingly heavy in his grasp. Then he wiped away the dust from the columned base. Each face of the hexagon bore an engraved glyph, of which he only recognized two: the green faery *F* and its mirror counterpart for the blue faery that was inscribed on the opposite face.

"Gyroscope…," Hank said. "Aren't those used in, like, planes and stuff for orientation? It does seem strange he would build one…."

"The technology is much older than that. Gyroscopes were first used in the 1700s, back when perpetual-motion machines were inventions of serious research."

"Perpetual-motion?"

Darren turned the device in his hand and studied the unfamiliar glyphs. "We should show this to Anne; she might recognize these other symbols and have some insight."

"Great idea," Hank agreed. He took a last glance around before going back up the stone steps.

Darren set the gyroscope device on the coffee table and trailed behind. "We should dress and go visit her."

A FEW minutes later, they met Anne in her parlor room. She bounced in her chair from excitement. "Great heavens. A secret basement workshop. And all of Cona's works weren't lost as believed. How delicious!"

Darren handed the gyroscope to her. "Are any of these glyphs familiar?"

Anne held the ivory artifact in her hands and turned it from one hexagonal face to the next. "Well, obviously, we have the green and blue faery glyphs on opposite faces. On this set we have the glyph of a mountain and on its opposite side is wind." Anne paused and studied the remaining two characters. "This one I don't recognize at all, and this one looks almost like the glyph for ocean, except for these extra little… peaks, or hills, I guess one might say." She turned her attention to the configuration of banded circles at the top. "I'll dig in the library and will surely turn up those symbols." She turned it over and looked at the bottom. "What the devil is this device for?"

"Maybe," Hank offered, "it's part of another clockwork machine?"

Anne traced her finger along one of the six grooved notches in the bottom. "Possible, I suppose. It does seem it was meant to fit inside a larger piece. But you didn't find anything else like it down there?"

"No," Darren said as he shook his head. "Just the watch pieces and a small clockwork."

"I wish I could go down there and make a thorough inspection," she said as she absently banged her hand on the arm of the wheelchair.

"I can carry you down the steps," Darren offered.

Anne blanched at the suggestion. "Besides the fact that I don't need you carrying me about like some crippled child, I should best avoid the dust. I doubt it would be healthy for my allergies."

"Probably not."

She glanced at Hank as she handed the device back to Darren. "Oh! Before I forget again," she said as she turned and dug into the leather pocket on the back of her chair. "Your plane tickets. Besides dropping the reschedule fees, I also got the airline to convert your departure to an open-ended date. So," she explained as she handed the tickets to Hank, "you just need to call when you're ready to leave, and they'll put you in the next available plane."

"Thanks, I guess," Hank replied as he took the tickets. "We could clean up all the stuff down in the cellar and bring it all up for you to see."

Anne frowned. "But, that breaks one of the cardinal rules of archeology. You must catalog not only *what* it is, but also *where* it is. The location of items can often prove to be very important."

"Oh, right," Hank agreed. "Like disturbing a crime scene."

"Exactly." Anne turned back to the leather pocket and pulled out her iPad. "I've just had a brilliant idea! Darr, go get your iPad and we can set up a Skype connection and you can use the camera down there and let me see everything!"

Darren beamed. "That *is* a brilliant idea. We can even record it for posterity. If you have any spare lightbulbs, we can probably fix the overhead."

Chapter 17

IT DIDN'T take long to get the Skype video conference connection running. Then Hank returned with Darren to the basement workshop. They replaced the bulb in the pull-string light, providing better illumination to the dark space. Unfortunately, the one feeble bulb left many shadows, so Darren had to continue using the flashlight to highlight sections. Holding up his iPad, he aimed the camera at the countertop and made a slow sweep. "Can you see this on your end?"

"Hold still a moment," Anne replied. "Let me adjust the color settings."

Noticing a collection of small items near the ballerina, Hank stepped forward and blew at the coating of dust. He instantly regretted the move, though, when the cloud of dust tickled his nose and threatened a sneeze. He stepped back and looked at the assorted bands and pieces of brass now revealed. They were obviously pieces of another clockwork, but he couldn't tell from the jumbled array of bits what the final form was meant to be.

"There," Anne said. "And quit doing that, Hank. The dust makes it hard to see."

"Sorry," Hank said as he stepped farther back and out of camera range.

"Is there enough light to get a picture?" Darren asked.

"I turned the contrast up to the point that it's almost like night vision now," Anne replied. "Step back a little and start at the stairs, so I can get the big picture."

Darren retreated a step and turned the camera to the stone treads, then started a slow sweep from right to left.

"Looks great," Anne said when the camera reached the opposite side of the stairway. "Now, where did you find the device?"

Turning the camera to the shelf above the watch pieces, Darren pointed the flashlight at the hexagonal imprint visible in the dust. "Right there."

"And nothing nearby. Let me see the ballerina."

Darren swung the camera around to point at the clockwork and took two steps forward for a closer view.

"My, that is exquisite," Anne said. "You can see all the detail of lace in the tutu. Point me down to the watch pieces."

As he swung the camera down, Anne yelled out, "Wait! Pan back up a bit."

Darren lifted the camera a bit.

"What's that rectangle shape in the corner?"

As he aimed the camera and flashlight at the corner, Darren stepped forward. In the very back, hidden by the shadow of the shelf, were a stack of books that they hadn't noticed earlier. He reached out and pulled off the top volume. "It looks like a notebook."

Darren and Hank winced when Anne let out a squeal of delight. "Cona's journals! They *weren't* stolen. Get those up here now!"

"Since we are here," Darren said as he frowned, "don't you want to see the rest of the room?"

"Well, yes. Of course," Anne replied.

After taking a step back, Darren slowly panned through the rest of the room.

"Didn't see anything else, now get up here with those journals."

Exchanging an exasperated glance with Hank, Darren picked up the notebooks before retreating to the stairs. They carefully made their way up the narrow steps.

Anne startled them with another squeal as they made their way around the confusion of furniture at the top of the trap door. "*Four* books! It only looked like two of them on the camera."

"When did you get here?" Darren asked in surprise as he stepped around the bookcase.

"Couldn't wait. I wheeled over while you made that last sweep." She held out her hands, clutching her fingers impatiently. "Hand them over."

As Darren passed over the notebooks, Hank moved aside one of the stacks of history books, then settled on the settee next to Anne's chair. She slowly flipped through the pages of the top volume. Hank could see many of the pages had sketches, like engineering blueprints of different things. Anne paused when she reached a page with a drawing of various details of the ballerina figurine.

"Curses," Anne spit out as she peered over the scribbled words. "I thought at first this might be Old Gaelic, but it's not. I can't make any sense of this language."

Darren stepped behind her and looked over her shoulder to study the pages. "That devil. Unfortunately, I don't recognize it either."

Hank also looked at the words, not that he really had any hope of understanding it. "You know, as paranoid as Cona seems to have been, it wouldn't surprise me if it's some kind of code."

"Of course," Anne replied with a wry smile. "The bastard most likely *would* have written encrypted notes."

"Not much help," Darren said with a shrug. "I still can't decipher it."

"Well," Hank said as he pondered aloud. "It looks like he could read it and write it on the fly, so to speak. So it must be something simple, like Pig Latin."

"Like *what*?" Anne asked.

"Pig Latin," Hank explained. "It's an old trick of moving the first syllable of each word to the end of the word and adding an *A* on the end of it. Like, 'An-cay oo-yay derstand-unay e-may?'"

"Es-yay," Darren replied with a grin. "I remember that now. We had a similar kind of code in the alleys, only we added an *E* on the end instead of an *A*. Never knew there was a name for it."

Anne shook her head as she looked over the scribbled text again. "Interesting, but not helping…."

They all spent a moment quietly studying the strange words on the page.

"Maybe," Hank ventured, "you should show it to Brigand. I'm sure Cona would have trusted *someone* in your Guild-thingy with the code key, just in case…."

"And," Anne said with a smile as she continued the thought, "he and Brigand were quite close friends at one time, so he would seem to be the likely candidate." Anne grabbed her right wheel and gave it a spin to turn herself toward the door. "Great idea, Hank. I'll go do that now."

Darren shook his head and ran to open the door for her. "All right, then. Let us know what he says."

"What about all the other stuff down there?" Hank asked.

Anne paused in the doorway. "You could get the duster, I suppose, and clean up the basement a little. I'll return in a bit."

"Reasonable," Darren said as she wheeled into the courtyard. He closed the door behind her.

Looking at the gyroscope device sitting on the coffee table, Hank tried to spin the centermost ring, but the band refused to move. It seemed locked into place by some kind of internal-gear mechanism.

Darren picked up the fire extinguisher still sitting by the back door. "I should grab the duster," he said as he carried the tank across the living room to the hallway.

"Maybe we could eat first?" Hank asked. "I can make some omelets with the groceries I got yesterday."

"Fine idea," Darren replied with a smile.

AFTER A quick breakfast, the guys returned to the cellar with a feather duster and a portable hand vac that Darren had also found in the broom closet. While Darren carefully brushed over the contents with the tips of the feathers, Hank held the vacuum a foot above the countertop and managed to capture most of the dust without disturbing the items.

Once all the watch pieces were revealed, Darren took a moment to study the array of gears and others bits. "Hum," he said with disappointment. "It just looks like normal watch pieces. I was expecting to see at least a few extra bits, to account for whatever else it does."

"Maybe the special parts are somewhere else?" Hank wondered aloud.

"That could be, I suppose."

They continued dusting the shelves above the counter, but didn't find anything new as they cleaned. The only other interesting bits were in the collection of loose parts by the ballerina. Removing the dust from the group of banded pieces of bronze revealed a small horse's head and a tiny pair of riding boots among the parts.

Darren looked around the cleaner cellar. "I wonder if we shouldn't take Anne's archeology analogy to heart and snap some photographs of the shelves before we move anything else."

"That sounds smart," Hank agreed. "We can put the gyro-thingy back where we found it and totally document the scene with pictures."

Darren left and returned a moment later with his digital camera. They had only taken two photographs when Anne yelled out, "Knock, knock."

"Down here," Hank yelled back.

After Darren took a few more quick pictures, they climbed back up the steps to find Anne holding the gyroscope. Darren put the camera down on the coffee table. "Learn anything?" he asked while looking at Anne.

"Yes, but not immediately helpful," Anne replied with a frown. "Cona had about a dozen encryption schemes, and would change which one he used from one page to the next. He also liked to write in Middle Gaelic, the bastard, so once each page is decrypted, it will still have to be translated." She held up the gyroscope. "I also took a moment to look for these glyphs. This one is ocean waves, but I couldn't find the other one, so still don't know about that."

"At least the books will be readable," Hank pointed out, trying to sound cheerful.

"Not before tonight, I'm afraid," Anne said. She let out a heavy sigh.

Darren gave his sister a hard look. "Why the urgency? What are you not telling us?"

"You heard the quatrain," she threw out as she pulled her lips into a grimace. "Isn't that enough?"

"It's plenty," Darren said as he continued scrutinizing Anne. "But, you're still holding out. What else?"

Anne hesitated before speaking. "I… we—it's too vague to mean anything."

Hank leaned down closer to Anne. "Is it about what I'm supposed to do?"

She shook her head. "No, I *still* don't have any notions on that."

"Then, what is it, Anne?" Darren pleaded.

After another hesitation, Anne finally whispered, "We won't be alone in the green."

"Not alone? What do you mean by that? Who else?"

"Like I said, it's vague. All shadowy. I don't know what it means." Anne set the gyroscope back on the table. "I should go check if Brigand has made any progress on the journals."

At her mention of 'shadowy,' Darren felt a sudden chill and he recalled seeing the reaver in her courtyard, but he tried not to show it on his face. "I suppose you should," Darren agreed as he followed her to the back door.

"Well then, we can rendezvous later," Anne said as she wheeled into the courtyard.

Darren closed the door behind her.

"We forgot to take the gyro downstairs for the pictures," Hank said as he walked to the coffee table.

"I noticed," Darren said. "I suppose we should do that."

They returned the device to its previous location on the shelf and took a few more pictures.

"Okay," Hank said. "What do we do now?"

"I suppose we wait," Darren replied with a shrug.

"I was afraid you'd say that," Hank said with his own shrug. "I hate just sitting around waiting."

"We can get the furniture into more of a semblance of order," Darren suggested as he motioned to the steps. "We can move the bookcases to that empty wall space near the front door and put away the clutter."

An hour passed as the men realigned the living room furniture in a way that left access to the door. Then they reshelved the various stacks of books.

"What now?" Hank asked as he plopped onto one of the settees.

Darren glanced at his watch. "We still have a few hours…."

"I figured. I hate the idea of just waitin' around the rest of the day."

"Well then," Darren said with a smile. "Let us fall back onto the time-honored tradition of a pint and board at the pub, to while away the time."

Hank chuckled as he stood. "You sound so damn Irish when you say that."

"I see," Darren replied with a shrug as he led Hank to the front door and opened it. "And, that's a bad thing?"

"No." Hank put his hand on Darren's shoulder as they passed outside. "Just you, I guess." He gave Darren's shoulder a gentle squeeze.

From their vantage point, neither man could see the coffee table, so they failed to notice the twitch of the gyroscope's inner ring. It drifted clockwise about an eighth of a revolution as Darren pulled the door closed.

Hank felt a chill in the courtyard as he waited for Darren to lock the door. He glanced around, but didn't see anything. Even the cat, who was such a fixture in his spot by the potted ivy, was absent.

Darren turned around, then hesitated when he glanced into the shadows.

"Everything okay?" Hank asked as he sensed Darren's pause.

"Of course," Darren said with a toothy smile as he pulled Hank through the courtyard to the street. He tried to remain jovial as they walked to the pub, but the sight of another reaver near the house left him chilled and concerned. He tried not to think of it as a bad omen.

They crossed two side streets; then Darren led Hank to the door of a flatiron-shaped building. Friendly nods and waves from the few people inside greeted them as they entered.

AS THE men enjoyed their ham sandwiches and beer, the phouka continued his desperate attempts to claw at the fiberglass sides of the cage.

He should have known better than to trust the dullahan. He had mostly himself to blame for this predicament. When the elder had found him hunting near the chapel, it had been all too easy for the dullahan to maneuver him near a row of rabbit-hutch cages, before grabbing him and locking him inside one.

The phouka gave up on using his claws and tried unsuccessfully biting the wood again. This cage, with its narrow spacing of fiberglass netting stretched tightly inside a wooden frame, had been designed to hold tenacious rabbits, but worked just as effectively for cats.

He finally gave up on his escape attempts. After hours of struggling, it seemed obvious he was not getting out by his own power. Being trapped wasn't too much of a concern. Since he had just eaten, he knew he could last many days before the need to eat would weaken him, but he also knew the dullahan had something planned. Some plan that involved the American.

With a nearly human sigh, the phouka curled against the back of the enclosure. He didn't know why he felt he had to intervene. In fact, it seemed rather foolish to get involved in a situation that certainly was of no concern to him. Of course, it also felt rather foolish to be locked in a cage.

Curse these claws, he thought as he glanced over at the latching mechanism on the cage door. With real fingers, he might be able to slide the bar aside, but these claws were too short and curved, leaving them useless for such an operation.

Hopefully, the caretaker would make his rounds soon to check on the rabbits.

BRIGAND LOOKED at the platinum watch on his wrist before closing the notebook and glancing across the library table at Anne. "It's nearly time."

"Shite," Anne breathed as she closed her own notebook and set down the pen. "And no great revelations yet?"

"Afraid not."

"Well then…," Anne replied. With a heavy sigh, she wheeled herself back from the table. "Let's go get this over with."

Brigand stood and followed behind as she rolled into the hallway. "You don't sound very hopeful."

"Unfortunately, this heavy pit in my gut leaves me feeling otherwise."

Chapter 18

AS THEY entered the Shamrock Green, Hank saw that he and Darren were not the first to arrive. Near the circle of stones, the beehive-haired lady was chatting with the old man, Mr. O'Keefe. They gave curt nods as the men stepped up.

Others filed into the garden, with Brigand and Anne the last arrivals. After a quick glance at the attendees, Brigand locked the gate, then stepped toward the circle.

Anne wore a tight smile as she waved to the others. "We all here?" she asked as she glanced around the group. After a quick head count, she rolled her chair back near the stone wall, then turned to Hank. "Could you be a dear and hand me the iPad from the back flap pouch?"

"Oh sure, no problem," Hank said as he rushed over and fished the tablet from the pocket on her wheelchair and handed it to her. She opened up some kind of calendar app covered with timers.

A short moment later, she gave a firm head nod to Darr. "It's time. Let's start the show."

Not knowing where else to go, Hank stood beside Anne as the others moved into positions around the circle, each behind one of the standing stones. Darr gave a firm nod to the others. Each one fiddled with their watch, held it out toward the center, then started humming very quietly.

AS THE young lass approached the cage, the phouka let out another painful mew. "Ah, poor kitty," she cooed to him. "Gone and got yourself trapped in a cage?"

The phouka replied with the most pitiful meow he could muster as he banged his paw on the cage door, right behind the locking mechanism.

Stepping up to the cage, the girl hesitated. The phouka banged his paw against the door again and let out a strangling noise.

"Well, it doesn't look as though you're *supposed* to be in there. Only rabbits are in here," the girl reasoned aloud as she looked over the other cages. She reached out her hand to the lock. "I'll let you out, poor kitty."

"Clarissa!" An older woman's voice echoed in the chapel garden as the girl twisted and lifted the cage bolt. "Where have you wandered to, child?"

"I'm in the garden, Ma," the girl yelled back.

The phouka reminded himself of his manners as the cage door swung open, so he leaped down to the girl's feet and purred loudly as he rubbed against her leg a brief moment, before darting into the alley. He felt he should have stayed longer to express more gratitude for his rescue, but he didn't have any time to spare. In his bones, he could feel the waning of the magic as the portal neared closing. He rushed through the alleys and streets, hoping he made it to Shamrock Green before it was too late.

HANK FELT disappointed as he watched the group standing behind the tall stones. Nothing appeared to be happening. Even looking into the corner of the walled space and using his peripheral vision, he couldn't see anything other than the floating, silvery globe, which looked the same as it had the night before. *If this were a Hollywood movie, there would be noises and exploding firework sparks to highlight such an important event,* Hank thought.

Of course, if this were a Bollywood *movie*—Hank chuckled quietly as his mental image amused him—*They would be dancing in sarongs and farting CGI rainbows. Wouldn't that be*—

His train of thought was rudely interrupted as his ring turned suddenly cold and he heard the screeching noise of the garden gate swinging forcefully open.

Hank and Anne turned to see a portly man wearing a priestly frock step into the garden with Paul. George trailed along behind them.

The priest shook his head with an exaggerated gesture. "Tsk, tsk," he scolded very loudly as they neared the circle. "It does appear they have started without us, Paul. How rude of them."

"Yes, quite rude, James," Paul agreed.

"Rude," George echoed as he stepped near Paul.

Hank briefly looked at Darren and the group at the circle, but they seemed unflustered and ignored the intrusion.

Anne pushed herself up from the armrests of the chair and stood on stiff legs. "This is a private event," she told them firmly. "I must ask you to leave."

Extending his hand, James dramatically twirled a key ring on his index finger. "Yet, we do have an invitation, of sorts. At least I do have a key...."

"A key which doesn't belong to you," Anne replied gruffly. "I do believe those are Kathy's keys."

With a dismissive flip of his hand, James turned to Darren and the group at the circle. "For all our sakes," he said in his smooth, oratory voice, "You should desist these efforts now."

Paul, who stood behind James, fiddled his fingers in an agitated way along the top of his cane. For the briefest moment, Hank thought he saw the cane grow transparent, but it must have been his imagination, for when he blinked, he saw only the darkly stained wooden shaft.

As the group ignored James and continued their humming, Anne took a wobbly step forward. "No. It is *you* that should desist. You have no place here," she declared strongly.

"Ah," James replied with a wizened smile. "But neither is it *your* place to interfere with the course of nature like this. Let the portal close, as it should."

AS THE phouka ran past the dumpsters and neared the green, he saw the entry gate standing wide open. He turned away from it and decided on a more stealthy approach. He ran around the corner and spotted a large branch that hung out beyond the wall. With agile cat paws, he scrambled up the stones to the top of the wall and leaped onto the branch before slowly walking along it, into the garden space. Using the trunk of the tree as cover, he hunched down and took in the scene below him.

The wheelchair girl actually stood up and confronted the dullahan and his friends. *Silly lass*, the phouka thought. *Brave maybe, but still silly.* Of course, she might not be able to see the bright glow that charged through the dullahan's aura, showing the strength of his energy reserves. A dullahan at full capacity was *not* someone to trifle with. The phouka hunched nearer to the trunk.

He would have to wait to make his move. He instinctively knew that the element of surprise would be his biggest weapon, and hopefully the dullahan would burn off some of that powerful energy before the time came.

ANNE AND James continued to argue, but Hank couldn't take his attention away from Paul, who grew more visibly frustrated. Drumming the top of his cane with his fingers, Paul rolled his eyes as the priest and girl bantered further. Then he seemed to reach some point of decision.

Paul slid his hand a little bit down the cane and grasped it. The cane grew transparent again as Paul hoisted it up, the wooden cane morphing into a nearly black, smoky glass sword. "Obsidian" was the descriptive word that popped into Hank's head while he watched, riveted to the spot, as Paul took hold of the sword's hilt with both hands and lifted the long blade above his right shoulder, like a professional baseball player up for his turn at bat.

Paul bellowed, "Enough talk!" as he swung the sword.

The blade moved so fast, it wasn't until James's head slid sideways and fell to the ground that Hank even realized the priest had been struck.

Paul stuck the sword through one of the loops of his belt, bent down, and grabbed the fallen head by the hair. George ran in front of him. With his free hand, Paul grasped the back of George's neck and leaped onto his back as the van driver morphed into a midnight-black horse. Paul shimmered before morphing into the figure of a headless horseman.

Held aloft by its short hair, James's head first blinked its left eye, then the right one. Its lips spread into a strange grin as the horseman turned his wrist so the slackened face looked at Anne and Hank. The dying mouth formed words, and Paul's voice issued from the decapitated head: "We've had quite enough babbling. Time to end this now."

FROM HIS observational perch in the tree, the phouka shook his head. *Such arrogance*, he thought, when he saw the dramatic display of the dullahan. *Always was an arrogant show-off, though.* He smiled at the way the dullahan's aura dimmed a bit after using his energy to transform.

The phouka felt no reaction to the beheading of the priest. It was well within the rights of the dullahan to dispense justice on a corrupted human.

With his cat eyes, he glanced at the group of humans surrounding the portal. He admired the way they continued on with whatever ritual they performed, managing to ignore the dullahan and his shenanigans. One thing he'd learned over the years was never to underestimate the tenacious stubbornness humans could muster.

The phouka looked back to the dullahan in his full form. *Show off some more, burn off that energy*, the phouka silently urged as he watched.

WHILE HANK stared down at the slumped remains of the priest, Anne found her voice. "I can't believe you just cut down an innocent man like that. I thought the dullahan had some kind of code of ethics, or something."

Hank looked up at the headless rider astride his black horse, watching as he lifted the head and placed it into the empty socket of his body. With both hands, the dullahan rotated the head to face directly in front of him. "James was no innocent. His heart had been blackened from greed and gluttony for many years." Finally satisfied with the placement of the head, he extended his right hand in front of his chest, palm facing up, where a small glowing ball began coalescing. The yellow ball of energy grew to the size of a basketball before he pulled back his arm and aimed for a throw.

Using the only tool she had in her hands, Anne held up the iPad and took a stiff step forward. As the dullahan pitched his arm, she threw the tablet at him, twirling it like a Frisbee. The pad zoomed through the air and hit his wrist, deflecting his toss and sending the ball of energy sizzling into the vines of Irish roses growing along the wall.

The vines crackled and burned. A gaping, smoldering hole in the greenery showed where the ball had landed.

"Nice throw," Hank complimented in a quiet voice.

"Not really. I was aiming for his head."

As a strange grin spread over his newly acquired face, the dullahan pulled on the reins, cantering George around to face in the pair's direction. With a tone that sounded almost admiring, he said, "A bit sassy, are we?"

QUITE A bit of sass, the phouka agreed. *But also a bit reckless.* Despite that thought, he found his level of respect for this new generation of Connell ticking higher. Especially the little spitfire one named Anne.

The dullahan's aura dimmed a bit more during his little show with the plasma ball, but the phouka didn't think it was dim enough yet. A few more of those, and he would fully deplete himself. He flicked his tail in anticipation, feeling certain that the dullahan could be counted on to keep up his theatrics.

"Ah, I do enjoy a sassy lass," the dullahan said with a lecherous grin, "but now is not the time or place for that." He cantered George toward the circle again.

"What are you going to do?" Anne asked.

Hank thought it was obvious what Paul's/ the dullahan's intentions were and guessed that Anne was trying to stall him with conversation.

With a grunt of frustration, the dullahan cantered George back to face Anne. "I'm going to have your silence now," he said coldly as he extended his palm and another energy ball formed in his hand. This bluish ball only coalesced to the size of a grapefruit before he yanked back and pitched it directly at Anne.

Hank reacted with a protective instinct and leaped to the right, putting himself in front of Anne. His body was still flying through the air at an angle when the plasma ball smacked him in the chest and deflected sideways as Hank's body twisted further. The Claddagh ring took on a deep glow as it siphoned most of the harmful energy out of Hank's body. The ball careened down and clipped Anne's left side, the force knocking her backward at an angle to land in her chair. Her upper right hip banged against the chair arm, and the chair tipped sideways, spilling her to the ground right after Hank collapsed in spasms.

While blinking tear-filled eyes as the searing pain coursed through his whole body, Hank saw Darren falter and lower his watch. "Anne!" Darren yelled out as he turned toward them.

Through clenched teeth, when he saw Darren pivoting in their direction, Hank hissed out, "Don't stop! If you stop, he wins."

Darren turned back to the center and lifted his watch again, but couldn't seem to give the task of holding open the portal his full concentration anymore. He kept glancing over with his brow scrunched with concern.

Hank tightly squeezed his eyes and reclined faceup on the ground as he endured the fires of hell burning on his chest. It felt like a bucket of acid had been thrown onto him, sticking to his skin and melting away his shirt and flesh.

WITH FRUSTRATION, the phouka dug his claws into the bark of the tree limb as he watched the attack from his perch. *Too far,* he thought concerning the dullahan's actions. *Entirely much too far.* The dullahan had significantly crossed the line by targeting those innocents. Although, the glow of his aura had dimmed considerably after the last foray. *Almost depleted enough. A little more.*

Then, the phouka saw the flash of green near Hank's knuckles when Hank lifted up his right hand. He peered closer to identify the source. *No, that* can't *be....*

AS HE consciously took in his breaths with shallow pants to minimize the movement of his skin, Hank watched the dullahan extend his palm again. Hank struggled to think of some way to stop him. Remembering a silly cartoon from his childhood, he let an inner instinct take over and raised his right hand. Despite the burning pain it caused, he took one deep breath, then yelled out, "By the powers of the faery ring, I call upon thee!"

The dullahan froze. The atmosphere of the green fell into anticipatory silence.

A moment ticked by.

Then, nothing happened.

The dullahan let out a hearty belly laugh. "And to think, for a moment I was concerned that you might be an actual threat. I seem to have overestimated your powers."

Feeling like a complete fool, Hank let his hand slump down in defeat as he slouched onto the ground.

THE PHOUKA felt the realization like a slap on the face as he stared at the ring on Hank's finger. *The Shay bridal ring. The American is a Shay!* Suddenly, his obsession over the man's welfare made perfect sense. As a long-ago appointed guardian of the Shay clan, this new fact completely changed the situation for the phouka.

His muscles taut with the urgent need for immediate action, the phouka hunkered down on the tree limb and dug his claws into the bark as he forced himself to wait.

AS HIS laughter subsided, the dullahan returned his attention to the portal and extended his palm again.

Managing to sit partway up, Hank was surprised when he glanced down at his chest. From the amount of burning pain he was feeling, he hadn't expected it to look so... unscathed. Other than a little dirt and grass from lying on the ground, his shirt looked fine and fairly clean. Only the agony searing his skin indicated that anything had happened.

As the dullahan created another of those yellow energy balls, Hank glanced at Anne. She lay on the ground next to her overturned chair, still in the position where she had fallen.

Then the air around them seemed to freeze, and Hank's ears suddenly popped. Movement in the center of the circle drew his gaze. A whole gaggle of little blue butterfly-like faeries began appearing in the air. A few darted in Hank's direction, but most stayed near the portal, buzzing around it in a loose circle.

The dullahan let out another laugh. "Really? A bunch of sprites? Is that the best you can do?" He pulled back his arm and threw the sizzling plasma ball at the throng.

The sprites around the portal formed a circular line, then held out their tiny hands. A misty spray formed in front of them that froze into part of an ice bubble, like a convex shield, protecting the portal. The plasma ball hit the reflective surface of the ice and deflected back, forcing the dullahan to quickly canter George the horse to avoid the return volley.

With a tone that sounded almost respectful, the dullahan said, "Ah, now that's a bit more impressive." He drew his sword from its sheath. "But is it impressive enough?" He held out the sword like a pointer, aiming it at the portal, and a very thin white stream, like a laser beam, flashed from the tip of it.

The sprites rallied and formed another ice bubble, but the beam was too precise and penetrated the barrier, striking one of the sprites on the forehead. With a squishing sound like a popped water balloon, the tiny sprite collapsed in a surge of water, showering to the ground.

The dullahan continued with more sword beams, and the ground below turned muddy as the sprites died and added more moisture.

FROM HIS tree limb perch, the phouka watched the dullahan's aura dim and darken with each blast. *Almost enough....*

AFTER DIMINISHING the number of sprites in the circle, the dullahan shifted the sword to his left hand and extended the right palm out again, drawing forth another ball. Feeling completely helpless, Hank watched as the rider drew his arm back and gave the ball a hard toss.

The sprites rallied again, but with so few left to create it, the ice barrier collapsed under the assault of the plasma ball, which crashed through the frozen shield, traveling a few feet farther before disappearing.

Without any accompanying sound, the air shimmered and vibrated, before a single loud thunderclap popped Hank's ears again. An incredibly strong gust of air rushed to the center of the circle as the portal collapsed, much like the strange air pressure changes Hank had heard tornado victims describe.

The powerful wind yanked everyone off their feet, pulling them toward the center of the circle. Darren managed to land on his knees and brace himself from falling completely, but many of the older members of the Guild didn't fare as well and fell face-forward into the muddy, clover-covered ground.

The unreal silence only lasted a few more seconds before the shrieking began.

Hank had to cover his ears from the wailing noise, which sounded like a siren of squealing baby pigs and fingernails scraping a chalkboard all mixed together.

Looking around, Hank could see that the horrible cries were coming from the few sprites still remaining. They flitted spastically in the air in an obvious torment. One by one, they each fell to the ground and dissolved into the earth.

FULLY DEPLETED! the phouka thought. With the confusion ensuing below, he finally found the opportunity he'd been waiting for. With a balancing flick of his tail, he leaped. As he fell through the air, he extended all four sets of claws and dug them deeply into horseflesh when he landed on George's rump.

George's painfully panicked whinnies joined the chorus of the dying sprites. The horse bucked, then forcefully dislodged his rider. The dullahan dropped the sword and nearly lost James's head as he slid sideways in the saddle.

The phouka released his grip and jumped forward, landing in the middle of the dullahan's back right before George bolted violently ahead.

The dullahan lost his balance as the horse charged. He fell to the ground with a thud, the head popping off of his neck and rolling into the clover.

Wasting no time, the phouka crawled his way up the dullahan's back and perched on his left shoulder. The exposed neck socket gave him easy access, so he used both front paws to claw his way down through the neck into the dullahan's body. The texture felt strange and gummy as he dug deeper, like pushing his paws into moist paper-mache.

The dullahan's hands groped in the grass until he found James's head. Grabbing it by the hair, he lifted it and turned his wrist so that the eyes faced his shoulder. "Cat!" he yelled in surprise. "What the devil are you doing?"

"Isn't it obvious?" the phouka replied as his claw encountered something cold and hard. "I am taking your heart." He snagged his claws into the harder bit and pulled it out of the body.

"Why?" The dullahan tried to use his left hand to dislodge the cat from his shoulder, but he couldn't get the proper angle and missed. "We've had our victory, dear friend."

"What victory?"

"For far too long, our kind have grown corrupted from exposure to this vicious world. No longer will our world be exposed to theirs."

The phouka shook his head. "I see only *one* of our kind that has grown corrupt, dear friend," he said sarcastically.

The cat held the golf-ball-sized lump aloft and examined it. It was quite boring looking, actually, and could easily be mistaken for just a black garden rock. He wondered if it had glowed before the magic ceased flowing. "Have you grown so arrogant as to think that a victory for you applies to everyone? This is a victory in no one's eyes. Certainly not in mine."

Feeling dramatic, the phouka had planned to eat the heart, but biting into it was like biting a piece of dried-out, splintery balsa wood, so he opted instead to shred it with his claws. Which proved more difficult than he anticipated, and only a paper-thin section peeled away. The dark and hardened lump was composed of packed layers, much like an onion.

"Stupid cat," the dullahan spit. "This accomplishes nothing. *I* am immortal. I will rise again when the full moon next ascends the horizon. I will be reborn."

The phouka chuckled as he continued peeling away the layers. "Your arrogance is showing again. I'm guessing your little restoration trick relies upon magic energies, does it not? So, since you have just sealed off the last flow of such magic, you are as pickled as the rest of us left behind."

"But," the dullahan countered as he took another swipe at the cat on his shoulder, "we're free now, no longer tied to the old ways. That's better for *all* of us."

"All? Then let us ask the sprites—oh wait, they all died when the magic was cut off."

"I *will* rise again, and you will pay for this insolence. I will change your form to that of a skittering roach, then smash you with my boot."

"Such arrogance," the phouka said as he continued the shredding. "Wouldn't that *also* require the magic energy?"

The dullahan made another swing at his shoulder, but with cat reflexes, the phouka easily avoided it and jumped to the other shoulder. "This isn't over. And you are quite out of bounds."

"Actually, as guardian of the Shay clan, I'm perfectly within my bounds to counter an attack. But even still, didn't you just say the old ways don't apply anymore?" As he pulled off the next layer, he was left with what looked like a dark wine-red glass marble, just a bit smaller than the marbles he had often seen children playing with. The phouka decided to go back to his original notion. He popped the marble into his mouth.

"No!" the dullahan yelled as he tried to punch the cat.

The phouka swallowed as he leaped off the dullahan's shoulder and grabbed the trunk of the tree with his claws. He scurried quickly up the trunk and back to the tree limb. He sat and watched as the dullahan's hand relaxed its grip, dropping the head with a squishy thump to the ground. He heard George start another round of painful whinnies.

He looked over and saw the horse in one of the corners of the garden wall, scraping at the stones with his front hooves and stomping into the ground in some fit of confusion as one of the female humans tried to calm him. George would survive, the phouka guessed. The horse was a twin spark of the dullahan that, much like himself, had been placed into an organic body. So, he should also endure the loss of magic.

The phouka looked at the humans, wondering if maybe he should speak with them, but he could see they were going about the business of tending their wounds. *Best leave them to their own,* he thought. He scurried along the limb to the garden wall to make his exit. *I can speak with them later.* Right then, he felt the urgent need for some water.

AS THE sprites died in squealing agony and fell around him, Hank heard Darren yell for Anne. Darren turned from the stone circle, then rush past him to his sister. Out of the corner of his eye, Hank saw something fall out of the tree and spook the horse.

Hank tried to sit upright again, but the movement of his arms caused another flare of fiery agony across his chest. "Fuck," he hissed under his breath as he looked down at himself. Once again, he was surprised at how normal his hoodie and T-shirt appeared. From the way his chest felt, he expected to see charred bits of cloth barely covering smoldering skin. He reclined back into the clover and closed his eyes, forcing himself to stay very still and take slow, deep breaths. The pain eased a bit.

"Is he alive?" Mrs. McCray asked from somewhere nearby.

"Hank?" Mike inquired.

He opened his eyes. "I'm alive, just not sure how hurt. My chest burns like holy fuck."

Mrs. McCray let out a frustrated grunt. "Someone please go help that horse. His whines are giving me a headache."

Mike bent down to one knee. "May I look?"

Hank nodded, sending another jolt of pain across his chest. As Mike unzipped his hoodie, Hank turned to look back at Anne. Darren had righted the wheelchair, gotten Anne reseated, and was now trying to lift up her shirt.

"It just barely nicked me," Anne yelled in a protesting tone as she swatted at Darren's hand. "Hank's the one that took the full brunt. Go check on him."

Hank winced when he felt the fiery pressure as Mike gently pulled down the collar of his T-shirt to expose the area a few inches lower. "Shite," Mike hissed under his breath.

"How bad?" Darren asked as he rushed near.

Looking down, Hank saw the harsh, dark-pink color of the small section of uncovered skin, but the alarming part was the texture. His skin looked all roughened with tiny welts, like angry bubbles marring the surface of his flesh.

"I definitely think he needs a healer," Mike said as he turned toward the circle. "Maybe Brigand knows—" Mike jumped to his feet as he yelled out, "Brigand!"

Along with everyone else, Hank looked at the circle. Brigand was still sprawled prone upon the ground. Mrs. McCray and Mike rushed to his side.

Another flurry of movement drew Hank's eyes toward the tree. He saw the dullahan sitting on the ground and the orange tabby cat sitting on his headless shoulder. The two seemed to be having some sort of discussion as the cat played with a black ball.

He turned his attention back to the circle. Now that Brigand was sitting up, Hank could see that he didn't look good. His pallor had faded to an ashy gray. So had his hair. Hank didn't recall Brigand having so much gray in his hair. Maybe it was just the dimmer evening lighting here in the garden that made it look that way.

Another blur of movement drew Hank's gaze to the tree. Paul's headless body now slumped lifelessly against the trunk. The cat had disappeared.

George shrieked out another painful horse cry. Hank turned and saw him scratching at the wall and bouncing fitfully as the woman tried to calm him again.

Then, Hank saw the ugly thing on George's leg. The dark and shadowy creature looked like some kind of overgrown slug covered with porcupine spines. The way its color seemed to fade and swirl, it looked like the thing was made from the stuff of solidified shadows. George jumped and kicked his rear leg back, trying to dislodge the creature as it writhed and slithered higher.

As the horse kicked fitfully at the wall again, Hank saw another creature slithering up George's front leg.

Darren called out, "Back away, Maggie! He's covered in reavers."

As the woman quickly backed away, more of the slug creatures worked their way up George's legs. Darren got behind Anne's chair and asked, "Hank, can you stand and walk?"

Trying to ignore the pain, Hank carefully pushed himself up from the ground. "I think so. What are those reaver things?"

Darren pushed Anne forward. "Later," he told Hank. In a louder voice he said, "Everyone out. Get to Brigand's."

Mike and Mrs. McCray helped Brigand to his feet. Mike put his arm around Brigand's waist to help support him while everyone else moved as quickly as they could to the garden gate.

The horse's cries grew into painful screams as they filed out of the exit in the wall. Hank got closer to Darren. "What about George? Can't you do something?"

"There's no help for him now," Darren said as he shook his head. "We must save ourselves."

Once all the Guild were outside, Darren closed and locked the gate.

As the group crossed the street, the horse's screams took on a muffled quality, sounding strangely distant.

Hank paused on the curb. The chest pain wasn't as intense now; it had changed and turned more into throbbing pulses. "What about the bodies?"

Darren led the group down the walk and around the corner. "It's doubtful there will be any bodies."

Hank paused again. "Those things are gonna eat him?"

Mike assisted Brigand up the short stoop, then Brigand fished out his keys and unlocked the door.

While the others filed inside, Darren turned Anne's chair around and pulled her up the two stoop steps. Hank saw the defeated look on her face, then realized she hadn't spoken a word in many minutes.

When all were inside the apartment, Hank closed the door. "Well?" he asked as he turned to Darren. "Are they gonna eat him?"

Darren pushed Anne into the living room as Mike escorted Brigand to the side chair. "I'm not sure that 'eat' is the right word. But they will… consume him."

"Paul too?" Hank asked, standing still to minimize the flares of pain.

"Most likely."

Chapter 19

DURING ALL the ruckus, the charred hawthorn flower had been tamped down and eventually buried in the mud inside the confines of the stone circle.

In the dark and warmth of the earth, water molecules began penetrating the crisp husk of the seedpod, slowly softening the outer shell.

Soon, the husk softened enough to allow the water to reach the shimmering green seed germ nestled inside.

As the seed absorbed the moisture of the fallen sprites, it began to swell. The cells of the energized hawthorn seed expanded and divided. The fledging taproot, one cell length at a time, stretched and grew, reaching down and aiming deeper into the ground.

AS DARREN stood with the group in Brigand's living room, he kept glancing between Brigand, sunken into a side chair, and Anne. His sister looked despondent and defeated, but Brigand looked so worn and withdrawn, he couldn't decide who he should attend to first.

Until he took a closer look at Hank. Mike had gotten Hank to stretch out on the couch, and after Mike had fully unzipped the hoodie and used a pair of scissors to slit open Hank's T-shirt, Darren barely stifled a gasp when he saw the horrible destruction wrought by the plasma ball. "Hank!" he cried out in concern as he rushed to the couch. "You never said it was this bad."

Through clenched teeth, Hank replied, "What part of 'my chest burns like holy fuck' did you not understand?"

Darren stared at the circle of seared flesh that stretched from his clavicle down to just below the sternum and across either side. It looked as if Hank's skin had literally boiled. "But your clothes didn't look burned at all. I didn't think it was this bad."

Brigand weakly spoke. "That kind of plasma only affects organic items. If the clothes were cotton or silk, you might have seen more result. I'm not surprised the synthetics didn't burn."

Darren turned to Brigand. "You've seen these kinds of burns before?"

Brigand nodded. "Had a dustup with a wraith many years ago."

"How do we treat it?"

"Anne, go get my rolodex. I have some numbers there that may be useful."

Darren looked at his sister, but she sat staring into space as though she never heard the request. "I'll go," Darren offered. "Where will I find it?"

Mrs. McCray cut in. "If no one needs anything from me, I'm going home now."

"First room on the right in the hall, the bookshelf at hand height," Brigand told Darren. He turned to the others. "I don't think there's anything else to be done. All of you can go home."

While Darren headed deeper into the flat, most of the others made their way to the front door. Darren found the rolodex and returned with it to the living room. Besides Brigand, only Mike, Hank, and Anne remained. Darren handed the rolodex to Brigand.

Brigand waved it away. "Look under *H* for healers; should be several listed."

Darren twirled through the collection of cards, then read the list aloud when he found the entry. "McCain, Smithers, and O'Dowd. Who should I ring?"

"Try O'Dowd first. Smithers is reliable, but cranky. Be careful if you have to go with McCain; he's a nonbeliever, but provides treatment with no questions asked, as long as you have cash in hand."

Darren looked at Brigand as he yanked the index card free. The elder slumped deeper into the chair. He seemed to be fading further with each passing moment.

Brigand cleared his throat, then spoke. "You should get Anne back to the main house." He turned to Mike. "Get Hank zipped up and help him over there."

Darren set the rolodex on the coffee table and stuck the card in his pocket. "I'll take care of Anne."

"Good luck," Brigand called out weakly as they left.

Once inside the main house, Darren motioned Mike and Hank to the parlor. "Stretch out and get comfortable on the long divan. I'll get Anne into bed, then call the healer."

After pushing Anne into the bedroom, Darren turned her chair around then walked around to the front. He knelt down and slipped the shoes off her feet. "There now. Stand up and I'll help you into bed." When he glanced up, he saw a streaming tear running down her face.

"I can't," she said quietly.

"You don't have to walk, just stand up."

"I can't!" she squealed in frustration. "My legs are numb and I can't move them."

"Okay, calm down. You probably just bruised your back or something. I can have the healer come look at it when they get here."

"No, Darr. It isn't just a bruise. I felt it when my back twisted as I fell over the chair. I felt my spine squeeze, then it all went numb."

"It's okay," Darren reassured as he moved to her side. Cradling one hand around her armpit, he slid the other arm under her legs before lifting her up. He transferred her to the bed. He stretched her out carefully. "I bet it's just temporary. Just swelling or something."

Anne reached up and grabbed a handful of Darren's shirt, then pulled him down to look into her eyes. "Darren. Listen to me. My spinal cord twisted. It's something that has always been a possibility, and it finally happened. This damage is not repairable."

When she let go of his shirt, Darren pulled back. He tried to keep his face calm and hold back the tears that threatened to burst forth. "I'll send in the healer anyway."

Anne stared up at the ceiling without replying.

"I'll go check on Hank," Darren said before he stepped out of her room.

As he entered the hallway, he took a few steps before the multiple painful blows of the evening threatened to overwhelm him. He stepped into the library and leaned over the back of the nearest chair, trying to hold it all together. In itself, Anne's injury was sad, but as she had pointed out, it had always been a possible fact of life.

No, what really hurt was seeing Anne's defeat. Defeat over the loss of the portal and her legs both in one night. It felt like she was just giving up. And now he would have to go and deal with Hank and his painful injuries. It was almost enough to drive Darren to lose his own hope.

He didn't allow himself time to wallow for long. As Darren pushed off the chair and stood upright, he blinked and wiped away the tears collecting in his eyes. He pulled out the index card and made a call to the number listed next to O'Dowd.

TAKING SHALLOW breaths, Hank lay with his eyes closed on the divan. He knew he shouldn't take it personally, but part of him felt that Darren had just dissed him again, in favor of Anne.

"Do you want to unzip the jacket?" Mike asked.

"No," he replied. "Exposed to the air actually makes it hurt worse."

"Oh, okay." He heard Mike pace across the floor. "If you don't need anything else, I have the early shift tomorrow, for work. Darren should be back momentarily."

"It's fine," Hank told him. "I appreciate all the help, but you don't need to hang around if ya got other things."

"Then… well, you'll probably go home soon, so I doubt we'll meet again. Good luck with everything."

Hank heard him walk away and go out the front door before he had a chance to reply. He hadn't liked that woeful tone in Mike's voice and had hesitated, trying to think of something reassuring to say.

He kept his eyes closed when he heard someone walk in a moment later.

"I've left a message with the medical answering service. We should get a call back soon, maybe."

Hearing that doubt in Darren's voice, Hank opened his eyes. "I'm sure they will," he replied, trying to sound positive. "How's Anne?"

Darren hesitated. "Her spine twisted when she fell. She will never have use of her legs again."

"Oh my God!" Hank said, feeling the burning pain in his chest as he reflexively tried to sit up. He forced himself to lie back down. "I'm... I'm so sorry."

"Not your fault," Darren threw out halfheartedly. "If you hadn't deflected it, and that ball hit her head-on, no doubt it would have killed her."

"Still," Hank said, trying to think of something elegant to say. Failing to think of anything, he just muttered, "That sucks."

Darren let out a sigh as he sat on the other divan.

The silence that stretched out only seemed to deepen the desperate mood. Hank tried to think of more conversation. "So Darren, what's the next step?"

"Next step in what?"

"With the portal."

"Don't you get it?" Darren barked out. "The portal closed. The war's over and we *lost*. There *is* no next step."

"Surely there's something we can do."

"Assuming we did come up with some grand scheme, there's no more magic to make it happen. This is it, laddie."

Hank closed his eyes. Instead of trying to debate, he kept his mouth shut. Darren was too unreceptive right now. Hank realized he had only been around a few days. But for Darren and the others, who had invested their whole lives into this fight, this defeat would be devastating. They would need more time to get past it.

The sudden chime of the doorbell startled both Darren and Hank.

"Who the devil?" Darren said as he went to the front door.

Hank opened his eyes and saw him return a moment later with a tightly buttoned young woman carrying an oversize designer bag. Darren seemed to be continuing some argument with her. "But, we were expecting a Malcolm."

The young woman looked down at Hank and stopped. She turned to Darren. "Malcolm is my grandfather, who retired five years ago. I've taken over his practice. Now, if this is the burn patient, let me take a look." She turned and bent down to Hank. "What's your name?"

"I'm Hank," he said as he reached up and gingerly pulled down the zipper of the hoodie.

With no regard for soiling the nice designer outfit she wore, the doctor got down to the floor on her knees next to the divan, then carefully lifted back the fabric. Keeping a neutral face, she said, "I see." She looked Hank in the eye. "And how did this happen?"

Darren cut in. "Plasma burns, from a welding torch."

The doctor's mouth tightened. "Welding, you say? I've seen welding burns. They typically aren't quite so evenly distributed over a broad area." She stared up at Darren. "The truth."

Hank took a deep breath. "Plasma, is the truth."

"Fae plasma of some sort? Was it a wraith?"

"No," Darren answered.

"Then what?" she asked with an exasperated tone. "I need to know what I'm dealing with before I can prescribe a proper treatment."

"A dullahan," Darren finally told her.

"For real? I've never heard of one using plasma. What color was the ball?"

Hank had to stop and think. "Kind of a bluish white."

The doctor opened her bag and rummaged inside, pulling items out and setting them on the coffee table. Along with three large tubes that looked like hand lotion, she also withdrew an empty glass jar, like the kind used for face makeup. She squirted equal portions of the three tubes of goop into the jar, then used a tongue depressor to stir the concoction together.

"This should do the trick," she said as she used the tongue depressor like a spatula to carefully spread a thin layer of the sticky mess over Hank's burns.

Hank bit his lip to keep from wincing when the salve was applied. The thick lotion felt so cold, it was a shock to his skin.

"What's in it?" Darren asked.

"Burn cream with a few extra herbal ingredients. You'll need to apply this several times a day. Don't let the skin dry out. Good news is, these Fae burns typically leave little to no scarring. And they heal rather quickly." Once she'd covered the burn area, the doctor put the lid on the jar and left it on the table. "Try to sit up now."

Hank carefully lifted from the waist. The skin still complained a little bit, but not with the searing pain he had felt before. He sat up. "Thank you, Doctor...."

"Call me Chelsea. I'm glad I could help," she said as she repacked her bag.

Darren bent down and offered a hand to help her stand. "There's also another patient, in the bedroom."

"Same burns?" Dr. Chelsea asked as she followed Darren down the hall.

Hank suddenly wanted out of here. Careful not to disturb the ointment too much, he zipped up the hoodie before standing. He grabbed the glass jar from the coffee table, then let himself out through the courtyard door.

He paused outside with the thought of lighting a cigarette, but he was also feeling thirsty, so he walked through the courtyard and entered Darren's apartment, making a beeline for the kitchen.

ANNE HAD heard the doorbell chime, but it seemed far away as she lay and stared at the ceiling. She knew she might as well let Darren bring in the healer, otherwise he would likely drag her off to some hospital or clinic.

She just didn't see the need for wasting a lot of time and effort before they declared nothing could be done. Anne knew her condition, as well as its potential consequences. It was unfortunate that the worst case had happened.

Her back was only a secondary concern. The primary concern was how quietly dead the world seemed now. Ever since the portal closed, Anne hadn't felt any presence of the ether. One of her senses had been brutally cut off, leaving her feeling as though she had gone blind. No more readings. The magic was gone.

Several times as she lay brooding, Anne thought she heard a woman's voice from somewhere in the house.

"She's in here," Darr said from the hallway.

No point in fighting it.

A moment later, Darr stepped in with a young woman in tow. "Anne," he said as the young woman approached. "This is Dr. Chelsea. She's here to look you over, and put a salve on your burn."

"Fine," she replied.

DARREN WATCHED Anne's face. She still had that look of defeat in her eyes, but now her lips pouted the way they did when she was just going along with something to avoid starting a fight.

He stepped behind Dr. Chelsea as she approached his sister.

"Hi Anne," Chelsea greeted. "Which side is the burn on?"

Anne pointed to her left side.

"Then, let's get you rolled onto your right side and have a look." The doctor turned to Darren. "Can you help? Just roll her legs and try to keep her hips in line."

Darren did as asked, and they settled Anne into a comfortable position on her side.

Dr. Chelsea lifted up Anne's shirt. As she had claimed, the burn mark just a tad above her hip was actually quite small, just a smear about an inch high and running four inches from front to back.

The sight that made Darren nearly wince, were the huge purpling bruises visible along her lower back and spine.

"Oh, that burn isn't much at all," Chelsea reassured. "You do seem to have some extensive bruising on your back, though." The doctor leaned over to take a closer look. "I see many surgical scars as well."

Darren spoke up. "Spina bifida myelomeningocele."

"Oh, that explains it," Dr. Chelsea replied. "And you had full sensation and mobility before tonight?"

"Not really," Anne replied. "Limited and weak."

"But the paralysis is new?"

"Yes," Anne said with a sigh. "Earlier tonight, I fell and twisted my back when the chair toppled. I felt the spine squeeze before losing all sensation. Such an event has always been a risk, and I don't want to waste time and effort fruitlessly trying to repair it." Anne sighed again. "So please, just put the salve on the burn, then leave me to get some sleep."

Dr. Chelsea stood up and glanced back at Darren.

"She's right," Darren reluctantly agreed. "It's always been a risk."

Opening her bag, Dr. Chelsea used the bed as a table and prepared another jar of the burn cream. It only took two swipes of the tongue depressor to cover Anne's small burn. She put the lid on the jar, left the jar on the nightstand, then put away the other items.

She stepped past Darren to the foot of the bed before turning back to face the siblings. "It will take several days for the swelling on your back to reduce, at which point I would like to do a full examination. I am aware of some… unorthodox methods that may be helpful."

Anne coughed dryly. "If those 'unorthodox' methods require magical energy, you won't get them to work now. The last portal closed and magic is gone."

"Rest," Darren told Anne. "I'll show the doctor out and come back to help get you into pajamas."

"Don't bother," Anne replied wearily. "Just let me sleep."

"Good night, then." Darren hesitated, thinking maybe he shouldn't leave Anne alone, but maybe this was better. Following her wishes, he turned off the light as they left her room.

They moved through the hall and into the entry foyer before the doctor spoke again. "Is that true? The last portal closed?"

Darren nodded. "That's where we were tonight, defending it from a dullahan. We lost."

"Scheisse," the doctor cursed in German. "What does that mean long-term?"

"Who knows?" Darren said honestly.

"Well, if Anne decides to explore options, give me a ring." The doctor opened the door and stepped out.

"What about your payment?" Darren asked.

"It will be minimal. I'll have my office ring tomorrow and get a credit card number. Good night, Mr. O'Connell."

"Thank you," Darren said before closing the door. He turned the lock bolts before making his way to the parlor.

He found the room empty when he arrived. He continued through the room and exited to the courtyard.

This space was also vacant.

Darren walked through and entered his flat. "Hank? Are you here?" he called as he stepped into the living room.

"Yes," Hank called from the inner hallway.

He found Hank in the spare bedroom, already in bed, stretched out on his back. "Oh, you're sleeping in here tonight?"

"Prob'ly best until the burn heals," Hank replied. "Good night."

Hank seemed so cool and distant, almost impersonal.

"Uh, good night," Darren said. He lingered in the doorway a moment, debating whether he should say more. Maybe Hank was just tired. After all, who knows what kind of herbs were in that burn concoction. One of the medications may be putting him to sleep.

Darren gave a quick wave before going down the hall to his own bed.

Chapter 20

IN THE dark and quiet of Anne's bedroom, Skeena trembled. She had felt the sudden loss when the main flow of energy ceased earlier in the evening. Yet at the time, enough residual energy existed in the house that she didn't feel any immediate concern. But now, as those traces slowly dwindled, she sensed the threat of losing her food supply.

She restlessly scurried along the floor behind the armoire, pausing occasionally to use her sensitive spidery legs to feel for vibrations of energy. On the side nearest the bed, she picked up a trace, a faint little tingle.

Skeena slowly ventured from behind the shelter of the armoire, feeling for the source. She crept along the baseboard, moving closer to the bed. When she reached the headboard, she slinked onto the bedpost and slowly climbed, drawing closer to the energy.

At the top of the mattress, she paused. The vibrations seemed to be coming from the woman on the bed. Normally, Skeena would avoid contact with any other creatures, especially humans, but the shortage of food spurred her urgent quest. Cautiously, she moved forward, one slow step at a time.

Skeena approached the woman, who lay on her side facing away. She stuck out her front legs, waving them slowly as she sought out the energy. The vibration came from higher up. Careful not to touch the woman's skin, she climbed onto the wide waistband of the denim jeans and slinked underneath the shirttail. Slowly, she moved upward, getting very close to that faint vibration.

Reaching the top, she froze on the woman's hip. The magic emanated just a little past the edge of the denim. Now that she was this close, Skeena felt something akin to disappointment at the weakness of the energy. This source wouldn't be able to sustain her for more than a day or two. But food was food.

She cautiously wiggled one front leg beyond the edge of the denim. She gently lowered it down to the woman's skin, wary of causing any disturbance to the slumbering woman.

When the tip of her leg encountered the sticky goo, she quickly yanked it back from the stinging sensation.

She scooted a little to one side and tried again. Her leg encountered more stinging goo.

In frustration, she paced back and forth along the denim waistband. There must be some way to reach the food and avoid the goo.

Methodically, Skeena followed the edge of the waistband, reaching out every few paces until she finally found a goo-free spot. One leg at a time, she cautiously crawled onto the dry skin. Once completely off the denim, she turned and reached up, but encountered more goo.

Skeena wanted to twitch in frustration, but the need to be very still kept her mostly frozen. Then the thought occurred that maybe she could avoid the goo by going underneath the skin.

Such a move would be rather risky, almost unthinkable if she weren't driven by a growing hunger. Yet, the woman did seem to be sleeping very deeply. If she phased into pure energy, a trick Skeena could briefly accomplish, then she could sink into the woman's body without disturbing her.

Going on instinct, she pulled in her legs and gently rested her abdomen on the woman's back. Then, she dematerialized her legs into a pure energy state and slowly pushed them into the skin.

Once buried halfway deep, she phased her body and let it sink as she pushed her legs deeper.

The woman twitched, panicking Skeena, who drove herself much deeper into the woman's body than she had intended. Disoriented, she turned the wrong way and moved farther down the woman's back.

Then, Skeena felt something different. A pulse of energy. She moved down farther and felt another pulse, then another. It wasn't the magical energy she had previously fed on, but it was still energy.

Sinking deeper, she nestled atop the thrumming weak spot of the energetic cable and fed briefly. She felt sustained from this infinite supply of new energy.

Well, not really infinite, since humans hardly survived a century. But a more reliable source than the one she had sought earlier. Skeena fed.

Her temporary energy state soon faded, and she returned to her body. She stretched her four front legs out along the cable and the other legs back, reaching as far along as she could from either end. She felt the movements as the woman's body twitched and shook. Then the woman tried to roll over.

Skeena sent a calming pulse into the cable. The woman's movements stopped.

In the quiet, Skeena resumed feeding.

PAINFUL THROBS from his chest woke Hank again when he tried once more to roll in the bed. He repositioned onto his back. The burn really sucked.

Remembering what the doctor said about keeping it moist, he gently reached up with his index finger and touched at the edge of the burn near his lower ribs. The skin still felt slick and oily. *Shouldn't need another coating yet,* he thought.

Hank couldn't get back to sleep. His hips and butt nagged complaints from lying in the same position on his back for so long. Maybe he should get up and walk around a bit.

Gingerly, Hank crawled off the bed. He pulled his jeans back on then decided against wearing a shirt.

He made his way to the kitchen, retrieved one of the water bottles from the fridge, and carried it to the living room. Recollections from earlier in the night kept tramping through Hank's mind. After learning that Paul was a dullahan, it made more sense now why the man was keeping tabs on him and being so insistent that he fly home. Maybe Paul had some idea of how Hank might have stopped him. Well, if Paul did, Hank would never know, since the dullahan was dead and eaten by those shadow worms.

The reavers. Hank never did get an explanation for what those things were.

After taking another sip of water, he set the bottle down on the coffee table near the hexagonal gyroscope. Hank eased back into the couch as he looked at the strange ivory device. Maybe they were supposed to have somehow used that thing last night. If only they'd had time to read Cona's journals. Or, maybe it wouldn't have made any difference. After hearing all the terrible things mentioned in that prophecy, maybe the old man was right. Maybe the whole situation was destined to turn to shit.

Hank wondered how Brigand was doing. The man seemed to have been affected the most by last night's bad events. Brigand had looked even more gray when they had left his apartment. Maybe someone should go check on him.

Then Hank remembered what Darren had said about Anne's back. Maybe she should get the prize for the one most hurt. Hank hadn't even known she could stand until last night in the park. *Green,* he corrected himself with the European terminology.

He closed his eyes and tried not to think about Darren. Hank had thought the two of them had made some kind of connection, but Mike had shown more concern for his welfare than Darren had. It felt like Darren had ignored him twice—no, three times, in favor of Anne.

He reached out and grabbed the water bottle again, his mind continuing to churn in a downward spiral of one negative thought chasing another.

IN HIS bedroom, Darren also struggled with falling asleep. He didn't understand the apparent shift in Hank's attitude. The excuse that Hank was just tired grew weaker the more Darren thought about it. Hank had been cool and abrupt toward him ever since they had left the green.

Hank, with that horrible burn on his chest, had probably suffered the most during the portal ordeal. It should be enough reason to excuse the Texan for having a grumpy mood.

Or maybe Hank was thinking of leaving now, since nothing remained to keep him here.

With that doubtful thought, the seed planted by Paul days before finally found nourishment and sprouted inside Darren.

Darren tried to tell himself not to worry about it so much. He worried anyway as the seed slowly grew around fears of Hank leaving, until Darren finally fell asleep.

Waking up the next morning, Darren rolled over. The gentle glow behind the window meant it was sometime just after sunrise. He kicked the covers aside and stood up, then made his way to the bathroom.

As he relieved himself, Darren thought about what to do next. He should check on Hank, Anne, and Brigand. He thought about them, but couldn't decide if any had a higher priority. From what the doctor had said, Hank should be fine in a few days, which left Anne and Brigand.

Brigand was the one who worried him. He felt neglectful now, not thinking to also have the healer check on the elder during her visit. Yet it seemed Brigand's troubles were more psychological, brought on by the trouncing defeat in the green. Darren would have to go look for himself, then ring the healer if it seemed necessary.

Darren should go over to help Anne out of bed and get dressed first before he checked on Brigand, he decided as he went back to his bedroom.

After putting on the pair of jeans and T-shirt he'd thrown over the chair the night before, Darren went down the hall, pausing briefly at the doorway to the spare bedroom. He peeked inside to find Hank still stretched flat on his back, snoring a bit with each breath. He should be fine for now.

Darren went through the flat and over to the main house. He froze when he stepped into Anne's room. Just like Hank, she was also stretched out on top of the covers, lying flat on her back, but her open eyes pointed up at the ceiling in a strange, glassy-eyed stare. "Anne?"

Not getting a response, Darren rushed forward. "Anne! Wake up," he said as he gently nudged his sister's arm.

She still didn't respond. She just continued staring blankly ahead.

"Anne!" he yelled again as he reached out and put his palm on her forehead, checking for fever. Her skin felt slightly cool and clammy. He waved his hand in front of her eyes. Her only response was a reflexive blink.

Darren reached for his phone with plans to call the healer, but his hand fell on an empty pocket. He cursed himself for leaving the phone in his bedroom. He rushed back to his flat.

He didn't slow as he passed by the snores coming from the spare bedroom. Darren found the phone and the index card on his nightstand. He quickly dialed the O'Dowd service number as he rushed back to Anne.

TWENTY MINUTES later, Darren left his vigil at Anne's bedside to answer the door. He rushed back with Dr. Chelsea.

"And she's been like this how long?" the doctor asked as she gripped Anne's wrist to check her pulse.

"I don't know, this is how I found her this morning." Darren paced at the foot of the bed. "What is it? Is she going to recover?"

"Give me some time to examine her," Dr. Chelsea said impatiently as she opened her bag and pulled out what looked like a metal version of a giant crab's claw.

Darren had no idea what the doctor was doing as he watched her first push the claw end of the device closed and place it on Anne's forehead. Then the doctor opened the claw all the way and put it around Anne's neck, like some kind of strange choker. As Darren paced, the doctor briefly put the claw in several more places on Anne's body.

The doctor put the claw back in her bag. "Good news is, her vitals are stable. She does have brain activity. So, I can't see any reason for the coma. Unless it is of a magical nature."

"Coma?" Darren repeated aloud. "What does that mean?"

"I don't know," the doctor mused aloud. "It's common with persons suffering brain injury, who will essentially 'shut down' as their bodies try to repair the damage. Maybe the spinal damage has somehow triggered it. Brain swelling can also bring about a coma." As if having a sudden inspiration, the doctor moved her bag from the bed to the floor. "Help me roll her over. Let's take a look at her back injury."

They soon had Anne rolled over onto her stomach. The doctor lifted the tail of her shirt to expose Anne's lower back.

If anything, Darren thought it looked worse than the night before. The huge purple bruise marks were now showing patches of yellow and almost a green color. "Is that normal?"

The doctor gently ran her hands along Anne's back. "Well, the bruises shouldn't be healing quite that fast, other than that, it's normal." She moved her fingers to feel along the spine. "I'm not feeling any major swelling."

"So, it's not her back?"

"Honestly, I don't know," Dr. Chelsea said as she pulled down Anne's shirt. "I'm a bit baffled."

Darren thought over what the doctor said. "Does that mean we should get her to hospital?"

The doctor wobbled her head. "She made it rather clear last night that she didn't want hospital involvement."

"But, isn't this more serious?"

The doctor took a deep breath. "I don't know. A coma is like a defense mechanism, a healing mode the body goes into. My instincts are telling me this has a magical cause and we should let it ride for now. She'll likely come out of it on her own in less than a week. I can set up a nutrient IV, to buy us a few days."

"Well." Darren nodded slightly. "I'll have to trust your judgment on this."

"After five days, if there's no change, we should consider taking her to hospital. Help me roll her over again, and I'll get the IV set up."

HANK STARTED awake from the searing twinge on his chest. Groggily, he touched at the throbbing burn, noting that it was feeling dry.

He scooted to the edge of the bed and opened the salve jar. After carefully smearing a layer of goop over the burn with the tips of his fingers, Hank closed the jar and went to the bathroom.

He relieved himself, then turned to the sink. He examined the burn in the mirror, to make sure he had the area well covered with the salve. *The doctor was right,* Hank thought in surprise as he looked at his reflection.

The burn was healing rather quickly. The color had already softened to more of a sunburn pink. Most of the welts had faded. Only a few lines of bumps still traced across his chest, like the spiderweb cracks of a broken pane of glass. In two or three days, the burn probably wouldn't be visible at all.

Which was both good and bad news. Having the horrible burn had delayed any thoughts of returning home, but once it healed, he would have to face the decision of how much longer he should stay in Ireland.

Hank turned to leave the bathroom, but suddenly turned back to his reflection. He didn't know why, but as he examined the pink, swollen-looking burn, he thought there was something familiar about it.

Shaking his head, Hank turned again and went down the hall to the kitchen.

GETTING ANNE situated had only taken a few moments, during which time his sister had showed no reaction or change to being moved or having the needle stuck in her arm. Darren gave a worried look to the doctor as she reached out and pushed Anne's eyelids closed.

Dr. Chelsea shrugged. "That's all we can do for now," she said as they watched Anne's eyes pop open again. "Come in and talk to her often, remind her that you're here waiting. It may help encourage her to pull out of the coma."

"Okay," Darren said as he followed the doctor to the hallway. "Oh, while you're here, could we run next door and check on our neighbor?"

"Was he also attacked last night?"

"Brigand was there, but he didn't suffer any injuries that I could see. Could we check anyway?"

"Of course," Dr. Chelsea agreed. "Lead the way."

Darren led her outside and around to the next stoop. When his knock at the door went unanswered, Darren started to use the master key on Brigand's door, but found the bolt still unlocked.

He turned the knob, and they stepped inside. "Brigand," he said loudly. They heard no reply as they walked through the foyer and into the living room.

They found Brigand still sitting in the side chair. He had visibly withered overnight, his face bearing the deep wrinkled lines of a shriveled prune under a mop of stark-white hair. His nose wheezed with each shallow breath he took. Looking shrunken and frail, his hands were loosely clasped in his lap.

"Brigand!" Darren called out as he kneeled down by the chair.

"Darr, who's this?" he asked as he raised his head to look at the woman.

"The healer," Darren replied, moving aside so she could get closer.

"Were you attacked?" she asked.

Brigand shook his head. "No. Since the portal closed, my gift is fading. No more magic to sustain the longevity."

Darren gave Dr. Chelsea an imploring look. "Isn't there anything we can do?"

Dr. Chelsea shook her head. "If what he said is true…." She left the sentence unfinished as she glanced at the notebooks spread out on the couch.

Brigand pointed to the couch as he reached out with his other withered hand and placed it on Darren's shoulder. "Make sure those get to Anne. I worked all night, noting the cipher used at the top of each page. It should be enough information for her to decode the journals."

"Okay," Darren agreed. "But she won't be able to use them yet. She went into a coma last night."

"Coma?" Brigand wheezed. "What of Hank?"

"Aside from the burn, he's fine."

Brigand paused, seemingly thinking. "Is she lying on her back, eyes staring open, even if you try to close them?"

Darren nodded and said, "Yes."

Dr. Chelsea leaned down closer. "Have you seen that condition before?"

Brigand coughed as he nodded. "Sounds just like what happened to Conrad."

Darren frowned. "Anything else you remember?"

"No. I don't think the doctors really understood what a coma was back then, especially not such an unusual one. They just watched helplessly as he weakened and died three days later."

"When was this?" Dr. Chelsea asked.

"1937," Brigand wheezed.

Dr. Chelsea didn't flinch at the date. "And do you remember if they used a feeding tube or maybe IV supplements?"

Brigand shook his head. "They didn't."

"Then," Dr. Chelsea said, "it was likely malnutrition that led to his death. We can at least make sure Anne doesn't suffer the same fate."

Brigand patted Darren's shoulder. "I'm sorry to leave such a mess behind."

"What do you mean?"

"With the Guild. I thought I still had many years. I hadn't bothered to start grooming a replacement."

Darren grimaced. "You're not dying yet. And since the portal closed, I don't think the Guild is of use anymore. There's no point in continuing it."

"Oh, right," Brigand agreed slowly. "But I *am* dying. All my years are catching up rather quickly." He looked over to the couch. "Make sure somebody reads those. It's likely that Conrad had something important to say."

"Okay, we will," Darren said as he reached over and gathered up the notebooks. He glanced back to Dr. Chelsea. "Are you sure there's nothing to be done?"

The doctor set her bag on the coffee table and rummaged through it. "I can give a vitamin shot, although I doubt it will be much good."

Brigand shook his head. "Don't. I don't think it matters." He let out another raspy cough. "You go now. Take care of Anne and Hank. And translate the journals."

"If you're sure," Darren replied with doubt. "I'll come check in later."

"Go," Brigand repeated as he slumped back into the soft chair.

After leading the doctor back outside, Darren used his master key to lock the bolt.

They returned to Anne's room and found no change to her condition.

Dr. Chelsea lingered in the doorway as Darren set the journals on the nightstand next to Anne's bed. "If there's nothing else, I should go."

"Oh, of course. Thank you for coming back again."

"You ring me if there is any change at all. Otherwise, I'll come back in two days to check her." The doctor turned and let herself out.

Darren sat on the edge of the bed and took Anne's hand. "I know this may not be the time for bad news, Sis, but without the magic, Brigand is dying."

"Do *what*?" Hank asked from the doorway. "What the hell's going on around here?"

"Tex," Darren greeted as he dropped Anne's hand and stood up. "You're awake."

"Yeah, I've been up awhile," Hank said as he stepped into the room. "What's with Anne?"

"I found her in a coma this morning."

"Why?" Hank asked. "I thought she just hurt her back."

Darren nodded. "Yes, she did. The healer was just here and she's rather confused about it all."

Hank frowned as he stepped closer. "What was that about Brigand?"

"Brigand is dying of old age," Darren replied.

"Well, holy fucking shit," Hank cursed. "Just when I thought it couldn't get any worse."

"You and me both," Darren said.

Hank let out a sigh. "Brigand still owes me some answers. You stay here with Anne and I'll go talk to him."

"Okay," Darren agreed as he reached into his pocket for his keys. He separated the master key from the others and handed them to Hank. "This will unlock his door. I doubt he'll answer a knock."

Hank took the keys without saying more. He turned and let himself out.

HANK UNLOCKED the door and let himself into Brigand's apartment. He walked into the living room. He had to stifle a gasp when he saw Brigand's shriveled condition. His stark-white hair was now visibly thinning and falling out.

Brigand looked up, squinting his eyes as he peered across the room. "Is that Hank?"

"Yes," he answered as he walked over and sat on the couch next to the elder's chair. "Darren said you weren't feeling well."

Brigand let out a chuckle that turned into harsh coughs. "You grow more Irish every day. You've mastered the art of understatement."

"At least you're well enough to be messing with me," Hank said with a grin.

Brigand leaned back and closed his eyes. "Did Darr send you?"

"No," Hank said. "I was curious about what you *didn't* say the other day. It seemed you were covering something up for Anne."

Brigand sat without answering. "Apologies," he finally said. "My mind is a bit fuzzy. I don't recall the subject."

"When we were talking about her readings. Now that she's in a coma, I can't ask her, but maybe *you* know."

"What about her readings?"

"Why I'm so frigging important, or might have been, or whatever."

"Oh," Brigand said before pausing. "I don't know much myself, Anne was never very clear about it, but she seemed to think that you and Darren were somehow the key to all this."

"Me *and* Darren? What do you mean by that?"

"I never understood it myself, so I can't offer explanation," Brigand said with a shrug. "You'll have to ask Anne when she wakes up."

"Okay, then. What do you mean by 'key'?"

Brigand was silent so long, Hank started to wonder if he was going to answer, but then he said, "She thought you were the answer to the portal problem."

"Are you talking about just keeping it open last night? Or do you mean she thought there would be a way to reopen it?"

Brigand shook his head. "Whatever her thoughts were, she never divulged them to me." He opened his eyes, then reached over and grabbed Hank's hand. "Just don't leave anytime soon."

"What if I have to?"

"Then none of this matters," Brigand said as he dropped Hank's hand. "Just move along. *I* certainly can't stop you." He ended his defeated statement with a raspy wheeze.

Hank just sat in silence, twirling the Claddagh ring on his finger. "What about the journals? Did you find anything in them?"

"No. My eyesight is already failing, I left them for Anne to…," he said, trailing off. "Leave me to myself, I grow weary."

"Ya sure? I could get you some food, or a drink, if you need it," Hank said, his concern deepening his Texan drawl.

Brigand shook his head. "Doubtful I could keep it down. Leave me."

Hank stood up. He looked at the Brigand's withered face and wondered if he shouldn't stay. It didn't seem as though the man had much time left.

Brigand closed his eyes and sank deeper into the chair. "I need a nap. Go check on Anne."

With one glance back, Hank left the living room and went out the front door, locking it before going back to the main house.

Chapter 21

THE MIDMORNING sun's rays eventually angled over to shine upon the muddy clover in the center of the green. The mud soon warmed and began drying out.

Tiny cracks grew on the surface of the ground under the sun's heat. The germ of the little hawthorn sprout expanded and stretched up in the loosening soil, its beanlike seed pods pushing higher and breaking through the dirt as it reached for the warmth. Green sparkles danced in the sunlight that shined on the surface of the seed pods as they spread apart to expose the first set of leaf buds.

Underground, the taproot of the hawthorn sprout received a spurt of growth. The cells at the tip of the root continued dividing, reaching deeper into the earth. Then, the cells sensed something to the east. Some exciting force enticed them.

The cells at the tip of taproot shifted their direction, stretching and growing sideways toward the excitement.

NO BIG surprise—Hank found Darren once again sitting at Anne's bedside. This time, when Hank walked into Anne's room, he noticed the stack of journals sitting on the nightstand.

"How is he?" Darren asked without looking up.

"Not good at all. His eyesight is gone and his hair is falling out. I don't think he'll last much longer."

Darren just nodded in acknowledgment.

Hank studied Darren as he sat on the edge of the bed, holding Anne's hand. He could see the mud and clover stains on the knees of Darren's jeans, and he looked almost as tired as Brigand. "What about you? How long have you been sitting in here?"

Darren shrugged. "For a bit."

"Then you should grab a shower and go get us something from the pub. I can sit with Anne."

When Darren didn't move, Hank stepped closer. "Go to the kitchen at least. Anne's bound to have some food there. Eat something."

Darren sat another moment. "Hank says I need to eat," he told Anne as he gently placed her hand upon her stomach. "I'll be back in a bit."

ANNE HEARD Darren leaving and wanted to scream again. She wanted to move, wanted to act, but her conscious mind couldn't seem to connect to her body. This was just like that dream she'd had of being trapped in a box, unable to move or call out for help.

She had lain here all morning, getting more frustrated. She tried again to move her hand. Concentrating, she willed the movement of her fingers, but nothing happened.

Changing tactics, Anne tried to take a deep breath, but her breathing didn't change; it just continued at the same, steady rate.

Darren, she tried to cry out again. Then, some force overwhelmed her and put her to sleep.

WHEN DARREN walked into Anne's kitchen, he noticed right away the notepad and pen his sister had left on the kitchen table as he crossed the room to peek into the refrigerator. Digging around, he found all the items to make a sandwich, but that seemed like too much trouble, so he simply grabbed a small block of the cheese and closed the door.

After fishing in the cabinet drawer for a knife, Darren sat at the kitchen table.

As he cut off a slice of cheese then slowly chewed on it, he glanced at the notebook. Anne had written a short list of names with phone numbers. Curious about what Anne might have been up to, Darren moved the notebook closer and turned it around. One of the names had a little star doodled next to it.

As he chewed another slice of cheese, Darren retrieved his phone from his pocket. Maybe Anne had gotten some kind of premonition and left these numbers behind for Darren to find. He decided to start with the one that had the star next to it. He dialed the number next to Nora's name.

After two rings, a female voice answered, "Hello?"

"Hello. This is Darren O'Connell and I'm calling on behalf of my sister, Anne."

"Oh. I hope I didn't misunderstand, I thought today's appointment was for 2:00 p.m."

Darren wondered what kind of appointment she had set, but he would likely have to cancel it. "I'm afraid she won't be up to it. Anne has taken a turn for the worse."

"I'm sorry to hear that," Nora said with sincerity. "Does she no longer require a home-care nurse? She seemed rather insistent I come by today."

Darren paused. Maybe his sister had foreknowledge of this illness and had already seen to the details of her care. That definitely sounded like something Anne would do, so Darren decided to go along with her wishes. "Actually, she does. But my sister slipped into a coma last night and I don't know if that's the kind of care you can provide."

"Of course it is. I am fully trained and certified. I can be there by 11:00 a.m. if you need me to start early."

Darren thought about it and saw no reason to delay. "That would be fine. I'll expect you at 11:00 a.m., then."

"Until later," Nora said before hanging up.

HANK SAT on the edge of Anne's bed, trying not to look at her as he waited for Darren to return. That glassy-eyed stare kind of creeped him out a bit.

Getting bored, Hank reached over and picked up the top journal notebook from the nightstand. He thumbed through it, but it was not much more than gibberish to him.

He put the notebook back when he heard Darren come in. "Did you eat?"

"Yes. I also discovered Anne must have foreseen this. Earlier in the week, she hired a nurse to start work this afternoon."

"Oh," Hank drawled out, not really sure how to respond to that. The burn on his chest started itching. He thought it might be time for more salve. "I'm going back to your place," he told Darren as he stepped by him on his way out. Darren didn't reply as he went to Anne's bedside.

After making the trek to Darren's spare bedroom, Hank grabbed the jar of burn ointment. He carried it down the hall to bathroom, thinking it would be easier to use the mirror as he applied the goop.

Once in the bathroom, he pulled off his T-shirt and coated the burn with the ointment. He felt relieved to see that the sizzled area looked even better than last time he had checked. Except for the spiderweb lines of welts. Those hadn't receded any yet.

Hank put the lid back on the jar and took it back to the spare bedroom. A yawn crept up on him. He looked at the bed. *Maybe a short nap*, he thought as he crawled onto the mattress. He stretched out, barely having time to finish another yawn before falling asleep.

HANK STARTLED awake. Thinking he had heard a noise, he lay still, listening. Then he heard a strange beep. He got up and slowly walked to the doorway. He heard an electronic crashing noise. It sounded like it came from the kitchen.

Still moving slowly, Hank stepped into the hall and noticed the aroma of brewing coffee as he walked to the kitchen. Inside the room, he found Darren sitting at the café table, playing with his phone. "Hey," he said as he went to the sink and rinsed out a mug.

Darren fiddled with his phone. "Get enough sleep?"

"What time is it?" Hank asked as he poured himself a mug full of coffee.

"1:59 p.m.," Darren replied without looking up. Another blooping noise issued from the phone.

"I figured you'd still be with Anne," Hank said lazily as he sat at the table.

"Nurse evicted me," Darren replied as he pushed at the phone screen. "Said I was hovering too much."

"How is she?"

"No change."

"What are you doing?"

"A silly app called 'Angry Birds,'" Darren replied without looking up.

Hank leaned over. "Oh, that game with the slingshot," Hank said. He took another sip of coffee. "So, what now?"

"What do you mean?" Another crashing noise came from the phone.

"I mean, have you looked at Cona's books? Can you decode them?"

"Not my bailiwick," Darren said absently.

"What about the garden—the green. Has anyone been to check? In case we need to clean up?"

"No need. Reavers don't leave much behind."

"What *are* those reaver things?"

"Evil shadows," Darren replied as another crashing noise came from the phone, followed by a short, cheery fanfare of music.

Hank didn't like this change in attitude. Only yesterday, he and Darren couldn't be in the same room together without touching each other, but now Darren was practically ignoring him. "Darren, put the phone away. I'm trying to talk to you."

"I'm talking," Darren replied.

"Not really. You're being rude," Hank drawled out.

Darren looked up with an edge of pain in his gaze. "Am I not being a proper host?" he asked sarcastically. "Everything last night was an utter disaster, Brigand and my sister are probably dying, but no." Darren pushed a button on the screen and set the phone down on the table. "Let's *do* make sure Tex is properly entertained on his visit." He looked at Hank with a hardened expression.

Hank lowered his eyes. "No need to be like that."

Darren sighed in frustration. "Then tell me how to be. What would make you happy?"

"Right now? Nothing really. This isn't much of a happy occasion."

"So sorry to disappoint," Darren said, the edge of sarcasm thickening his Irish accent. He looked down at his phone. "Maybe you should return home."

Hank flinched back. Of all the things Darren could have suggested, he honestly hadn't expected that. He studied Darren's stoic face. "Do you want me to leave?"

"Do *you* want to leave?"

Hank took a deep breath. If Darren was going to continue to be so cold, maybe going home *would* be the best option. Yet doing so would be a final move. He didn't want to give in to defeat so readily. "I still keep thinking there's some way to fix things. We haven't even *tried* to do anything yet."

"And what do you suggest we do?"

"I don't know," Hank said in frustration. "But there have to be options."

Darren shook his head. "Wishing for options won't make them appear. With the magic gone, there isn't anything to work with," he said with a tone of defeat.

Hank reached across the table, resting his hand near Darren. "I'm not giving up yet."

Keeping his hands in his lap, Darren shrugged. "I don't think you have a choice."

Hank nudged his hand closer to Darren. "All the other shit aside, what about *us*?"

Darren looked back with a flat expression. "What *about* us?" He shook his head. "We had some fun, it was nice, but now it's time to move on."

Hank pulled his hand back as he felt the insulting sting. "*Nice?* Really? I thought it was a hell of a lot more than just 'nice.'" He studied Darren's face, looking for any signs of emotion under that flat expression. "Didn't you *feel* anything? I sure as hell did."

Darren's face showed a flash of sad remorse before going flat again. "Maybe I did. Maybe, if circumstances were different, there might have been something. As things are now, it doesn't matter."

"What circumstances?"

After a frustrated sigh, Darren said, "The most obvious one being that you live 5,000 miles away. In a foreign country. That kind of long distance rather limits our contact."

"But that can change," Hank argued.

"Oh? Are you moving here?"

Hank paused. "There's nothing preventing that, if I had a reason to. And I wouldn't necessarily have to be the one to move. You could come to Texas."

Darren let out a bitter laugh. "You've thought all of this through already, have you? That seems *quite* premature." He paused. "With Anne's current condition, I don't want to leave the house, much less move to another country."

With a sigh, Hank sank back into his chair. "Why are you giving up so easily?"

"I'm merely being practical," Darren replied, his accent sounding more crisply British.

They both sat in a silence of unspoken words, avoiding each other's gaze.

Moments later, Darren stood. "I should go check on Anne."

Hank nodded. "Have you been to look in on Brigand lately?"

Darren fished his keys out of his pocket and tossed them onto the table before he turned to leave. "*You* may do so."

AS HE passed through the connecting courtyard, Darren let out a heavy sigh. He struggled not to lose his resolve. He hated treating Hank this way, but it was for the Texan's own good. Hank would be better off if he extracted himself from this ugly mess and fled while he still could. Darren only wished he had the same kind of exit options, but there was no way he could abandon Brigand or Anne to face their fates alone.

Darren stepped into his sister's room. Nora, the elderly nurse, had brought in one of the dining room chairs, where she now sat with a book next to Anne's bed. He cleared his throat to interrupt her reading. "Any change?"

"None, sir," she replied without looking up.

Darren saw the pile of dirty clothes in front of the nightstand, and he noticed Anne was now safely tucked under the bedcovers. The nurse must have bathed and changed her. He walked over and sat on the bed. "Anne," he said gently to her as he took her hand. "If you need more time, Sis, that's okay. But make sure to wake up once you're healed. We're all worried about you."

Anne showed no sign of response.

INSIDE HERSELF, Anne struggled to be heard. *Help me, Darr, I'm here,* she tried screaming with her mind. She tried taking control of her eyelids and blinking without success before something put her to sleep again.

HANK LET himself into Brigand's apartment. Stepping into the living room, he saw the emaciated body of Brigand. He was so thin and frail now, he hardly looked like more than a stain on the overstuffed chair in the dimly lit room. Brigand's face had withered so much, it brought to mind one of those old horror-movie mummies.

Thinking the man had passed away, Hank startled when Brigand took a wheezy breath. "Brigand?" he called out softly.

Not dead, just asleep, Hank thought. He stood for a moment and watched the elder's slow, shallow breaths.

Hank turned to leave. The tempo of Brigand's inhale changed. He thought he heard Brigand say something, so he turned back and sat at the end of the couch. "Did you say something?"

"Stay," Brigand repeated in a soft whisper.

"Sure, I can stay with you," Hank reassured. "Would you like some water, or maybe a bite to eat?"

Brigand shook his head with tiny movements. "Talk," he whispered.

"You want to talk?" Hank asked. "What do you want to talk about?"

"Stay."

Hank felt uncomfortable. Not only was the man struggling just to get out each word, now he was repeating himself. Unless he meant.... "Are you asking me to stay in Ireland?"

Brigand nodded ever so slightly. He seemed relieved as he took a deeper breath. "Mike."

"What about Mike?"

After another breath, Brigand said, "Languages."

"I don't understand."

"Notebooks," Brigand wheezed out before a phlegmy cough overtook him.

Hank took a second to put it all together. "You're saying Mike can help decode Cona's journals?"

Brigand nodded slightly as he slowly raised a hand and pointed to the coffee table.

Looking over, Hank saw the rolodex. He reached out and picked it up. "Mike's number is here?"

Brigand coughed again. "Families."

Hank twirled the old rolodex until he found the *F* entries and a subtab for "Families." He saw some familiar names of the Guild members on the index cards as he thumbed through them. He soon found the one for Mike O'Reilly. He pulled the card out of the device. "Okay. I'll call him."

Slowly, Brigand moved his hand back to his lap. "Hope," he said.

"What do you mean? Is that someone else I should contact?" Hank asked as he looked through the index cards again, searching for the name "Hope."

Brigand shook his head. "Keep."

"Oh." Hank suddenly realized. "You're saying to keep hope, don't lose faith."

"Everybody."

"Everybody? What do you mean?"

"All fading."

Hank thought aloud as he recalled Darren's mention of the Pandora's Box story. "You mean, hope itself is fading for everyone?"

With a nod, Brigand coughed again.

"I'm trying to keep hope," Hank said as he put the rolodex back on the coffee table. "But Darren's not making it easy. He told me to go home."

"Don't," Brigand wheezed out.

"I won't. I promise. And I'll call Mike."

"Yule."

"Stay until Yule? That's near Christmas?"

"Yes."

Hank shrugged. "I'll try, I don't know if I can promise that long."

"Please?"

"Okay, I'll do my best."

Brigand nodded, then closed his eyes.

Hank stood up. Brigand seemed so near to death, Hank vacillated between thoughts of leaving or staying.

"Go call," Brigand said.

"Okay, I'll go," Hank said. He walked to the door and quietly let himself out.

After returning to the main house, he went to Anne's room. An unfamiliar woman sat in a chair next to the bed. Hank thought she looked like an old crone as he glanced over. Her chiseled wrinkles made him think of the Cliffs of Moher he had recently visited.

Hank stepped to the head of the bed. "Hey, Anne," he said as he drew near.

The nurse looked up from her book. "And you are...?" she asked pointedly.

"I'm Hank. The…." He paused, not really sure how to describe himself to the nurse. "A houseguest of Darren's."

"I'm Nora; don't stay too long," the nurse said. "I'm going to try and spoon-feed her in a bit. See if she takes to it."

"Okay." Hank took a step back to the nightstand. "I'll come see you later, Anne." Hank reached down and picked up the notebooks. "Brigand said I should borrow these for Mike," he said as he turned to leave.

The nurse didn't look up as Hank carried the journals out. He decided to settle in the large parlor. He set the books on the coffee table and got out the rolodex card. Now he just needed a phone. Hank scolded himself for not thinking to borrow Brigand's.

Maybe Anne has a house phone, he thought. He hadn't seen one in the parlor area, so he walked over and peeked into the kitchen. Glancing around, he didn't see a wall phone of any sort, but then he spotted the cell phone sitting on the kitchen counter by the sink.

After calling Mike and asking him to come to Anne's house, Hank put the phone back on the counter and looked in the fridge. He took one of the bottled waters before returning to the parlor to wait.

Chapter 22

IT DIDN'T take too long for the doorbell to chime. Hank went to the entry hall and opened the main door. He smiled at Mike. In the evening light, Mike's spiky red hair reminded Hank of flames.

"Hello, Hank," Mike greeted.

Hank noticed how Mike fidgeted on the stoop, looking a bit nervous. "Come in," Hank said as he opened the door wider.

"What's this about?" Mike asked as he followed Hank to the parlor.

Mike relaxed visibly when Hank explained about translating the journals and how it was a favor for Brigand.

After telling Mike that he couldn't take the books home to work on, Hank had to hunt around in the library room for a blank legal pad and a pen.

Hank left Mike in the parlor to work on the project and stepped outside into the adjoining courtyard.

He lit a cigarette and took a heavy drag. It seemed boringly normal out here now without undefined shadows, mysterious movements, or strange cats lurking about.

Hearing the doorknob turn, Hank looked over to see Darren leaving his apartment. He wanted to ask why Darren had been avoiding him but thought that might be too antagonistic, so he just said, "Hey."

"Did you check Anne?" Darren asked as he stepped closer.

Hank couldn't help but notice how Darren still stood almost three feet away, like he was keeping a buffer zone. "Yeah, nurse kind of hustled me out, though. She's gonna try spoon-feeding."

"Oh. Then I should wait a bit longer. Is Brigand…?"

"Still alive," Hank said. "Told me to call Mike about the journals. He's in there now, working on them."

"You called Mike?"

Didn't I just say that? Hank wanted to snap back, but he held his tongue. "Yes. I'm getting the feeling that you don't like Mike."

"I *do* like Mike, it's just…."

"What?"

"He has a bit of a reputation, and it makes me anxious when he's around you."

Hank almost chuckled. "You mean, you're jealous?"

"Of course not," Darren defended quickly. Then he just shrugged.

"What do you mean by 'reputation'?"

"Mike's well known for promiscuity. Plus, he often ignores boundaries."

"Ah, he's a slutty ring-chaser. Got it," Hank said, puzzled over the implications. If Darren felt nervous about having Mike around, then he must think of them as being some kind of couple with boundaries to protect. *So why did Darren try so hard to pretend he* didn't *care and tell me to leave earlier today?*

"Ring-chaser?" Darren asked.

"Someone who gets off on pursuing married or otherwise committed people."

Darren nodded slowly. "That sounds about right."

Hank stomped out the cigarette, then picked up the butt before putting it in his pocket. "Don't you think I can take care of myself?"

"It's not *you* that I'm concerned about."

"Don't worry, I can handle Mike," Hank said while studying Darren. Then, he recalled how nervous Mike had been when he arrived earlier. It was doubtful Mike would be afraid of *him,* so that meant…. "But it isn't me *or* Mike you're really worried about, is it?" Hank said pointedly.

Darren didn't say anything.

"Do *you* have a reputation?"

Stiffening, Darren didn't reply.

"Tell me what's up," Hank urged.

After a moment, Darren's shoulders slumped. "I've told you my past. The alleys are still part of me in a way. Sometimes, my first reaction to things is anger and…." Darren dropped his eyes. "I can be a little aggressive. It's not something I'm proud of. But it's mostly in the past."

Mentally, Hank translated Darren's statements from Irish to Texan: *I still have a rough edge and a hot temper, driving me to beat the shit out of people when I get defensive.* "How many fights have you had?"

"Just a few, not many. I'm working to manage it."

"How many?" Hank asked again. When Darren didn't reply, he added, "Are we talking three, or a dozen, or a hundred?"

Darren looked wounded when Hank mentioned a hundred. He shook his head. "Maybe half a dozen serious ones."

"Okay," Hank said, internally feeling a sigh of relief at the relatively low number. It worked out to less than two incidents for each decade of his life. "When was the most recent?"

"Over three years ago." Darren took a step closer.

"That doesn't sound like it's *too* out of control. It doesn't bother me. Like you said, it's the past."

Darren relaxed a bit more, but he didn't smile. "We should see if Mike is making any progress."

"Sure," Hank agreed as he led Darren back into the main house.

GRATEFULLY, DARREN noticed Mike proved to be quite a whiz with the decryption. He burned away in the parlor—already consuming two journal pages and starting on the third one. "May I?" Darren asked, peering over to read the legal pad.

Mike suddenly looked up. "Oh, hi. I didn't hear anyone come in," he said while putting down the pen and then pushing the pad across the table to Darren.

Darren read the decoded Gaelic, shaking his head. "Diabhal," he muttered under his breath.

"What does it say?" Hank asked as he sat on the divan.

"He's talking about the arc movements of suspended water bodies, whatever the devil that's supposed to mean." Darren handed the notebook back to Mike. "Keep going. Hopefully, *something* useful is buried in his ramblings."

Mike picked up the pen and went back to the task.

Hank stood up. "Let's go peek in on Anne."

Without reply, Darren led the way down the hall. They stepped into Anne's room. The nurse was in the dining chair reading, but she must have been up at one point, for one of those hospital tables now extended over Anne's bed. "How did the feeding go?"

"Not well," Nora replied without looking up. "She chewed, but didn't swallow properly. Maybe I'll try again tomorrow."

Darren rolled the table so it hovered over Anne's feet, leaving room for him to sit on the bed next to his sister. "Hey Anne. I'm back. Did the food taste good?"

Anne showed no reply.

Darren suddenly realized how rude he was for not making introductions. "Pardon me. Nora, this is Hank."

"Hello," Nora replied.

"We met earlier," Hank said.

"Oh right, of course." Darren turned back to Anne and gently cradled her hand. "Mike's busy working on the journals. Even after translating them, they still don't make much sense. We need you to wake up, Anne, so you can help us."

ANNE AWAKENED again when Darr took her hand. She heard his words and wondered what the devil was going on out there. *How is Brigand?* she tried to ask aloud. No one had mentioned Brigand.

She had to give them some sign that she could hear. Focusing again on her eyes, she tried to take control and force a blink. *Come on, blink,* she thought as she struggled to move the eyelids.

Nothing happened.

Another wave of sleep overwhelmed her and she went under.

ONCE AGAIN, that chaotic noise from above bombarded Skeena. The situation was growing more uncomfortable for her. She could continue sending out blasts of calm, but each one required almost as much energy as what she collected.

This wasn't the best use of resources. She sent out another calming pulse of energy to quiet things down while she pondered another solution.

OUT OF the corner of his eye, Darren saw the nurse put down her book and turn their direction. "My replacement, Tyler, should be here soon. We'll both be here for twelve-hour shifts until we can line up a third nurse."

"Is it already 11:00 p.m.?" Darren asked.

"Nearly so," Nora replied.

"Thank you," Darren said. "My sister made a good choice in hiring you." Nora seemed steady as stone when it came to her job. "How shall I pay you?"

Nora shook her head. "No need. Anne already set up a payment system with the agency we work through. That's all settled, as far as I know."

Darren nodded. "Thank you."

The chime of the doorbell echoed through the house. Darren patted Anne's hand before letting go. He moved quickly to the front door and opened it to find a small young man smiling up at him. His windswept, wavy, charcoal curls fanned away from his face, looking stark beside his cloudy blue eyes.

"Mr. O'Connell?" the man greeted.

"Darr," he corrected, motioning the man in. "You must be Tyler."

"Yessir," Tyler said as he breezed through the door. "Your sister is the one in need of care?"

"Right this way." Darren led Tyler to Anne's room. His initial reaction was that the guy seemed a little young. Yet, Nora was a very down-to-earth kind of lady, so he decided to trust her judgment. She was too no-nonsense to pick someone unqualified for her team. "Anne," he announced as he stepped into her bedroom. "This is Tyler."

Tyler stepped in. "Good evening, Anne, Nora," he said, nodding his head to each woman.

"Come, Tyler," Nora called, pulling out her iPad. "Let me go over some notes with you."

While Tyler hurried around the bed, Darren waved. "I'll leave you to it." Not thinking of any other place to go, Darren made his way to the parlor. Hunched over the short coffee table, Mike continued his steady blaze of progress, having scorched through one journal and started another.

Darren loudly cleared his throat. "Would you be more comfortable in the library?"

Mike looked up. "No, this is fine. What time is it?"

"11:00 p.m."

"Shite!" Mike exclaimed as he jumped up. "I'm late for work." He flared past Darren and aimed for the door.

"I didn't know your schedule, or I'd have let you know," Darren yelled before he heard the front door close.

Darren sank down to the divan and picked up the legal pad of decoded words, starting the slow process of reading through the Gaelic. He felt disappointed as he continued reading. Most of it was scatterings of strange phrases that didn't make much sense, or even seem to relate to each other in any way.

Trying to maintain some optimism, he flipped to the second page and read more. Then he found a section that jumped out at him:

> Lights in circling dance. Twirling. Enhancing energy. Two Fae magnifying magic with four elements. Intensify, Focus, Rectify, Cauterize. Six in the center: three circles around. Amplify and Mesmerize.

Could that have something to do with the device? Darren wondered with a touch of excitement. The gyroscope had three bands, and the other section could refer to the six symbols on the hexagonal base. They had already identified three of the symbols for the cardinal elements: wind, mountain, and ocean. *Maybe the last one is fire? If that's the case, then it sounds like the device was meant to amplify energy somehow.*

Farther down the page, Darren found:

Sister, Friend, Elder, Youth, Contain. Brother, Lover, Conjoin. Ignition intense.

The last phrase seemed peculiar because those two words were written in English. But as he thought about it, Darren realized there wouldn't be a way to really express that thought in the older Gaelic language. The concept of machine ignition would be too modern for Middle Gaelic.

He read through the rest of the phrases Mike had finished decoding so far, but didn't find anything else that seemed relevant.

With a disappointed sigh, Darren flipped back and read those notable passages again. He tried to ignore the demoralizing decline he felt as he put the notebook back on the coffee table.

Darren got up and walked through the courtyard and into his own flat.

He saw the hexagon gyroscope still sitting on his coffee table as he passed by. He stopped to look at it, thinking about what he had just read as he peered over the ivory rings and carved symbols on the base. Even if his deduction were true, if this device did somehow amplify magical energy, it would be useless now. It wouldn't be possible to amplify something that no longer existed. He felt like he had gotten his hopes up for nothing.

As THE moon climbed higher in the midnight sky, the clouds thinned enough to let its light shine into Shamrock Green.

The bright moon rays fell upon the tiny leaves of the hawthorn sprout nestled in the clover. Its unique properties illuminated sparkles on the sprout.

Like an excited living thing, the green energy pulsed and flowed around and through the sprout's leaves while basking in the compatible silver glow of moonlight. The tiny plant grew quickly as the energy grew, expanding its leaves, its stem stretching and reaching up to the cool light as new leaf buds swelled on the stem's surface.

Underground, the taproot also experienced the surge of growth and reached farther east in spurting steps, growing closer to that enticing spot.

HANK SAT alone at the kitchen café table, slowly nursing a bottle of Harp. He kept thinking about what Brigand had said. His statement that everyone was losing hope seemed to be holding true. Hank had seen signs of it from Brigand, Mike, Darren; even Nora the nurse didn't seem very optimistic. *So,* Hank wondered, *why am I the only one who can see it and not be affected?*

He reached out to pick up the beer bottle. The clink of his ring against the glass drew his attention. The ring had been so "quiet," he'd almost forgotten he was wearing it. Thinking back as he took another swallow of beer, Hank hadn't "felt" anything from the Claddagh ring since last night—not since the portal closed, he realized.

After setting the bottle down, he pulled his hand near his face to look at the ring. He saw nothing peculiar; even the spangold had lost its mysterious shimmer. Now, it was nothing more than a compressed carbon stone, set in a band of dead metal, wrapped around his finger.

He looked up when he heard someone coming into the hall.

Darren stepped up to the café table and stopped. "Mike completed quite a bit of the cipher, but the ramblings are useless. We probably shouldn't bother to have him waste his time on continuing."

Hank couldn't help but notice Darren had positioned himself with the café table acting as a buffer between them. "If Mike wants to continue, I see no harm in letting him finish," he argued. "How's Anne?"

"Still the same. The nurses are a bit close-lipped about her condition."

"Nurses?" Hank asked. "There's a new one?"

"Tyler, he'll be on the night shift."

"Oh, of course. I'm sure Nora would wanna go home."

Darren stepped to the cabinet drawer and pulled out his pack of cloves. "I'm going outside, then to bed. There's a deli sandwich left in Anne's refrigerator if you get hungry."

"Thanks," Hank said as Darren left the kitchen. "Good night, then." Trying to ignore the downright chilly attitude, he twirled the ring with his thumb.

Maybe, Hank thought, *the ring isn't so dead after all. Maybe it's protecting me from this loss of hope everyone else is suffering.*

LEANING BACK against the old brownstone bricks of the courtyard wall, Darren looked up at the sky and the hazy moon. He used to get comfort from simple joys like this, but he felt nothing from it now. He took another drag of the spicy cigarette.

The responsibility of Anne and Brigand weighed heavily on him. He didn't expect the elder to survive the night, which would lead to all the fuss over dealing with his death. Then there was Anne. Despite her wishes, if she didn't show any improvement soon, he would have to consider sending her to hospital. Doing so would be almost a form of betrayal.

Darren took one last drag, then tamped out the unfinished butt against the brick wall. He always got the kind without filters so he could leave the butt in one of the courtyard planters to break down into compost. Even when he was young and lived in the alleys, he never liked littering.

He glanced up at the moon again, trying not to think about Hank. He would probably still be up, still sitting in the kitchen. Maybe Hank's burn would be healed well enough to accept an invitation to join him in bed. *No,* Darren scolded himself. *Quit thinking with your gonads and keep your distance. No matter what he says right now, Hank will soon abandon us and go home. He has no reason to stay and deal with all this. No sense in clouding the issue further with sex.*

As if the sky reinforced his point, a thick bank of clouds slid in front of the moon, leaving him to make his way back into the flat in near darkness.

HANK DOWNED the last of the beer while watching for Darren to return. He didn't like leaving things this way; their distance felt so wrong to him. He wanted to make some sort of positive connection with Darren before they went to sleep.

When he heard the outside door open, Hank got up. He grabbed the empty beer bottle and dropped it into the glass recycle bin on his way out of the kitchen. He intercepted Darren in the hallway.

"I'm going to bed," Darren said.

Hank reached out to touch Darren's arm. "Can't we talk first? We haven't really seen each other all day."

Darren shook his head. "There's too many things in the air right now, if you hadn't noticed. I'm sorry I don't have time to entertain you properly."

"I'm not talking about that, and you know it. You've been so distant...." Hank trailed off as Darren pulled away from his touch. Hank followed his gaze to the guest bedroom doorway.

"We can talk in the morning. I think you should go to bed now," Darren said before going down the hall to his own bedroom.

Hank stood frozen in the hallway, paralyzed by the squeezing grip in his gut from being excluded. "I don't understand," he yelled out. "Why are you acting this way?"

Darren paused in his doorway and turned back. "Since you're leaving, there's no point in complicating things."

"Who said I was leaving?" He thought about mentioning the promise he had made to Brigand, but that seemed like a bad move, so he didn't say more.

"It's inevitable," Darren said. He turned and stepped into his bedroom, closing the door behind him.

Hank's gut squeezed so hard that he could barely breathe. Seeking support, he took a step nearer the wall and leaned against the doorjamb. Hank closed his eyes and lifted his face to the ceiling, breathing through his nose as he slowly regained his composure. His eyes had started to fill, but thankfully, he had managed to stave off any real tears.

Seeing no other choices, Hank decided he would just go to bed. He went down the hall to bathroom for his nightly ritual.

Gazing in the mirror as he pulled off his T-shirt, Hank felt dismayed at the sight of his chest. The lines of welts had reduced considerably, but now they had the appearance of pink scars, like the design lines resulting from the body decorating practice of scarification. A practice that Hank had never understood.

He couldn't even bring himself to go as far as getting a tattoo. It just seemed like too bold and immutable a statement. What if you get tired of seeing it and change your mind? Too bad, you're stuck with it.

He grabbed the burn cream and applied it liberally, hoping to make the scar lines eventually fade away. He didn't want this giant spiderweb on his chest to be a permanent mark. How would he explain the scars to his mother? Or to anybody for that matter? He couldn't imagine himself actually saying aloud, *Oh that? Just a war wound from when I fought an evil dullahan in Dublin.*

Hank took a deep breath as he stepped around the tub to the toilet. At least the shock of seeing the ugly marks had eased his wrenching gut. After relieving himself, he brushed his teeth, trying to avoid looking at the mirror's reflection of his chest. He then went to the spare bedroom for some sleep.

Chapter 23

DARREN WOKE the next morning. The light glowing through the curtains seemed so dim, he assumed it must still be early morning. He wasn't looking forward to what probably awaited today. He rolled over to try and sleep more, noticing the clock displayed 8:47 a.m. It was much later than he thought.

Despite the time, he didn't get up right away. He knew the next few hours were likely to be busy, so he rolled onto his back and stretched out his legs, enjoying a few moments of quiet before the hectic day began. As he closed his eyes, Darren listened, but didn't hear any rain outside. It must merely be a soft morning.

Turning his head, Darren looked at the clock again and saw 8:52 a.m. *Might as well get to it,* he thought, as he rolled to the edge of the bed and dropped his feet to the floor. He got a clean pair of jeans and a simple light sweater from his armoire. After dressing, he spruced up in the bathroom and made his way to the kitchen.

The aroma of the coffee worked its way into Darren's nose when he was halfway down the hall, so he guessed Hank must be up already. He hesitated. Darren didn't know if he'd be able to face him just yet. The previous night, it had taken all of his resolve to maintain the distance and not cave in to the Texan's charms. Darren didn't know if he'd have the strength to resist Hank this early in the day.

Darren did have the thought to just bypass the kitchen and go directly to Anne's. But the scent of the coffee was so enticing. Then he recalled leaving his pack of cloves in the kitchen drawer. He would have to go in eventually. Darren straightened his spine, put on a stage smile, and strolled into the room.

He moved quickly past Hank at the café table and aimed for the sink. After rinsing a mug, he poured some of the coffee into it. He turned around and leaned his butt against the counter, holding the mug in front of him like a shield.

"Morning," Hank said quietly as he thumbed through a book.

"Morning," Darren replied. He looked over but couldn't tell what book Hank was reading. Then he noticed Hank also had the Tiffany box on the table and felt a jolt of protectiveness. "What's that doing in here?"

"Just wanted another peek at it," Hank said. Then he closed the book and looked up. "Why don't you ever wear it?"

"*Wear* it?" Darren scoffed, thinking it was a stupidly silly question. "It's a precious ancient heirloom, valuable beyond measure." He turned to the upper drawer and retrieved a clove fag from the pack and lit it.

"But it's also a necklace, meant to be worn," Hank countered calmly. "Meant to be worn by an O'Connell. Right?"

"That doesn't mean I *should* wear it," Darren said, as he took another drag, then thumped the ash into the sink. "It's better protected if it stays in the box." He watched as Hank absently twirled his Claddagh ring with his thumb. "Where is all this coming from?"

Hank shrugged. "Just a notion." He picked up his mug and took a few big swallows.

"A notion of what?"

"Well, I'm not as up to speed with all this magic stuff, but...." Hank paused, looking at the box as he searched for words. "I've been watching everybody. Then Brigand told me he could feel hope fading, and I remembered the Pandora's Box story you mentioned. Everybody else is losing hope, but I seem to be unaffected." Hank shrugged again. "I thought, maybe the ring is somehow protecting me. And maybe *your* charm would do the same for you."

Darren's first instinct was to argue that he wasn't losing hope, he was simply being realistic, but he stopped himself from saying that. He took one last drag as he thought over Hank's words. *Maybe he's right.*

He turned on the sink tap enough to get a small stream and doused the tip before throwing the butt in the waste bin. *It does seem as though everyone else is losing hope.*

Hank spoke again. "It couldn't hurt to at least wear it for the day, see if it makes any difference."

Darren looked at the stained glass box. He'd only been brave enough to wear the faery-tree heirloom once in his life and that had been to Aunt Oli's funeral. *Hank's right, it can't hurt,* he thought as he stepped across the room and opened the box.

Reaching inside, he gently lifted the spangold pendant. He noticed that the tree didn't seem to have quite the pearlescent shimmer he recalled from before. The metal looked more like mottled silver. *Maybe it's just the kitchen's poor lighting,* he tried to tell himself, avoiding thoughts of the closed portal.

He tied the leather cord around his neck, letting the tree sit on top of his sweater. He felt a bit silly wearing the large ornament. "Maybe I can also get some complimentary fat gold chains, then I can look like an LA rapper," he joked.

"Put it *under* your shirt, against your skin," Hank said.

Darren lifted his sweater collar and tucked the charm behind it. The metal felt cold against his upper chest. "I should go check on Brigand now," he said as he patted his jeans pocket to make sure he had his phone. He felt the reassuring solid rectangle. "You still have my keys."

"Yeah, and I'm gonna go grab that sandwich you mentioned," Hank said, pushing back from the table and standing. He pulled the keys from his pocket and set them on the café table.

Darren grabbed the keys, and then they walked into the living room without speaking more. As Darren stepped out the front door, Hank called out, "Later."

INSIDE THE tomb-like gloom of Brigand's flat, Darren made his way to the living room. He moved quietly, feeling self-conscious about disturbing the subdued silence surrounding him.

Brigand's parched and frail body had sunken deeper into the overstuffed chair; his unfocused eyes stared into his lap. Darren stood over him a moment, wondering who to call first. Anne and Brigand usually took care of all the funeral arrangements. He'd also have to remember to turn on the tolling bell.

The Persian cat let out a yowl from somewhere in the kitchen.

After hunting around in the cabinets, Darren found some cans of food and opened one for her. She seemed too impatient to wait for him to put it in her bowl, so Darren just set the can down on the floor before returning to the front room.

Darren stepped over to Brigand's chair, then leaned down to push the elder's eyelids closed. The sudden grasp of bony fingers on his wrist startled a squeal from him. His knees nearly buckled under him as he pulled back.

"Journals?" Brigand's voice asked in a strangled whisper.

"The journals?" Darren echoed, trying to re-collect his composure. "Mike is working on them."

"Helpful?"

Darren shook his head. "A few interesting tidbits, but nothing really helpful yet."

Brigand let go of his wrist. "Love?"

"Love?" Darren repeated, confused by the strange shift in conversation.

"Hank."

"Love Hank?" Darren still wasn't quite following.

"You," Brigand struggled to wheeze out.

"Do I love Hank? Is that what you're asking?"

Brigand bent his head in a tiny nod.

"Isn't that a bit premature?"

"Love Hank?" Brigand asked again.

"He's only been here a few days, how can—"

"Love Hank?"

Darren leaned closer. "It wouldn't be wise. He'll be leaving soon."

"Yah or nah?"

Feeling a rising frustration at being grilled like this, Darren replied, "It's too complicated for such—"

Brigand grabbed Darren's wrist again. "Love Hank?"

Darren tried to deflect the question. "Why are you asking?"

Squeezing Darren's wrist and pulling him closer, Brigand whispered, "Yah or nay?"

Frustration boiling over, Darren blurted out, "Maybe!"

Brigand let go of his wrist.

Darren stood and started pacing around the chair. "Despite all the reasons I shouldn't, I *could* love Hank. I don't know how I could get this close to him so fast." He stopped in front of Brigand. "Why are you asking that? Is there something you're not telling me?"

"Nap," Brigand said, closing his eyes.

"Oh, no you don't, old lad," Darren said as he leaned down and put his hand on Brigand's arm. "You spill first. *Then* you can have a nap."

Brigand's mouth pulled into a little smile. "Ask Anne." He closed his eyes again.

Darren patted the wrinkled skin of the arm. "It would be easier if *you* just tell me," Darren said as he stroked the old man's arm and rubbed his bony knuckles.

Brigand let out a coughing chuckle. "Your gift. Won't work. On me."

"Bastard," Darren said as he withdrew his hand from Brigand and stood up. "Anne's still in a coma. *You* have to answer."

Keeping his eyes closed, Brigand ignored Darren.

Darren paced again. "I hate it when you two do this. You know more than you're telling, I know you do." He stopped in front of Brigand. Obviously, the man wasn't going to say more. He let out a frustrated sigh. "Fine, then. I'm going."

ENTERING ANNE'S room, Darren saw Tyler sitting in the chair with the iPad in his lap. He could see on the screen that the nurse was playing one of those match-up-style games with rows of colored balls.

"Morning," Tyler greeted as Darren stepped up to the bed.

"True, soft morning," he replied. He sat on the edge of the bed and took Anne's hand. "I'm back, Anne. I hope you're feeling better today. Nora said she would feed you again when she gets here. I'm guessing you'd like some food."

As Darren sat silently stroking his sister's hand, he thought about the interrogation he'd gotten from Brigand. If only Anne were awake, he could entice the answer out of her. "If you wake up, I can get you some of that tandoori chicken you like so much."

ANNE AWAKENED again when Darren took her hands. She held back the panic this time. Relaxing herself, she listened to her brother's soothing words.

She could still feel something foreign lurking around, but it didn't actually seem like something threatening. The situation was odd. Anne could still see through the open eyes that refused to close, feel Darr's touch, and hear everything in the room around her. It was the connection to her body that seemed somehow lost, or blocked.

She wondered if it was possible that the dullahan had infected her with something when he attacked. *Could this be some kind of poison running through my system?*

Maybe relaxing more was what she needed to do. She needed to avoid the panic and meditate. Maybe then she could determine what kind of poison had paralyzed her.

ONCE AGAIN, Skeena felt the presence of the woman, but this time it wasn't the angry assault of noise. This time the presence felt calm, soothing almost. Skeena relaxed, letting her guard down a little. She felt the presence spread, slowly flowing out as it reached for more room. No longer feeling threatened, Skeena allowed the presence more space.

ANNE RELAXED and ignored the sounds when she heard others moving around the room. Cautiously, she let her presence expand, reaching for control of the lung function. Anne visualized changing the shallow breaths to a slower, deeper breathing.

When she felt something change, Anne kept herself in a meditative mode and held her focus. She visualized the deep breathing. Her body responded, taking in a slightly deeper breath.

Still meditating, Anne then shifted the focus to her eyes, visualizing the lids pulling closed and the room going dark. After several long minutes, she felt a twitch in her left eyelid.

Anne took a deep breath. Her body actually listened this time, slowly drawing in a lungful of air. Anne concentrated on holding her breath. Her lungs stayed full for a few seconds before releasing the air in a sudden exhale.

DARREN TURNED to Nora and Tyler as they conferred in the doorway. "Did you see that?"

Everyone waited, watching Anne, but her breathing resumed its shallow rhythm.

Nora stepped over to Darren. "Changes like that happen occasionally, so just one occurrence doesn't really mean anything."

Darren gave Anne's hand a gentle squeeze. "Wake up, Anne. We're all waiting."

SKEENA FELT the woman's presence spreading, reaching out. The calm energy posed no threat, so she remained relaxed and didn't send another pulse.

She felt the inhabitant drifting closer.

ANNE LULLED herself into a deeper meditation trance. She imagined a tidal pool. She visualized her consciousness as being like the water in the tidal pool, slowly flowing out and filling her brain in small, smooth waves. With each tide of the waves, she visualized the water activating the different parts of her brain as it moistened and flowed over them.

She felt Darren squeeze and rub her hand, urging her to wake up. Anne ignored her body and relaxed further, deepening the trance as far as it would go as she visualized.

Slowly, her mind spread into all the nooks and crannies. Then, somewhere past the edge of the water, she sensed another presence. Maintaining her calm, she took a deep breath and imagined the waves moving forward, slowly surrounding the other occupant.

DARREN GREW excited when Anne took another deep breath. He looked up and saw that Tyler had already left for the day and Nora was sitting in her chair with another book. "She did it again," he said quietly to the nurse.

"I heard," Nora replied without looking up.

Darren sat vigil with Anne, watching her closely, but he failed to see any more changes. A rumble in his gut reminded him that he hadn't eaten breakfast yet. He gave Anne's hand a squeeze then set her hand on her stomach. "I'll be back in just a little bit, Sis. Keep fighting, or whatever it is that you're doing."

SKEENA QUIETLY fed as the woman's presence moved closer. The soothing lull of slow, rhythmic waves kept her calm as the presence grew larger around her. This felt like a comforting place now.

Until the waves suddenly crashed over Skeena, overwhelming her and drowning her in the alien energy. With the next wave, the energy flooded into her. The next crash pushed the energy through her. Skeena fought back, sending one of her calming pulses, then a stronger one, until the overwhelming tide stopped.

AS DARREN passed through the parlor on his way to the kitchen, he saw Hank and Mike sitting on the long divan with the journals. He called out a friendly "Hi."

Darren dug through the refrigerator and cabinets, pulling out three plates and all the things he would need to make roast beef sandwiches. He spent the next few minutes layering the items, before taking the plates back out to the parlor.

"I come bearing food," Darren said as he walked up to the coffee table.

Mike looked up with a blazing smile as he pushed away the notepad to make room. "Thank you, Darr. How'd you know I hadn't eaten yet?" he said as he took one of the plates.

"Just a guess," Darren replied as he handed a plate to Hank.

Hank reached out for it and set it on the table. "Thanks. The deli stuff was kinda dried out, so I didn't eat much of it."

Darren skipped around the coffee table and sat on the end of the divan near Hank. "I'm sorry. We should have taken time for a proper breakfast this morning."

After they each had a few bites, Hank looked at Darren. "How's Anne?"

"Actually doing better, I think. She's taken several deep breaths, and things seem to be changing."

Mike nodded. "At least there's good news somewhere. I've decoded more, but it still just seems like a bunch of rambling nonsense."

"Keep at it," Darren warmly urged. "From what I read yesterday, his writing style is very free-form, like a flow of consciousness. Different tidbits scattered throughout may fit together in the end, when we read it front to back."

Mike shrugged as he chewed. "If you say so." Mike looked at Darren. "How's Brigand?"

"Still with us, somehow."

"What do you mean?"

Darren had just taken another bite, so Hank jumped in to answer. "Well, he's aged rapidly. All of his one-hundred-fifty or however-many years, caught up with him at once. Kinda creepy looking, but he was still talking last time I was there."

With a nod, Darren added, "He's shriveled a bit. Yet he's still Brigand, trying to run the show." He looked over and smiled at Hank when he recalled his last conversation with Brigand. "Still stubborn and secretive as always."

AFTER FINISHING their meal, Darren cleaned up the plates, then followed Hank to the side courtyard, leaving Mike to burn through more of the decryption work.

He saw Hank looking around as he fished out and lit a fag. "What's wrong?"

"It just seems so quiet, almost dead out here now."

"Oh, I know what you mean," Darren said. He hadn't realized how much of a presence the Fae had kept at the house until they were all gone.

"So, Brigand's really still alive? How?"

"Don't ask me," Darren replied with a shrug. "But I don't think the man has moved from that chair since...." Darren trailed off, not wanting to think about the disasters at Shamrock Green.

"Yeah. I keep offering him food and drink, but he won't take any."

"It won't be much longer before he succumbs to dehydration, I suspect."

Hank nodded. "Probably not." He dropped the remainder of his cigarette to the ground. He stamped on the ash with his foot before bending down to pick it up.

Darren enjoyed watching the way Hank moved, every action of his muscles both quick and precise. Hank also had a really nice rear end, Darren noticed with a sly smile. His cock also noticed, responding with a swelling twitch.

As Hank put the cigarette butt in his back pocket, he smiled at Darren. "You seem to be in a much brighter mood today. Is it the necklace that's helping?"

Darren shrugged. "I don't know. I think Anne's signs of improvement have more to do with it."

"Well, whatever it is," Hank said as he flashed a grin, "keep it up."

Darren pulled his gaze away from Hank as he tapped his clove cigarette against the wall. He tried not to notice how Hank's eyes sparkled when he grinned at him, making him look so handsome. *It would be easy,* Darren thought as he stepped over to the planter to dispose of the butt. *So very, very easy to open my heart to this man.*

So what? part of Darren debated. *I can enjoy Hank's company, even have a little fun without going* that *far. Don't I deserve it? It's been a long while since I relaxed that much.*

Which was quite true, he knew. During the recent trysts with Hank, Darren hadn't fully relaxed; he had always held back a little of himself.

"What's up?" Hank asked. "You seem to be in some rather deep thoughts over there."

"Oh, nothing," Darren said as he stepped back to Hank.

"No really, you were a million miles away. What were you thinking?"

"Just… everything I guess," Darren said dismissively. "I should go check on Anne again."

"Sure. Whatever," Hank replied.

HANK TRIED not to scowl as he watched Darren go back into the main house. *Damn it all to hell,* he thought. *Why does he keep doing that? Just when he starts to loosen up—bam! He slams shut like a frightened clam.*

Maybe Darren didn't think he'd noticed, but Hank was well aware of being watched, as well as the resultant swelling in Darren's crotch. *The more telling part was when Darren went to the planter, that's when he'd felt a rush of warmth followed by a sudden hesitat—*

Hank brought that thought to a screeching halt. The first part, about being watched, that was all based on body language. Hank could understand deducing that.

As for the second part, though, how could Hank have any idea what Darren was feeling? That wasn't the same kind of speculation. Hank hadn't put together various body language clues to make a reasonable deduction. Instead, something inside Hank claimed to *know* what Darren felt.

Hank shook his head. *People don't run around with the capacity to know what everybody else feels. That would lead to chaos, wouldn't it? How would you know if the feelings belonged to you and not to someone else? Madness.*

Memories of the Guild meeting popped into his head. Hank recalled how everyone had seemed so insistent that he must have a gift. At the end, that Mrs. McCray lady had said something about sensitivity.

That wasn't the first time in his life Hank had been accused of being sensitive.

Hank shook his head again, trying to clear all these useless thoughts away. He decided to go back inside and see if Mike had found anything interesting.

After closing the door, Hank walked over to the divan. "Anything good?" he asked Mike as he sat near the end.

Mike shook his head as he scribbled another word on the notebook.

Hank suddenly felt brave. "Is there such a thing as a sensitive gift?"

Tilting his head, Mike stopped scribbling. "You mean, something besides being an empath?"

"Is there anything else?"

Mike chewed on the pen as he thought. "Can't think of many. Empath or projector is all I know of that involve emotion."

"Projector? What's that?"

"Someone who can push a desired emotion onto someone else."

"How do you mean 'push'?"

Mike set down the pen. "Think of it as being like an antenna. Empaths can receive emotion, and projectors can transmit them. From what I understand, someone with this kind of gift is actually capable of both transmission and reception, but their 'wiring,' so to speak, naturally slants more to one side or the other."

Sitting back, Hank recalled the post-market incident in the kitchen with Darren, when his anger had quickly calmed. "Is Darren one of these projectors?"

Mike gave a crooked smile. "I've always suspected as much, but Darr has never claimed to have a gift."

Empath, Hank thought. Despite some evidence, he couldn't take the leap and believe that he had that gift.

It seemed more likely that Darren had projected his emotions into the courtyard so strongly that Hank had felt them. *Even so, wouldn't I have to be at least a* little *empathic to pick them up?*

Mike stood up and looked at his phone. "I should move along. I don't want to be late for work again."

Hank stood also. "Thanks for the talk. If you hadn't guessed, I don't know much about this magic stuff."

"I don't mind helping a newbie," Mike said with a broad smile. He took a breath like he was going to say something else; then he just waved. "I'll see you."

Chapter 24

IN THE heat of the late-afternoon sun, the three-foot-tall sapling stalled a bit, its cloak of green energy dwindling and shrinking into the leaves. The taproot also slowed its growth, taking time to rest in the warm ground.

DISAPPOINTED, DARREN sat near Anne. He hadn't seen any changes in a while.

Nora looked up from her book. "You should tend to other things. I'll yell if there's any change."

"I can't leave," Darren said.

"Yes you can, and you must," Nora said firmly. "You'll need to be strong and healthy when she wakes up. Anne will likely face a rocky road and need you for support."

"Maybe."

"You won't be of any use to her if you run yourself down. Now shoo. I'll try spoon-feeding her again."

Darren stood. "Then I'll go." He turned to Anne, looking for any signs that she might be waking up. "I'll come back later, Sis."

He stepped out of the bedroom and made his way to the parlor. He saw Hank sitting alone at one end of the divan. "Where's Mike?" he asked as he sat on the opposite end.

"Work," Hank replied. "How's Anne?"

"The same."

Hank closed his eyes and leaned back. "Can I ask you something?"

"I suppose."

"Do you have a gift?"

"Not really," Darren replied.

"Are you sure? I had an interesting talk with Mike before he left. All about projectors."

"And you think I'm one? How did you come to that conclusion?"

Hank sat up. "I keep remembering in the kitchen when I got back from the store. I was so angry, but you touched me and I calmed down, like, immediately."

"I do have that," Darren admitted. "But only a touch, and it isn't very reliable, or useful. I wouldn't really call it a gift."

"Hey, anything's better than nothing." Hank leaned forward a little. "What makes you think I'm leaving?"

Darren shrugged. "Well, you have to eventually."

"But not now. Not for a week, or even a month."

It felt like Hank was scrutinizing him. "And that makes it better how?"

"We'll have time to work on this portal thing," Hank explained as he put his hand on the center cushion between them. "And time to work on us."

Darren shook his head as he ignored the invitation of touch. Hank just didn't get it. But Darren didn't want to start an argument over it. He stood up and fished out his phone. "I'm calling for Chinese food," he said as he went into the kitchen.

HANK GREW more frustrated as Darren left. *Why is he fighting this so hard?* Hank wondered. It was obvious to Hank that Darren felt something. Yet Darren continued to avoid it.

Once the food arrived, they ate in Anne's kitchen in relative silence. The only real conversation happened when Nora stepped in.

She looked down at the cartons on the table. "Maybe I will have just a bit of rice," Nora said to Darren as she walked to the table and picked up one of the plates.

"Please," Darren said with a hand gesture. "Help yourself. I got enough for all of us."

"Thank you, Mr. O'Connell." Nora dished out some of the steamed rice. "I'm in the habit of bringing my own lunches, so you needn't concern yourself with feeding me."

"Just call me Darr. It must get a bit boring, eating sandwiches every day."

Hesitantly, Nora sat at the table and picked up a fork. "It's fine, I don't mind it."

At least I'm not the only one who can't use the chopsticks, Hank thought as he glanced at Darren, who used the Asian utensils like a pro. He looked to Nora. "Darren said Anne showed some improvement today?"

"She has shown changes," Nora replied with a head nod. "But it's difficult to know if it's actual progress. Time will tell."

"I think it's progress," Darren said.

Hank looked from Darren to Nora, then back to Darren. It seemed that the necklace did help Darren, at least in some ways. His attitude was definitely more positive than Nora's. Which only frustrated Hank more because that hopefulness hadn't spilled over to include him. *Yet. It hasn't spilled over yet,* some part of Hank insisted.

Nora finished the last of her rice and stood up. "I should get back. I shouldn't leave a charge unattended."

"I understand," Darren said. "Just leave the dishes. We'll clean up."

"Thank you again." Nora turned and left the kitchen.

Hank finished off the portion of beef with broccoli on his plate, trying to think of something to say that might reach Darren and get him to open up. He hadn't thought of anything by the time Darren put down his chopsticks.

"I'm *quite* stuffed now," Darren announced. "Were you going to want more? Or should I box up the rest?"

"I've had my fill," Hank replied.

As Darren went about closing up the cartons and moving them to the fridge, Hank watched in silence, picking at the remainder of food on his plate.

After finishing the chore, Darren announced, "I'm going to my flat," as he walked out.

AFTER THE sun made its slow arc through the sky, the afternoon heat faded to the cooler air of evening. Slowly, the sapling revived.

A BIT later, Darren returned to Anne's room, carrying his guitar. He'd thought that a bit of song might help revive her.

"Hey, Anne," he greeted, noticing she still looked the same. He rolled the table down to her feet and sat on her bed, resting the guitar on his thigh. "What would you like to hear?"

Nora glanced up, then returned to her book.

Darren strummed a few scale bars, watching Anne for any signs of life. None appeared.

Maybe I should play one of the songs Anne detests. That might get a reaction out of her, Darren thought.

"Okay then," Darren said with an evil grin. "I'm in the mood for 'Dúlamán.'"

Using the tempo of a dirge, he strummed the chords slowly. Just to make it worse for her, Darren decided to sing it in English.

"Oh gentle daughter," he sang, dragging out each syllable as miserably as possible. Darren thought he saw Anne's left eyelid twitch.

"Here come the wooing men," Darren continued. Anne showed no other reaction.

He went on with a few more lines, but Anne failed to respond further.

Trying to hide his disappointment, Darren rested the guitar on the floor and leaned over to his sister. "It's okay if you're not ready to wake up yet. I'll sing again later," Darren promised as he reached out and patted Anne's hand.

Hiding his teary eyes, Darren picked up the guitar and turned to leave.

Nora looked up. "I've never heard your group play. I hope that wasn't an example of your best work."

Darren thought she was trying to cheer him up, but it didn't lift his heavy heart. "Of course not, that's one of Anne's least favorite songs and she'd hate hearing it. I was thinking maybe a little anger would help her. I suppose it was a silly idea."

Nora shook her head. "Not silly at all. Might actually be helpful." Nora returned to her book as Darren left.

INSIDE HERSELF, Anne continued her stalemate with the alien force. She would awaken and overwhelm the presence until the stowaway put her to sleep again.

Hearing Darren's horrible song, Anne felt a bit ticked off. *How dare my brother annoy me like this. It's just plain mean*, she thought bitterly before another sleeping pulse hit her.

Fueled by anger, Anne revived very quickly, and channeled her annoyance into the crashing waves.

AFTER ANOTHER disheartening visit with Brigand, during which the man slept most of the time after Darren fed the cat, he decided to seek out his place of solace. Hugging the guitar close, he jogged across the street and entered the Shamrock Green.

Once inside, he approached the ring of stones. Even though the portal was gone, Darren remained outside the confines of the circle. He still felt a deep sense of respect for the sacred space.

Drawing near, he noticed the new sapling growing near the westernmost standing stone. It had sprouted near the obelisk, right along the circle's imaginary line. The young hawthorn was nearly a meter tall, so it must have been growing awhile, but Darren didn't recall seeing it before.

Any other sort of weed or plant so near the sacred space Darren would immediately remove, but his strong reverence for the faery trees made him hesitate. He decided it would be best not to disturb it.

Facing the circle, Darren sat down on the ground cross-legged, then raised the guitar to his thigh. He strummed a few random bars just to relax and warm up. He sat up straight and settled himself, opening up to the music inside in a style of meditation he found soothing. After a cleansing breath, Darren stopped guiding his fingers, letting his inner muse take over and play through him.

His fingers changed pace and slowed, picking out a few sorrowful-sounding notes, then the song moved into a series of more determined triplets of notes. Darren recognized the Metallica song as his fingers played the opening of "Nothing Else Matters."

Then his rhythm changed, and the notes took on a quicker pace. As his fingers played The Eurythmics' song "Here Comes the Rain Again," he hummed along, bursting into song after a few phrases. "I want to dive into your ocean. Is it raining with you?"

His fingers changed tempo again, and he let them go as they would. The next chords came out much harder, more like an '80s metal ballad, and Darren soon realized it was a Bad English song. He jumped in and sang along.

"Baby, there's nothing in this world that can ever do what a touch of your hand can do. It's like nothing that I ever knew. Yeah."

When he sensed a presence behind him, Darren stopped singing "When I See You Smile," but he stayed in the zone. His fingers changed tempo again, turning to more of a 3/4 beat. It took him a minute to recognize the Olivia Newton John song.

From behind, he heard Hank sing, "Come take my hand… you should know me… I've always been in your mind."

Darren stopped playing and rotated as he stood up.

Hank froze about a meter and a half away and dropped his head. "Sorry. I didn't mean to interrupt."

"It's fine," Darren said with a sincere smile. "I was just relaxing; I like to meditate out here sometimes." He took a step closer to Hank. "How did you find me?"

"I was going to check on Brigand and thought I heard guitar music. I peeked around the corner and saw the gate open, so I wandered in." Hank flushed slightly. "Really, it was nice hearing you play; I shouldn't have sung along and interrupted. I just couldn't help it. The song 'Magic' has always been one of my favorites."

"I don't mind. You have a nice singing voice." Darren chuckled. "How did you call yourself a skeptic back in the '80s, if that was a favorite song?"

Hank shrugged. "Maybe down deep somewhere, I always wanted to believe." Hank took a step closer. "You said that was some kind of meditation?"

Darren nodded and took another step closer. "I tried, but I can't just sit still and chant the way Anne does. I discovered that I *can* do it with the guitar. I just relax, get into a zone, then let the music come out."

"So, you just let yourself play whatever comes to mind?"

"Exactly," Darren said with a grin.

"Then, all those song choices were subconscious. Interesting...."

"Why say that?"

"Think about the songs you played," Hank said with a sly grin. "All songs about lovers."

Darren had been trying to ignore that fact. Leave it to Hank to not only notice it, but throw it at his feet. "I suppose they were."

"More specifically, they were songs about getting together, or sticking together with a lover." Hank dropped his grin and cocked his head slightly. "Is there maybe a bit of conflict?"

Feeling put on the spot, Darren didn't want to answer that. After letting out a sigh, he decided to try and explain it. "I still think it's in your best interest to leave now."

"But," Hank countered. "You don't *really* want me to, do you?"

Darren hesitated. He didn't want to reply, but he had come to notice Hank's stubborn and tenacious nature. Hank wouldn't leave this alone until he finally got an answer. *Might as well get it over with,* Darren thought as he took a deep breath. "No," he said quietly.

"Then why all the pushing away? I don't understand. Is there something about me that you don't like, or trust?"

"No."

"Are you afraid of me?"

That question was quite a bit closer to the truth since his reasons did involve fear, but not *so* close that he couldn't answer with "No."

Hank must have sensed the dread Darren felt as he anticipated the next question, for Hank's eyes softened and looked less interrogatory. Quietly he asked, "Then, what *are* you afraid of?"

Hesitating, Darren took a deep breath. He knew there wasn't any way to tilt or spin this, short of being evasive. He had no doubt Hank would pick up on any evasion and not let it slide. He took another deep breath. "I fear falling in love with you."

"Okay," Hank said as he nodded calmly. "And why is that something to be afraid of?"

"For reasons we've already discussed, and many more."

Hank leaned against the nearest obelisk. "Distance and skepticism are the only things I recall discussing. And at this point, I think we can cross 'skeptic' off the list. The distance is also solvable; let's ignore that one for now. So, what else? Tell me the 'many mores.'"

Darren tried not to cringe at Hank's behavior as he leaned on the standing stone, which he felt bordered on disrespectful of the sacred space. Yet, not inconsiderate enough that he felt the need so say something, so Darren let it go. "Many mores?" He stopped to think. "Actually, I was going to say my career, but with Anne in her current state, we may never have a band again. So it's likely moot."

"I know it may seem like a cruel reality to hear right now, but I'm sure Celtic Cantrips could hire another keyboardist. That's beside the point, though. If the group did start working again, how is that a reason not to fall in love?"

"Because it's not exactly 'banker's hours' kind of work. When we tour, we're gone for long stretches of time. You'd either be left alone or dragged around with us. Neither one would be fair to you. Being alone wouldn't be fair to me, either."

"Okay," Hank said with a nod. "Let's mark that one as a potential concern, then. What else?"

Darren thought a moment without finding anything else. "I think that's mostly it."

Hank looked up at Darren. "Forgive my bluntness, but the 'mostly' bits seem like excuses. I think the remainder, whatever thing you *haven't* mentioned, is the real reason."

Darren was taken aback. Yet he had to admit upon review, that those *were* just excuses, details that could be ironed out with a bit of work and planning.

"So I ask again, why are you afraid of falling in love with me?"

Darren stammered, not sure of the answer.

After a moment of quiet, Hank said, "I'm guessing it isn't the *love* part you're afraid of, but some potential later consequence."

Darren looked at Hank, trying to judge what he was getting at. "As in?"

"Oh," Hank said with a dramatic wave of his hand. "Let me just take a stab in the dark and say you're afraid of falling for me, then having your heart broken if I leave."

Yes, Darren had to admit to himself. He did have that very thought just the other night, right after the green— No... it wasn't until they went to bed later that night, when Hank was being a bit aloof, that Darren had the thought.

"Am I right?" Hank asked.

"That does seem accurate."

"On that point, I should tell you I already made a promise to Brigand that I would stay until Yule. Assuming you can put up with me that long...."

"I think I can manage," Darren said with a crooked smile. "Now let *me* ask, why were you so aloof the night after the green?"

"You mean, besides the fact I had that painful burn all over my chest?" Hank gave back his own crooked smile. "Well by then, with the lotion and all, it wasn't so painful. I guess I was still a little miffed that you'd dissed me for your sister, and Mike showed more concern toward me." Hank shook his head. "I *do* get it though, she's your blood, and at the time you didn't know my burn was as bad as it was."

"Right," Darren agreed.

Hank pushed off the obelisk and stood up straight. "So, can we hug and forgive, and get all this behind us?" He took a step forward.

Darren leaned down and carefully rested his guitar flat on the ground. "That sounds like an idea." He stepped forward to meet Hank. Tentatively, Darren put his arms around him and gently pulled him close. Although he knew his caution was pointless now. His biggest obstacles were his silly doubts and fears. Darren bent down and kissed Hank on the forehead, allowing his heart to open to the rush of emotion he felt building. Overwhelmed by so much joy, the seed of doubt buried inside Darren withered and died.

ON THE coffee table inside Darren's flat, the innermost ring of the gyroscope vibrated and twitched slightly, but it was too far away from the magical source to draw any power.

HANK RESPONDED to the forehead kiss by pointing his face up and lifting onto his toes so his mouth could meet Darren's. They gently played with each other's lips as Hank hugged closer to him. Darren reveled in the tiramisu taste of Hank, created from his recent smoke and all the coffee he drank. He'd never kissed a man who tasted so delicious.

In the sapling slightly behind them, the dwindled green energy recharged, expanding out of the hawthorn leaves and dancing around the foliage.

Hank pulled back and let out a contented sigh. "That was one hell of a hug, Mr. Rock Star."

Darren was too happy to even really argue. "Not a rock star" was all he replied. He bent his knees slightly so Hank wouldn't have to strain his neck so much, then went in for a deep kiss. Darren just let everything go, enjoying their moment of bliss.

Hank eventually dropped down flat on his feet. "Not that I couldn't kiss all night long, but my calves are getting tired."

Darren chuckled. "I think my knees will lock soon. Why don't we relocate to someplace more comfortable?"

"You read my mind," Hank said with a grin.

They pulled apart. Darren bent down and picked up his guitar, then followed behind Hank as he exited Shamrock Green.

WHEN THE doorbell chimed a second time, Nora glanced up from her book. *Is no one here to answer?* Come to think of it, she hadn't seen the brother or any of his friends in quite a while. She dropped in the bookmark and set the book on the dining chair before she made her way to the front door.

ANNE ALSO heard the doorbell. *Enough of this nonsense,* she thought. *Hey you,* she yelled out in her mind. *Stop fighting me.* The response was another of those intense urges to sleep, but Anne was angry enough to resist them now. She sent another wave of her own out within herself.

Changing tactics, Anne took a deep breath (and it felt like her body actually did), then sank herself into a deeply calm meditation. She let herself gently ebb and flow into all of herself, washing into every crick and hollow she could find.

The stowaway seemed to calm and relax.

Now, Anne said in her mind. *You don't fight me, and I won't fight you. We can exist here together.*

Anne felt another pulse, but this one echoed her own calm.

That's more like it. We can cooperate.

NORA OPENED the front door. Outside, Tyler waited. "Nora," he greeted with a head nod as he stepped through the open doorway.

"Sorry Tyler, I didn't realize it was 11:00 p.m., or I would not have made you wait."

"No trouble. How is she?" he asked as he followed Nora down the hall.

"Actually, a few more deep breaths and some eye twitches. Enough to make me more hopeful."

When they stepped into Anne's room, they both noticed right away that her eyes were closed.

"My stars," Tyler said. "I'm also agreeing."

Nora stepped over to the chair and retrieved her things. "I don't have much to report that hasn't already been mentioned. Keep an eye open," she said before letting herself out.

Pulling off his backpack, Tyler went to the dining chair and settled in.

Chapter 25

WITH AN arm motion, Darren held open the door to his flat and ushered Hank in first. He followed as they headed for the kitchen.

"I suppose it's too late to make coffee," Hank mused aloud as he opened the refrigerator. Darren tried not to stare at his butt when Hank bent over. "Beer or water?"

"I'll take a beer," Darren replied, thinking the alcohol might help with the sudden nervousness he felt. "We can make coffee if you'd like."

When Hank hesitated, Darren walked to the counter, grabbed the glass carafe, and took it to the sink.

"Thanks," Hank said. "You must think I'm a nut wanting to drink it this late."

"Not at all." Darren busied himself with the task as Hank took the beer bottle to the café table and sat down. "I know you enjoy your coffee."

As the coffeemaker began brewing, Darren went to the table. He noticed Hank was fidgeting his leg. "Are you nervous?" he asked as he grabbed the beer.

"A little," Hank admitted. "But I don't know why. It's not like we haven't... been in bed together before."

"That's true. Tonight feels somehow different, though."

Hank looked up with a slightly fearful yearning in his eyes. "Like maybe, the stakes are higher, somehow?"

Darren set down the beer bottle, then reached over the table and took Hank's hand, putting as much warmth and desire as he could into his grasp. "We don't have to go any further than what we're ready for."

"I know," Hank said in a resigned tone as his leg stopped bouncing.

When the coffeemaker beeped, Hank got up and went to the sink for a mug. He retrieved two ice cubes from the small freezer cubby in the fridge and put them in the mug, then filled the mug with coffee.

Darren admired Hank as he paced around the kitchen with his quick and precise movements before drinking from the mug. That was one of things about this little American man that enthralled Darren so much. Hank had such a uniqueness about him with everything he did.

Hank set the mug in the sink, then reached over and turned off the coffee pot warmer before returning to the table. He stood next to Darren, for once having the height advantage. He reached out and ran his hands over Darren's clipped head, sending relaxing waves of comfort coursing through Darren as his follicles tingled. "I love your short hair," he whispered.

Darren scooted his chair back from the table and wrapped his arms around Hank. He had planned to wrap them around Hank's chest, but remembering the injury, he lowered his arms down to Hank's waist. "How's the burn?"

"Don't even notice it anymore," Hank replied as he turned slightly, then sat down in Darren's lap.

Darren's heart pounded with excitement as his cock swelled in his jeans with painful restriction. He raised his knee and lifted Hank briefly so he could readjust his jewels. Darren thought he heard some small sound in the living room, but it didn't concern him enough to really notice.

"Am I too heavy?" Hank asked before leaning forward and running his lips along Darren's forehead.

"Not at all." Darren lifted his hands to Hank's shoulders. He massaged as he pulled Hank slightly lower so their lips could meet.

When their lips touched, a "vroooom," noise echoed from the living room and they separated quickly. Hank stood up, asking, "What the *hell* is that?"

Grabbing Hank's hand, Darren stood, then they nearly ran into the living room.

On the coffee table, Cona's gyroscope twirled with life. As all three bands rotated, the round assembly on top revolved, briefly creating a low-pitched hum before the bands slowed down. The sound changed to more of a swishing as the bands slowed further.

Hank squeezed Darren's hand. "Holy shit. *That's* the freakin' noise I've been hearing almost every night."

The gyroscope slowed further, the swishing turning into a triplet beat as each band passed some imaginary line. The top's revolution ceased. Only the two inner bands continued rotating, dropping to a staccato "thump, thump," almost like a heartbeat, as they slowed.

"I'm guessing it was nights when we snogged," Darren replied, watching the bands settle into a slow rhythm. He realized he was still holding Hank's hand. He turned slightly then leaned down for another kiss.

He heard the "vroooom" and pulled back.

"Tease," Hank said as he wrapped his hand around Darren's neck and pulled him down for a real kiss.

Darren was too distracted to really get into the kiss as he watched out of the corner of his eye. Inside the hollow center of the rapidly rotating bands, a tiny, an ethereal wisp of turquoise energy swirled. The gyroscope spun with a low-pitched hum until he pulled away again. The wispy energy vanished.

Hank rubbed his hand up Darren's neck, brushing against the short hairs on the lower part of his head as the sounds of the device slowed. "I wonder what happens when we…?" he asked with a twinkle in his eye.

"I don't know," Darren said. "I don't understand why it's doing this. The snippet I found in the journal said something about the gyroscope amplifying magical energy. Or at least, I assumed it was the gyroscope it was referring to."

"Then, we must be *making* energy somehow, for it to have something to amplify."

"From what I understand, though, some fundamental physics law prevents any creation from happening in our dimens—"

The ringing of Darren's phone interrupted. He fished it out of his pocket. "Hello?"

"Darr, get over to Anne's," Mike nearly yelled. "I've found something."

"Anne's? I didn't even know you were there," Darren said as he wrapped his arm around Hank's shoulder and turned him to the back door.

TAKING A deep breath, Anne opened her eyes as she came fully awake. Still groggy, she cleared her throat. Something seemed to be sticking to her arm, so she reflexively reached over to pull it off.

"Stop, Anne," an excited male voice said. She paused her hand and turned her head to see a strange young man standing up from a dining chair near her bed. *What's a dining chair doing in here?* she wondered.

"I'm a nurse," the man said soothingly. "Name's Tyler. Just take some slow, deep breaths and don't move around too much."

Anne did as he asked and breathed deeply.

"You've been in a coma for a few days, so don't rush anything," Tyler said as he leaned over the bed.

Coma? Anne wondered. She tried to think back. She remembered coming home from the disaster at the green, then Darren putting her to bed. After that, she recalled some vague, foggy dream of being trapped and fighting aliens.

"I'm going to take out the IV now," Tyler said in a soothing voice as he gently took hold of Anne's arm. "Can you speak yet?"

"I—" she managed to say, but her scratchy and dry throat didn't want to cooperate further.

Tyler wrapped some kind of sticky bandage around her elbow. "I'll get you some water. Be right back."

HANK FOLLOWED Darren through the courtyard and into Anne's parlor.

He saw Mike pacing near the coffee table. "Come look," he said to Darren.

Sitting down on the divan, Hank watched Darren pick up the legal pad as he dropped his butt to the cushion and started reading. "Listen to this," he said before reading it aloud. "Emotion. Exude. Moving the static. Feeling flow in synergy. Synergy equals energy. Give and take creates." Darren put down the notebook.

Mike grinned. "I thought you'd want to see that."

"I didn't even know you were working on it," Darren said as he looked at Mike. "How'd you get in?"

Hank noticed Tyler breezing into the kitchen.

Mike sat down, but he kept bouncing on the cushion, like he couldn't contain his excitement. "I tried calling, but didn't get an answer, so I just used the hidden key and let myself in."

Tyler breezed out of the kitchen carrying a small bottle of water and a straw. The nurse didn't even seem to notice them in the parlor as he hurried back to Anne's room. Hank turned to Darren. "Forgive me for being slow, but what does that mean?"

"It means," Darren explained with a huge grin. "Emotions aren't governed by physical laws. Therefore, they are capable of generating magical energy."

"Which emotions? And how does it generate?"

Darren paused. "Since he mentions synergy, or working together, it must be a shared-bond emotion."

"Like love," Mike threw in.

With a nod, Darren said, "Most likely. Mutual hatred might also work, I'd think."

"Then," Hank thought aloud. "This 'give and take' is what somehow creates it? Then it wakes up the gyroscope?"

Mike looked confused. "What gyroscope?"

"Come." Darren stood and motioned Mike to his feet. "There's a few things we need to fill you in about."

ANNE GRATEFULLY slurped the chilled water through the straw after
Tyler helped her sit up a bit. As the nurse propped the pillows up
behind her, Anne asked, "How long?"

"This is only my second night here, so it can't have been very
long."

Anne leaned back against the pillows and closed her eyes.
"Where's Darr?"

"He had been in the living room earlier. Excuse me; I'll check
while I call the head nurse," Tyler said as he stepped out the door.

A few moments later, Tyler returned. "Not there. He's been in
and out the whole time. But as late as it is," Tyler said as he glanced at
his watch, "11:47 p.m. Darren may have already retired."

Anne nodded. Her brother never was much of a night owl.
Hearing a soft noise, she opened her eyes to see Tyler with one of those
Chinese takeout cartons as he rolled a table toward her.

"Nora is coming by in the morning. In the meantime, are you
hungry? I found some rice in the refrigerator you could eat."

At the mention of food, she suddenly felt ravenous. "Oh, yes
please."

"Would you like it cold, or prefer it heated up?"

"Cold is fine," Anne said as she sat up a bit more and put her
hands on top of the table.

Tyler set down the carton and a spoon next to the water bottle.
"You probably feel very famished, but your system hasn't had any food
in some time, so eat slowly, very small bites. You will probably feel
full quickly."

Anne nodded that she understood as she took a small spoonful of
the rice and ate it. The plain steamed rice tasted a little dry and bland.
"Did you see any soy sauce or duck sauce packets?"

"Let me check," Tyler said as he blew out of the room again.

DESPITE THE utter vileness of the act, the phouka dug through his
latest scat, once again finding nothing. Well, nothing except clumpy
hair and poop.

He swirled and washed his paw in the nearby fountain of the rectory garden. For days, he had been watching for the return of that "marble," the center of the dullahan's heart that he had so impulsively eaten. He had yet to void the nasty ball, which left the phouka with a growing concern.

Is the devilish thing stuck somewhere in my bowels? Or is it possible that my body has absorbed it? If his body *had* absorbed it, what exactly would that mean? *It probably doesn't matter,* he thought as he shook his paw to dry. *Without magic here, the situation is likely moot and inconsequential.*

The phouka once again had the thought to go visit with the Connell clan. After all, it would be the responsible thing to do. But as a general rule, phouka weren't known for being very responsible. *Maybe tomorrow.*

AFTER BRINGING Mike up to speed on the gyroscope and their latest discoveries, Darren watched Mike as he examined the ivory device again.

Feeling his phone vibrating in his pocket, Darren pulled it out and answered as he stepped into the hallway. "Hello?"

"Ya must be Darren," a gravelly old woman's voice said in his ear. "I'm Gwen Lear. Harrison's mother."

"Hello, Mrs. Lear. Hank's right here, I—"

"Whoa there, hold yer horses," she said quickly. "I'd like a word with ya first."

Darren stepped all the way down the hall and into his bedroom. "Of course m'lady. What would you like to discuss?"

"For starters, you can tell me your plans for whatever this situation is."

"Mrs. Lear, I'm not sure I understand what you mean by 'situation.'"

"I mean, is this just a summertime fling, then yer gonna kick him out with a broken heart in a week or two?"

Darren sat on the edge of his bed. "No, ma'am. That is not the situation at all. And why would you think Hank is that serious?"

Gwen tsked in his ear. "A mother knows her children. I could hear it in his voice when he called earlier. My boy's head over heels with you."

"I wasn't aware he had called earlier," Darren admitted.

"Yep, he did. And this idea of his staying until Christmas don't sit well with me."

"Hank told you that?"

"Of course he did. And ya didn't answer my question yet, Darren. Are you doing right by my boy?"

"Mrs. Lear," Darren said before he took a deep breath to try and compose his thoughts. "As far as any plans go, we, Hank and I are just following this along, seeing where it goes. I can't make any promises for the future, but I *can* assure you that this isn't just a summer fling for me. I'm as serious about this situation as I believe Hank is."

"Well," Gwen said a bit resigned. "That's something, at least."

"Truly, you have nothing to worry about. I'm very hopeful."

"At least somebody is. If it turns out ya lied to me, I can send my other son out there with a can of whoop-ass for you."

Darren suppressed a chuckle at her strange expression. "That won't be necessary, Mrs. Lear."

"Fine, then. You just keep in mind what I said. I won't cotton to no bullshit."

"I promise, no bullshit," Darren replied. "Did you wish to speak with Hank now?"

"No need. I just wanted to say my piece with you. I suppose you're decent enough. You boys have a good night, Darren."

"We will, Mrs. Lear."

"Might as well call me Gwen, seein' everybody else does."

"I shall. Good night, Gwen."

Darren shook his head as he stared at the dead phone. Having never really known his own mother, he hadn't expected Hank's mother to be so protective. Yet, he realized, if Aunt Oli were still around, she would probably react the same way on his behalf. He stood and put the phone back in his pocket, hopeful that he had passed inspection with Mrs. Lear.

HANK LOOKED up when Darren returned from the hallway. He noticed the strange crooked grin spread across Darren's face, and was even more curious about the phone call.

"What's up?" he asked when Darren walked over.

"I'm not sure," Darren said as he looked down at Hank. "That was your mother."

"Oh, jeez," Hank said. "I hope she didn't grill you too badly."

"Not too badly, considering the circumstances. I do think I passed her inspection. She wished us a good night."

"That's good," Hank said as he stood up and put his arm around Darren's waist. Behind them, the gyroscope started up with a swooshing noise. "What all did she say?"

"Other than trying to suss out my intentions, she also mentioned you had a brother with a can of whoop-ass."

"Jeez," Hank said while rolling his eyes, trying not to feel embarrassed.

"You never mentioned you have a brother, I don't think."

"I didn't? Well, his name's Shawn. He's five foot eleven and built like a pit bull." Hank wrapped his other arm around Darren. "I can't believe she threatened you with him. Sometimes, I think she forgets that I'm a grown man."

"She's a mother. You will always be her young boy. Did Mike leave?"

"Yeah, he wanted to decode some more. He said he'll let himself out later."

With a sparkle in his eye, Darren leaned down. "That means we're all alone now."

Hank pushed up into the kiss, hearing the "vroooom" noise from the coffee table behind him.

Darren pulled back. "That gyroscope is a bit distracting."

"I noticed," Hank agreed. Tightening his grip around Darren's waist, Hank pulled him over to the settee and sat down. "Speaking of, now that it seems we have a source of that magic energy, is there some way to harness it for reopening the portal?"

"I haven't thought much on it. It's more along the lines of what Brigand or Anne could help with."

Hank frowned. "I was afraid you were gonna say something like that."

Darren's phone rang. He stood and then retrieved it from his pocket. "Hello?"

"Be right there," he said excitedly as he grabbed Hank's arm and pulled him to his feet. "Anne's awake!"

Darren grabbed the gyroscope, and they jogged through the courtyard and into Anne's flat.

Tyler was sitting in the dining chair playing some kind of game on his iPad while Mike and Anne continued chatting about Cona's writings.

Darren pushed past everybody then set the gyroscope on the nightstand. He surrounded his sister in a big bear hug. "Anne, you don't know how great it is to see you awake."

"Darr, ribs," Anne hissed out.

"Sorry." Darren released his grip. He looked at Tyler. "Did anyone call Dr. Chelsea?"

"I will, if you think there's a need," Tyler replied. "Nora will be here by first light."

Anne cut in. "I don't think I need the healer." She punched Darren in the arm.

"Ouch! What was that for?"

"I had a dream that you were mean and sang a terrible song to me. That wasn't a dream, was it," she said pointedly.

"No. I sang 'Dúlamán' in English. But I didn't do it to be mean. I was trying to reach you."

"Well, it must have been somewhat effective, since I still remember it," Anne said with a smile before her face turned more serious. "Mike's been filling me in about the journals. How's Brigand?"

"Aging rapidly," Darren said. "Refusing to eat or drink."

Anne grimaced. "I should go visit with him in a bit." She looked at the nightstand. "Why'd you bring the device in here?"

With a broad grin, Darren said, "Watch," as he reached out and took Hank's hand. The two inner bands of the gyroscope began spinning, making the swoosh noise. Pulling on Hank's hand, Darren drew him closer and leaned down for a kiss. When their lips touched, the gyroscope cycled up with the "vroooom" noise again.

"Look!" Anne yelled as she pointed at the device.

Inside the hollow center of the globe of bands, a wispy, purplish-red ball circulated. It looked like a fragile and undefined bruise before it faded away as the gyroscope slowed down.

Anne reached her hand out to it. "Do that kiss again."

Hank moved a bit to the left around Darren, so they could both see the device as they kissed again. After the "vroooom," the faint, wispy energy appeared again.

Holding her hand near the globe, Anne frowned. "It *is* magic energy, but it seems somehow raw and unrefined, like it needs filtered."

Mike spoke up. "It didn't do that purple when you guys showed me earlier. I wonder what's different."

"Maybe being in Anne's room?" Hank thought aloud.

"No," Darren suddenly exclaimed. "It must be the people. One of Cona's strange notes said… shite, I don't recall well enough to recite it. Let me go find it."

When Darren left the room, Hank stepped closer to Anne's bed. "How are you feeling?"

"Feeling good," Anne said with a smile. "And still a touch strange. I had some unusual dreams." She shivered when the strange word 'Skeena' popped into her mind.

"I can imagine," Hank replied as Darren came back in with one of the legal pads.

"Here," Darren announced. "Sister, Friend, Elder, Youth, Contain. Brother, Lover, Conjoin. Ignition intense." He glanced up. "Oh, I should read the other one for Anne's benefit," he said as he flipped to another page.

Darren read, "Lights in circling dance. Twirling. Enhancing energy. Two Fae magnifying magic with four elements. Intensify, Focus, Rectify, Cauterize. Six in the center: three circles around. Amplify and Mesmerize."

Anne grabbed the legal pad. "Let me see that; your Gaelic never was very advanced." She spent a moment reading over the handwritten notes. "Well, it seems like you got it right, Darr."

Hank kept thinking about the first line. "Yes Darren, I think it's the people. He mentioned six, and there's six symbols on that device. I don't think that's a coincidence."

Anne picked up the gyroscope, and studied the hieroglyphics carved into each face. "Two Fae, the blue and green faeries. Four elements." Anne scrutinized one of the glyphs. "Campfire!" she said excitedly. "That's the one we didn't identify."

Hank looked at Mike with his flaming red hair. "For some reason, I always think of fire when I look at Mike," he announced.

Tyler stood up and set down his iPad. "I apologize for eavesdropping, but I have a bit of affinity with air."

"Then you must be the youth, and Mike is the friend," Hank thought aloud. "Of course, Anne is the sister, and the elder is next door. Maybe we should go get Brigand."

Darren cut in. "But, Anne doesn't have any elemental ties, do you?"

"I never thought so, but I recall dreams of the ocean and tidal pools when I was… resting. Maybe I'm tied to water."

Tyler raised his hands. "Speaking of resting, I think we should break this up for the night. We can resume in the morning."

Darren huffed. "Not when we're this close to deciphering it all."

Tyler gave him a firm but gentle look. "You and Hank look dead on your feet. Anne also needs her rest. This can resume tomorrow. Since Anne is awake, I'll go sit with your friend next door."

Hank stifled a yawn. "I have to agree," he said to Darren as he took hold of his arm.

The gyroscope swooshed to life again. Anne looked at it. "Take that noisy thing with you. I'll never get any rest if you guys shag later."

Darren blushed. "Anne!" he said as he picked up the gyroscope.

"I'll be back in the morning," Mike said as he waved. "Night, all."

"Good night," Hank said as he tugged on Darren's arm to get him moving to the door.

Once in the hallway, Hank let go of Darren's arm so the gyroscope would stop. They made their way to the side courtyard. "What're we gonna do with that thing?" Hank asked. "I don't wanna have to hear it again all night."

Darren looked at the sky, then stepped to the wrought iron lounge table next to the wall and set down the device. "I think it would be safe enough to leave it here. Being outside, we probably won't hear it."

"Let's hope." Hank followed Darren into his apartment.

Chapter 26

UNDER THE bright moonlight, the green energy danced around the foliage of the hawthorn sapling, fueling a new growth spurt. As its trunk and stems stretched wider and higher, the taproot underground resumed its quest for the exciting spot with renewed vigor.

The root lengthened with each new cell division, steadily reaching farther east before it began angling up.

ONCE INSIDE his flat with the door firmly closed behind them, Darren took hold of Hank's hand. He listened, but didn't hear any annoying noise. "It seems to be insulated well enough," he said to Hank with a smile.

"Yeah, I don't hear it at all."

"Would you like to come to my room tonight?"

Hank stepped forward and wrapped his arms around his waist. "You could talk me into it," Hank said teasingly.

Darren bent down and kissed his forehead. "Then, shall we?"

"Let me hit the bathroom first," Hank said.

Darren went into his bedroom to wait. He pulled back the covers and fluffed up the pillows, feeling grateful that Anne was awake. Nora had warned him that his sister would still have some recovery ahead, but Darren felt hopeful that the worst lay behind her.

Hank stepped into the room a moment later. He walked in slowly and sat on the edge of the bed. "You know," he said hesitantly. "I haven't... been serious in a while. I think I already mentioned that at the baths."

Darren stifled a yawn as he sat down next to Hank. "For tonight, my only plans are to hug against your naked body and fall asleep."

"Sounds good."

"As for the other," Darren admitted. "What *I* didn't tell you at the baths is that it's been over ten years for me."

"Oh," Hank said after a chuckle. "Then I don't feel so bad. Sometimes, I've felt broken as a gay man, since we're supposed to be so promiscuous and all. Casual just doesn't work for me."

"Nor me," Darren said as he pulled off his sweater. He noticed Hank staring at his chest with a strange expression. "What is it?" he asked, glancing down.

"No fucking way." Hank yanked off his T-shirt. "Look!"

Darren looked at the spiderweb lines coursing over Hank's chest, then looked down at his own chest. The Celtic-knot rope borders separating the tableau of tattoos matched, in mirror image, the pattern of scarred lines on Hank's chest.

Hank leaned his chest close to Darren's. The tattoo ropes and pink scars lined up nearly perfectly. "I don't think you should doubt Mike's premonitions anymore."

"It would seem I shouldn't."

Looking down, Darren saw the faery-tree pendant still around his neck. He'd been wearing it long enough to have grown used to its presence and had nearly forgotten the artifact. He noticed that where the tree rested against the upper part of his sternum, an empty panel, vaguely diamond shaped, framed behind it. *Had Mike intentionally left that one blank, just to accommodate the necklace?*

"Wait," Hank said as he pointed to one of the tableaux on Darren's chest. "Isn't that the gyroscope? I remember looking at that tat the other day, thinking it was a chalice."

"Bloody devil," Darren cursed as he looked down. "It sure is."

"Spooky," Hank said with a crooked grin. "I think we'll have to have a talk with Mike soon."

"Tomorrow," Darren said before yawning again. "We really should get some sleep."

The men finished undressing. Darren turned on the nightstand lamp, then turned out the ceiling light. He carefully removed the necklace and set it on the nightstand.

"You're not gonna wear it?"

"Don't wish to strangle myself in my sleep. Or cut one of us with its sharp, pointy edges."

"Oh, I suppose not. I always sleep with the ring on."

Darren worked his way under the covers first, then raised his arm and held open the side of the sheets with a tent-like flap for Hank to crawl in beside him.

Darren nestled against Hank, careful not to put any pressure on the other man's chest. "I like this," he said before sighing.

"Me too," Hank agreed as he reached turned off the little lamp.

As THE sun's glow warmed the eastern sky with the rays of dawn, the phouka pushed out his front paws in a long stretch. He uncurled from his sleeping position under the hawthorn tree and stood up, then arched his back in another stretch.

Looking up into the branches of the tree, the phouka saw nothing but leaves. He glanced around his claimed corner of Shamrock Green, noticing how quiet the place was. He hated to admit it, but ever since the other Fae had fled through the portal before it closed, he found himself a bit bored. Even daresay, a bit lonely.

Maybe it's time for that social call with the Connells, he thought. *At least it will be something to do.* He rubbed the side of his head against the hawthorn tree, now empty of the pixies that once called it home. After a quick scratch, he scampered to the exit gate, then made his way across the street.

As he approached the old brownstone house, the phouka's whiskers began to tingle. He paused, puzzled by the reaction. He took a few slow steps, sniffing at the air. As he neared the wall, he picked up the faintest whiff of magic.

Magic? he thought. *That can't be.* The phouka stalked his way toward the source. Getting closer to the courtyard's outer wall, he heard the strange sound at nearly the same time he felt pulsing vibrations that made his whiskers twitch in syncopation.

He slithered through the space under the gate and into the woman's narrow courtyard. Everything inside the space was bathed in an unusual purple color. Glancing around, he quickly saw the source of the light.

Some sort of device twirled with swooshing noises as it generated a faint purple essence of magic. The strange artifact looked to be one of Cona's contraptions. The phouka approached it for a better look, cautious of the wrought-iron furniture.

As he neared the iron table, the phouka felt all of his hairs standing on end before some bizarre surge coursed through him. He could feel the dark-red energy coursing as it condensed and collected. The darkness grew stronger as it neared his heart.

"Bloody shite!" he exclaimed aloud as he realized what must be happening. He quickly turned and rushed back to the gate, crawled out of the courtyard, then dashed across the street as quickly as possible.

He slowed, but kept a scampering pace as he distanced himself from the tainted energy and aimed for the rectory garden.

Finding a secluded spot near the fountain, the phouka sat. He could still feel the dark force moving around inside, but its churnings had slowed.

The only conclusion, the phouka reasoned, *is that I must have absorbed the dullahan's heart—his essence.*

If the energy had time to completely condense, he had no idea what the final result would be, but the phouka guessed it would not be a good thing. *As long as I stay away from that bloody magic, I can keep it at bay.*

After a quick drink, the phouka scampered up the wall facing the Connell's street, then perched atop it. He would have to keep an eye on things, from a safe distance of course, and confer with one of the Connells the next time they ventured from the house.

EARLY THE next morning, Anne woke in confusion, feeling both ravenous and the urgent need to urinate. Careful as always not to twist her back, she rolled onto her right side. She didn't see the wheelchair near her bed. At some point, it had been pushed into the corner by the closet door.

A dry patch of skin on her left heel itched. She unconsciously reached down to scratch it as she thought how best to get to her chair. *Maybe I should call Darr,* she thought. Anne looked at the nightstand, but didn't see her phone.

Slowly, Anne realized she had bent her knee in order to move her foot closer to her hand. She consciously thought to straighten her knee out again. The leg complied. *What the devil?*

Anne lifted the covers and sat up on the edge of the bed. Tentatively, she put her right foot on the floor, then slowly pushed herself to stand on it. The leg held her weight. She put down her left foot and completed the stand.

This shouldn't be possible, she thought as she pulled her right hand up from the bed and stood fully unsupported. Her injury the other night should have left her completely paralyzed.

With her right foot, Anne took a slight step. Not only did her leg muscles respond, they worked with such vigor it nearly toppled her forward.

"Anne!" a rumbling old woman yelled. She looked over to see Tyler and an older lady rushing through her door.

Tyler reached her first and put his hands under her armpits to support her. "You shouldn't be out of bed." He gently lifted and guided her to sit on the edge of the bed again.

"Do you know what day it is?" the older woman asked.

"I'm not sure; they said I was in a coma for several days. I'll take a wild stab and say it is Sunday." Anne looked up at the woman. "And who are you?"

"Nora, the head nurse," she said with a nod, presumably reassured as to Anne's cognition. "It's actually only Saturday. Now lie back down, dear. I shall call Dr. Chelsea soon."

"But," Anne argued as she tried to stand again. "I need the facilities."

Nora went over near the closet, then wheeled Anne's chair to the bed. "In that case, I shall escort you."

Anne felt coddled as Tyler helped her to sit in the chair. She always hated being treated like an invalid child, but for now, she would play along.

"Let's get you taken care of," Nora cooed as she wheeled Anne out of the room. She turned to Tyler. "You can go now. I'll see to it you get payment for the full shift."

"Thank you. Good luck, Anne," Tyler said as he gathered up his belongings.

They had barely made it into the hall before Anne heard the front door open. Nora wheeled her around the corner, nearly running over Brigand.

Seeing the frightful state of the elder, Anne understood what her brother had tried to explain. Brigand looked so old now. The wrinkled skin of his face, covered with darkened age spots, sagged from his cheeks. His stark-white hair, which seemed much shorter than it used to be, showed a visible receding hairline. Anne thought he looked like a seventy-year-old man now.

"Anne," he said in a weak voice as he stepped to the side. "You're awake."

"Bathroom," she announced urgently.

As Nora wheeled her forward, Anne said, "Wait in my room. I'll be back in a minute."

Once in the bathroom, Anne fussed with Nora, who persisted in lifting her from the chair to the toilet before finally leaving her alone in the room.

Anne took care of business, then got herself back into the chair and wheeled to the door.

Nora pushed her back to her room, then insisted on helping her back into bed.

"I'm glad to see you awake," Brigand said.

"Glad to be awake," Anne said. "You look like shite."

Brigand chuckled. "I see your nap didn't temper your diplomacy any." He stepped forward. "I'm actually feeling much better today. I've just felt... energized all night long."

Nora tucked in the sheets around Anne. "I'll go call Dr. Chelsea."

Anne waited until Nora had left the room, and then she grinned at Brigand. "I'm feeling better too," she said as she yanked back the sheets and turned to sit on the edge of the bed. "Look," she said as she stood up.

Brigand's brow scrunched with puzzlement. "But couldn't you always stand?"

Anne took a step from the bed, then bent her knees and jumped about a foot off the ground. "Not with this much mobility."

SLOWLY WAKING, Hank settled into the loving warmth that surrounded him. He realized he was laying on his side with his head on Darren's chest as he nestled in the fold of Darren's arm.

He gave Darren a squeezing hug. "Morning."

Darren pulled him closer. "Good morning."

Hank opened his eyes. "What time is it?"

"Don't care," Darren said as he angled his neck down and kissed the top of Hank's head.

Hank gave him another squeeze before he tried to sit up. Darren resisted, firmly holding Hank in place with his surrounding arm. "We really should go check on Brigand and Anne," Hank pointed out.

"So soon?" Darren asked playfully as he moved his right hand to Hank's free arm and gently pulled it to his groin. "I was hoping you could help me with a problem I have."

Hank felt the solid erection under his palm. "I see," Hank replied. He moved his hand up to Darren's stomach. "But we should check first. We can come back to bed later."

Darren sighed loudly as he let go of Hank. "I suppose you're right."

Hank rose up and kissed Darren on the cheek. "We can check quickly," he said with a grin.

"That better be a promise," Darren said teasingly as they got out of bed and fished up their clothes from the floor.

"I won't even stop for coffee first."

After getting dressed, Hank picked up the faery-tree pendant from the nightstand and handed it to Darren. "Don't forget this."

Once Darren put on the necklace, Hank took his hand and led him through the apartment to the adjoining courtyard. As soon as he opened the door, he heard the swish-swishing sounds of the gyroscope spinning. He turned to Darren as he closed the door behind them. "I wonder if it ran all night?"

"Probably so," Darren replied as they went to Anne's door. "Probably as long as we were touching in some way."

They walked through the parlor and into the hallway. Then Hank thought he heard Brigand's voice. He yanked on Darren's arm and quickly hurried to Anne's room.

Hank stepped in and found Brigand standing near the bed, talking to Anne. He was shocked to see how the elder's condition had changed. He still looked much older than he had before the whole portal thing, but Brigand had lost that horror-movie-mummy appearance and now showed more normal signs of old age.

Darren let out a gasp of surprise. "Brigand! You look so much better."

"I *feel* much better," Brigand said with a grin as he turned to them.

Anne looked at her brother. "What do you mean, he looks better? I think he looks like crap."

Hank gave her a crooked smile. "Trust me, he looked *much* worse yesterday." Hank turned to Brigand. "What happened?"

"All through the night," Brigand explained, "I felt some peculiar energy… it was like it was feeding me."

"The gyroscope?" Hank asked as he looked at Darren.

"Possibly?"

"What about the gyroscope?" Brigand asked.

Anne reached out and grabbed Brigand's hand. "I hadn't gotten around to mentioning that yet. We've had a few discoveries." Anne looked at Darren. "Where is it? We need to show him."

"I'll get it," Hank said as he let go of Darren's hand and hurried to the courtyard.

By the time Hank got there, the gyroscope had slowed to a near stop. He picked it up and carefully carried it into the house. He was still marveling over the incredible improvement in Brigand's condition. *This thing must be much more powerful than we suspected,* Hank thought as he looked at the device.

Hank carried the artifact into Anne's room and set it on the nightstand before going back to Darren's side. "Watch," he said as he pushed up on his toes and touched his lips to Darren's. The gyroscope started its swishing sounds.

Disappointed it didn't fire up fully, Hank dropped back down. "What's wrong?"

Darren rubbed his hand along Hank's head and rested it on the back of his neck. "Just close your eyes. I think it has to be a *real* kiss." Darren surrounded him with his other arm and leaned down. Hank relaxed and enjoyed the passion of another deep kiss.

The "vroooom" sound echoed loudly in Anne's small bedroom.

As Hank pulled away from Darren, Brigand muttered something in Gaelic. He looked at the device in time to see that the inscribed runes on the base, all six of them, glowed briefly, as though illuminated from behind. The purple color of the energy circulating inside the globe washed out and turned a brilliant white.

"What the devil is going *on* in here?" Nora yelled as she froze in the doorway. She glared from one visitor to the next. "The doctor will be here momentarily. Everyone out," Nora demanded. "Anne is still convalescing and doesn't need all this excitement. So scoot."

Hank ran to the nightstand and grabbed the gyroscope. Like scolded children, he, Brigand, and Darren filed past Nora and silently made their way to the parlor.

Chapter 27

HANK FOLLOWED as Brigand slowly sat on the divan. Darren stepped past the elder and sat next to him. As Hank set the device on the coffee table, he noticed Brigand staring at it and shaking his head. "I'm still amazed," he said.

Hank sat beside Darren as he said, "I can't help but think it could have helped the other night, somehow."

"No," Darren said. "I don't think it was designed for that."

"Then what was it designed for?" Hank asked.

"Maybe the problem we are facing now. The part I'm trying to understand is why does it keep changing color?"

"Oh, you noticed that too."

"What do you lads mean?" Brigand asked.

"Well," Hank explained, "the first time it fired up, the energy inside was kinda turquoise. Then the next time, when we showed it to Mike, it turned more orangey red. Then last night, when we showed it to Anne, it took on that purple, bruised color. Then just now, it changed to white."

"The runes," Darren said. "Don't forget the runes. When it was just us, I didn't notice anything with them. With Mike, three of them sort of lit up. Last night, I think all but one did."

"And last time, they all lit up. I noticed that," Hank added.

Brigand looked deep in thought as he listened to their discussion. After a moment, he asked, "Anne said something about some significant notes in Cona's journals?"

"Yes," Darren said and picked up the legal pad from the coffee table. He flipped to the proper page. "This one," he said, pointing to one of the paragraphs as he handed the pad to Brigand.

After Brigand read over it, Darren said, "And the top of the next page."

Brigand flipped the page and read the second one. "I see. I'm thinking, it was tuning itself, since the changes occurred when those different elemental people were around." He put the pad back on the table. "Try it again."

"If you insist," Hank said with a grin before he grabbed the back of Darren's neck and pulled him into a hot and heavy kiss, so hot in fact, he sprouted an erection. He kept at it long after they heard the "vroooom" of the device. Hank had to angle around to see the ball of pure white energy inside before he pulled away from Darren.

"Quit doing that," Darren said with a teasing grin as he reached down and adjusted the crotch of his pants. "I'll have to hold you to your promise soon."

"What promise?" Brigand asked.

Hank and Darren both chuckled. "Never mind," Darren said. "You probably don't want to know."

"It would seem that now it is tuned, it will stay that way without requiring the presence of the others," Brigand said as he nodded his head. "Which is good news, I do believe."

"How so?" Darren asked.

"Its future use won't require all six of us together in some grand ritual." Brigand leaned back into the divan and thought a moment. "I'm still bothered." He sat up and looked at Hank. "That first phrase of Neil's quatrain keeps coming to mind. It's haunted me for several days. 'With a song in his heart.' We still don't know what that means."

Darren grinned broadly. "Maybe *I* know. And it gives me the idea for what we need to do next," he said as he turned to Hank.

Hank couldn't follow Darren's thoughts.

Darren added, "The song I played in the green. The one you sang along with."

"Oh," Hank said with realization. "The one that's been one of my favorites. 'Magic.'"

"A magic song? You boys will have to clarify that for me," Brigand said as he shook his head again.

"No," Darren explained. "An '80s song named 'Magic.' I think we need to take that device into Shamrock Green, then have Hank sing the song while I play it on my guitar."

"But," Hank asked. "Won't the thing have to be running first?"

Darren gave him a seductive look. "I think we can take care of that easily enough," he answered with a teasing tone.

"Well what are we waiting for then?" Hank asked as he stood up. "Let's go for it."

The swishing noise started right after Darren took Hank's hand to pull him back to the divan. "I want to hear from the doctor first, to make sure Anne is truly on the mend." Darren turned to Brigand. "And it wouldn't hurt to have her examine you as well."

"Quite right," Brigand agreed.

They didn't have to wait much longer before the doorbell rang.

DARREN LET the doctor in and followed her to Anne's room. He stood out of the way against the far wall as she began the examination of his sister.

Dr. Chelsea didn't seem surprised by Anne's recovery from the coma, but she spent quite a bit of time poking and prodding at Anne with her peculiar claw devices, puzzling over the restoration of her spine. "Frankly, it's nothing short of a miracle," she finally announced. "It will require a CAT or MRI to really determine the extent of repair."

"I'm fine," Anne declared. "And I won't look a gift horse in the mouth. No tests."

"Yet, not knowing the 'why' of it makes me fearful of long-term prognosis," Dr. Chelsea argued. "Without understanding, I can't say for certain if you mayn't relapse at some future point."

Anne shook her head. "I don't think I will. I don't know why, but I believe wholeheartedly that the repair is permanent."

Dr. Chelsea threw a pleading look at Darren.

"I have to comply with my sister's instincts and wishes," Darren said. "So, can you come to the parlor and take a look at Brigand?"

As she packed her things back into her bag, the doctor said, "This is against my best judgment, but so be it." She followed Darren to the parlor.

The doctor paused when she saw Brigand but recovered her professionalism quickly.

"Hello again, pretty doctor," Brigand greeted. "I must say, you are a sight more attractive than Malcolm O'Dowd. Where is the old lad?"

"Probably tootling around the Riviera," Dr. Chelsea said. "I'm his granddaughter, Chelsea." She sat beside Brigand and took his wrist to check his pulse. "And I must say, you look much better than the last time I saw you."

"Thanks. It's a wonder what a good night's sleep can do," he said with a wink to Darren.

Chelsea opened her bag and pulled out a pointed scope, then used it to peek inside Brigand's ears, nose, and mouth. "You seem like a fit sixty-year-old," she declared as she put the scope back in her bag. "Any problems or pains?"

"Not today," Brigand said. "I'm sorry this was a silly waste of your time."

Dr. Chelsea smiled. "Better safe than sorry. And I'll tell Gramps you asked after him the next time we speak." She stood up to leave.

Darren led her back to the door. As he opened it, Chelsea stepped close and spoke in a lowered voice. "Anne's situation concerns me greatly. Something… unusual has happened in her lower lumbar region. Please, Darren, see if you can convince her to investigate this further, for her sake."

"What do you mean 'unusual'?"

"That's the thing, I can't say. Her bruises are completely gone, and the instrument I use to detect auras is registering something… peculiar with her spine, but I can't determine what it is. I don't know."

Darren nodded. "Let me speak with her and explain your concerns. But she's a stubborn lass, so I can't make promises."

"I understand," Chelsea said as she stepped out. "At least try."

"I will. Good day, Dr. Chelsea," Darren said before he pushed the door closed behind her.

THE PHOUKA started to leap down from the wall when he saw the two lads exiting the courtyard gate carrying a beat-up guitar and blanket, but he froze when he saw the American was also carrying that ivory contraption with him.

Bollocks, the phouka thought. The device wasn't running at the moment, but who knew if it mightn't spark to life as soon as he approached.

Regretfully, the phouka made the decision to follow them at a distance. Maybe he would be able to approach them later.

DARREN LOCKED the gate behind them after they entered the green. He didn't want to risk any interruptions if things got as intense as he expected they might.

As he turned toward the circle, he thought he saw a flash of light come from the grass by the southernmost tree. Darren walked that way as Hank trailed behind him.

Moving his foot through the taller tufts of grass near the tree trunk, Darren's toes bumped into something solid. He reached to the ground.

"What did you find?" Hank asked from behind.

Darren took hold of the hilt and picked up the obsidian sword. For something that looked so thin and frail, he found it exceedingly heavy.

"Wow," Hank exclaimed. "I forgot about the sword."

"I'm surprised it's still here," Darren said.

"You mean, the reavers could eat it?"

"No, they only consume soft things, as far as I know," he said as he held it up to the sun and admired its smoky transparency. "I mean, I'm surprised that it *stayed* a sword. I would have thought it would revert back into a wooden cane when the dullahan died."

"Oh, I see your point," Hank said. "There's a lot about these Fae that I don't understand."

"I'm beginning to feel the same way," Darren agreed.

"Where should we set up?" Hank asked.

Darren pointed toward the ring of standing stones with the sword. "Over there, about where I sat yesterday; does that seem acceptable?"

"Sure." Hank walked partway to the circle, then stopped and stared at the ground.

Darren saw that Hank was looking at a dark puddle-shaped stain on the clover.

"I've been meaning to ask," Hank said. "What about the priest? Should we call the police, or something? Let somebody know that he's dead?"

"And say *what* exactly?" Darren asked.

"I know we can't tell them the truth, but—"

"Without a body, it's doubtful they could do much to pursue it anyway. Believe me, I feel remorseful that we can't do more. It's an unfortunate situation."

Hank frowned. "I suppose."

Darren stepped past Hank and walked to the southern edge of the circle, hating the way the mood had suddenly collapsed into something so melancholy. He would have to think of a way to lift their spirits. Hopefully, the singing would help.

Darren set down the sword and his guitar, spread the blanket over the ground, then folded it in half to create a double thickness on the hard ground.

"Where should we put this?" Hank asked as he held out the gyroscope.

"Since the east is the point of creation, it should go over there." Darren pointed to the right.

"Why creation?"

"Since we are striving to create a portal, doesn't that seem appropriate?"

"Oh, right," Hank agreed with a slight smile. "Makes sense."

As Hank put the device on the ground next to the easternmost stone, Darren picked up the guitar and sat cross-legged in the center of the blanket. Since he hadn't played this one in a while, he spent a few moments plucking and tuning the strings.

Darren had decided not to return with his good, Spanish ten string. Since they were attempting a bit of magical work, he had chosen instead to bring the old six string that had been passed down from his great-uncle. This guitar didn't have the same richness, but it never hurt to stack the deck with heirlooms.

After playing a few chords and feeling satisfied with the tune of the strings, he looked up at Hank. "Are we ready?"

"Don't we have to get the thing running first?"

"Sit in front of me," Darren said with a smile as he rested the guitar on his thigh and let it hang from the neck strap. He put both hands in front of himself, palms facing out at about shoulder height. "Now, put your hands on mine."

They faintly heard the swoosh as the gyroscope started turning.

"Have you ever heard of tantric?" Darren asked.

"Isn't that some kind of weird sex from India?"

After a chuckle, Darren said, "Apologies for laughing, but I've never heard it referred to as 'weird' before. It's the same as regular sex, only slower, and you work on sharing the emotional feeling as well as the physical ones."

"Oh." Hank smiled. "Then that's not weird. It's kinda the way I like to do it anyway. I'm tantric at heart and didn't know it," he said with his own chuckle.

"Close your eyes and push slightly into my palms," Darren directed.

Darren slowly pulled his hands closer to his shoulders while Hank pressed gently against them. Darren leaned forward and warmly kissed Hank, using his gift to push his emotion through his hands as he did so.

The resulting "vroooom" sounded louder than before. As the gyroscope continued, Darren heard that steady hum at the pitch of middle A. He opened his eyes and glanced at the gyroscope, noting the even swirl of the white energy ball inside the globe.

TO THEIR left, neither man noticed that the dim, green energy of the hawthorn also began to swirl around the tree's leaves.

PULLING HIS hands all the way against his shoulders, Darren first slipped out his right hand, letting Hank press directly against his shoulder. He then slipped out his left hand and dropped it to the guitar neck. Without breaking the kiss, he strummed a middle A chord. The white energy pulsed. He strummed a middle C chord and the energy ball pulsed again.

Hank pulled his mouth back from the kiss, and the hum ceased as the gyroscope slowed down.

"Bollocks," Darren said. "I was hoping it would keep running on high without kissing you."

"Well, it's still running on low. Let's try the song."

Darren played the intro to "Magic" and watched the gyroscope, but the swirling energy didn't pulse along with his chords as it did before.

When Hank began singing the lyrics, Darren still saw no change in the energy.

At the chorus, Darren jumped in and sang along, "You have to believe we are magic, nothing can stand in our way…." He trailed off when his additional voice had no effect on the gyroscope's energy, then stopped playing.

"Why stop?" Hank asked.

"Because it isn't making any difference with the gyroscope. We'll have to try something else."

"Maybe it's not the right song," Hank said with a sudden excitement. "Shouldn't it be a song about Ireland?"

"That would make a certain amount of sense, I suppose," Darren said as he nodded.

"Then play 'Greensleeves,'" Hank said. "I'll sing it the way Granny taught me."

Darren first played a flourish intro, and then Hank sang an arrangement of lyrics Darren had never heard before.

"Go back, go back, to the Eire of old,
where the shamrock blooms on earth so cold,
Go back, go back, to the Eire of old,
to the isle your heart does hold."

Thinking the tempo was a bit dirge-like, Darren sped up the beat as he played the bridge.

"Dance, dance, feet bare in June,
under the shining silver moon,
Sing, sing, with a raptured tune,
in the isle your heart will swoon."

Responding to Hank's song, the green energy on the hawthorn grew stronger, granting a new growth spurt to the taproot underground. Faster, the root stretched and lengthened, reaching toward the center of the stone circle.

"Sing and dance in the Eire of old,
where the faeries' tales are often told,
Sing and dance in the Eire of old,
for your heart, love's magic does hold."

Darren played the end of the song, trying not to feel disappointed. He'd kept a careful eye on the gyroscope and failed to see any changes throughout Hank's rendition.

"Nothing?" Hank asked.

Shaking his head, Darren said, "Unfortunately not."

"Maybe we need to be closer to it?" Hank thought aloud as he turned around to face the circle. The shimmering of the hawthorn tree's leaves immediately snagged his gaze.

"Don't think it matters," Darren replied.

"When did the tree start doing that?" Hank asked as he pointed.

Darren looked to the left and nearly gasped when he saw that the faery-tree sapling was now twice as large as it had been yesterday. He'd been so busy concentrating on the music and the gyroscope that he'd failed to notice when the green aura had appeared around the tree's foliage. "I don't know," he admitted. "I wasn't looking that direction."

Hank got up and moved around Darren, kneeling behind his back and wrapping his arms around Darren's chest, presumably so he wouldn't have his back to all the action. "We must be going about this the wrong way. How about a faery song? Something peppier?"

"No," Darren said as he shook his head. "I don't think music is the way to go."

"Then, what is?"

Darren tapped at Hank's hands with his fingers, then reached up to the guitar strap around his neck. Hank released his grip long enough for Darren to set the guitar down at the edge of the blanket near the sword. Before he lost his nerve about undressing in a public place, Darren grabbed the collar of his T-shirt and pulled it off before pulling off his shoes.

"Oh," Hank said as he pulled off his own shirt and shoes.

They moved around to face each other and sat on their knees in the center of the blanket.

Darren reached out his hand and lightly stroked his index finger along Hank's cheek, then traced a line down to his jaw. Hank gazed at him, and a feeling of nervous excitement whirled in Darren's abdomen as he looked upon those bay-water-blue irises. He heard the swooshing tempo of the gyroscope speed up as they locked eyes.

Darren ignored the gyroscope. He focused only on Hank, on his eyes, letting himself be taken into their depths.

Chapter 28

FROM HIS safely distant vantage point on the tree branch, the phouka watched the two lads on the blanket, wondering what they intended next. With their earlier music, they had energized two triangular points, so they only needed a third now, to finish whatever goal they strived for.

Almost teary-eyed—he probably would have shed tears if he hadn't been stuck in this feline form—the phouka felt a warm flutter of goose bumps from hearing the Shay travel song after so many... must be several centuries now. Although, it was a bit peculiar to hear it in English instead of the Gaelic he remembered.

In puzzlement, the phouka watched as the Connell lad put aside his instrument. After stripping off their shirts, they just kneeled on the ground, staring at each other. This didn't seem to be accomplishing anything.

HANK GAZED into Darren's face as the finger stroked along his cheek, feeling the almost electric charge where their skin made contact. He zeroed in on Darren's eyes, the green of them reminding him of summer fields full of growing cornstalks—vast fields of green that Hank could easily get lost in.

Pushing down the sensation of butterflies as his heart beat faster, Hank leaned closer to Darren and put his right hand on Darren's bare shoulder. The sense that he was embarking on something significant continued to fuel his nervousness.

Darren lowered his hand to gently grasp Hank's forearm. Hank tried to ignore all the sudden thoughts about empaths and projectors that surfaced in his mind when he felt another surge from Darren's touch. Right now, thoughts didn't matter. He took a deep breath and tried to settle himself into only this moment, truly feeling it.

Hank placed his other behind Darren's neck and slowly brought his hand around to the top of Darren's head with a light touch, feeling the bristly tickle of Darren's short hair move along his palm.

Darren closed his eyes and let out a contented sigh.

Hank saw the dancing opalescence of both his ring and Darren's tree pendant as he applied a little more pressure, enough to feel Darren's skin underneath the hair, then reversed the stroke of his hand. He closed his eyes and took another deep cleansing breath, settling his mind away from more thoughts.

Darren released his forearm. Hank felt an intensified sensation of desire on his chest as Darren gently ran a finger along one of the burn scar lines.

When he heard Darren shifting his position, Hank opened his eyes. He saw the deep desire, almost a hunger, in those green eyes as Darren placed his hand behind his neck, just at the shoulders. Darren eased him forward into an open-mouthed kiss.

Hank felt all of Darren's emotions flowing from his hand as he tasted the spicy cloves of Darren's mouth. Warmth, desire, love, passion, need—he absorbed them all in a sputtering jumble.

Pulling away his mouth, Hank put his hands on Darren's shoulders, then moved his head to the side to ever so softly lick along the folds of Darren's ear. Darren responded with blissful moans as gratitude and comfort added to the mix of emotions radiating from Darren's hand.

As he gently worked over Darren's ear, Hank focused on his own hands, willing them to project, wanting to share all the emotions he felt in the same way Darren shared his. Hank wasn't sure if it worked or not. He didn't want to engage his thoughts enough to make deductions, so he just followed his instincts.

Darren put his other hand on his lower back, sending an intense, tingling charge into his spine as he pulled him closer, pushing their bare chests together. Hank felt like a battery about to burst from overcharging as so much body contact filled him with Darren's glorious emotions.

Then Hank felt a quiver in his hands, and his whole body shook as he pushed all the gathered emotions back into Darren. Darren groaned aloud ecstatically as the gyroscope took on a much higher-pitched hum.

Hank could no longer ignore his swollen cock as the tight denim around it began chafing uncomfortably. He pulled away from Darren enough to reach down and unbutton the waistband, then unzip the jeans, giving his cock more room to expand. Resting his head on the top of Darren's shoulder, Hank reached his hands across and did the same for Darren's jeans, feeling that the other man would also be grateful.

After working open Darren's zipper, Hank raised his hands a bit higher and put his palms on Darren's stomach, gently rubbing and kneading with his thumbs and fingers at the firm, muscled flesh lightly dusted with fine hairs. Darren moaned blissfully again.

Without speaking—the pair were so in tune they didn't need words—Darren leaned back to rest on the ground and they assisted each other in wriggling out of their jeans.

Once fully naked, Hank straddled Darren's stomach as Darren retrieved something from his jeans' pocket. Hank put his palms on Darren's chest just to either side of his necklace, sharing through his hands the new, consuming need he felt to have Darren inside of him.

Hank closed his eyes and moaned with anticipation as Darren's slickly lubed finger stroked along the fold between his spread cheeks. The finger rubbed and teased at his entry point, making Hank itch for more.

NEARBY, THE taproot of the young hawthorn tree finally reached that point of excitement it had searched for and emerged from the ground. It pushed up against the torn scar in the veil created by the dullahan's sword days before, seeking a way inside.

The torn fissure had not yet completely mended. A tiny space, barely wider than one of the taproot's cells, still existed, leaving a pinprick tunnel that led to the other side.

The taproot found the space. The cell at the very tip of the root divided, pushing the new cell inside the entrance of the tunnel.

HANK CLOSED his eyes as he pushed back, slowly filling himself with Darren, so he failed to see the tiny, green spark that leaped from the Eirestone in his Claddagh ring to the bluestone in the tree pendant. He moved his hands closer together as he arched his back.

Another spark, only blue this time, jumped from the bluestone to the Eirestone as he rested on Darren's hips briefly before pulling forward and pushing back again.

"Bloody devil," Darren whispered among moans of pleasure as the humming pitch of the gyroscope escalating higher. Hank felt Darren put his hands on his hips, sending pulses of pleasure into Hank through his fingers.

As Hank slowly rocked forward and back, more sparks leaped from both stones. They met in the air and turned turquoise, the bolt catching and dancing erratically as it sparked between the two artifacts.

Gathering up all of the pleasure and gratification he felt, Hank pushed those emotions into his hands, sending them through his palms and into Darren as he bucked up and down with more vigor. Two, then three more turquoise energy bolts formed, sizzling between the ring and the pendant.

Feeling the pressure building to a finish, Hank slowed his movements. Darren lifted his knees and pushed up from his feet, taking over the work. Hank stilled, then lowered his back a fraction, changing the angle and letting Darren drive them to the end.

INSIDE THE tunnel, the single line of cells continued dividing, pushing deeper and nearing the edge of the faery plane.

THE PHOUKA watched from what he thought was a safe distance as the two lads coupled, fascinated by the unusual turquoise aura that grew and thickened around them. Then he saw a flash of light from the center of the standing stones and the energy around the tree brightened, changing from green to white.

The phouka looked to the gyroscope. The white energy ball created by the machine's rapid movements continued growing larger, expanding beyond the boundaries of the spinning rings by nearly a meter now.

HANK CLIMAXED first. His orgasmic cries and squeezing spasms brought on Darren's climax. Darren clutched firmly on his hips. Their feelings of ecstatic love flowed from Darren's hands, into Hank, then out from Hank's hands and back into Darren in an escalating feedback loop that nearly drove Hank to swoon, and he collapsed on top of Darren.

The sparking bolts on the artifacts thickened and crackled outward, some of the turquoise sparks surging to the hawthorn tree while the rest leaped to the gyroscope.

When the turquoise sparks hit the device's white energy globe, now nearly two meters in diameter, the globe silently exploded and flashed, sending a wave of charged energy ripping through the air.

As the exploding energy blew through the center of the stone ring, it yanked on the tiny bit of exposed taproot, ripping the fabric of the veil and tearing a tiny stress fracture.

Hank looked up when he felt the sudden gust of air rush over him, but saw nothing unusual. The gyroscope had slowed back to its swoosh-swoosh rhythm.

Trying not to feel disappointed, Hank rolled off Darren and nestled against his side.

THE PHOUKA didn't have time to run when the exploding blast of the gyroscope's energy came his way. The energy washed over and through him, reawakening the dark-red energy inside. He felt the red sparks resume condensing and settling into his heart.

He turned and ran to the end of the branch, fearing some horrible consequence of the dullahan's essence, but he slowed when nothing happened. Maybe he was just overreacting. The phouka turned to look back at the lads and sat down on the branch as they lay panting on the blanket in their postcoital bliss.

He glanced at the contraption, then at the hawthorn tree, not seeing anything significant. Since the phouka didn't know the nature of the lads' intentions, he couldn't tell if they had accomplished whatever action they sought. Or maybe they weren't trying to accomplish anything, other than a lover's tryst.

No, he thought. *They must have had some other goal. Otherwise, why bring that machine along?*

HANK FINALLY spoke. "Looks like it didn't work."

Darren sighed next to him. "I deduced as much, when I sensed your disappointment a moment ago." He rolled onto his stomach and pushed up onto his elbows before looking toward the stone circle.

"What now?" Hank asked as he rolled onto his back and covered his eyes with his hand to block out the sun overhead. He heard the gyroscope slowing to a stop since Darren had moved beyond his touch.

"Wait," Darren said excitedly. "I see… something."

Hank sat up and turned around to face the circle. He didn't see anything of note in the empty space over the carpet of clover.

"In the center, on the ground. Use your peripheral," Darren said.

Hank turned his eyes to the gyroscope. Then he saw just the tiniest shimmer of silver appear briefly on the ground. Hank moved his eyes a bit, and it appeared again. "What is that? Another reaver?"

"No. I think it's a tiny crack. Maybe."

"A crack?" Hank asked.

"In the veil. Maybe we can make it bigger," Darren seemed to think aloud. "Come wrap your arms around me and let's try another song."

Hank smiled as Darren grabbed his guitar. He waited until Darren had the strap around his neck before nestling his chest against Darren's back and wrapping his arms under Darren's armpits. "Which song?"

Darren hit the side of the guitar with the end of his finger in a quick tap-tap-tap. "I'm thinking, your suggestion of peppy faeries may be in order." Darren hit the front of the guitar with his palm several times, making a thump-thump-thump noise.

Hank closed his eyes and listened as Darren hit the guitar with quick thumps and taps again.

tap-tap-tap-tap-tap, thump, thump, thump

tap-tap-tap-tap-tap, thump, thump, thump

HANK RECOGNIZED the rhythm of the Celtic Cantrips instrumental song, "Faery Fungus Jig," as Darren proceeded to play the plucky, staccato notes. Then Darren surprised Hank by singing some lyrics that weren't part of the CD recording.

With quick, bursting breaths, Darren sang:

"Prancing and dancing—the faeries fly,
Bouncing and leaping—from toadstools high,
Buzzing and cooing—the faeries sigh,
'Our magical hour draws nigh.'"
tap-tap-tap-tap-tap, thump, thump, thump

As Darren banged out the percussion line, Hank thought he saw a breeze moving the leaves of the hawthorn tree that grew next to the circle, but he felt no wind. With his ringed hand, Hank absently tapped and slapped lightly on Darren's chest in beat with the rhythm. A green spark jumped from the ring to the nearby pendant.

Darren sang the second verse:

"Calling and crooning we—sing their song,
Raising our voices up—bold and strong,
Urging to rights what—once went wrong,
Guiding them where they belong."

Hank heard the swoosh of the gyroscope speed up while Darren continued the song. He glanced at the machine. In his peripheral view, the silver sparkle stretched and lengthened upward, like some invisible hand was using shimmery silver chalk to draw a line up from the ground. The hairs on the back of his neck stood up as more turquoise sparks coursed between the heart-shaped stones of the artifacts.

tap-tap-tap-tap-tap, thump, thump, thump
   "Calling forth, calling forth—let them rise
   Piercing this veil—between the skies
   Watching the mists with—open eyes
   Their magical hour arrives!"

The gyroscope kicked into high gear with another "vroooom" before the atmosphere went deathly silent. Hank watched the center of the circle as the air buckled.

A turquoise bolt of energy shot from the artifacts into the center of the stone ring, colliding with something near the ground.

The air rippled convulsively, then tore open with an echoing thunder.

A mass of tiny flying creatures spewed forth from the ripped gap, all chanting so fast that they sounded like the drone of a happy beehive.

Hank watched in awe as the procession of faeries, pixies, and sprites poured out of the torn veil and scattered out into the world.

INSIDE HER library, Anne looked up from her book when she felt the ether coalesce and return to the atmosphere. She closed her eyes and let out a grateful sigh. With her gift no longer silent, the world felt alive and normal to her again.

Anne opened her eyes and grinned at Brigand, who sat across the table from her nursing a cup of tea.

Brigand smiled warmly back. "They must have succeeded."

"I told you, if we leave them be, they would solve it on their own."

"So," Brigand asked as he put down the teacup. "What of the second quatrain? Did you ever tell your brother, or Hank of it?"

Anne chuckled. "I really don't see how a pregnancy can come from all this. That quatrain must be referring to some other event."

"If you say so," Brigand replied in a doubtful tone.

Anne closed the book and stood up. "I'll go get my cards, now that I can do readings again."

SEVERAL OF the green faeries and sprites flew toward Hank and Darren. Repeatedly, they chanted a short phrase in Gaelic as they swirled around their heads, which Hank assumed must have been a show of thanks, for Darren replied in English, "You're welcome, ladies."

The faeries quickly scattered back as a slightly larger green faery approached. Hank noticed she wore some sort of silvery crown on her head. She hovered in front of Darren's face as the other faeries flew in circles and chanted, "A boon. A boon. A boon."

The crowned faery quickly darted up and kissed Darren on the forehead.

Still resting against Darren's back, Hank felt a strange surge rush from Darren's body to his. "What just happened?" he asked as the faeries scattered away.

Darren turned his head and flashed Hank a crooked grin. "It seems, we were given a Fae blessing of some kind."

Hearing the rustling in the grass, Hank turned to see the marmalade tabby phouka strolling up. "Let us hope it doesn't go awry like the last Connell-Shay blessing did."

"You know of that?" Darren asked as the phouka sat in front of them. The cat seemed to disregard their naked condition.

"Indeed. Its memories haunt me. It was I who was tricked into stealing the bride's ring at the dullahan's behest." The phouka turned to Hank. "I'm glad to see that you have recovered it. Was it with you in America?"

"No, I found it in an antique store in Galway."

The cat tilted his head. "A bit puzzling. I would have thought that once the dullahan squirreled away the ring, it would never be seen again." The phouka shook his head. "No matter how it surfaced, I suppose," he said as he stood up. "I wish you lads peace and contentment."

With a flick of his tail, the cat sauntered to the circle.

Raising up onto his knees, Hank leaned against Darren as he gave him his own kiss on the forehead. Then he lowered his kiss to Darren's lips.

THE PHOUKA left the lads and approached the opening to the other side. With the magic flowing unimpeded once again, he might be able to get rid of the wearisome cat body. At least he could try, anyway.

He sat in front of the jagged-edged, shimmery fold, then stuck his paw inside. He willed himself back into his normal form. Almost immediately, he felt his body painfully stretching and twisting, choking him briefly before he managed to suck in air again.

Still shivering from the transformation, the phouka lay on the ground. He brought his paw up to his face and looked at his pudgy, fur-covered hand. He didn't need a mirror to know how ugly he looked now. He clearly recalled his past appearance—like that of a hairy and wrinkled troll child.

Still sensing that essence of the dullahan in his heart, the phouka had an interesting thought. Maybe he would be able to tap into it somehow and use the dullahan's gift of form changing. *It's worth a try,* he decided as he crawled back to the ripped veil and stuck his hand inside.

He concentrated on what kind of form he would want.

Definitely taller, he decided, but not *too* tall.

Keep the hair only on the head, and maybe a short beard too. Those looked rather nice on men.

He also decided he didn't like the pale and freckly skin; he wanted something with more of a tan to it.

The brief visual of an American movie star came to mind when he thought of a new face.

As he held all of those images in his mind, the phouka felt that dark-red energy stirring in his heart.

Then, the painful pulling and wrenching commenced again, but not nearly as badly as before, since his natural form was already modeled on humans.

Once completed, the phouka lay on the ground with his eyes closed until the shivers subsided. He opened his eyes and pulled his hand to his face.

Very nice, he thought, admiring the dark golden color of his hairless fingers. He glanced down to his naked body. His form was still slightly thin, but with the tight musculature of his cat form. Even his penis looked very adequate.

He would have to track down a mirror before knowing, but he suspected his face would also be just as attractive.

Bloody bollocks, the phouka cursed at himself as he scratched a flea in his short beard. He should have thought ahead to retrieve some clothing before he attempted this. He darted over to the seclusion of the hawthorn trees. He would have to wait until dark before wandering the city naked.

"I THINK it's time to get dressed," Darren suggested after he finally pulled away from Hank's steamy, congratulatory kiss.

"Sure."

As they pulled their clothes on, Darren asked, "Have you given more thought to moving here?"

"Unless you plan on moving to Texas," Hank said with a quirky smile before he retrieved the gyroscope.

"I'd rather not," Darren said as he gathered up the guitar and sword while Hank folded and picked up the blanket. "Someone will have to stay and guard the new portal."

Hank chuckled. "Yep, somebody will, I guess."

Darren turned his peripheral to look at the silvery rip, which reached up from the ground about two meters in height.

The comforting sight reminded Darren of the slightly parted gap of a stage curtain. It didn't appear nearly as elegant as the hovering silvery globe, but hopefully, this fracture wouldn't be governed by the same laws of physics that had left the previous portal so vulnerable.

As they turned around and walked to the gate, Darren felt a sudden queasiness coming from Hank.

"What's wrong?" Darren asked as he rushed to Hank's side and wrapped his arm around Hank's waist.

"I was just wondering," Hank said. "How am I going to explain all this to my mother?"

JACKSON CORDD first attempted writing in junior high, when he put together an eight-page comic book. His lack of drawing skills doomed the work to failure, though. In high school, he learned to rely on the words alone, and placed third in a regional short story contest his senior year. (He still feels he didn't get first place only because of the homoerotic elements.)

To get a steady paycheck, he works in the software industry writing and proofreading programs and manuals, but he returns to weaving the tales of his hunky fantasy men at night.

Visit Jackson on Facebook:

https://www.facebook.com/profile.php?id=100003616877972.

Duanta Beads Book One by JACKSON CORDD

http://www.dreamspinnerpress.com

Duanta Beads Book Two by JACKSON CORDD

JACKSON CORDD

LAVENDER

SKIES

PART 2 OF DUANTA BEADS

http://www.dreamspinnerpress.com

Romance by Jackson Cordd

JACKSON CORDD

CLEATS
in CLAY

http://www.dreamspinnerpress.com

Brian's
Mate

HOLLIS SHILOH

SUI LYNN

ADEL'S
PURR

Also from DREAMSPINNER PRESS

Book One of The Sleepless City

Shades of Sepia

Anne Barwell

http://www.dreamspinnerpress.com